# Spirits Eat Ripe Papaya

# Spirits Eat Ripe Papaya

BILL SVELMOE

RESOURCE *Publications* · Eugene, Oregon

SPIRITS EAT RIPE PAPAYA



Resource Publications
An Imprint of Wipf and Stock Publishers
199 W. 8th Ave., Suite 3
Eugene, OR 97401
www.wipfandstock.com

ISBN 13: 978-1-60899-520-2

Manufactured in the U.S.A.

*For Lisa*

# Chapter One

THE SMALL PHILIPPINE AIRLINES jet shook as it surged from the steaming runway into Manila's muddy wet air. A thin mist, which began forming as soon as the outside doors closed and the air conditioning began its battle with the saturated tropical air, swirled about the cabin and settled into the aisle. The windows and overhead luggage containers were slick with condensation. Philip watched, fascinated, as a drop of water formed next to the stewardess call button above the seat two rows in front of him. As the airplane nosed even more steeply upward and then banked sharply left, the drop gained independent life. It ran toward the window, then, as the jet pulled out of its bank, raced down the overhead paneling toward Philip gaining size with every inch until, as the airplane jolted sharply in an air pocket, it released its hold on the air vent above him and plummeted like a kamikaze onto the bridge of his nose. "What the hell," he muttered, as he shook the water from his eyes. He turned to say something to the Filipino man next to him, but the white haired gentleman in the intricately embroidered Barong Tagalog was already asleep. Or maybe he was praying. His face was relaxed, but he was gripping what appeared to be a crucifix through the gap between two buttons on his fancy shirt.

Philip took a deep breath then looked around him. Nobody appeared to be panicking. The two young women across from him chatted as if a jet cabin filling with fog was an everyday occurrence. One of them held a magazine over her head to fend off the water drops. He listened to the engines. He was no expert, but these sounded functional, although they seemed a good bit louder than on airplanes back home. The mufflers are probably rusted through, he thought. He mustered his courage and peeked outside. The wings were still attached. The plane was leveling off now. When Philip looked down he noticed they were over the coast. They were flying south toward Mindanao.

If his stepmother had been with him, she would have leaned over and said, "Relax. Don't you see those angels holding up the wings?" Secure in the knowledge that she was all prayed up for "journeying mercies," she probably would have slept like a baby all the way to Cagayan. Philip didn't see any angels, and, in fact, he had a difficult time believing there were any out there, at least not any charged with keeping this particular airplane in the sky. Sure, he retained enough of his evangelical Protestant heritage to have muttered a prayer for safe travels that very morning, but he did so with a wink and a shrug. It was a harmless superstition. If something went wrong with the internal workings of the PAL jet, and Philip had been in-country long enough not to be surprised if something did, it would plummet out of the sky like Icarus. God, and the torturer's horse, would notice, but neither would bestir themselves to help. Presumably God would weep with those who wept, and he would oversee the ushering of the departed souls to their final destinations, but he had long ago set this old world to working according to a certain set of rules, and, although he perhaps reserved the right to cross those rules when he wished, the Almighty wouldn't intervene to save Philip Andrews from a watery grave. Billy Graham maybe! He might intervene for Billy. But Philip? Not bloody likely. Or at least that's how Philip had it figured.

The equatorial sun reflecting off the tops of the bright clouds fatigued his eyes, and he felt a nap coming on. Surely, even in the third world, airplanes didn't fall from the sky as a matter of course, so the odds were good he would reach his destination unscathed. He pushed his seat back as far as it would go and tried to fit his legs under the seat in front of him. But the seats were designed for Filipinos, not six-foot Americans, and he couldn't find a comfortable position. Still he managed to drift a bit. Maybe now that I'm a missionary, he thought, God *would* dispatch an angel or two to keep my airplane in the air. His last conscious image, before his mind became a jumble of half-formed dreams, was of an old college friend chuckling, as he saw Philip off at the airport in Los Angeles, at the crackbrained notion of Philip going overseas as a missionary. It might be better for the advancement of God's kingdom in faraway lands if this plane *did* go down, Philip muttered somewhere inside himself. That made him want to smile, but then he was asleep.

<center>~~~</center>

Heat and silence. Three hours later these were his primary impressions of the mission center whose name, Ilusan, he was still learning to pronounce. ("Most a's are soft in the Philippines, almost like an o." He'd heard that twice in the past few days.) The generator that kept the mission outpost supplied with electricity during key hours of the day was off for the noon siesta, and a silence so palpable it hummed in his ears descended over the high plateau. Ilusan was situated in a sprawling rectangle along Kulasihan Creek, a slow-moving green river along the center's western edge that rarely received a clean shot of sunlight, so thick were the overhanging trees. Located roughly in the middle of Mindanao, the large southern island in the string of islands that made up the Philippine archipelago, Ilusan was one of the most significant missionary bases in all of Asia. The Bible Translation Mission, which operated the center, was the largest North American Protestant missionary organization in the world, with outposts in countries literally around the globe. After getting its start in Mexico and Latin America, the mission, which focused on Bible translation for indigenous groups, began making inroads into Asia in the 1950s. In 1956 the first Asia area director, following logging roads onto the high plateau that dominated central Mindanao, stumbled across the clear frosty springs which gave Ilusan its name and immediately recognized its potential. He wasted no time in securing a one hundred year lease from an accommodating local land owner. By 1978 when Philip arrived, while the springs remained its crown jewel, the dozens of tropical fruit trees, neat two story homes arranged around broad grassy plazas, grade school and four boarding homes to look after the children of hard-working Bible translators, recreational facilities including basketball and tennis courts and several grass volleyball courts, and regular flight service to the scattered mission outposts throughout the jungles and islands of the southern Philippines had turned Ilusan into the envy of mission boards around the world.

Philip had survived the jet flight and the hubbub of the airport at Cagayan, where he had kept his hand firmly on his wallet while besieged by a pack of luggage porters all eager to earn the exorbitant sums that could be extorted from an obviously out-of-place American, until he was rescued by Tom Jacobson, the smiling clean-cut mission pilot. Tom led him to a blessedly quiet end of the terminal away from the majority of the travelers. He had rested there with a cold bottled soft drink while Tom collected his luggage for him. There followed a wary forty-five minute flight in one of the mission's single engine Helio Couriers during which Tom tried to size up the newcomer and Philip tried to avoid being too closely sized up. The welcoming committee at the center had been small. The base hostess seemed apologetic. "Folks are looking forward to meeting you at church on Sunday," she said while driving him in an ancient army surplus "Carry-all" to the house that would be his home for the next year.

Now, alone, he slumped, exhausted from what seemed like days of travel, in a chair constructed of weathered strips of woven bamboo. The chair sat next to a small wooden table on the back porch of his house. Sitting here, Philip could see little of the mission center itself, as his gaze was directed east, away from Ilusan's heart. To his left a line of thick trees shielded his view of the dirt road that connected the center to the main highway somewhere across the corn field that lay immediately in front of him. The tree line turned sharply at the corner of his property, before proceeding down the row of houses that, like his, had a back porch facing east. Someone had clearly planted them with the intention of shading the homes from the intense equatorial sun, a job they fulfilled quite admirably. The primary object in his view was the corn field, but just off center to his left, he could make out the rough wooden beams of the water tower which supported the enormous tank that supplied the center with running water. If he leaned forward to permit his vision to clear his roofline and looked up and to his left, he could see the silver side of the tank through the tops of the trees. At its base, he noticed a sign painted in bright yellow, urging its readers not to climb the tower. He thought that he would climb it soon, probably in the next few days, as it must provide a nice view of the center. It struck him that anyone walking or driving down the road to Ilusan would see the water tower first, and that they would immediately recognize that this was no Filipino village, but that Americans, with their money, technology, and know-how lived here.

But now he leaned back and gazed out across the corn field which began about thirty yards from his porch. The field was held back by a barbwire fence that ran from the water tower to the far southeast corner of the center. He had already observed that approximately ten homes stretched in a loose southerly line from his house before giving way to an empty field which appeared to occupy the far end of the center. He knew from flying over it less than an hour ago, and from the mimeographed map which lay on the side table next to him, that almost seventy buildings filled the acres behind him before running out of room against the river that meandered along the western periphery. He felt the weight of those buildings now, and the weight of all those people he would soon have to meet. He picked up the map again. It was damp from the humidity and stuck to his fingers. He glanced over it, noticed the spring fed pool just off the river, and picked out the buildings that weren't private homes: the four children's dormitories, the generator shed, workshops, lumber shed, library, two public bathrooms, meeting hall, several office buildings, nursery, post office, commissary, a radio shack up the hill at the extreme northern end of the center by the airplane hangar and runways, and finally, also by the hangar and at the highest elevation on the center, the three buildings that made up Samantha Stoddard Memorial grade school. He wondered briefly who Samantha Stoddard was, then set the map down. Plenty of time for that later. He hadn't even unpacked yet. Right now he wanted to sit on his porch and stare. He wanted to feel that he had finally arrived and that this place was utterly foreign. He thought he might take another nap.

The heat had been working on him ever since he arrived shortly before noon, and now he ran his fingers idly along his arm, tracing a line through the moisture saturating his skin. It was not an unpleasant feeling, as it had been in Manila, the capital city on the west coast of the northern island of Luzon, where the heat, humidity, and raw smoke billowing from the thousands of buses, taxis, and jeepneys had nearly suffocated him. He felt there like he was constantly moving through a hot light rain, although it hadn't rained a drop during his two days there. A light rain dancing off a blazing skillet. The hair on his head had been fiercely hot to the touch. If he hadn't been so constantly wet, he might have worried about spontaneous combustion. Still, he caught himself wincing when a taxi driver flipped a cigarette butt in his direction. At Ilusan, however, on the high plateau in the center of Mindanao, miles from the ocean and one thousand feet above sea level, the shade trees and the breeze kept the heat, and more importantly the humidity, to manageable levels. He imagined the evenings might be pleasant enough to permit sleep. Maybe later he would follow his map to the swimming pool, that legendary watering hole whose glories mission personnel had sung to him from the moment he'd arrived at the mission's group home in Manila a few short days ago.

He'd been sitting there for twenty minutes when he noticed a girl perched about half-way up the tree directly between his house and the water tower. She was in the deep shade on a branch next to the trunk. She was watching him intently. He was startled, but thought he hadn't betrayed his knowledge of her presence. He decided to wait her out. He turned his chair so he was directly facing her, stretched out again, intertwined his fingers on his stomach, and eyed her as intently as she observed him. She appeared to have long hair, the color he couldn't tell, as the shade was too deep. Gangly, he thought. She was wearing either shorts or a short skirt. One bare leg in a patch of sunlight told him that much. Probably shorts, or she wouldn't be up a tree. She must have noticed the leg exposed in the patch of sun, as she suddenly made a small move to withdraw it, then caught herself and remained absolutely still. They continued staring at one another for what seemed to him like ten minutes, but were probably really just two or three.

"I see you," he finally said.

She didn't betray herself for another long minute. Finally, "Took you long enough," she said.

"I was expecting monkeys in my trees, not little girls."

"I'm not little."

"Sorry, it's hard to tell when you're sitting in a tree."

With a few expert movements, which startled Philip with their sure speed, she was standing on the ground. She stepped hesitantly into the sunlight. He saw that her hair was a sun-bleached yellow-brown and reached the middle of her back. She was wearing a light blue tank top and red shorts. She was barefoot.

"See, I'm really tall for my age," she said.

"Not if you're twenty-five."

"I'm not twenty-five. That's obvious! I'm thirteen. I'm in eighth grade."

"Really? I'm the new teacher for the seventh and eighth grades." She took this news calmly.

"I know that."

"What you don't know is that I'm going to grade you extra hard for spying on me."

"How can you if you don't know my name?"

"You think you're going to go an entire school year and I'm not going to figure out your name?"

She considered this for a moment while she rubbed her toe in the dirt. "No, I suppose not." Then, "It's easy to spy if you're quiet. People always leave their windows open."

"It's easy to give bad grades."

"It wouldn't matter. I always get bad grades."

"Really, why is that?"

"School is boring."

"You've never had me for a teacher." He was surprised at the confidence of his retort. She took a step closer.

"Can you make Math interesting?"

"Nope, sorry, not even I can do that."

She came the rest of the way uninvited and sat on the steps. She leaned forward with one elbow on the porch. "What *can* you make interesting?"

"Maybe history, maybe literature, sometimes art, although I'm not an artist."

"Can we study about President Carter? My daddy says we have to pray for him because he's a Christian president."

Philip raised his eyebrows. "You all are a bit behind on your news over here aren't you?" The girl just looked at him. "Never mind," he said.

"What about science?" Philip thought she moved on from Carter almost as fast as people were back home.

"Science is interesting, but I can't explain it."

"Then how are you going to teach it to us?"

"Maybe I won't."

Her eyes opened a little wider. "You have to. What are we going to do during Science period?"

"I don't know. Maybe we'll put some frogs in a pot, light a fire under it, and see if they jump out when it gets hot."

She didn't get the reference. "Why on earth," emphasizing "earth" in her girl's voice, "would we do that?"

"To see what the frogs do. That's what scientists do. After they've tested the frogs, they put in cats, maybe a bird or two."

She looked conflicted, like she didn't know whether to laugh or be horrified. She chose puzzled skepticism. "The cat would never stay in the water while you lit a fire."

"Maybe not, but I think we have to try. It's not a good experiment if you don't test all hypotheses."

"I think I remember that word from last year. I don't remember what it meant."

"I don't really know what it means either. I just like to say it because it makes kids like you think I know a lot."

At this she smiled. "You're weird." She said it over several times under her breath. "Weird, weird, weird . . . ." It was the purest smile he'd ever seen.

She thought for a moment. "Can you make the Bible interesting?"

"The Bible?!" He was caught off guard.

"Yes, in Bible class."

"Don't they teach you that in Sunday school or something?"

"Of course. Aunt Audrey teaches the older kids. We're studying Romans, and I have to tell you," he was struck by how adult she suddenly sounded, "I have to tell you, I don't understand it most of the time." She stared off into the corn field. When she looked back at him, she seemed mildly irritated. "But you still have to teach us Bible class three times a week."

"So I see." The news did not set well.

"Can you make it interesting?"

He was suddenly nervous. This was someone's child, someone who would expect him to play the role assigned him. What exactly was that role? He hadn't known it included the pastoral. He'd scarcely thought about his role at all until this moment.

"Well the Bible's very important to know." He paused. He wondered how he could end this interview. But the girl gave no inclination of leaving any time soon. He knew that the Bible was, in fact, extremely important to evangelicals. Many believed it was inerrant, not one false word, not one mistake. Everyone on this center had dedicated their lives to transmitting the Bible to indigenous cultures. He'd better get this right. Finally he said, "The Bible is very interesting I think."

"And why do you say that?" Another curiously adult phrase. He was stuck and he knew it.

"It tells interesting stories." Her eyes, which rarely left his face, seemed much older than the rest of her. He wanted to ponder this phenomenon, but he had to focus. This was what they would have called a God-arranged special opportunity back in Bible college. He should have known how to handle this. If only his tenure at Bible college had lasted a little longer, been a little more successful. What should he say to this kid? He tried to be profound. "The Bible tells us about God. It's important to know about God don't you think?" O.k. Maybe it wasn't so profound. He wasn't sure he knew how to be profound on this subject. The girl said nothing. "Look around you. I haven't even seen much of this place yet, but it seems beautiful and very interesting. The person who made all this must be interesting." It was lame, and he knew it. He noticed that a cow had wandered through the corn. It was chewing its cud, lazily staring at them through the fence. Maybe humor would throw her off track. "Cows are interesting. Do you think someone who made that cow might possibly be interesting? Maybe that's what we'll do in Bible class. We'll talk about that cow."

She looked at the cow, then back at him. "Weird," she said. "Weird, weird, weird . . . ." Then, "You're really in trouble aren't you?" Philip stared at her. He couldn't get a handle on the girl. She parsed every flip thing he said much too closely.

"You think so? How come? What do you mean?"

"You must read the Bible." The way she said it meant, you're here, so you must be a Bible reader, but Philip worried she was starting to wonder.

"Of course!" But then he was too weary to do the work necessary to resurrect who he used to be, or who he was supposed to be now, at least not with this kid. He'd have to dissemble enough in the days ahead. He didn't have the energy to start now. Time to cut his losses. "O.k. I'm going to give it to you straight. Are you ready for the truth?" She nodded. "I've never taught school before." She didn't even blink. "I've gone to school a long time, and I know lots of stuff. And I've always wanted to be a teacher. I heard you guys needed a teacher, so I came over here to teach for a year. But I didn't know I was going to have to teach the Bible. I really didn't. I like the Bible, and when I was your age I had to read it a lot. My Dad was a preacher. So I'll brush up on it and I'll make it interesting I promise. We'll only study the cool parts." He leaned back again in the chair. He was glad she didn't ask for elucidation as to which parts of the biblical record might be aptly characterized as cool. "I'll make you a deal," he continued. "I'll try really hard to make school, even science and the Bible, interesting for you this year. And you have to promise to stop asking so many questions."

"I don't know if I can do that."

Philip finally had to laugh. "You are really something else, aren't you?" She regarded him with a straightforward gaze. Philip couldn't tell if she thought his remark was a compliment or an insult. "Actually, you're right. No teacher should tell a kid not to ask questions. Strike that comment from the record please."

She nodded her head. Philip took it as compliance. "But at least, as your part of the deal, don't go telling people that I'm weird or in trouble. Actually, on second thought, since you know this place a whole lot better than I do, if you really think I'm about to get in trouble, warn me. Is that a deal?"

"O.k." She must destroy the other kids in stare contests with those brown unwavering eyes. "I don't talk to very many people anyway. I seem to prefer to be alone. My mommy says I'm dreamy." There it was again. Was she thirteen? Eight? Thirty? Philip realized he didn't know much at all about thirteen-year-old kids. Probably not a good thing considering he was about to spend a year with them in the classroom.

The conversation seemed to have run its course. The girl was silent; she played with her hair, looking now around the yard, now sneaking peeks at Philip. Philip tried in vain to figure out a way to probe the girl's last remark.

"You have long hair," she finally said.

Somewhere he heard the generator start up. A light that had been left on in the room behind him suddenly burst to life. She jumped up. "I was supposed to go with my mom to the commissary." She started to dash down the path.

"Wait! I have what?! What were you doing in my tree?"

She stopped. "I climbed the tree when they announced your plane coming in." He must have looked puzzled, because she added, "They always announce over the loud speaker when one of the planes is landing and they say who's on it. It almost always goes right over this corner of the base, and I like to watch it take off and land. So I climb this tree almost to the top. Sometimes when there's a strong wind, the airplane almost stops in the sky right up there. It stops." She looked at him like she didn't think he would believe her. "It really stops."

"I believe you. I've heard that your mission planes are like that."

She sighed. "You just happened to get the house right next to my favorite tree. I didn't know they were going to put you here."

"Well, it's still your tree. Climb it any time. You don't have to ask permission. Just don't spy on me."

"I wasn't spying." The words were emphasized in mock exasperation. "At least I wasn't planning to. I was just watching the airplane and then I was enjoying the tree and then you were there and then," she fumbled for how to put it, "and then I was embarrassed. O.k." She suddenly turned, ran down the path, and disappeared around the corner of the neighboring house.

"Goodbye to you too," Philip muttered. "Usually you say goodbye, maybe say see you later, maybe wave. Usually you don't just stop talking and then run away. Or am I missing some strange Filipino custom?" He had noticed that in the movies people rarely said goodbye when talking on the phone. They just abruptly hung up. Maybe it was like that here. Conversation over, hang up. Oh well, he wouldn't be seeing any movies for at least a year. He wondered what kind of radio reception they got out here. Probably just Voice of America. Who knows when he'd find out if his beloved Cincinnati Reds made it to the Series. He wondered if missionaries were sports fans. Probably not, unless they could tie it somehow to the Bible. Did you know that God invented baseball? No, did he really? Yes, when he created the earth in the Big Inning. The most you could say for evangelical jokes was that they weren't dirty. Unfortunately they usually weren't funny either. He entered the house, remembered he had never learned the girl's name, hurried back to the porch, but of course she was gone. He sat down wearily on the steps. He looked for the cow, but it had also wandered off. He was alone.

He found that the conversation with the girl had left him feeling melancholy. He envied her confidence, her dash down the path into the interior, the ownership she felt of trees, of a place and of a people. How she immediately recognized that he didn't quite fit. He could only hope the adults weren't as perceptive. He was reminded of what an enormous step he had taken, or rather "fallen ass backward into as usual," as a friend of his would have put it. And the friend would have been right. Philip had washed up here as he had washed up most places in his life, at someone else's initiative. His physical location at Ilusan seemed symbolic somehow. Here he was once again on the outskirts of a tightly-knit community literally facing away from something of which he longed to be a part, but also desperately wanted to flee. He had been a member of a religious community as a child, the way the girl was now. But he had lost his place in his community, drifted away, rejected it, did it really matter how? He had tried to join other communities, loose secular bands of friends, but had never been able to do so with an open heart. The religion of his childhood haunted him. He carried about with him a vestigial sense of doom, and his enjoyment of his life apart from his church had been always skin deep, flecked with bitterness.

But when he'd been a member of his church, enveloped by his parents' community, he had also felt a nagging estrangement. When he'd been in, he had wanted out. He had desperately longed to be what he thought of as a normal person in the world, not publicly stamped with his parents' fierce devotion. Philip thought now that his life consisted of two neat halves lived by two different people. One wanted out; one wanted in. They slumbered in peaceful coexistence for the most part, neither really acknowledging the other. He felt now as if he was struggling to push the wrong two ends of a magnet together. He could force them close but ultimately they resisted the connection. He hoped this trip to the Philippines might help him reverse the poles. He longed to jam the two halves of his life together, to wake up the two Philips and force a reunion. It remained to be seen, once awake, just how they would get along. And that he'd come thousands of miles for this little experiment? A whim of fate perhaps, or, just maybe, a necessary step. He was alone here, no family, no friends. It was an ideal setting in which to reinvent himself.

He looked around once more and then went inside to unpack. He went first into the bathroom. As he passed the sink he caught a glimpse of himself in the mirror. He turned his head from side to side, skeptically observing the hair that curled over his ears and touched his shoulders. "You have long hair," the girl had said. He wondered if the remark was her first word of warning.

# Chapter Two

"Have you been swimming yet?" The question was asked by Lillian Troyer, a red-headed bespectacled missionary who Philip estimated was probably in her mid-fifties. Her glasses had wings in the corners, and she wore them on a chain around her neck, perhaps worried that at any moment they might leap into flight in a desperate bid for freedom. They were an odd color, a mix of black and burnt-orange, like an embarrassed wasp. She looked like a good humored librarian, the kind who twinkled at you when you talked rather than shushed you.

Lillian and her sister, Evelyn, along with their aging mother, Dorothy, were his nearest neighbors, occupying the house two doors down. Both of the houses next to his were empty at the moment, the residences of missionaries who were currently out in their allocation. Someplace in the jungle as far as Philip knew. The four of them were sitting on the women's back porch, the sisters together on a bench swing, the old woman on a chair next to them, and Philip facing them on a chair brought from the dining room. The sisters wore 1950s era vintage dresses. They had covered their mother's lap with a blanket, and Dorothy sat rocking slightly and staring straight ahead across the corn field. Her mouth moved as if she was praying, but no sound came out. "Mom isn't always with us," Lillian had whispered to Philip, but clearly the sisters tried to include her in their daily activities.

The Troyer women were the first stop on his dinner tour, a four-day schedule of meals arranged at different homes by the base hostess, designed to keep him fed for a few days and to introduce him to a few of the center's regulars. He had found the schedule on the dining room table in his house neatly typed and placed in an envelope along with a welcome letter and an information sheet. When Lillian asked Philip if he'd been swimming yet, the women had just introduced him to a local beverage. It was kalimansi juice, a tiny citrus so sour it would ruin the sweetest disposition Lillian said with a wink, but when mixed with a pound or two of sugar made an astoundingly delicious drink. Philip decided immediately that his refrigerator would never be without it. It was a vow he quickly forgot, as he was too lazy to do anything in the kitchen that wasn't absolutely necessary to keep him alive and functioning at a minimal level. Besides there were plenty of soft drinks available in the commissary that only required a bottle opener to tap their life-giving resources.

He had in fact been for a swim that afternoon. He hadn't needed much time to unpack or acquaint himself with his home. There were two rooms on each side of the central dining room/living area. Two bedrooms on one side, a study and kitchen on the other. The kitchen cupboards and the refrigerator had been modestly supplied with staples, sort of a missionary starter pack. His first real shock came when he noticed that the only milk to be had came out of a box. He followed the recipe on the large blue container and decided that it would be preferable to simply soak a white crayon in water. Maybe if he doubled the amount of powder it might at least provide a suggestion of milk. He imagined a marketing slogan—"Hint 'o Milk." Some cereal, rice, and tins of meat completed his starter pack. A hand of bananas sat by the sink. He thought he'd better get to the commissary as soon as possible.

The bathroom and shower could be entered from the back porch or the back bedroom. There might have been a tussle for that bedroom if he had a roommate, but he had specifically requested that he live alone, and, as there was no shortage of housing on the center due to the number of missionaries in their allocations at any given time, the center administrator had somewhat reluctantly agreed. There was a porch on either side of the house, but he had already decided that the back porch would be his primary reading and work space. Facing away from the center, and situated as his house was on the perimeter, it promised a good deal of privacy.

The house was built about four feet off the ground, almost high enough to string a hammock under. It rested on posts grounded in cement footings. He would later learn these were precautions to avoid termites. The posts were of irregular thickness, and some weren't perfectly straight, but they seemed sufficient to the job. While the interior of the house was paneled, the exterior was crafted from split and then tightly woven strips of bamboo, giving it the look of an Indian basket. Much of the furniture was constructed from this same material. The roof was steeply angled and appeared to be made of sheets of corrugated tin. In spots it glowered with rust. At the corner of the house under his bedroom window, a downspout funneled into an equally rusty red rain barrel. It was only half full, and he noticed what he thought were tadpoles darting just beneath the surface of the water. Every window and doorway was screened. Philip saw what looked like two large torpedoes around the corner under his kitchen window. A closer inspection revealed that these were the propane tanks that fueled the stove and refrigerator. The dials indicated they were both full.

After inspecting his house, he had decided it was time to venture out, and, what with the heat of the afternoon, the pool seemed the logical place to visit first. He changed into his swim trunks, and, in a moment of uncertainty, put on a tee shirt as well, before throwing a towel over his shoulders, donning flip flops, and exiting his front door for the first time headed for the interior of the center. With his map in his suit pocket just in case, he followed a path down a slight hill between two rows of houses.

"I guess I shouldn't have put on that tee shirt," he said now to the Troyer sisters. He had decided they had a sense of humor, or at least Lillian did, so thought he would share his first moment of humiliation with them. They looked at him expectantly. "I hadn't even gotten to the bottom of the hill when a woman calls from an upper story window and asks me if I would take her little girl swimming with me."

Evelyn Troyer glanced at Lillian, then covered her mouth and murmured, "Oh my."

"Yes. I turned to see who was talking to me, and when she saw me, she threw her hands over her face, blurted, 'I'm so sorry,' and disappeared into her house."

Lillian didn't understand. She looked at Evelyn. Evelyn was embarrassed. She touched her hair and then gave a meaningful glance in Philip's direction. Lillian began to laugh. She also said, "Oh my." Then she covered her mouth with her hand. "I'm sorry," she said through her hand. "I guess a man with your hair is an unusual sight at Ilusan. But I can't believe someone mistook you for a woman! Who was it? What house was she in?"

"It was at the bottom of the hill on the left."

Lillian clucked her tongue. "Oh, Loretta, Loretta. I bet Loretta didn't have her glasses on. The Montgomerys haven't been to the States in a long time, and I'm afraid Loretta is even more out of touch than the rest of us."

He asked, "So what kind of sign is it that my first day here, the first time I walk out of my house, I get mistaken for a woman? I didn't think my hair was that long!"

"Dear Jesus!" This sudden interjection from Dorothy startled Philip. The old woman was staring at him. "Jesus," she said again.

Evelyn reached out and touched her mother's arm. "Are you o.k., mother? Are you warm enough?" Philip didn't see how warmth would ever be a problem for anyone here, but the woman was quite elderly.

Dorothy didn't respond, only lapsed back into her rocking and whispering.

"She's o.k.," Evelyn said to Philip. "She'll interject something every now and then. It's usually a prayer or a section of Scripture. That seems to be all she remembers now, which is a great comfort to us."

"So she wasn't responding to what I said?" Philip was relieved.

Lillian got up and poured him some more kalimansi juice. "I don't think so. But if she could see your hair she might have a thing or two to say. Mother was a strong woman in her day." She sat back down and smiled at Philip. "Most of the men here wear their hair pretty short. Some of the high school boys, when they come back from Faith Academy, have longer hair, but even Faith doesn't let them grow it very long. You'll definitely stand out." She paused and sized up his appearance for a long minute. "If you ever want a trim, Evie cuts my hair."

"Lillian!" Evelyn exclaimed. "He doesn't want a haircut. I've never cut a man's hair."

"Dear God," said Dorothy.

"Well," said Philip, with a glance at Dorothy, "maybe I should get it cut if it's going to be a problem. I don't want to offend anybody. So, Evelyn, you might get to practice on a man yet. You can give me your best Jesus cut." He regretted it as soon as he said it, but Lillian laughed, and even Evelyn smiled.

"You'll have to grow a beard," Evelyn said, and then insisted they all come inside for dinner.

As the sisters helped their mother into the dining room, Philip considered his position. He was glad he'd shared the story with the sisters. He knew that at an isolated outpost like Ilusan, Loretta's story would make the rounds quickly; maybe a dozen people already knew it. By tomorrow night everyone would. Better to get an alternate version out there, a version that said he could be a good sport about such things, that he could acknowledge with a smile his differences even as he refused to flaunt them. He desperately didn't want to draw undue attention to himself; his goal was to fly beneath the radar as long as he possibly could. He knew now he should have cut his hair. But coming from a college campus in California in 1978, he had realized too late that it might be a problem. When he arrived in Manila, his uncle had quietly suggested a haircut, passing it off as a tip for keeping cool, but Philip knew the real reason for the remark. He had half intended to comply, although he was just stubborn enough to resent the implication, but with everything else he had to get done during his two days in the capital city, he had simply never gotten around to it. Besides he was as vain as the next person. He thought he looked good with long hair, and you never knew when a girl worth impressing might pop up. He had to admit now that, as usual, he hadn't thought it through carefully. It was the Apostle Paul who argued that long hair dishonored a man, and Philip knew most missionaries took the Apostle's suggestions very seriously indeed. He could only hope that most of them would find Loretta's story funny rather than threatening.

An hour later they were enjoying dessert and Philip was remarking in mock horror at the carnage unleashed outside the screen window. The sun set shortly after 6:00 p.m. which probably explained why the dinner invitation had been for 5:00. He supposed everyone ate early, went to bed early and got up early, a thought which caused him some regret. As soon as the sisters turned on the interior lights, the screens began to fill up with all manner of bugs, small flapping moths, longer stick-like creatures with buzzing wings, fat flyers with waving antennae, what looked like red ants with red-rimmed translucent wings, and even a black-shelled creature with horns like a rhinoceros. Now nearly a dozen lizards bivouacked on the screen. Gray with very pale bellies, about five inches from head to tail, they were clearly in no danger of starvation. The most sincerely converted native could not have been happier for the arrival of the missionaries than these lizards, which with the flick of an electric switch found a rich smorgasbord laid out for them nightly. A sudden dart forward or to one side, a snap of jaws, and wings beat helplessly against the lizard's beatifically closed eyes. After a long moment, during which the wings gradually slowed, the lizard's throat worked convulsively as it swallowed the hapless creature whole. But as fast as they ate, more bugs filled the screen. Despite the screens, bugs already flocked to the interior lights, and lizards crept along the ceiling, moving easily upside down, gorging themselves on any insect that landed nearby.

"Does this slaughter go on every night?" Philip asked.

"Every night," said Lillian. "Now you know why we sleep under mosquito nets." She watched a lizard on the roof for a minute. "I scarcely notice the bugs anymore," she said. "Although I could do without the roaches."

"And the ants," Evelyn chimed in. She proceeded to instruct Philip on the fine art of ant avoidance in the kitchen, how everything, every scrap, had to be carefully put away in the refrigerator, how the counters must always be clean, how jars with anything sweet inside should always be washed so that no particle of jam or peanut butter remained on the lid, etc. He half listened, sipping his coffee and taking irregular bites of chocolate cake.

He had thoroughly enjoyed his meal with the two women. It had been simple, rice and chicken and some steamed greens. They told him how to cook rice, as they assumed he, like they, would fix it for almost every meal. He thought he probably would. He couldn't live for a year on corn flakes, although he was tempted to try. Anyway, rice seemed easy enough. Just add water and cook. Soy sauce was the universal condiment. The sisters soaked the rice, chicken, and even the greens in it.

As they ate, they quizzed him about his life. He told them the parts he thought they'd want to hear, practicing for the life story, or testimony, he knew he'd have to tell over and over during the next few weeks. He had grown up a preacher's kid in a pious and very conservative Protestant home. He focused most of that part of the story on his father's ministry, which had been quite successful for a time, avoiding his own peccadilloes and uncomfortable adventures with various authorities. He did mention the Bible camp when he was fourteen, where, around a roaring camp-fire, he had "turned his life over to the Lord," something which, if he'd been honest, he would have been obliged to report he had done virtually every night of his young life. He had often confused a need to repent with a need to start over at the beginning. He had a vivid imagination, and sermons and biblical verses about hell toyed mercilessly with his young mind, and he had determined at an early age that it was better to be safe than sorry. The Lord, essentially, had an open invitation to enter his heart and take over his life, an honest invitation which, judging by the activities to which the boy had been constantly drawn, the Lord had for reasons of his own apparently refused. But during high school Philip had achieved a certain respectability within the community, or at least ceased for a few years to be a blight on his father's ministry, so now he played up those years, talking about his leadership at Young Life events and his victory in a Young Preachers' Contest his senior year.

When his life story reached his college years, he became somewhat of a fabulist, fabricating and bowdlerizing where the interests of good taste outweighed the requirements of conscience. He avoided any mention of his unfortunate sojourn at the Bible College of San Diego, instead reporting that after high school he had "sought the Lord's will" while working various meaningless jobs, before deciding to major in history at San Diego State. While there, or so he now suggested—in fact he made this part up on the spot—he had "felt led by the Lord" to become a teacher. This sentence, which bordered on the fantastic, stunned him even as he said it, and he was forced to pause for a moment to recover. It was only later that evening, as he reflected on the story he had told, that he decided he must have said it in an attempt to provide a natural rationale for his coming to Ilusan. It certainly had a nicer ring than the truth, which was that his uncle, who happened to be the director of the Philippine branch of the Bible Translation Mission, suggested his exotic sojourn as a way to help him find direction in his life, and, not just coincidentally, fill a position for a year that the branch desperately needed filled.

The truth was that he had not decided in college to become a teacher, and in fact, had always wondered what that phrase "I felt led by the Lord" actually meant. Everyone he had grown up with said it so casually, but, despite often asking for leading from the Lord, he had never actually felt led about anything. But, having committed himself before the sisters to this version of his story, he had plunged on, attributing his going on for a master's degree in history, also at San Diego State, to this certain leading. It did, he had to admit, make for a nice transition to his arrival now at Ilusan to teach the seventh and eighth grades just in time to fill the mission's vacancy. "Mmmmm, mmmmm," said the ladies, "God's timing is perfect."

Now, after Evelyn finished her dissertation on ant avoidance, Philip asked the sisters to tell him their story. How did two sisters wind up as a missionary team in the Philippines?

Evelyn looked at Lillian. "Lillian is a better storyteller," she said.

"Well," began Lillian, "it's what we've always wanted to do, and, since we couldn't talk any men into marrying us, we decided to team up with each other."

"I don't believe that for a minute," said Philip. "Besides there must be a lot of available men around here."

"There are lots of men," said Lillian, "but they're all married. Very few single men go overseas as missionaries, nowhere near the numbers of single women. I think it's because men have so many options at home. They can be pastors and teachers, and of course they can ask anyone to marry them. But being a missionary is one of the few options women have if they want to serve God."

"Which means, by the way," said Evelyn, "you'll be a rare commodity Philip. I can think of several young women here at the center who will have their eye on you."

"Keep your eyes on Jesus," exclaimed Dorothy loudly enough to bring the conversation momentarily to a halt. She was once again staring at Philip. She seemed to want to say something else.

"We will mother, we will," said Evelyn. "Now, Lillian, start from the beginning. Tell him about father and about Guatemala. Philip can take it. Besides, he got mistaken for a woman today. He deserves a good story." Philip couldn't read how she said this. Her eyes were neutral, but her voice seemed weary. He glanced at Dorothy. The old woman's eyes were rheumy and red. She might have been crying.

"Well," he said, "that got my attention."

Lillian started over. "O.k., but you have to understand that our story isn't typical, or at least, our parents weren't typical." Philip promised not to judge. He figured he knew how the story would go. Their parents hadn't been Christians, he supposed, which at Ilusan would probably make them stand out. He was quickly proven wrong. The sisters' parents were very Christian, in fact had been medical missionaries with the Latin American Indian Mission. "We grew up in Guatemala," Lillian continued, "where our folks were stationed in a small town by a beautiful mountain lake called Atitlán. Do you remember Atitlán mother?" Dorothy was still gazing at Philip. "Evie and I loved swimming in that lake. Father was a wonderful man, but," here she glanced at Evelyn, "he was his own bird. You might say he was a bit eccentric. One day when we were quite young, maybe twelve and ten, Father sat down at the dinner table, tucked a napkin into his shirt, which he always did, and announced, 'Mother,

I've closed the clinic. We've seen our last patient. Jesus is coming back very soon, and we've got to get these Indians saved. Lancing their boils won't save their souls.' He had been studying the book of Daniel, and he was convinced, absolutely convinced, that the Guatemalan president was being groomed to be the Antichrist. Apparently the president had some socialist leanings and was talking about closing churches."

"I think the Antichrist is supposed to be from the Middle East," remarked Evelyn.

"Maybe your father thought Daniel meant Middle America," said Philip. Again, he instantly regretted it. He wasn't sure the sisters had given him permission to enjoy the story on that level. But Lillian immediately said in mock seriousness, "I hadn't thought of that," and Philip relaxed a bit more. He had to constantly remind himself that most evangelicals had a better sense of humor than his father.

"Anyway I think now it might have just been an excuse," said Lillian. "Father had always loved evangelizing. He could go up to anybody and start questioning them about their beliefs. It was quite inconvenient for the family sometimes; we missed a lot of trains. He could spend half the day arguing with a willing Catholic, and we were in a Catholic country! Anyway I think now he just wanted to be a fulltime evangelist. It caused the mission a good bit of trouble, as they had to find a replacement doctor, but Father never saw another patient. He got up the next morning, saddled the donkey, and rode into the hills. When he got back that first night, he was exhilarated, absolutely flushed with excitement. He had bruises on his back. They'd actually stoned him in some small village. He told them that Mary was not a virgin her whole life, that Jesus had brothers. Imagine that topic for your first day. We had a hard time getting the story out of him. He just kept saying over and over, 'It was Paul at the Acropolis, it was Paul at the Acropolis.'"

Philip decided he did not know how this story would go. Here was something new, interesting, worth remembering, perhaps to repeat to friends at home. He sat up straighter. "Did he keep on evangelizing?" he asked.

"Of course," said Lillian. "He was thrilled to be persecuted for his faith."

"What did the other missionaries think of his techniques?"

"Some of them tried to tone him down a bit, but you have to remember, the missionary enterprise then wasn't nearly as sophisticated as it is now. There weren't graduate programs in linguistics and anthropology. There weren't airplanes and radios. Nobody had any real training. So everyone just did what they thought God wanted them to do."

"Remember Miss Stenson?" said Evelyn.

"Yes, she's a good example," replied Lillian. "She was a single woman who spent months every year riding a donkey by herself from jungle village to jungle village. Rain, mudslides, lodgings where she was the only female, being called terrible names, having rocks and even manure thrown at her, nothing stopped her. She was a legend in Central America. Priests were terrified of her. I remember one time she had a horrible infection on her face. Father was treating her, and warned her that it might leave a scar. 'Praise God,' she said. Father must have looked puzzled, because she said, 'I've always prayed that God would make me homely, so no man would ever want me. I don't want to be bothered when I'm by myself out in the jungle. He's given me this boil in answer to my prayer.' It did leave a scar."

"I think some of the Indians thought she was a witch," Evelyn said. "We used to hide when she came to the house when we were little. She frightened us to death." The sisters laughed. Philip had never heard stories like this from his uncle, or when missionaries visited his church.

"Anyway, Father had been evangelizing for several months when he had his greatest brainstorm," said Lillian. "He came home early one day. He had something wrapped in a large bag. He gathered us all around the table and said, 'Mother, daughters, I have discovered a tool that will revolutionize evangelism. With this tool, and if all the missions work together, we can evangelize all of Latin America in just a few years.' We were breathless with excitement, carried away with his enthusiasm. He was praising God for giving him this profound insight."

"What was it?" asked Philip. He was engrossed.

Lillian and Evelyn looked at each other. Evelyn shrugged. "He finally uncovered his prize," said Lillian. "It was a megaphone. And not some fancy electronic one like you see today. It was simple, but huge, almost as big as I was, like what cheerleaders use. I think it was blue. He must have seen that we were puzzled, because he began pacing the room. 'This will multiply the efficiency of missionaries many fold,' he said. I still remember that 'many fold.' 'Just think Mother,' he said, 'the largest town can be evangelized in just a few minutes, and remote villages reached without hard walking. With a boat I can evangelize the entire coast of

South America in a year.' I don't think missionaries understood back then just how many languages were spoken in some of these countries. Father thought everyone knew Spanish."

"Did you try to talk him out of it?" Philip asked. The pictures in his head made him want to laugh, but he kept control of his emotion. "What did your mother think?"

They all looked at Dorothy. She was rocking again. She seemed to have increased her pace, and she shot looks at Philip.

Lillian sighed. "Mother was a reasonable woman and she tried to make Father think about what he was doing. But you didn't talk Father out of his brainstorms. He would get utterly focused on something and wouldn't let it go until in his mind God told him to stop. And that only happened when the one commitment was superseded by something newer and stronger. He was a wonderful musician in college, but one day walked into the office, dropped all his music classes, and signed up for biology and chemistry. God told him to be a doctor. Now God had told him to be a megaphone evangelist. That very night he dashed off letters to his superiors back in Texas, trying to convince them to equip everyone with a megaphone. When they didn't listen, he wrote to every mission working in Latin America. The more rejections he received, the more feverishly he evangelized. He would find a hill outside a village and start preaching through the megaphone at 5:00 a.m., because he wanted to reach the Indians before they left to work their fields."

"5:00 a.m.!" Philip groaned.

"Yes, he'd often get up at 3:00 or 4:00, put on his tie and jacket . . ."

"Tie and jacket?!" Philip couldn't contain himself.

"Oh yes, you always dressed impeccably for the Lord's work. 'It's warfare,' he used to say to me, 'and I want the devil to know what he's up against. I want the devil to know he's up against an educated Spirit-filled Yankee, not some dumb local yokel.'" Lillian looked at Philip, seemed to think she should explain that last remark, but finally simply shrugged and said, "It was a different time." When Philip didn't respond, she went on. "Father referred to his megaphone ministry as 'attacking' a town with the gospel. Sometimes the town attacked back. He got shot at a few times. One time a shotgun exploded in an Indian's hand, and father actually went down and treated him. One village beat on tin cans to try to drown him out. Another time he climbed up on the roof of a store owned by a Protestant, and the villagers burned down the building.

Fortunately there was a tree nearby that Father jumped to. He barely got away alive. It took a long time to get the smoke smell out of his suit. The mission paid for the store. Father would come home and breathlessly tell us his adventures, and he would always end by saying, 'Faith cometh by hearing.' And the ones who didn't listen, well, 'They've heard the gospel, so they're without excuse.'"

"Hell awaits," Philip muttered to himself.

The women hadn't heard him clearly. He apologized. "It's just something my brother and I used to say all the time when we were kids. We were mimicking my father. Sometimes in one of his sermons he'd list various sins, drunkenness, smoking, going to movies, dressing provocatively, all manner of sexual sins, and after each one he'd shout 'Hell awaits.' 'Are you drinking? Hell awaits. Are you giving your money to Hollywood? Hell awaits. Are you lusting? Hell awaits.' So naturally my brother and I picked up that line and we'd use it with each other all the time. Anything we didn't like we'd look at each other and say, 'Hell awaits.' We thought it was funny, but of course we were scared to death too. I said it one time at the dinner table in reference to my mother's cooking and got thrashed. Anyway, your father's 'without excuse' line reminded me of that."

During the last few minutes of conversation Dorothy had begun rocking faster and faster. She was staring fixedly now at Philip. By the time he finished speaking, the old woman had reached full boil and she popped like a turkey thermometer out of her seat. Philip hadn't imagined she could move so fast. She staggered toward him, her face alight with something akin to rapture. She seized his arm and wheezed, "I love you." Her running eyes fastened on his with frightening intensity. "I love you." She began to moan, and, suddenly running out of strength, sank to her knees before him. She buried her face against his leg and wept.

Both sisters were out of their seats tugging on their mother's arms, but she had Philip's leg in a death grip. By the time they got her pried loose, she was wailing "Jesus" over and over. Philip said, "You don't suppose she thinks . . .," but he couldn't finish his thought. It seemed sacrilegious to say. The sisters were trying to move their mother toward her bedroom, but Dorothy was inconsolable. Almost without thinking, Philip stood and went to the struggling women. "Dorothy," he said, "I think it's time to rest."

She immediately reached out for him and clung to him like a long lost son. "Oh yes," she said. Philip gingerly put his arms around her and slowly her sobs subsided into incoherent whispers. He looked helplessly at Lillian and Evelyn who both were staring at him in astonishment. He shrugged.

"Where's her room?" he asked. The two women led Philip and their mother to her room. By the time he sat her on her bed she was compliant and smiling. "Sleep well Dorothy," he said.

"Yes." The old woman said it so softly Philip wasn't sure he'd heard her. "I can sleep now."

"Thank you," said Evelyn, "we'll get her into bed and be right out."

Five minutes later they were sitting in the living room, and, at Lillian's suggestion, Evelyn served kalimansi juice.

"Well," said Lillian, "I've never seen anything like that before."

They discussed whether maybe Philip looked like someone their mother had known in the past, but decided that the Jesus theory was as good as any. "At any rate I prefer that idea," said Lillian. "Mother's eyes aren't so good, and with your hair, maybe you look like Jesus to her. I think mother will enjoy thinking Jesus is just two doors down."

Philip was skeptical, and decided he should probably avoid the old woman when possible. He didn't want her to think he was a vision of Christ and that her time was up. Who knows what a shock like that might do to her! She had gotten pretty worked up tonight.

Eventually the talk returned to the women's father. Philip wondered how his megaphone adventures turned out.

"He kept it up for almost two years," Lillian said. "He was struck by lightning and killed when he was evangelizing a village early one morning from a tall tree. A storm came in, and Father was so focused on his sermon that he didn't notice. A villager later said the lightning struck before anyone heard any thunder."

"I'm sorry," Philip managed.

"I think it's how Father would have wanted to go," sighed Lillian. "The priests of course had a field day, proclaiming that God had killed the Protestant as a warning to all against converting. We never saw the megaphone again. We heard it was quite charred, but the villagers turned it into a shrine under the tree where Father died. The Indians always respected heroic efforts in the area of religion. They didn't become Protestant, but at least one village thinks Father is a saint to this day."

"What did your family do after your father died?" Philip asked.

Lillian replied, "Mother moved back to the States. She remarried and went back to the mission field, this time to Africa. Evie and I went along of course, at least until we were college age. Our stepfather was a good Christian man. He died several years ago of heart trouble. Mother loved him, but one time she told Evie and me that she still missed our father. 'Your stepfather is a good man,' she said, 'but your father, now he knew how to live.' I've always thought that was the most beautiful thing." After a pause, she continued, "For a long time Evie and I were embarrassed by our father's story. We used to never tell it. But I'm not any more. He was my daddy." It was the first time she had referred to him as anything other than father.

The sisters rounded out the rest of their story. After attending Bible college in Ohio, they had joined the Bible Translation Mission. After a summer's training in linguistics and anthropology, they were assigned to the Philippines. They had been here twenty years, splitting time between Ilusan and their allocation in the jungle in Davao province. They had learned the language of a small indigenous group, created an alphabet, taught the people to read, and were now laboriously translating the New Testament into their language, all while nursing diseases and wounds, interceding in family and tribal quarrels, and living under extreme jungle conditions. It was clear that the sisters loved their work, both of their homes, and the people who had become their family.

Philip was genuinely astonished at their story. Their voices flowed over him. Despite the evening's bizarre events he wasn't on edge. He found he understood the sisters. They were like a well-worn and out-of-date favorite shirt, comfortable, if a trifle embarrassing in the wrong setting. He had been out of these circles for a long time. He recognized the lingo, but it didn't irritate him as it once had. The sisters were genuine and they wore their hearts on their sleeves. Besides, it was nice to be mistaken for Jesus rather than for his opposite number. He'd had some experience with that as well.

At 9:00 p.m. Evelyn remarked that it was probably time for Philip to go. She wasn't being rude. The generator went off at 9:30, and she was concerned that he be settled, or at least have a lamp, candle, or flashlight ready. Philip appreciated the warning. As they said their goodbyes on

the back porch, Philip was struck by the intensity of the insect noise. "Are the evenings always this loud?" he asked.

"Louder," said Lillian. "You're hearing cicadas primarily. But just wait till the rains come and the frogs join in. I find it wonderful background to sleep by. The only thing better is hard rain on these tin roofs."

Evelyn remembered something. "You never told us what you thought of the pool."

"Absolutely amazing," Philip said. "Beautiful! And so cold. What a gift to have the center built around a place like that." He wasn't exaggerating to please the women. The spring-fed pool occupied an area about the size of a football field on the western edge of the center. After his unfortunate encounter with Loretta, Philip had hurried between the meeting hall and the post office in the direction indicated on his map. He immediately saw an area of towering trees and thick undergrowth and knew he had found the legendary swimming hole. The coolness radiating from the pool struck him as soon as he passed beneath the trees and started down a set of rough cement steps. There was a subtle smell as well, a cool smell, a smell of damp undergrowth, moss, and deep springs. The stairs continued right down into the water, but he stepped off onto a wooden pier covered with wire mesh. A young boy was sitting on a diving board, and two girls were talking on the pier, but otherwise the pool was empty. It extended approximately one hundred yards to where a distant spillway carried water into Kulasihan Creek. The primary swimming hole was a deep blue and appeared to be about twenty feet deep. Philip saw small fish swimming around the legs of the pier.

The children watched him as he took off his shirt, left his map with his towel, took a deep breath, and plunged in. He would remember the shock of the cold water on his sweating skin for the rest of his life. "It was one of the most refreshing feelings I've ever had," he told the sisters, and he meant it. He decided to swim to the spillway. After twenty yards or so, the going was more difficult. The water grew shallow, and his legs tangled in thick seaweed. When he put his feet down, he could stand. The water stayed fairly shallow all the way to where it rushed briefly over rocks into the river beyond. Philip stood for a moment in the spillway, feeling the urgent tug of the water almost pull him off his feet. A bridge spanned the spillway above him and beneath it he got a narrow glimpse of the river and thick vegetation beyond.

When he turned back he noticed a small pier on his right. Drawing near, the ground fell away into a crater much deeper than the first one. He couldn't see the bottom here, and the water felt considerably colder. He noticed a rope swing hanging from a tree, its free end knotted around a railing on the pier, but there was no one swimming here at the moment. He rested on a fallen tree. After a few moments he walked down the trunk until it left his grasping toes, disappearing into the dark below him. Treading water, he felt briefly uneasy. Just how deep was it here? What sort of cavern might open up beneath him? He smiled at his own fears. No one would put a rope swing and a pier around a dangerous swimming hole. Nevertheless he began to paddle quickly back toward the main swimming area. Climbing out on the ladder by the diving board, he knew that he would be stopping here daily.

"It lives up to its billing," he said as he wished Lillian and Evelyn a good night.

His house was only a few minutes away. Once outside the warm light cast by the sisters' home, he paused. The sky above him was a distant cacophony of stars. There seemed scarcely a point of darkness that wasn't in danger of being crowded out by the light. He had never seen anything like it. What must the moon be like here? When the generator went off in a few minutes, there would be no source of light for miles around. That thought made him realize again just how far he was from home. It wasn't a bad feeling. He was enveloped in the warmth of the night breeze, the cicada chorus, the universe of light above him.

His reverie was broken by the largest winged creature he had ever seen. Or at least that's how he remembered it later. It passed no more than ten feet above him. The only reason he saw it at all in the dark was because it blotted out the stars as it silently slid by through the thick night air. Philip gasped and ducked. The wing span seemed wider than he could reach his hands. His mind immediately conjured up images of every Dracula movie he had ever seen. He suddenly didn't want to be caught outside when the generator went off, plunging the entire center into darkness. Who knows what might actually be abroad at night in a place like this! He began to run toward his house. Why hadn't he left a light on? He couldn't go very fast because it was difficult to see. Why hadn't he brought a flashlight?

He thought he saw the opening between the trees that marked the path to his back porch. He hurried through, ducking in case the winged creature had landed in one of them. He was about five paces from his porch, when a bright light suddenly shone in his face. It was a flashlight. A girl's voice said, "There you are. I wondered when you'd finish your supper."

He recognized the voice. "Well, if it isn't the tree girl," he said, but he found it difficult to speak. Even though he'd run only a few yards, the adrenaline that shot through him had his body on high alert. The light still shone in his face.

"What's the matter with you?" Her voice sounded mildly amused.

"Let's turn on a light. Shine your flashlight at the door." She obeyed, and he climbed the stairs, reached inside and turned two switches. Both the living room and the porch immediately flooded with light. He collapsed beside the girl on the stairs. "God," he gasped. "What was that thing?"

"You shouldn't say God," she said. "It's sacrilegious."

"What?" He was nonplussed.

She repeated her injunction against taking the Lord's name so cavalierly.

"How do you know I wasn't praying? Maybe I was crying out, God save me from that giant winged creature."

"It was probably just an owl or a fruit bat. You also shouldn't say geez or gosh or golly. They're all short for the name of Jesus."

"How is golly short for the name of Jesus?" But that really wasn't important. He wanted information about fruit bats.

"I don't know, it just is," she said primly. "You also shouldn't say darn, and especially not gosh darn. They're short for, well I can't say it, but they're bad."

He thought he had her. He could explain that gosh couldn't be short for Jesus, if gosh darn was short for God damn. But he couldn't figure out how to explain it all without using any of the taboo words. Besides he really didn't care. He was focused on fruit bats. Owls he understood. But fruit bats?! He pumped her for information.

"They're just huge bats that eat fruit. They eat papayas mostly. The Filipinos say the spirits eat the ripe papayas." She said the last casually, as if papaya-eating spirits were simply part of the local fauna. "Anyway, fruit bats don't bite people. It's the little bats that might bite, but only if you corner them or knock them out of the air with a tennis racket."

"What! They're so thick in the air around here that I might knock one down with my backswing?!"

"No, silly! When they get into your house and you chase them with a tennis racket."

That made perfect sense. "I think I'll just open a window," he said.

"Look, I brought you some fruit." She had a bag beside her. She shook its contents out on the porch. "This," holding up a green fruit the size of a lemon, "is a guava." He had seen guavas before on a trip to Hawaii. He'd never seen anything like the next two objects she held aloft. "This is a rambutan." It was about the size of four large marbles. It was red and had soft spines. She showed him how to dig his thumbs into its side and pop it open. The fruit was white and very sweet. It had a large seed. Next she handed him a yellow fruit the size of an apple and shaped like a star when looked at on end. "It's a balingbing. You eat the stars like corn on the cob."

Suddenly the lights dimmed dramatically then surged back to life. The girl jumped up. "I have to be home by lights out. That means you have ten minutes before they go out."

"Does everybody go to bed at 9:30?"

"Usually, although sometimes I read with a flashlight in bed. On weekends Daddy lights the lamp and we get to stay up till 11:00. But I still have to be home before the generator goes off."

"Well thanks for the fruit."

"Oops, I almost forgot." She pointed. "That's Mr. Bumbles."

Philip followed her finger and saw a large gray cat taking its ease on the railing of his porch.

"My mom thinks Mr. Bumbles has a mind of his own. She doesn't like that. They don't get along. So I thought Mr. Bumbles might want to stay with you." She looked at him as if the gift of a cat ten minutes before lights out on his first night in Ilusan was perfectly normal.

"I can't take your cat," Philip protested.

"He's not my cat. He's Mr. Bumbles. He lived at our house, but now he'll live at yours. I can tell he already likes it."

Philip didn't know what to say. "What do I feed him?" he finally asked.

"Rice and sardines," and she disappeared into the night. Her voice came back to him from somewhere down the trail. "He finds other things to eat too." Then it was quiet.

Philip picked up the balingbing and took a bite. It was somewhere between sweet and sour. He wasn't sure where exactly. He looked at Mr. Bumbles. "You're not going home?" The cat stared back impassively. It yawned and then began to polish its ear with its paw. "Unbelievable," Philip muttered.

The lights suddenly dimmed, then went out completely. From somewhere at the center of the base, he heard the generator wind down and go silent. He was alone on his porch with a large gray cat and some fruit. There was no light except for the stars. The cicadas kept right on singing. In the dark now they seemed to crowd out every other sensory experience. He took a deep breath and let the night noise sweep over him. He pushed aside his fears and enjoyed the moment.

Soon he began to hear another noise over the cicadas. At first he thought perhaps the generator was coming back on, but this was a deeper, nearer sound. It wasn't until Mr. Bumbles rammed his head into his side that Philip realized the cat was beside him purring. The purring had the sound of a motor boat making its way through a swamp. It was hearty, yet muffled, and it stopped and started at times as if the propeller were snagging on hidden debris. Bumbles rammed him hard again with his head, and Philip decided it best to make friends and start petting him. "Well Bumbles, your erstwhile owner dumped you on me. She left without saying goodbye again, which I find very strange, and you know what? I still don't know her name." He couldn't believe he had again forgotten that basic rule of social etiquette.

Eventually he decided he had better try to find his way to bed. He thought he remembered the basic layout of the place. Tomorrow he would find a flashlight and a lamp. He wasn't sure he wanted to get used to going to bed at 9:30. He got up and made his way to the door. "I have a feeling you're going to come in," he said to Mr. Bumbles. He was right.

It wasn't until later, as he lay in bed, that he remembered he'd left the rest of the girl's gifts outside on the porch. He considered retrieving them, but then decided to leave them be, perhaps as an offering to any wandering spirit with a fancy for fresh tropical fruit.

# Chapter Three

THE NEXT DAY WAS Sunday. When Philip woke he was sweating lightly. It didn't take him long to figure out the reason. Not only had the night been warm, but Mr. Bumbles was crowded against him, sleeping soundly with his head on Philip's shoulder like a lover. Bumbles was snoring like a dragon. Philip felt the humid puff of each exhaled breath on his cheek. "Holy shit" was his first thought. He immediately started up and looked around, then, remembering that he was alone, relaxed again. He was going to have to rid his subconscious of such words. In a world where geez was blasphemous, some of his kneejerk expressions might get him banished. At the very least they would bring upon him the suspicion usually reserved for the willfully lost.

Bumbles hadn't stirred despite the commotion. Philip felt discomfort on his cheek and rubbed it with his left hand. The discomfort turned to pain. He stared at his fingers. They were crusty with scab. He rubbed his cheek again. This time his fingers came away with fresh blood. Then he remembered. "Damn Bumbles," he muttered. He smiled to himself and tried again. "Gosh darn you Bumbles." That sounded better on a Sunday morning.

The night before, after the generator's silence plunged his world into darkness, Philip had crawled under his mosquito netting and, as he'd been instructed by the Troyer sisters, painstakingly tucked the net in all around the bed more by feel than by sight. But he had neglected Mr. Bumbles, who stared at him disapprovingly from the opposite side of the net. Or rather Philip assumed the disapproving stare by the sound of the moan emanating from the darkness a foot from his pillow. Philip pulled up enough of the netting to let Bumbles in, only to discover, once they both settled down, that, despite his care, a mosquito had managed to slip through his defenses. After five minutes of fruitless hand clapping in the dark, Philip decided the sound of one single-minded mosquito was worse than the roar of legions. But it was difficult to be grateful when the diabolical whine ceased for a few moments, because then he was left to wonder upon what part of his anatomy the tiny demon was feasting.

After one long moment of silence during which Philip imagined goblets of his sweet blood being slowly savored by the crepuscular insect, or worse, malarial juices being pumped through nasal tubes into his veins, the maddening hum drew near once again. Philip steeled himself, determined to let the bug light on his face where he stood a better chance of killing it with a well-timed swat. A second later, just as he felt the satisfying prick on his left cheek, Mr. Bumbles, apparently equally incensed by the mosquito's presence and deciding to take matters into his own hands, launched a full body assault on the offending bug. Mr. Bumbles' entire weight crashed onto Philip's chest even as he felt a stinging blow on his cheek from Bumbles' paw. At the time, Philip had yelled and pushed Bumbles away, but as long moment after long moment passed with no reoccurrence of the mosquito's war cry, Philip's painful shock had turned to admiration for Mr. Bumbles' adroit coup de grâce. He apologized to the cat and thanked him for ridding them both of the noisy nuisance. He had been amply rewarded by Bumbles' rollicking purr as he drifted off to sleep. It was the scab from Bumbles' open-clawed attack that he had just rubbed open.

Philip's next shock came after he managed to slip away from the sleeping cat and stumble into the shower. A lone pipe ran up the cold aluminum wall in front of him. Philip's eyes followed the pipe to the shower head; it was a simple fitting with one large black hole in the center. He bent over to examine the temperature controls. A single lever stuck out at right angles from the pipe. His early-morning brain began to slowly comprehend the ordeal that awaited him. Throw that lever and the earth's subterranean floods would be unleashed upon him with no intervening device to modulate temperature, at least as far as Philip could see.

"This can't be good," he said out loud. He repeated the phrase under his breath several more times. He was right. As the frigid water cascaded over him, he whooped and jumped, and, he was ashamed to admit, warmed the steely air with imprecations of a sort far viler than had likely been spoken at Ilusan since before the arrival of the missionaries. Philip apologized to God for the verbal slips as, now wide awake, he vigorously toweled off. He was sincere in his apology. He didn't want to get on God's bad side so quickly, or rather, having felt himself living in God's doghouse for many years, he hoped that his journey to the Philippines had begun his climb back into the Almighty's good graces, and he wanted to avoid any needless setbacks. A respectful first Sunday at Ilusan would continue the progress he had been making, and he determined to focus diligently on the worship services before him. He dressed in tan slacks and a light cotton shirt, poured a bowl of corn flakes and white-flavored water, and ate while combing his hair and shaving.

Church was at 9:30 and he had to hurry. He was out the door and down the steps before the thought struck him that it might be good to bring a Bible. He had two. One was a hardback edition with critical commentary. The other had been his grandmother's and then his father's. It was a soft-cover red-letter edition of the King James Bible. Scarcely a sentence in it had gone unlined or uncircled or otherwise unmarked by some generation of Philip's family. It had a leather cover with an engraved sword on the front. It was an easy choice. You never knew who might glance over your shoulder. Philip left the house a second time, this time armed with the very prominent sword of the Lord.

The meeting hall where the community assembled for church was the largest building on the mission base. It stood approximately in the middle of Ilusan immediately beside the center's main road which ran from the highway all the way to the small cluster of southernmost homes down by the banana orchard. Like most of the houses, it was built off the ground on rough posts, and the exterior was constructed of woven bamboo. The interior, which consisted of a couple of storage rooms, bench seating for maybe two hundred people, and a small platform with pulpit in front of a stage complete with curtained wings, was paneled. A piano and organ rested on opposite sides of the pulpit. Open windows lined both sides of the hall. As Philip approached, a man was whacking a large rusty bell which hung from a wooden frame next to the dirt road. People were streaming toward the hall from all corners of Ilusan.

Just before he reached that uncomfortable moment when his forward progress would bear him inevitably into the orbit of strangers whom he would then have to either greet or nervously ignore, a black Suzuki motorcycle roared up beside him. The man who greeted him was handsome and looked like all the world's testosterone could be mined from his veins. He was short and the hair on his arms needed mowing. Thick black curls crawled over the top of his undershirt. He already had a five o'clock shadow, although Philip knew he had recently shaved, because the nick on his chin was still fresh. He introduced himself as Matt St. Clair, the base superintendent. He asked Philip how he was getting settled. Philip thought his accent was strange, sort of a mixture of Alabama and New Jersey. They chatted pleasantly for a few minutes.

As often happened with Philip in conversations with new acquaintances, at one point an off-the-beaten-path neuron fired in his brain and he blurted, "I'd like to climb the water tower by my house and look around if that's possible." Matt, who had just been explaining to Philip that the men on the center took turns preaching on Sundays, took Philip's comment in stride. "Sure," he said. "We don't want the kids climbing up there, but, hey, I'll come by before church tonight and take you up myself. Then I'll give you a lift to church."

"That would be great," Philip said. "I'd just like to get an overview of the base."

"I'll see you about 5:30 then." Matt excused himself to go find his family, but then turned back to Philip as he started up the meeting hall steps. He tapped his own cheek and said, "If you need stitches in that cheek, see the nurse after church." Then he laughed and went inside.

Philip entered the hall and quickly found a seat in the second to last bench on the left side of the aisle. He had forgotten about the scratch on his cheek and figured it must be pretty angry by now. But, as there was little he could do about it, he tried to ignore it. Glancing around the room, Philip estimated there must be between one hundred twenty five and one hundred fifty people, including children, in the pews. A few turned around and smiled at him. Others stole more surreptitious looks and appeared to reserve judgment. They needn't have bothered being coy, because a few minutes later Philip was standing with every eye on him.

Tom Jacobson, his pilot from the day before, was leading the service, and after welcoming everyone, he announced that there were several newcomers to Ilusan. He invited the newcomers to stand, and then, beginning with Philip, asked whoever had hosted the new arrival for dinner the night before to introduce them. Lillian Troyer stood, gave a very brief overview of Philip's life, including the fact that he was the nephew of the Philippine Branch director, and then announced that he was here for a year to teach the seventh and eighth grades. This created no little buzz, and every head turned to look at him.

"Welcome Philip," said Tom, and they all politely clapped. Philip smiled and nodded, struggling to control the burn creeping up his face.

He noticed Dorothy sitting beside Lillian and Evelyn. She was gently rocking, staring straight ahead. Just before he sat back down he saw the girl from his tree sitting with her family on the far side of the room. She gave the briefest hint of a wave, before returning her hands quickly to her lap and glancing at her mother. Philip thought she must have decided a larger wave would be outside the bounds of church decorum.

A young couple from Tennessee was the next to be introduced. They would remain at Ilusan only until an allocation had been chosen for them somewhere in Mindanao or one of the other southern islands. They were Bible translators, and Philip thought they looked as wholesome as a Smokey Mountain morning. The applause for them was unabashed and celebratory, where Philip's had been speculative and nervous. A single man and single woman were the last to be introduced. The young woman had come to work as a literacy consultant. The man was a Bible translator who would help out around the center wherever he could until his partner, another single man he had been paired with over the summer at training camp, finished raising his financial support and came to join him.  Too young for the Troyer sisters, Philip thought.

After their applause died down, Tom announced that the new arrivals would be giving their testimonies in the evening service if that was all right with them. Philip glanced wildly at the couple from Tennessee, but they provided no help, as they eagerly nodded their assent. He imagined himself jumping to his feet and blurting, "I choose not to give my testimony," but he didn't have the stomach for such histrionics. He had known all along that to immerse himself back into the culture of his youth would require him to fashion his life story into some semblance of the approved narrative. He had already begun to do so last night with the Troyer sisters. That his story did not fit easily into the dramatic arc of repentance and conversion was his own fault. He had never been one for stark choices; he had always drifted, and there wasn't much drama in drift.

The uncomfortable fact was that he found himself now in a setting that required him to be on the far side of repentance and conversion, but he had not yet actually repented, at least not of his most egregious recent sins, and the conversion he relied upon was tied up in the *Sturm und Drang* of his youth. He was the prodigal son, but it was as if, instead of the son voluntarily returning home, the father had traveled far to rescue him from his desperate situation, and he was now restored to some semblance of his rightful place but without ever purposefully removing the slop from the pigs which still clung to his clothing. That he hoped to soon do so didn't count. He was a fraud and he knew it. But he was a practiced fraud. He knew the language, and to maintain his seat at the table he would have to rely on the well-intentioned naiveté of the community and the inheritance of rich semantic code which spiraled through his veins. Christianity was in his blood, if not bubbling from his heart.

After the congregation heartily, even expertly, sang a few hymns, Tom got up to preach. Philip sensed his discomfort in the role. Apparently not all the men enjoyed their turn in the pulpit. He began by apologizing for his sermonic ineptitude, and Philip winced, recognizing the common rookie mistake. The audience politely prepared to listen; some made encouraging noises. Tom's theme was the greatness of God, and he began with the standard gambit that ran all the way back to the Enlightenment, how the marvelous complexities of creation demonstrated the necessity for a designer. "Consider the human body," Tom said. Philip perked up. "Consider the ear for example," Tom continued. Philip perked up even more. Tom took out the World Book Encyclopedia volume five, "E." He opened it to the article entitled "Ear." Philip smiled; this was going to be interesting.

For the next fifteen minutes Tom read sections of the encyclopedia article. He recited the names familiar to grade school students everywhere—hammer, anvil, stirrup, tympanic membrane (otherwise known as the eardrum), semicircular canals, and cochlea. He waxed eloquent about how all the parts worked together, nervously pointing to the tiny diagrams, his face desperately trying not to register his dawning realization that nobody further than three feet from him could possibly make them out. Philip was forced to admit that the ear was a fascinating organ, and it was, indeed, hard to imagine that a designer hadn't been involved at some point. He glanced around. Bodies were positioned in a manner which conveyed attentive support, but Philip could tell minds were elsewhere. He tried to help Tom out by keeping his eyes riveted on him, nodding with the best points. Soon Tom seemed to be preaching only to him.

Together they were sharing the intricacies of the Eustachian tube, when Philip noticed that his pew was shaking. No one beside him appeared to be the culprit. Philip glanced behind him. A man, sitting alone at the end of the last pew, was bouncing his right leg rapidly up and down. His head was down and he appeared to be silently shaking with laughter. The man glanced up and caught Philip's eye. He raised an eyebrow and they measured each other for the briefest moment. When Philip turned back around, the man stopped bouncing his leg.

After the service, Matt St. Clair found Philip and introduced him around. Loretta Montgomery had just finished profusely apologizing for her mistaken identification the day before, although she never precisely named the nature of her mistake, when Philip noticed the girl from his tree standing with her mother waiting to be introduced. He excused himself from Loretta, turned to the girl and said, "So, am I ever actually going to learn your name?"

"This is Sally, and I'm Beverly Fraser," said the woman. "I hear the two of you have already met."

"Yes. Your daughter has been a one-person welcoming committee. She's introduced me to some of the native fruit. And I've promised to return the favor by making school interesting this year." It wasn't the correct order of events of course, but Philip thought it best to stay far away from his first conversation with the girl.

"Really!" Beverly looked at her daughter. "Sally will be happy for that, won't you Sally?"

Sally didn't answer the question. "What happened to your face?" she asked. "Did Mr. Bumbles do that?"

"Yep, but it was an accident. We were locked in battle with a mosquito. My cheek was collateral damage, but we got the mosquito." He briefly described the incident.

It suddenly occurred to Philip that Beverly might be unaware that the family cat was now residing with him. "I'm not sure why your cat stayed with me," he said. "I'd be happy to return him."

"I'm delighted he's gone," said Beverly. "That cat has far too much a mind of its own for my taste. But I can't believe you let him sleep with you. You don't have to do that. He'll be happy enough outside. You have to be firm with cats, like with kids. He might fuss, but don't give in. Don't be weak."

Don't be weak. Philip had heard that before. But he let it pass. "I don't mind," he said. "I'll enjoy the company. I think we're going to be friends." He noticed that Sally, who seemed disturbed with her mother's comments, smiled at that. "At any rate I'm going to enjoy having Sally in class this year. She seems like a wonderful young lady."

Beverly said, "Yes, she's a good kid." She asked Philip if he knew that the adult Sunday school class met in the sanctuary. "It will begin in a few minutes. Sally, don't be late for your class. I've got to help prepare the *merienda*." Philip looked puzzled. "It's the word for snack," she said, then hurried away.

Philip looked at Sally. "You don't mind us talking about you while you're standing right there do you?"

"Adults always do that." She didn't pass judgment on the practice one way or the other. "Did Mr. Bumbles really sleep in your bed?"

"Yep. He's still there now as far as I know."

"That's really neat. I always wanted him to sleep with me, but Mom never let him. She didn't even want him in the house."

Standing there in a crowded hall their conversation felt awkward, but Philip clung to it. The girl was already a lifeline of familiarity in a sea of new faces. "Are you ready to start school on Wednesday?"

She made a face. "I guess. I wish it could always be summer."

"It certainly still feels like summer. In fact, technically it still is summer. It's July after all." Starting school in July seemed outrageous to Philip. But in a land of endless summer, endless heat, endless sunlight, it didn't matter much how you arranged your school year. The classroom would always trample on the freedom of the warm outdoors.

Before he could go on a voice behind him said, "Don't worry. They're not all that bad." The man speaking to him was rather disheveled. His graying hair was thinning and his sunburned scalp could be seen through long unruly strands, none of which seemed committed to carrying on in the path blazed by its fellows. The top buttons of his shirt were unbuttoned and the tails were only haphazardly tucked in. From time to time as he talked to Philip he hitched his pants up, made half-hearted attempts at reinserting his shirt tails, and passed his hands through his hair without ever successfully resolving the issue as to what general pattern the strands were intended to conform. He wore wire rimmed glasses and a carefully trimmed goatee, the one startlingly neat aspect of his appearance. Philip recognized the man who had been sitting behind him vibrating his bench with his bouncing leg. "Not quite like your sermons back home, was it?"

Philip was cautious. "No, this was quite different. But I enjoyed it."

"What are you, a masochist?" The man eyed him quizzically. "No, you're just being polite. Very commendable. But unnecessary."

Sally, who was still standing there observing the exchange, broke in and saved Philip the need to say anything further on the subject. "Uncle Joseph, I was talking to Mr. Andrews, and you rudely interrupted."

Philip was surprised. "Is this your uncle?" he asked Sally.

The man answered. "No, that's just a figure of speech. You'll be Uncle Philip, or Uncle Phil, to all the munchkins. We're all uncles and aunts here. One of our quaint customs. Just one big happy family."

"No, he's Mr. Andrews. He's our teacher," said Sally indignantly.

"Oh right," said the man. "Mr. Andrews to you young lady. Now shoo. Don't you have a class to get to? I want to talk to Mr. Andrews here."

Sally rolled her eyes. "You need to learn manners Uncle Joe. I'm going to tell Uncle Tom you said his sermon was bad."

"I already told him," said the man. "And don't call me Uncle Joe."

Sally moved to leave. "O.K. Uncle Joe." She laughed and ran off.

"Hi," said the man. "I'm Joseph Haaf." They shook hands. After a moment's silence, Joseph said, "So I'm looking at you and I'm wondering how in the world this guy got by the gatekeepers."

Philip felt his stomach lurch. "What do you mean?"

"Look at your hair. You're wearing sandals. You have a suspicious look to you. And that Bible! Where'd you get that thing?" Joseph began shaking again with laughter. "Believe me I'm on your side. Don't try so hard. It's a red flag."

Philip was utterly nonplussed. But before he could open his mouth, the leader of the adult Sunday school class called everybody to order. Joseph said, "Better go," and walked away still chuckling to himself. Philip felt a bit dazed. He quickly found a seat. Was it that obvious? He was in trouble if it was. Maybe this Joseph character was unusual. He certainly didn't seem to conform to any normative standards of human intercourse, at least initial human intercourse. For the next forty-five minutes Philip tried to concentrate on the Sunday school lesson, but found it difficult. He kept stealing glances at his rumpled interlocutor. What was the man's agenda? He found that he really had no idea.

The class was led by Bruce Carlock, a Bible translator who had contracted polio out in the jungle. The braces on his legs made it difficult for him to get around, so he spent most of his time at Ilusan working with members of his assigned tribal group flown in to help with the translation. The lady next to him helpfully imparted this information *sotto voce* through shallow gasps for air. She was a large woman and the day was heating up. Philip noticed that she referred to the native translation helpers as informants, a term that startled him. It seemed to put a negative spin on their work, as if they somehow betrayed their culture even as they exposed their families and friends to the light of the gospel.

The class was studying the Old Testament book of Nehemiah. Someone helpfully passed Philip a study guide. As he glanced through it, he felt the nudge of depression that had lately seemed to infect him whenever he was summoned to a Bible study. The booklet appeared to be the kind of well-meaning and slickly-produced study that must have powered the Sunday School in every church he'd ever entered. The cover had a polished attraction. He glanced at the first chapter. "The leader should spend five minutes introducing newcomers and letting regular attendees catch up." The words were printed in a highlighted box. Next came a summary of Nehemiah Chapter One, followed by several pages of questions. Little pseudo-handwritten notes were neatly arranged in the margins. A cartoon or two made an appearance. Some "Food for Thought" and "Suggested Activities" in bold letters rounded out the chapter.

As a kid he had excelled at getting the right answers to the questions, but by the time he was in college he found the exercise mind-numbing. Most of the questions were the easiest sort of softball, some so painfully obvious they were embarrassing to answer in public. The leader would ask, and Philip and his friends would look at each other to see who wanted to read the verse back to him. He stole a glance at the people sitting next to him. Most had done their homework, dutifully filling in the spaces after each question. Philip opened his Bible to Nehemiah.

The class spent ten minutes arguing over whether the Artaxerxes mentioned in Nehemiah was the same man that the book of Esther called Ahasuerus. They eventually decided that Ahasuerus was Xerxes the Great. Someone's massive study Bible was helpful in this regard, as it noted that Xerxes was known as an impatient, hot-tempered womanizer, a description which seemed to match the Ahasuerus of Esther. Therefore the Artaxerxes of Nehemiah must be the son of Ahasuerus, Artaxerses I, who ruled from 465 to 425 B.C. Philip was glad to have this cleared up, although he hadn't spent much time previous to this Sunday worrying about the matter. But it was at least mildly interesting to know the date of Nehemiah's adventure.

Someone then read the passage describing how Sanballat and his friends mocked the Jews who were hard at work rebuilding the wall of Jerusalem. The study question read "Have you ever been mocked? If so, how did you feel about it?" Several folks disclosed their personal experience with mockery. They felt pretty bad. The next question read "How did the Jews respond to their enemies, and what does this suggest to us?" Sure enough the Jews had prayed about it and kept on working. Someone helpfully pointed out that perhaps when Christians today were faced with mockery, they should pray about it and keep on working for God. There were lots of nodding heads and "Mmms."

Philip glanced at Joseph. His head was down, buried in his Bible. Suddenly he raised his hand. Bruce acknowledged him, although Philip thought he detected a note of resignation in his voice. Joseph said, "Their prayer is interesting. They don't seem very forgiving of their enemies. They ask God to 'return the reproach of their enemies on their heads and give them up for plunder in a land of captivity.' Then they ask God to refuse to forgive their sins. Is that how we're supposed to pray for people who mock us?"

There was a long silence. Philip glanced through his study guide to see if it addressed the issue. It didn't. Finally a woman said, "There's a note in my study Bible that says that this is an example of imprecatory prayer, and that sometimes God leads us to pray this way because he knows that the person's heart is so hard that they'll never repent. My Bible says it's almost like prophecy, and should only be used when really led by the Spirit."

A man said, "I agree. It wouldn't be very Christian to pray against somebody like that. We're supposed to love our enemies. So we shouldn't feel like that about them."

Someone else said, "Maybe this is an Old Testament thing." A woman then told a story about how, when she was working her way through Bible college, a co-worker had tried to get her fired, but she prayed that God would help her love her enemy, and then she had asked her boss to give her co-worker a raise that was rightfully due her, an action which had so amazed her co-worker that she had repented and become a Christian. This story unleashed a flood of similar stories, and the class spent the next ten minutes sharing their best love-your-enemy stories. Philip enjoyed this much more than the actual Bible study, so he was glad for Joseph's question, although he didn't feel it had been adequately addressed. Apparently Joseph felt the same. Philip noticed that his leg was drumming up and down as he glowered at each missionary who shared a triumphant story. But he remained silent.

Finally Bruce looked at his watch and announced that it was time to take prayer requests. Hands went up all over the room. Things proceeded comfortably until Joseph raised his hand.

"Aha," Philip thought, "the agent provocateur is about to strike again." He thought he was beginning to figure out Joseph's game.

A woman had asked prayer for her sister whose marriage was under Satanic attack. Apparently her husband had been discovered having an affair with the church organist. Bruce had just assured everyone that attacking Christian marriages was indeed one of Satan's top priorities these days, when Joseph politely remarked, "I think you can assure your sister that her marriage isn't being attacked by Satan."

A woman with bright red hair wearing a long earth-toned dress whirled on him. Philip recognized her as the base hostess from yesterday. "Honey, how can you say that? Of course she's being attacked by Satan." The woman was sitting several rows away from Joseph, but, as nobody appeared startled by the term of endearment, Philip figured he must have just been introduced to Joseph's wife. She wore her hair in a thick ponytail. She was tall, not willowy, but not oakish either. Her face was covered with freckles and her earrings clanked on her shoulders when she moved.

"Haight-Ashbury," thought Philip.

"I seriously doubt that," said Joseph. "Who is Satan?" When nobody responded, he went on. "He's a fallen angel. He's a finite being. He can't be everywhere at once. Only God is omnipresent. Don't you think it more likely that Satan is rabble rousing in Vietnam or stirring up the Khmer Rouge or whispering in Brezhnev's ear than focusing on Janice's sister's marriage?" Philip raised his eyebrows. He had never thought of that. Apparently no one else had either. They gaped at Joseph, a response Philip was beginning to think was probably a regular occurrence on the center.

Finally someone said, "O.k. Maybe it's a figure of speech. It's one of his demons attacking Janice's sister's marriage."

"Maybe," said Joseph. "But you have to figure Satan has a limited number of demons. There are billions of people in the world, and the chances that he has assigned one of his minions to Janice's sister are remote."

"Well what do you think it is then?" exploded a man sitting directly in front of Philip. The man was lean as a crowbar with short cropped graying hair. Philip thought he would have been handsome if his face weren't contorted in anger.

"I think Janice's sister's husband is perfectly capable of lusting after the church organist all on his own. He doesn't need Satan's help for that. Blaming it on Satan just lets everyone avoid responsibility. The man's a cad, a bounder, a mountebank. The earth is filled with such men. The church is filled with such men. Satan has very little to do with it." Joseph folded his arms across his chest and glared around the room, daring anyone to challenge him.

"I think you need to read your Bible," said the gray-haired man. "Satan roams the earth seeking whom he might devour." The man's jaw worked as he stared down Joseph.

The heightened energy in the room seemed to galvanize the class. Study guides were cast aside, Bibles came out, and for the next fifteen minutes Philip witnessed an extraordinary display of biblical dexterity. Verses were quoted from hither and yon, Greek and Hebrew phrases tossed about, and heated arguments broke out about how best to translate a verse into indigenous languages. Before long Janice and her sister were long forgotten in a discussion about how various translators described Satan to their people. Philip was fascinated. He realized at one point that his mouth was hanging open as he watched the show. Now this was how a Sunday School class ought to be run, he thought. Ditch the study guides and let the pros have at it.

Joseph's wife eventually called the class back to prayer. She reminded the class they needed to pray for Janice's sister. "And Janice," she said, "don't listen to Joseph. What does he know? I think it's perfectly possible that a demon is attacking your sister." She looked around for support. "In fact, I think that's exactly what's happening." There were a few nods. She got up and sat by Janice, who appeared to be quietly sniffling. "So we're going to pray. We're going to pray for your sister, and we're going to rebuke Satan."

"Thank you Celia," said Janice. "I just know this is a Satanic attack."

"You're right dear." Celia gave her a hug. "Satan is the one organizing all our opposition, so whether he's there or not, he's there." She glared briefly at her husband and then addressed the group. "Well, are we going to pray?"

And so they did. They closed this meeting as they closed every meeting. They prayed. But their prayers seemed somewhat desultory. Philip knew what prayer warriors evangelicals could be, but after Joseph's questioning of the working assignments of the underworld, those who prayed seemed reluctant to invoke the name of the great enemy of their souls, and without their dark nemesis, the prayers lacked their usual snap and focus. But Philip knew this would be only a momentary setback. To be evangelical was to live on the battle line. It was a spiritual battle to be sure, but no less real to anyone in the room for that. And whether he was there or not, Satan was always there.

The meeting broke up a few minutes later. Philip noticed that most of the missionaries avoided Joseph on their way out. Philip wanted to speak to him, but instead wound up in a brief conversation with Tom Jacobson. Tom wanted to talk some more about ears; he apologized for the size of the World Book illustrations, and asked if Philip would like to see them. Philip politely obliged him, and, after a few minutes, was rewarded when Tom said, "I do quite a bit of flying out to the allocations, taking folks mail and supplies. Some are way out in the jungle with some pretty hairy landing strips. If you ever want to come along, just let me know, and if I have room, I'll be glad to take you."

"Are you kidding?! I'd love that." Philip had hoped to get into the jungle at some point. Plus, he had always enjoyed flying.

"Why don't you get your feet on the ground in the classroom," said Tom, "and then let me know when you have some free time, and I'll see what flights I have coming up."

Philip thanked Tom profusely. They chatted about the problems of jungle flying for a few minutes. A few others joined the conversation. Evelyn Troyer tapped Philip's arm and said, "Why don't you come over for lunch?" And then to those around, "Poor thing, he probably doesn't have much to eat in his house." Back to Philip, "Come over about 1:00. That will give us time to get mother down for a nap. We don't want to get her all worked up again."

When Philip turned back to the group, Tom was looking at him quizzically. "It's a long story," Philip said.

When he walked into his bedroom, Mr. Bumbles was on his back in the middle of the bed, feet curled up on his stomach. Seeing Philip, he yawned, stretched his legs straight out above him, and then flopped over onto his side. Philip was inordinately glad to see him. He sat beside the cat and rubbed his head. "Bumbles," he said, "I met your previous owner. I think you're going to like me a lot better." He rubbed the cat's ears. "Did you know that you have amazing ears and that your ears prove the existence of God?" Mr. Bumbles gave another enormous yawn. Philip had difficulty believing he could get his mouth open that wide. At the yawn's termination, Bumbles snapped his mouth shut with an audible pop. "Yep," said Philip, "that's how most of the audience felt this morning too."

True to his word, Matt St. Clair thundered up to Philip's back porch at 5:30 p.m. "Maayo," he called as he shut off his bike. Philip was putting on his shoes at the dining room table. He yelled to Matt to come in. When Matt entered, he asked him what it was he had called. "That's the Filipino version of a doorbell," Matt said. "The correct response is 'dayon.'"

Philip repeated the two words a few times. "Easy enough."

On their way to the tower, Matt stopped at his bike and pulled a large pair of binoculars out of one of the saddle bags. He handed them to Philip. "This'll give you a better look around."

Matt unlocked the gate to the stairs. They were made of rough wood and wound back and forth up the northern side of the tower. A few were loose and rotting. Matt, who went first, pointed them out to Philip and muttered that he'd have to get a workman to replace them this week. They quickly reached the platform. There was room to walk all the way around the tank at its base. Matt stopped on the side above Philip's house and leaned against the rail. "This is a good place to start," he said. "You can see almost the entire base from here." But Philip first looked east, away from Ilusan, in the direction his back porch faced. A heavily loaded logging truck was moving at a fair clip along the highway on the far side of the cornfield. A thick cloud of dust billowed behind it.

"I'd hate to live right next to that road," said Philip.

Matt grunted. "Wait till you have to drive into Malaybalay sometime. That's the worst road you'll ever be on. It's a real axle breaker. And if it's been raining, then you're lucky to make it at all. Turns into a river of mud." They followed the truck with their eyes. Philip could just make out a small town in the distance. Matt noted where he was looking.

"That's Bancud. It's a small barrio, too small to really be useful. A few Sari-Sari stores and a few houses are about it. Quite a few of our Filipino workers live there. But we do most of our shopping in Malaybalay. It's the provincial capital."

The landscape to the east of Ilusan was flat, except for one mountain jutting up from the plain. Philip had noted it earlier from his porch. It wasn't very large, but it looked impressive sitting alone on the plateau. It reminded him of the Lonely Mountain in Tolkien's *The Hobbit*. The perfect place for a dragon to slumber and keep one eye on the plains around him.

"That's Mt. Capistrano," said Matt. "We take the older kids to climb it a couple of times a year. I even stayed overnight with them once. It's a good day climb, quite steep, and the views from the top are impressive. We'll get you over there pretty soon."

Philip wasn't a big fan of physical exertion, but he didn't dare mention that to Matt. "That sounds like fun," he said.

"The real climb is over here." Matt led Philip to the west side of the tower. To the west and south the flatlands gave way to jumbled hills which, as they marched north, formed themselves into mountains. All were heavily forested. The steadily rising landscape culminated in an impressive mountain, the tallest Philip could see in any direction. "That's Katanglad. It's an active volcano. You can't do that in one day, so you have to overnight at the top. Maybe when the high school kids come down from Faith Academy in September, we'll take my son, Benjamin, and a few of the older boys, and spend a few days climbing it. But they might want to climb Capistrano instead. That and a downriver trip are their two favorite things to do when they come home on vacation. And those are things the younger kids can join them in, so it's fun for everybody." Philip thought both of those options sounded better than struggling for a day up a volcanic peak.

"Going downriver sounds great," he said.

They spent another twenty minutes on the tower. They fell silent as they gazed about them, at times through the binoculars, but more often taking in the setting with the naked eye. Finally Matt said, "It's a long way from the States. You miss it for a while, but then one day you wake up and realize you're in Paradise." He was looking out over the center as he said it. Philip didn't respond. He could tell Matt had more to say, but needed a minute to work his way toward it.

Just when Philip was beginning to worry that his lack of response might have ended the conversation, Matt said, "It happened for me early one morning quite a few years ago. The night watchman woke me up early, about 3:00. A couple of drunk Filipinos from Bancud had come through the fence and were wandering around. The watchman didn't know what to do with them. We opened up the office in the shop and I made some coffee. We chatted for about an hour." Here Matt stopped for a second, shrugged, then continued almost apologetically. "I had only been here about a year at the time, and didn't know Visayan, the local language, very well. But in the towns around here, everyone knows a little English. So I gave them Visayan Bibles and told them why we were here and tried to witness to them a little bit." He winced at the memory, although it clearly pleased him. "Finally I prayed with them and then gave them both a ride on my motorcycle out to the highway where they could catch a jeep home. The sun was just coming up when I got back. You could hear roosters crowing on the farms close to the base. I parked my bike and decided to go for a swim. As I walked to the pool I felt so good you know. It was so peaceful. Just birds. And so beautiful, with all the trees, and of course the pool."

Matt paused again. He glanced at Philip and then continued, but Philip thought he seemed almost embarrassed. "But it wasn't just how beautiful it was that made me feel so good. I had done the right thing with those two drunk guys. I hadn't read them the riot act for trespassing or for being drunk. And I had witnessed to them a little bit. And I never could have done that in the States. You're a teacher. You're probably good at that sort of thing, but I'm not very good at talking." Philip wanted to interrupt, but Matt was in a rush to get it out. "I'm a good mechanic, and an o.k. administrator; I can help the translators do their jobs. In the States, where even the non-Christians know as much about Jesus as I do, well I can't argue with them. But here so many of the people haven't heard the basic story. And I could tell them the story." He looked out over the base and then turned back to Philip. "And that," he said, "made me feel like I was home. I was where God wanted me to be."

"I think you're pretty good at talking," said Philip. "I wouldn't have handled the situation nearly as well as you did. For one thing I never could have gotten out of bed at 3:00 a.m."

Matt laughed. Philip was pleased to see that his instinctive skills hadn't left him; he was still the master at the non-response response. It was a necessary survival tactic he had learned growing up, how to turn a conversation that threatened to get uncomfortably spiritual back to neutral ground, but without giving his conversation partner any reason to doubt his sincerity. It was a benign magic act that left both parties feeling relieved. It required a feint toward your partner, preferably one in which you flattered them somehow. The second step was the key. While they were processing the flattery, the conversation had to be vaulted in an entirely new direction. Philip had discovered that humor provided the best counter. If you were skillful, the counter was like a judo throw; utilizing their own momentum, something they had mentioned themselves, you launched their thoughts in a new direction. Philip had written the manual for the non-response response, and he had just pulled it off like the master he was. But this time he felt regret along with relief. He would have liked to respond honestly to Matt, but he simply didn't have it in him.

Matt was already pursuing the new line of conversation. "You better get used to getting up early and going to bed early. Almost everyone is up by 6:00. You'll hear Bobby Sorenson practicing the piano in the meeting hall at 6:00 every weekday morning. You can set your watch by him. You'll know what he's working on by heart. And when he's struggling with a song . . . well let's just say it's better to get up and get about your day than to listen to that." Philip put his head on the rail and groaned. Matt clapped him on the shoulders. "Don't worry. If you go to bed when the lights go out, it's not that hard to get up. And you'll soon discover that it's the best part of the day. Great time for a run."

"I'm sure it is," said Philip. "I'm sure it is."

The sun was setting and as they looked over the base they could see people starting to make their way to the meeting hall for the Sunday evening service. "We better get going," said Matt. "Folks are eager to hear from the newcomers."

"Great," said Philip. "You'll find out I'm not much of a public speaker."

Among the people streaming toward the hall, Philip could see children running ahead of their parents. The Troyer sisters came out of their house and waved up to the two men on the tower. Then Dorothy inched down their porch steps, and the three women moved slowly toward the center of the base. Suddenly, as if a switch had been thrown, cicadas began to sing in the trees below them. The evening air was warm and lightly wet. The top of Katanglad was shrouded in cloud, but everywhere else the sky was clear. A motorcycle left the airplane hangar and began to move toward the hall. Philip felt compelled to say something else. He owed that much to this good man with him on the tower. "I think I can understand why you love it here," he said.

Matt led Philip toward the stairs. "You'll fit right in," he said.

Philip's chest began to twitch before the Smokey-Mountain-pure Bible school couple even began to speak. It was a familiar response to the stress of public speaking. In college just raising his hand to ask a question would set his chest and arms to twitching so violently that he usually had to forgo the question. When he had something important to ask, he either approached the professor in private or wore a sweater to class to better cover his vibrations. A college friend once told him that if he'd lived in Salem and done any public speaking with his shirt off, he'd have been hung for a witch. Fortunately Philip had his shirt on for this particular inquisition. But, as it was a hot night, it was a thin covering, and Philip thought that speaking to a group of missionaries was probably as close as he'd ever get to Salem. He'd be lucky to get out alive. He began to pray, begging God to help him calm down. The twitching got worse.

Philip could tell the audience loved the Tennessee Bible translators. They stood in front of the group together, holding hands. The man let his wife speak first, and as she shyly told her story, he beamed at her, radiating a wholesome love. When he spoke, it was clear she adored him as well. Only the lack of a child sleeping quietly in her arms kept the picture from being perfect. Philip thought that with a child they would have butchered the competition at the Christmas pageant casting call. "Dear God," he thought, "don't make me follow them."

He didn't, but things only got worse. Next up was the single man. Two minutes into his story, Philip's twitches had increased to a frightening level. He hugged his arms tightly to his chest and took deep breaths.

From long experience he knew that the only testimonies evangelicals appreciated more than holy family stories were radical conversion stories, especially male stories. Wild young women, even ones who rivaled St. Theresa for saintliness after their conversion, made them nervous. But men had to go pretty far indeed to cross the line for what was acceptable pre-conversion sin.

Evangelicals collected conversion stories like trophies. It was a way of counting coup on the devil, and the greater the sinner, the greater the coup. For years his saintly aunt had been praying for Mick Jagger, convinced that if this titan of turpitude, this potentate of prodigality, this doctor of degeneracy, ever actually got saved it would cause a cosmic tidal wave large enough to put out the very fires of hell. The devil would be so shamed he'd slink into hiding, and enlightened sinners would dash headlong into the kingdom.

The man standing before them now wasn't quite Mick Jagger, but as he detailed the hair-raising transgressions of his youth the response of the audience built to a fever pitch. The "mmmms" and "praise the Lords" followed hard on each other. Philip knew that while he might be able to match the speaker sin for sin, this young man's moral failings occurred pre-conversion. Philip, a life-long Christian, understood that his transgressions would arouse the suspicion accorded a traitor. He would play Benedict Arnold to this fellow's Saul of Tarsus.

But then things got better. Philip, it seemed, was destined to go last. The next speaker, the young linguistic consultant, was clearly very nervous. She said "um" a lot, and the more distraught she grew the longer she spoke. She appeared to have been an exemplary young woman, and eyes began to glaze over. Philip breathed a prayer of thanks for her rhetorical incompetence, but then felt guilty and began to pray that God would help her get through her story. But his heart wasn't in it. He wanted her to fail, so that the audience would be grateful when she sat down and predisposed to look on him kindly. The longer she talked, the more his twitches died down. When at last it was his turn, he almost felt good, even cocky. He'd be funny, get some laughs, stretch some things, leave out some things. He thought he knew how to entertain Christians. He walked to the front with a bounce in his step.

As soon as he turned to face the assembled missionaries and his introductory applause died down, his mind stopped functioning, or at least it refused to take its cues from his will. He wasn't twitching. He was preternaturally calm. But he couldn't remember any of his carefully planned opening lines. He saw each and every face before him, noted their studied appraisal, and all he could think was, "Why didn't I cut my hair?" He felt their judgment. He remembered Giles Corey at Salem. He had refused to speak, and the Salem elders piled rocks on him until he suffocated. Philip wondered what it would feel like to have rocks piled on him until his chest caved in. His chest began to feel like it *was* caving in. From somewhere far away, as if he saw the words approaching like headlights through a thick fog, he thought, "My name is Philip Andrews." Had he said that out loud? Well if he hadn't, it was a good place to start.

"My name is Philip Andrews," he said. Then that troublesome neuron fired, and he seized on it. "My father was a minister and he named me after Philip the evangelist." The minister part was true, but the naming bit was a lie; but it was something his father might have done. The neuron fired again. Aha, a terrific laugh line. "So if you know any eunuchs who need to get saved, send them to me." They didn't laugh. Eyebrows went up all over the room. Wives looked at their husbands. A few boys snorted. Sally was staring at him intently without an ounce of comprehension. She was just waiting for his story. What a sweet kid. Joseph Haaf, in the back row, quietly applauding, head thrown back in silent laughter. Why wasn't Joseph's wife sitting with him? Did she never sit with him? Where was she? Philip's mental activity accelerated to warp speed. He grasped for another sentence. Something to divert disaster.

And then a monkey named Jeremiah rescued him. Philip found out later the monkey was indeed named for the Old Testament prophet. The monkey belonged to a boy named Anderson Thomas. Anderson had once made the mistake, during one of his father's black moods, of remarking that he was bored. Anderson's father whirled on him and shouted, "Do you need something to do? Go to your room and read the Bible." He made Anderson read all fifty-two chapters of Jeremiah before he left his room. Anderson had named his monkey in mocking reference to his father's discipline.

Jeremiah spent his days in a large cage in the yard of the Thomas family home, where the teasing of the center's children drove him to fits of prophetic rage. Miraculously, and Philip half believed it was a genuine case of divine intervention on his behalf, Jeremiah had either found a way to throw the latch, or someone had left the cage open. Instead of fleeing to the jungle, Jeremiah apparently decided to unleash his wrath on his human tormentors. He now appeared in Philip's hour of desperate need, leaping up and down and shrieking, in a window at the rear of the auditorium.

A frozen moment and then pandemonium. Jeremiah swung effortlessly from window to window screaming at the assembled missionaries. To Philip's left a man stood and yelled at his son sitting with his friends in the rear, "Anderson grab your monkey." Anderson ran toward Jeremiah even as the women and children nearest the windows screamed and ducked behind their men. It seemed to Philip as if the entire right side of the auditorium was moving en masse toward the center. When he reached a window at the middle of the room, Jeremiah leapt like a mad kamikaze into the crowd. He landed on the perfectly coiffed head of the shy Tennessee Madonna. Her terrified scream galvanized her husband who gallantly swung a fist. But Jeremiah was much too quick. Taking a handful of blond hair and dark roots with him he rollicked at madcap pace across the pews and with a final gargantuan leap landed on top of the piano. From there he screamed his triumph, urinated with surprising energy all over the front pew, then leapt down onto the keyboard and capered with wild abandon, pounding out a cacophonous score that only the most infatuated devotees of modern music might have appreciated. It was there that Anderson captured him. Indeed, once Jeremiah discovered music, he blissfully ignored the assembly. Caught up in tuneful carnage, he was an easy capture. He seemed almost calm as Anderson carried him out. He only cast a few wistful glances back at the piano.

Slowly order was restored. Two women comforted the weeping new arrival who had been most directly attacked. Several other women found a role of paper towels and wiped down the front pew. Another cleaned up the piano. Most of the adults were laughing. Matt St. Clair shouted to Philip, "Welcome to church in the Philippines." Indeed many seemed to attribute the evening's entertainment to Philip, as if he had somehow summoned the monkey. They crowded around him laughing and patting him on the back. If anyone remembered his eunuch remark, they weren't letting on. Eventually Tom Jacobson, whose Sunday duties included leading the evening meeting, called everyone back to order. He apologized to Philip for the interruption and suggested he begin again.

"Are you kidding?" Philip said. "Apologize to me? That was the coolest thing I've ever seen." The audience cheered and laughed. Even the teary-eyed Tennessee translator smiled. Philip kept himself under control. When that neuron fired and reminded him of a monkey joke he'd once heard, he shut it down without a moment's hesitation. When Dorothy, about five rows back, reached both hands toward him and said loud enough for those near to hear, "Thank you Jesus," he merely smiled at her, and the sisters quickly quieted her down. He expertly repeated his testimony more or less as he'd related it to the Troyers the evening before. By the time he began to recount his graduate school years, his semantic DNA was firmly in control of all his faculties. There would be no more neuronal coups tonight. He smoothly related how the Lord had led him step by step to Ilusan. The appreciative "mmms" and nodding heads told him he had won his audience.

There were only two worrisome notes in the evening's triumph. As missionaries gathered around afterward and welcomed him to Ilusan, Joseph leaned into the circle from behind him and whispered into his ear, "You're scheduled to be at our house for dinner Tuesday night. Good thing. You need some help."

And, alone, leaning against a back window, the very one Jeremiah had first entered, the lean handsome gray-haired man from the morning's Sunday school class watched Philip's every move. As Philip walked slowly toward the door, greeting and being greeted by various families, whenever he glanced that way, the man was observing. His gaze never wavered.

When Philip got home he collapsed onto the bed. He didn't have the energy to fix something to eat. He lay there for a half hour reliving the events of the evening in his mind. What a start! He finally got up, took off his clothes, turned out the lights and went to bed early. He was still going over the day in his mind when he heard Mr. Bumbles approach the bed. Philip untucked the mosquito net and the cat readily jumped in next to him. As they settled down together, Philip said, "Well Bumbles, now you know my secret. I'm not supposed to let you sleep with me. But it's as your previous owner said. I'm weak. My father thought I was weak. The chaplain at Bible college thought I was weak. My girlfriend *knew* I was weak. What can I say, I'm a weak man. I give in to people. I'm nice to cats. Is that such a bad thing?" Mr. Bumbles didn't seem to think so.

## Chapter Four

THE NEXT MORNING PHILIP got up very early and had devotions. He attended to neither the getting up nor the devotions with any real enthusiasm. By 5:30 there was already a good bit of light in the room. At 5:40 Mr. Bumbles thought about starting his day. He edged against the mosquito net and whisked his tail back and forth across Philip's face. At 5:50 Philip let go his tight grip on Bumbles' tail, pulled the corner of the mosquito net from under the mattress, and a purring Bumbles leapt down and left the room, tail high and twitching.  At 6:00, from a great distance, Philip heard scales being played on a piano. Over and over. In his mind he saw a tiny pair of hands, one, two, three, four fingers, cross the thumb under, one, two, three, four, five fingers, back and forth, up and down. "I'm going to strangle that kid," he muttered. He imagined that all over Ilusan adults were having a similar reaction. Who scheduled piano practice at 6:00 a.m.? But then a worse thought hit him. What if most of the adults at Ilusan had been up for an hour or more already? Matt St. Clair had probably already finished a ten-mile run. He imagined busy wives preparing breakfast while husbands in their studies memorized unpronounceable lists of jungle words, and pious children dutifully read their Bibles and prayed. That last image cracked his eyes open. "I should have devotions," he thought. "God, I hate that word."

He got up, threw on some shorts, and managed to reach the kitchen with his eyes still gummy slits. He found the matches, went to the stove, turned the gas on in the front burner, then held a lit match next to the sooty ring. This last act brought him wide awake. He held his breath, preparing to be incinerated. Not this morning. The burner flamed to life with a satisfying whump. He filled the coffee pot with water, set it on the burner, and then returned to the bedroom. By the time he hit the bedroom door he was already running. Better to get through the next ordeal quickly. He was out of his shorts, into the shower, and dancing under the frigid deluge before his mind could form even one of the words of choice for such moments. By the time he collected his coffee and Bible and sat in his favorite chair on the back porch he was feeling pretty good.

Philip wasn't sure where, maybe over the Pacific on his way to the islands, maybe when his uncle welcomed him to Manila with the gift of a book titled "Your First Thirty Quiet Times," maybe not until a few moments ago with the vision of children bathed in the lambent light of early morning dutifully reading the Scriptures, but somewhere he had formed the notion that he had better start having devotions again. But he had the wrong Bible. Staring at the heavily marked passages, he knew immediately that this particular Bible was too steeped in his family's piety for him to ever find his own way. He switched to the heavy hardback. There were only a few marks in this one. His stepmother had given it to him the day he went off to Bible college, but he had been invited to leave the school before he had made much headway in turning the study Bible into a multi-colored monument to his spiritual journey. Embittered by that experience he had thrown his Bible into a corner where it had remained all through college and graduate school. It was only as he packed for the Philippines that a phone call from his stepmom had reminded him to "take your Bible dear." And now here he was embarking once again on that discipline central to the evangelical spiritual life, the setting aside of an early hour for Bible reading and prayer.

He almost got up to get a pen, but then rejected the idea. To read with pen in hand would be to give in to all the faces from his past that peered over his shoulder as he opened his Bible on his back porch at 6:25 in the god-awful early morning in an obscure corner of the Philippines. He could feel their misty-eyed approval; he saw them nod to each other and smile; he heard a chorus of "mmmms"; the hours they had spent in prayer for him were paying off; the prodigal had come home. The vision made him squirm.

"This kid ain't gonna be his momma's evangelical," he blurted out loud to the assembled hosts. The sound of his voice in the early morning quiet made him pause, but he went on. "If you think I'm going to be doing word studies, you're wrong. If you think I care for one second whether Paul said Christ was coming 'for' or 'with' his saints, and what that means for the rapture, well you're wrong. And I'm not going to build a federal case on the difference between *agape* and *phileo*. I couldn't care less whether there was one or fifteen Isaiahs or whether Moses ever actually put pen to paper. In fact," and here he lowered his voice, glanced around the porch, and then muttered with an intensity stoked by years under the thumb of his father's preaching, "if you think I'm going to worry for one second about inerrancy, you're wrong. If you think I'm going to feel guilty if I miss a morning's devotions, you're wrong. If you think I'm going to reference anything any of you ever taught me when I read this book, you're wrong. I'm going to read it like a book. I'm going to assume nothing. And furthermore I'm never going to pray before I begin."

He stopped suddenly, surprised at his own anger. "Damn," he muttered. "I've got issues." He said it again, "Damn." His mind began to clear. He said it a few more times. He felt better. He looked around. No visions peered over his shoulder. Only Mr. Bumbles, who appeared to be having his own devotions over the mangled body of a small rodent, had witnessed his tirade. The cat looked at him expectantly; he had blood on his chin. "Good grief Bumbles," said Philip. "I've got to get you some food."

Philip decided to read one of the Gospels. John was too talky to start out with, too repetitive. I and the Father are one. All right, we get it already. But he had always liked John's poetic sensibility. He'd get to John later. He decided not to begin with Matthew because the Sermon on the Mount showed up too quickly, and he didn't think he was ready for a three-chapter-long sermon that fingered his failures at every turn. But Mark was too prosaic. A lot of running around and a really weird ending. So he decided to read Luke. That would make a nice transition to Acts. Then maybe he'd try one or two of Paul's letters. He found Luke and began to read.

But then, despite his resolution, he felt guilty about not beginning with prayer. And he felt doubly guilty for the words he'd just used in such close proximity to his devotional time. Philip groaned. Sometimes it was hard to put one foot in front of the other with his mind so filled with the past. He leaned back in his chair.

"O.k. God, here we are. I'm sorry I said those things. I wasn't mad at you, but all those people who were just here were crowding me. I want to do this on my own. I don't know if you care that I said 'damn' or not, but if you do, I'm sorry. Try to think of it as a modern version of the imprecatory psalms." He glanced at Mr. Bumbles. The cat was in the process of tearing his breakfast in half. The rodent came apart with a long stretch and an audible pop. Something green spilled on the porch. Bumbles licked it up.

"Thank you for my new friend, Mr. Bumbles," Philip said. "He's the first thing that's shared my bed that hasn't gotten me in a lot of trouble. Thank you for my other new friends too. Thank you for all of these good people. Please help me do right by them. Help me be a good teacher. And help me figure out what's up with that Haaf character. Oh, and the gray-haired man too. What the hell is his game?" He sipped his coffee and thought for a few minutes. "And God, I'd appreciate it if before this year is up, you'd step out from behind the curtain. Even if all you do is moon me like you did to Moses. Just a glimpse is all I'm asking." He began to read Luke. But his past wasn't finished with him yet. Philip spoke again. "By the way, I guess the prayer is over. I know I didn't end it how you're supposed to. But you're smart; you'll figure it out." He took a sip of coffee. Besides, he thought, maybe I'm not done talking to you yet.

Philip had read five chapters when an exclamation point dropped out of the sky onto his Bible, highlighting a verse that Philip would forever privately believe was God's personal message to him. The exclamation point was black, but perfectly accented by a white dot on one end. Philip had seen the exclamation points before, scattered around the house in corners and on window sills that hadn't been regularly cleaned. But those were calcified. This one was fresh and damp. It stuck to the page. Philip looked up and saw the lizard directly above him, tail still twitching, clinging upside down to one of the ceiling crossbeams. "You're lucky that missed me," Philip said.

But the lizard wasn't lucky. Mr. Bumbles followed Philip's eyes and apparently decided that dessert had arrived or else that this insult to God's holy word must be avenged. He launched himself like Michael the archangel at the lizard. Unfortunately for Philip, he was the only one who witnessed the resulting feat, and consequently, much to his disgust, was never believed when he later told the story.

Philip first noticed the cat was up to something when it leapt to the porch railing. Bumbles crouched, tail lashing, and eyed the lizard for a long second. Then he abruptly whirled and raced to the far end of the railing. There he turned, crouched again, then shot back down the rail toward Philip. The cat reached takeoff speed directly in front of Philip's boggled eyes where he hurled himself up a vertical beam. He appeared to only touch the beam twice before he reached the ceiling. Bumbles twisted in midair during his last leap so that when he touched down for the final time in the corner of the ceiling he was bunched in a tight ball. He was only in contact with the corner for an eye blink before he launched himself spitting and snarling directly over Philip's head toward the transfixed lizard. As he sailed under the gawking reptile Bumbles twisted again and swatted the creature ferociously with his right paw. Philip heard the lizard smack off the back door a half-second before Bumbles sailed over his head and crashed to the floor behind him. Philip leapt to his feet. Both cat and lizard appeared stunned. The lizard gathered itself first; it made a mad dash for freedom, running right out of its tail which remained twitching next to the door. But the cat was far too quick. In two great bounds it was on its prey. Bumbles held the lizard down with one paw, looked back at Philip, then seized the twisting head in his teeth and ripped it off.

"And thus shall the Lord's enemies be dispatched," breathed Philip. He sat down a bit shakily. The cat was soon back in the position he had left only moments before, only this time with two bloody sets of remains before him. "Don't forget the tail," said Philip, but Bumbles ignored him. His rattling purr filled the porch.

It was only then that Philip noticed the verse which the inspired lizard had accented. He flicked the dropping off his Bible with his finger, grimacing at the damp smear on his fingernail. But before he got up to wash his hands, he glanced back at the Gospel open before him. A stain in the shape of an exclamation point clung like a ghost to the page. It was perfectly positioned at the end of Luke chapter five verse twenty. Philip read "Friend, your sins are forgiven you" exclamation point. "Bumbles," he said, "I think you've just decapitated the Lord's messenger. But then they did stone the prophets didn't they!"

At 10:00 that morning Philip was sitting at a table in the library of Samantha Stoddard Memorial Grade School. Arranged around the table was the staff of the school. Fossia Gertrudes, the school's principal, was welcoming them to the start of a new school year. And Philip had fallen immediately in love, not with Fossia, but with the school's young librarian sitting next to her. He had only known her for ten minutes, but the symptoms were sure. "I'm in trouble," he thought.

Philip had arrived at the school for an appointment with Fossia an hour ago. Fossia was East German. She was thick and very blond. The hair on her arms was almost as pronounced as Matt St. Clair's. She could throw a football farther than anybody on the center. She addressed Philip as Mr. Andrews. In fact she never used a first name with anyone, adult or child. The smallest baby was Mr. or Miss. "Mr. Andrews," she said, "let me show you around your classroom."

Samantha Stoddard Memorial Grade School consisted of three buildings lined up on a hill at the extreme northern end of Ilusan. The top and back side of the hill opened up for the two perpendicular airstrips and the hangar and tower. The school shared the front side of the hill with a twin-sided public bathroom and the radio shack, where Matt St. Clair's wife, Julia, kept in daily contact with the missionaries scattered throughout the surrounding jungle. Philip's seventh and eighth grade classroom occupied half of the furthest building, with the fifth and sixth grades in the other half. The two rooms were separated by a storage closet. The middle building housed the library and an auxiliary classroom. The first and second grades shared the first building with the third and fourth graders. The staff consisted of a teacher for each homeroom, the principal, and the librarian. Various specialty classes were taught by other missionaries as they became available.

Philip was delighted to learn from Fossia that lesson plans for the entire year rested neatly in files in his homeroom. Apparently the regular seventh and eight grade teacher had been there for ten years and was a perfectionist. "You're welcome to deviate from her plans," Fossia told him, "but when she returns from furlough next year, if she doesn't think the seventh graders have been prepared adequately for eighth grade, she'll hunt you down and crack your head." The eighth grade kids would be off to Faith Academy in Manila for high school, so Philip could at least avoid being evaluated on half of his work. That provided some measure of relief. "I'm sure I'll stick pretty close," he informed the principal.

Fossia gave him a class roster. Philip would teach eight eighth graders and three seventh graders. The principal ran down the list throwing a few pointed comments in the direction of each student. First the eighth grade. Madeline Broderick (Fossia said, "Miss Broderick"): "tall, striking, just back from furlough . . . hope she got smarter"; Sally Fraser: "sweet kid, but hard to tell if she's too smart or too dumb for school" . . . after a pause, "at any rate she's never hit her stride, doesn't try"; the Meyer twins, Donny and Danny: "good luck telling them apart," but then, "the task is made easier by the fact that they don't like each other"; Mary Michaels: "smartest kid in school, but kind of" . . . the principal paused, glanced at Philip, then placed her thumb on the end of her nose and tilted it upward . . . "doesn't like to get her robes dirty"; Timmy Mullen: "troublemaker . . . but you'll never convince his parents of that"; Elaine Pauley: "she needs help"; and finally Bobby Sorenson: "smartest boy in school . . . if you need help with anything, I'd ask him before Mary . . . he won't remind you of it the rest of the year." Then the seventh grade. Charlie Pilarski: "last year was his first year here . . . struggles to fit in . . . picked on a lot . . . has flat feet"; Marcia Proud: "biggest ears I've ever seen on a kid that age"; and Drew Sorenson: "Bobby's brother . . . strange kid . . . if dead bodies ever turn up around here, I'm checking with him first." With that she stood and said, "The classroom is yours Mr. Andrews. I'll see you in fifteen minutes for our first staff meeting." Philip felt like clicking his heels and saluting, but decided to suppress that notion. He nodded and politely thanked her. He wondered how her notes on him would read. "Long-hair hippie type . . . doesn't have a clue . . . must be hard to get short-termers out here if this is the best we could do."

Twenty minutes later, after an opening prayer and Fossia's welcome, the staff were introducing themselves to Philip. Jerry Van Kleek shared Philip's building. He taught the fifth and sixth grades. Jerry was probably the most educated fifth and sixth grade teacher in the world. He had a PhD and was the world's foremost expert on the book of Enoch, an obscure Jewish text that maybe eight people had read. Jerry had retired five years ago from a distinguished professorship at Princeton to teach at Ilusan because his daughter married a missionary stationed in Mindanao and his wife wanted to be close to her grandchildren. Jerry used words like "eschew" and "desuetude" in sentences like "Kenny, why don't you eschew bothering Susie" or "Class, if we don't engage in some writing exercises our grammar skills will fall into desuetude." He presided over his homeroom in a haze of benign neglect and dry wit, and his students adored him. Philip would spend the entire first semester listening to shrieks of childish laughter from the room next door and hearing his three seventh graders complain "But that's not the way Mr. Van Kleek did it." What Jerry's secret was, Philip never discovered.

Philip would have less to do with the two women who occupied the classrooms two buildings away. Peggy Margaret Mitchell taught the third and fourth grades. She was a southern belle; her middle name functioned as a compound first name. Although she was at least a fifth generation evangelical from the Bible Belt, her family came from money, and consequently she chafed against certain of the time-honored cultural constraints. She once asked permission, for example, to teach the "little monkeys" in her class to dance, feeling that might improve their manners. Permission was denied. She drank pitchers of kalimansi juice, but longed to enhance the flavor with just a touch of gin and a hint of mint. She had married a wealthy oilman, but he died under mysterious circumstances when he somehow fell off one of his rigs into the Gulf. There had been rumors of an affair with his rig foreman, but Peggy Margaret never permitted the wild stories to dampen her grief. In her despair she applied to Bible college, and in a spasm of muddled thinking akin to how girls in previous generations wound up nuns, she went forward at a missionary meeting and woke up in the Philippines before it occurred to her that there might have been other ways to process her loss. Now, surrounded by monkeys both real and figurative, with no dances or mint juleps within five thousand miles, she oscillated between days of sugary sweetness and others of vituperative bile the likes of which kept the rest of the staff on their toes until they figured out which Peggy Margaret graced them with her presence that day. On one particularly rough Monday, Jerry would poke his head into Philip's room and remark for both Philip's and the children's benefit, "If your meanderings take you to the far building today kids, pack your sangfroid. Mrs. Mitchell is sedulous in her pursuit of scalps."

The youngest children on the center were instructed for six hours every day by Annabel Abbott. Although in her mid-thirties and possessed of a bewitching ethereal beauty, she had never married, and in fact had never dated since the day, when she was seventeen, that she left the old Annabel sitting in her pew and fled to the altar at a revival meeting to be reborn into a sparkling new creation. To possess the new Annabel in a carnal way simply never occurred to most men. She deflected male concupiscent desire with an adamantine integument of holiness that separated her from normal human intercourse all her adult years. She was in love with Jesus and had yet to meet a man who measured up. She was the owner of a stunning soprano voice and on those Sundays when she stood shyly before the assembled missionaries, lifted her eyes to heaven, and filled the meeting hall with melody fit for the courts of heaven, women fanned themselves extra briskly and men felt beads of sweat shimmer on their brows. And they thanked God for her. They all loved Annabel, but few knew her. She lived in a small house at the southern end of the center next to the St. Clairs, and although Matt and Julia invited her to dinner at least twice a week and Matt gave her a ride to school every day on his motorcycle, few others mustered the courage to speak to her. Her first words to Philip were, "I've been praying for you every day for three months ever since I heard you were coming. I know God is going to use you mightily in the lives of our children."

But most of this knowledge was future for Philip on this July day. The greetings were polite on all sides, but, although Philip tried to avoid looking only at her, his attention was fixed on the young librarian. Her name was Kari Trainor and she fell immediately into that category in Philip's love life marked "Turns brain to porridge." Philip had always had an easy way with women and they loved him for it; but when, usually inadvertently, he loved one back, he could come up with no good reason to speak a word to her. When he did decide to speak, he said things like "Do you like grape nuts?" or, "Have you ever been to Honduras?" Consequently most of his dating relationships had been with women he didn't really care for; they were attractive of course, and he enjoyed their company, but all the while he longed for someone else.

Philip was old enough now that he could articulate exactly why he fell hard for the librarian. It usually began for him with hair. He always looked twice, maybe a dozen times, when he saw long, straight hair tinged with amber highlights. Irresistible! Then a certain lissome quality to the limbs, a sweet and youthful timbre to the voice, perhaps a freckle or two, and finally, and most importantly, something in the eyes that spoke of both innocence and fun. Philip would be the first to admit that he had made errors of judgment in the past, especially where these most important elements in the equation were concerned. Eyes could be hard to read with any degree of certitude. His last serious love interest, at least the last one he had actually mustered the courage to approach, had majored in fun and only minored in innocence, despite her sterling credentials as the daughter of a prominent evangelist. It was her idea of fun, coupled with her father's idea of justice, which had curtailed his stay at the Bible College of San Diego. Still he had to admit that what he had seen in her eyes had been accurate. He had had a great deal of fun, followed, unfortunately, by a great deal of shame. But it was hard to read future shame in eyes that sparkled with fun.

When the meeting broke up shortly before noon, Philip immediately stood and began to speak to Jerry. He did this, not from any immediate desire to chat up the distinguished professor, but because he desperately needed to keep his eyes off the librarian. Jerry was just asking Philip if he liked to golf when the librarian swept by. She cheerily waved at Philip, gave Jerry a big hug, then jumped on a bicycle and peddled down the hill. Philip followed her with his eyes. "Golf?" he asked Jerry.

Jerry failed to notice Philip's distraction. He didn't notice much when he thought of golf. As far as Jerry was concerned it had been easy to give up father, mother, job, even country to follow God's command. But only when God asked him to give up golf did Jerry finally understand the steep cost of discipleship. Jerry had carried his clubs across the Pacific, had even managed to play once or twice in Manila, before arriving at Ilusan to discover that there were no golf courses in central Mindanao as far as he could see. But, as he now explained to Philip, after a brief period of mourning and after a lengthy discussion with Tom Jacobsen and the other pilots, he had set up a nine-hole course of sorts on the airstrips. The course consisted of tiny piles of firmly packed dirt no bigger than an ant hill to mark the tee boxes and yellow paint on the grass to mark the greens. Painted red circles served as holes. Every time the airstrips were mowed, the greens had to be repainted. The pilots got a kick out of the measled look of their strips from the air, and the most they ever felt was the smallest of bumps when they rolled over one of the tee boxes. And although putts never ran true and every shot was basically played from the rough, Jerry had enough of a golf course to keep him from speaking ill of God's call on his life.

Philip had indeed taken up golf in graduate school and, now that the librarian was out of sight and he could fix his attention on Jerry's story, he was enthusiastic. "If I'd known I could golf I would have brought my clubs," he said. Philip thought Jerry was probably excited to finally have a golf companion, although it was difficult to be certain from his reaction. Jerry's face rarely ceded ground to his moods. Whether admonishing a sixth grader, eating papaya, or crouching over a putt on a painted green, Jerry always appeared to be addressing a second century text.

"Indeed," he said. "Indeed. Perhaps my clubs might be rationed for the two of us." He suggested a Saturday morning outing. "It would behoove us to begin at an early hour, as Saturday can be a busy flight day and it's a trifle disconcerting to be driven from the field by approaching airplanes. The quotidian activities at our exclusive club must be accounted for." They set a date for 6:30 a.m.

Philip spent most of the next two days in his classroom preparing for the first day of school. He did, however, take time out for several visits to the pool and for a much needed trip to the commissary to stock up on rations for both himself and Mr. Bumbles. Most of the families on the center had house girls, as they were called, to do their shopping for them, local Filipino young women who were thrilled to be employed by the westerners. They shopped, cleaned house, and cooked. Many lived on the center in the homes of their employers, only going home on the weekends. Others commuted in from surrounding villages on a daily basis. Laundry was taken care of by another set of women, ingeniously labeled laundry women, usually older Filipinos who were specialists in the art of washing clothes in the river. Philip had been assigned a laundry woman and informed of the day during the week when she would stop by to pick up his dirty clothes. He was not assigned a house girl, however, as the mission felt uncomfortable with the idea of local girls popping in and out of the homes of single men. Once his tour of introductory dinners was complete, Philip would do most of his own cooking and cleaning. He didn't really mind. Although one part of his mind felt the restriction on house girls rather silly, another part was relieved that he wouldn't have a strange woman from a strange culture in his home. His cuisine might suffer, but his psyche would rest easier. He thought it a sound tradeoff.

The commissary opened four days per week with alternating morning and afternoon hours. It occupied the lower floor of a duplex next to the swimming pool. The upper floors were reserved for short term visitors to the center. Celia Haaf, who served as both base hostess and commissary manager, was sitting behind a desk just inside the door examining a ledger book when Philip entered. She appeared to be fighting a losing battle with her sums. Bits of eraser were scattered over the pages and just before she noticed Philip she mimed driving her pencil through her temple.

"Hey you," she said, looking up at Philip, "I've been expecting you. I figured you'd have to come by and get some food sometime." She asked Philip how he was getting settled, and after a brief conversation, during which she mentioned that she and Joseph were looking forward to seeing him for dinner the next evening, she handed him a basket and turned him loose. "Lots of strange things in here. Let me know if you have any questions."

Just then two boys emerged from behind some shelves and made for the door. "Just a minute Timmy," said Celia, "you're not going anywhere until you turn out your pockets. You too Bobby." The boy called Timmy laughed and pulled a small handful of candy out of his pockets. He was a large boy, chubby, and wore thick black glasses with gray tape holding the frame together at several spots. His hair was brown and straight and hung long in a bowl cut around his head. He pulled out a wad of money and change and cheerfully paid his bill.

"You don't think I'd try to steal from you do you Aunt Celia?"

Celia smiled. "Of course not, at least not as long as I keep my eye on you."

The boy called Bobby had closely cropped hair. He was slight but not short. He had a sensitive face, and when he smiled, large perfect teeth. "I'm not getting anything Aunt Celia," he said. He turned out his pockets as proof. "Wish I could, but I don't have any money."

Celia looked at Philip. "Boys, have you met your teacher yet? This is Mr. Andrews. Philip, this is Timmy Mullen and Bobby Sorenson. They're both in your eighth grade class."

Philip held out his hand. "I recognize the names." The boys shook his hand. They regarded him with what Philip took to be a mixture of shyness and curiosity.

"Sorry about the monkey last night," said Timmy. The boys looked at each other and laughed.

"Saved my" . . . he almost said ass, but caught himself in the nick of time . . . "butt," finished Philip. "I was getting a little tongue tied. That monkey showed up just in the nick of time."

Timmy suppressed a snicker. Bobby was staring at him astonished. Celia looked a little pale, but she recovered first. "Well boys I've got to help Mr. Andrews shop. I doubt he'll recognize much of what we have in here. You run along. You'll get to spend plenty of time with him once school starts."

The boys said goodbye. As they righted a couple of bicycles that had been casually flopped on the ground outside, Bobby looked back at Philip. After a moment he waved, then pedaled off. Philip turned to Celia.

"What?! What was that? What did I say?"

"Nothing. Don't worry about it."

"I didn't say . . . the other word for butt."

Celia sighed. "I know. That was good." She sat on the side of her desk. "Look, there's an innocence here that will take you some time to get used to. Joseph and I embraced the sixties," she raised her eyebrows as she said it, "and it took us awhile to settle in too. The kids, when they're just with themselves, can seem like kids anywhere. Having the boys turn out their pockets, well that's sort of a game we play, but I wouldn't doubt that Timmy would sneak some candy if he could. Bobby never would, but I didn't want to single out Tim. But in mixed company, or with adults, anything that even gets within hinting distance of body parts that normally remain covered is simply unheard of. If you had said . . . the other word for butt . . . you would have knocked them over. As it was, they never expected the first words out of their teacher's mouth to refer to a private part of the human anatomy. You might have gotten away with it if it had just been the three of you, although even then they wouldn't have expected it from an adult. But with me here, well that just added to the discomfort. What can I say, that's the way it is." She looked at Philip and laughed. "No harm done. Just be careful until you get the lay of the land. And never say anything even remotely risqué around the girls."

Philip groaned. "I know. I've already gotten the clean language speech from Sally. I said God when I had been spooked by a fruit bat. I got a lecture."

"And what a sweetie she is. You'll love these kids. I can't get enough of them." She got up. "And you'll love Ilusan. But it isn't the States. It isn't even stateside Christianity. It's its own world with its own issues. You'll get the hang of it."

Celia spent the next half hour helping Philip shop. His basket filled with rice, sardines for both he and Mr. Bumbles, a good selection of canned and fresh vegetables, bread, peanut butter, an interesting jam-like substance called coco-honey, canned juice, papaya, pineapple, bottles of Pepsi, and other staples. He wound up making two trips back to the house to carry it all. Before he left on his final trip Celia informed him that a buyer drove into Malaybalay, the provincial capital, every weekend, and all the way to Cagayan, a much larger city, once a month. She showed him a list where he could sign up to have the buyer look for any special requests he might have.

As Philip left, he glanced quickly around, then said, "Thanks Celia. You saved my ass."

He was gratified, as he quickly walked away, to hear her choke with laughter.

Philip was working at his desk on Tuesday afternoon when Kari poked her head in the door. Philip didn't notice her at first as he was glumly intent on an eighth grade math textbook. It was beginning to dawn on him that math at this level was going to be more than simple addition and subtraction. Philip thought the equations before him looked an awful lot like algebra, something he hadn't encountered as a kid until high school. He was just wishing that he had paid more attention to Mr. Dinwiddie in ninth grade algebra, when he heard the librarian's shy hello.

When Philip looked up to see the object of Monday's fantasy standing before him, the rush of feeling immediately overwhelmed any keenness of mind promoted by his razored focus on eighth grade mathematics. "Hi," he said. He stared at her for a long moment from behind his desk. She shifted her feet and gave a small wave. Neither of them spoke. It occurred to Philip that it was customary to invite people who came to your door to enter. "Come in," he said. She stepped inside the door.

"Thanks." She was wearing a straw hat with a floppy brim. Philip had always loved hats on women, and this librarian was stunning in her hat and sundress. Add that to the long hair with amber highlights, the freckles, the lissome limbs, and the sweet voice, and she stomped hard on all his infatuation buttons. He forced his lungs to operate.

Finally he managed, "Do I already have overdue books?"

"No," she said. Then, "Do you want a bicycle?" It was this question, so startling in its suddenness, so simple, yet so oddly out of place, that gave Philip his most satisfying flash of intuition in all his relatively young life. The librarian was nervous. She was perhaps as nervous as he. Only one logical corollary to this hypothesis came to mind; he was having an effect on her similar to her effect on him. As this suggestion catapulted through his mind, his senses immediately began to canvas their surroundings searching for corroborating evidence. Corroboration was everywhere. She began to apologize, to explain her sudden outburst. His ears picked this up. His brain said check. Her cheeks were touched with red, her eyes flitted down and away, one foot lifted slightly in the air and came to rest at its mate's heel where it began a rapid tapping, her left hand passed briefly across her eyes then settled on its opposite elbow where it clung just a little too awkwardly. His eyes took this in. His brain said check, check, check, check. Was there a touch of perfume in the air that hadn't been there yesterday? His nose inhaled deeply. His brain said checkmate.

Philip surged from his seat. In the process he slammed the little toe on his left foot hard into the leg of the desk. His flip-flops were sitting by his chair, and the pain in his unprotected toe was excruciating. "God," he blurted, but then a long lost friend fired up an emergency flare in his brain, a friend Philip had forgotten he had, and he gagged his words off into a strangled croak.

Some referred to it as a conscience, but Philip preferred to think of it as his holiness neuron, that spark from deep in his brain that protected him from ungodly responses to worldly stimuli. He much preferred it to his speak-without-thinking neuron that typically dominated such moments. His conscience, however, had grown lazy in the years since he deeply humiliated it by purposefully overriding its frantic appeals and addressing the Dean of Students at Bible college as "you hypocritical Lucy," an admittedly recondite, albeit felicitous at the time, allusion to her simian appearance and Neolithic ethics which he immediately regretted, although the reference passed quite over her head. That this slight to his conscience was carried out shortly after yet another purposeful override with the lovely daughter of the evangelist was the last straw. His holiness neuron had refused to weigh in on his actions for the past several years while nursing its admittedly legitimate grievances. But Philip was gratified to see that since arriving at Ilusan it appeared to be returning to its post, if still a trifle sluggish after its period of hibernation.

At any rate, it saved him now in his initial one-on-one encounter with the librarian. Philip took two quick hops and collapsed in a chair behind a student desk. The librarian was shocked out of her nervousness and earnestly inquired after his well-being. She asked if he thought it was broken and whether she should get some ice. All Philip could do for the next fifteen seconds was hold his foot and bang his head on the desk, but his desperate attraction to the librarian quickly reminded him that there might be better ways to make her acquaintance than showing the weakness he would have undoubtedly indulged if he had been alone. "I'm fine," he gasped, "just give me a minute. Nothing worse than a stubbed pinkie toe." He winced, then tried to cover up. "The little toe, I hit the little toe on my foot." Curse the day, he thought, someone referred in his presence to a pinkie toe.

The librarian appeared willing to overlook his lapse. "I'm so sorry. I know how much that hurts." She reached out and touched his arm, then quickly withdrew.

"It's your fault," Philip said. Both their eyes widened a bit. Philip laughed to cover up his confusion as he realized he'd spoken out loud.

"What do you mean, it's my fault?"

"Well, you know, it's a guy-girl thing." He let that hang there, hoping he wouldn't have to go on. But she just looked at him. He decided the only way out was to go forward. "You know, a guy is sitting there working, a beautiful girl suddenly comes to the door, and, you know, he turns to mush. He does idiotic things. He rams his toe into desks and humiliates himself in front of said girl. It's a law of the universe."

"Oh," she said. "Oh." And then she smiled. And then she said, "That's very sweet. Thank you." And they both laughed. And they were a little embarrassed, but even more, they were delighted. Something had been named, and in the naming came intimacy. Philip felt a shiver of possibility pass between them. They were two young people cast ashore in a small community of expats far from their pasts. They knew nothing of each other, but in that moment Philip, at least, longed to begin a process of exploration.

"You said something about a bicycle," Philip said.

"Oh yeah. It's nice to have a bike to get around here, and we, I live with Fossia, we thought you might like a bike. Fossia never uses hers, so we thought you could use it. It's a girl's bike," she was apologetic, "and it has a basket on the front, but the colors aren't girly," she laughed, "and actually as teachers the basket comes in handy to carry books. And you'd only have to use it until you get your own."

"Thanks. That was thoughtful of you." Philip tested his foot. "I think I'm o.k. to walk, so let's go take a look at this girl's bike that isn't girly. And since certain people already think I'm a woman, it shouldn't matter much anyway."

She didn't know what to make of that revelation. So as they walked outside to the bike rack in front of the school, Philip told her about his confrontation on his first day with Loretta Montgomery. "Oh no," she said, "that's terrible. I can't believe she thought that. I don't see how anyone could mistake you for a woman just because your hair is kind of long." Philip found that statement absurdly gratifying.

They reached the bike rack. "Here it is." She pointed to the ugliest bicycle Philip had ever seen. It was painted a shimmering gold. It was definitely a girl's bike, and the frame swooped down and thickened remarkably toward the base. Philip thought it would be like peddling about on the back of a gold swan. A white basket was mounted in front of the handlebars. The basket was decorated with a large painted red rose.

"No, it's not girly at all," said Philip. The librarian burst out laughing. "That's quite possibly the most ridiculous bicycle I've ever seen."

"Now that you mention it," she said through her giggles, "it is pretty awful isn't it! I don't know what I was thinking."

Standing there with the librarian gazing at the bicycle, both of them laughing, caught up in the charged moment of initial exploration, Philip felt exultant. He was surviving an encounter with a woman he was utterly attracted to. He wasn't just surviving; he was doing quite well indeed. The world was all good, and it was wonderful to be alive. "I'll take it," he said. "I accept it as a well-meaning gift from the librarian of Samantha Stoddard Memorial School, knowing that it's probably been years since she was in the States and saw what a real bicycle looked like. And I will peddle it about proudly all my days at Ilusan, accepting the scorn of neighbors and friends, and more than likely of total strangers as well. Thank you." With that he bowed deeply.

"It's not just a gift from the librarian," she said. "It's from the principal as well."

"All the more significant. Although I don't think I would have stubbed my toe over the good principal."

Kari looked at him. "You're terrible," she half-whispered, but Philip knew she meant just the opposite.

"So how long has it been since you've seen a real bicycle?"

"I've only been here two years," she replied. This exchange launched them into a relation of their pasts. She had already heard Philip's story the previous Sunday night, or at least the version that Philip was comfortable telling. But he had much to learn about her. She was an MK, a missionary kid. She had grown up in Peru on a mission base similar to Ilusan and with the same mission she now worked for. "It was paradise for kids, just like Ilusan is for our kids. Swimming, climbing trees, running through the jungle, making up all sorts of games, we had the run of the place. I absolutely loved it." But, as with all MKs, when she finished high school in Peru, she had to return to the United States for college. "Growing up overseas in such a sheltered environment doesn't really prepare you for life in the United States," she admitted. "Even though I attended a Christian college in Texas I was blown away by American culture. We landed in Los Angeles. I had never seen anything so immense. Driving to mission headquarters to check in, we passed all these adult shops. I couldn't conceive of such things." Her voice trailed off.

"I can imagine," said Philip. But he really couldn't. He was already learning that the kind of innocence possessed by MKs was beyond anything he'd known at home.

Her adjustments had been of the daily variety that made for stories both humorous and tragic. Simply being waited on at a restaurant by a white person was an initially disquieting experience. The only white people she had ever known had been missionaries or diplomats. She had never seen a white laborer. She had never seen a white criminal. She worked at a pizza parlor during her first summer home. One weekend night, after closing at two and then cleaning up and talking with her boss until well after three, they had emerged from the rear of the store to find four men loading televisions from the shop next door into a van in the alley. It never occurred to her that anything untoward was going on. She did the Christian thing. She waved to the men and asked if they needed help. Her boss grabbed her arm and literally threw her into his car. "They're robbing the place you idiot," he hissed as he roared out of the parking lot. "Where can we find a cop?"

Although stunned, she demonstrated that she was a quick study where American culture was concerned. She suggested they try the local doughnut shop. Sure enough three squad cars were parked out front. The news that Griffey's TV was being robbed was exciting enough that the men didn't begrudge leaving their doughnuts. As they ran out they ordered her boss to follow them back to the store. Her boss was too shaken to immediately comply, however, and ordered doughnuts and coffee first. By the time they drove back to the parlor, a helicopter with a blazing spotlight was circling overhead and the strip mall was swarming with squad cars, officers, and their dogs. Her boss parked in the pizza lot as far from the TV store as he could get. It was a warm summer night and she had opened her door and was sitting with her legs resting on the pavement enjoying the show next door. Then, in a surreal moment that she now described to Philip with the same wonder with which she first experienced it, she had glanced at the line of pizza delivery trucks parked in front of the parlor. A man was lying under the near truck staring fixedly at her. "Hey boss," she said, "what's that guy doing under the truck?"

When her boss saw what she was looking at, the torrent of frightened abuse that poured from his lips for her idiocy exceeded anything she'd heard from him to date. He ended with "get in the car you fool," before leaping from the car himself and yelling for the cops next door. Unfortunately when one of the canine handlers heard the commotion, he let go his grip on his German Shepherd. The dog bounded around the corner and the first people he saw were Kari, still sitting with her feet resting on the pavement, and her boss, now standing at the front of the car. The dog accelerated across the parking lot in a terrifyingly silent blur of brown and black; all Kari heard was the rapid click of its nails on the pavement. Kari had never seen an animal move so fast. She had never seen her boss move so fast either; he didn't even have time to curse before he was slamming his door. Kari, however, was transfixed. As if in slow motion she saw her boss lunge across her, pull her legs inside the vehicle, and slam the door. A second later the dog crashed against the side of the Buick, rocking the car. Its face contorted in rage and now howling at a demonic pitch, it slathered her window with spittle as it desperately sought a way in.

If possible, however, what happened next was even worse. The dog's handler yelled its name. The dog turned. The fugitive emerged from under the truck and began running. The screams of rage from the dog and the assembled men still haunted her. The dog seemed to use her door as a launching pad as it hurled itself in the direction of the fleeing thief. In a few great bounds it was on him, and dog and man crashed to the pavement in a welter of screams, growls, and struggle. A moment later a young policeman joined the ruckus. He wrenched the thief's arm high up between his shoulder blades, jammed a revolver into his cheek, and with the dog howling and slobbering inches from the terrified man's face, screamed, "How many were you? Where did they go? Were you armed?" All the librarian remembered now was the helpless man yelling, "No, no, no," whether in response to the questions or to his general life situation, she did not know. But, she told Philip, she had vowed right then she would get out of the United States and back to the mission field as soon as she possibly could. A fifty dollar gift certificate from Griffey's TV a few weeks later had done little to change her mind.

When Philip asked about her experience at Bible college, her face clouded a bit. "It was o.k.," she said. But she exhibited no enthusiasm as she recounted a few generic stories, and Philip thought that she must have struggled to fit in even there. After college her parents had suggested she return with them to Peru, and she spent a year at the Peruvian jungle base working in the nursery. Then she had heard of the need at Ilusan for a librarian. Philip knew she had been here for two years, and the light in her face as she spoke of her life on the center told him that she had made the right choice. He hoped Ilusan would be as good for him. As he watched her walk down the hill, he thought that it just might.

At 5:30 p.m. Philip was standing on his back porch trying to decide whether to walk or bike to the Haafs' for dinner. There was no question it was convenient to have a bicycle to get around the center, but Philip wasn't quite reconciled, despite his gallantry in the presence of Kari, to peddling about on the monstrosity that perched quietly on its kickstand next to his porch. He wasn't sure his dignity could handle the comparison to Matt St. Clair on his Suzuki. "What do you think Bumbles?" he asked. The cat was sitting in the middle of the porch steps. He appeared to be regarding the bicycle with a measure of disdain. "Oh to heck with it," Philip muttered. "What do I care what these people think of me? I'm only here for a year. Besides," he said to Mr. Bumbles, "it's the librarian we want to please."

He paused to scratch Bumbles' head on his way down the stairs, then mounted the bike. As he put up the kickstand, Mr. Bumbles got up, stretched, and strolled toward the bike's front tire. "Looks pretty silly doesn't it?" Philip said to him. The cat paused in front of Philip, tensed for a moment, then leapt nimbly to the top of the tire. From there he stretched up and inspected the basket. "You're not thinking," Philip began, but Bumbles was thinking just that. He jumped into the basket, turned around two times, then settled down facing forward with his head peering over the rim. Philip just gaped at him. The cat turned around, looked at him, then faced forward again and began to purr loudly. "Unbelievable," Philip muttered. As he sailed down the hill in front of his house toward the heart of the center, he had to admit it was a lovely evening for a ride. He crossed the main road, then peddled across a large grassy area toward the pool. Crossing the secondary road by the pool he waved to a small group of kids. He recognized Bobby Sorenson among them. Several of the kids pointed; he wasn't sure if it was at him, the bike, or Bumbles.

Joseph Haaf was sitting on his porch as Philip peddled up. He began laughing even before Philip came to a stop. "Celia," he called into the house, "get the kids and come get a load of this."

Philip obligingly waited on his bike as Celia and three little girls crowded onto the porch. Celia shook her head. "You are quite a sight," she said.

"Are you referring to me, my bike, or my cat?"

"The entire ensemble," Celia replied. The girls crowded around and reached for Mr. Bumbles. Bumbles gave Philip a quick look that Philip took to mean, "If I'd known there were kids here I never would have come," then leapt over the girls' heads, pranced up the porch steps and jumped onto the porch railing. Celia told the girls to leave the kitty alone, that it might not want to be bothered.

"I have two questions," said Joseph. "Where did you get that contraption you're riding, and where did you get the cat?"

After parking the bike and finding a seat on the porch, Philip explained the origins of each. "That Sally is a strange kid" was all Joseph said.

"She's a total sweetheart is what she is," chided Celia. "And so is Kari," she added with a meaningful look at Philip.

"I think I agree with both of Celia's sentiments," said Philip.

Joseph just grunted. Philip noticed that he was engrossed with a fly that had landed on his leg. "Watch this," Joseph muttered. "I'll show you how to kill a fly." Celia groaned and started to go inside but Joseph barked at her to freeze. She froze. Slowly he lowered both hands until they were opposite each other on each side of his leg. He smiled in triumph and then abruptly clapped his hands together above the fly.

"What good did that do?" asked Philip. "You just scared it away." Joseph slowly took his hands apart, gazed at them for a moment, then with a look that said "Oh ye of little faith" showed Philip his hands. Sure enough the fly was smeared across both palms.

"You better wash good before dinner," Celia said. "We're almost ready to eat. It'll just be a few minutes." She went inside.

Philip looked at Joseph. "Well?"

Joseph was clearly enjoying his triumph. He wiped his hands on the edge of the porch, then said, "In this country it helps to know how to kill flies. You don't always have a swatter handy. And usually you can't move your hands as fast as you can whip a flyswatter, so if you just try to smash them they'll be gone before you get there. Plus they see your hand coming from above. So one day when we were waiting to have our food served in a pretty seedy restaurant in Malaybalay, of course all the restaurants there are some variation of seedy so it's a fine distinction, I did a little study of fly escape techniques. They were all over the table cloth, so I had lots of subjects."

Philip raised his hand. "Let me get this straight. You did a study of the escape techniques of flies! I think this story is going to tell me a lot about you."

Joseph raised his right eyebrow and gave him a long look. "When you're in the presence of genius, it's best to just be quiet and attend to the lessons they teach. I'm about to show you what will be perhaps the most useful bit of information anyone has imparted to you since you arrived in the Philippines." He paused. "Now are you ready to listen and observe?"

"I beg pardon." Philip bowed his head. "Please, carry on."

"O.k. I noticed two things when I brought my hand slowly down toward them. First, they always freeze and crouch. Second, as my hand approached, they always sprang straight up in the air before buzzing away. They have to get off the ground before they can fly."

"Makes sense."

"Good. Now here's the part where the genius kicks in. I figured, why not use their own instinctive action against them. So I started bringing both my hands down beside them. They're confused because enemies seem to be approaching from all sides. Then as I clap my hands together, I clap above the fly, and its first evasive action, springing directly up, brings it right into my trap. Smash. No more fly."

"Yes, but do you really want smashed fly all over your hands?"

"If you don't want to get a little bloody, don't go to war." Joseph inspected his hands again. "Besides, in this country, you should probably wash your hands at least once every fifteen minutes anyway. You have to always be vigilant."

"What am I looking out for?" Philip decided that it might be fun to humor Joseph.

"Snakes and spiders for starters. You're relatively safe here on the center, but it's a freak fest off the base. I don't mean the people, I hasten to add. They're fine. Well some of the tribes out in the jungle are pretty scary." Joseph shuddered. "But the critters. The germs.  Spiders as big as your hand. You step foot off this base, all bets are off. And if you have to go to the bathroom, wait till you get back home. That's my best advice. I don't eat for twenty-four hours if I'm going off the base. Squatting over a hole with tarantulas leaping at your backside is the definition of gruesome humiliating death as far as I'm concerned."

Philip laughed. "I'll remember that."

"You laugh now; just don't say I didn't warn you. And I haven't even mentioned the mountain lions yet."

"And you're not going to start." Celia came up behind him and covered his mouth with her hands.

"Ugh, where have those hands been?" exclaimed Joseph.

"Just in the food that you're about to eat," said Celia. She invited Philip inside. "Is your cat coming in?"

"Mr. Bumbles? He does whatever he wants. Right now he looks pretty content right where he is." Bumbles did indeed look content. His paws were curled beneath him and his eyes were narrow slits. He might have been a monastic with his eye turned inward searching his soul; he might have been a Roman patrician with stuffed belly and sated sexual appetite. From what Philip had seen of the cat so far, he would have guessed the latter. Either way, Bumbles had that look of contentment that only cats can achieve.

"I never would have pegged you for an ailurophile," grunted Joseph. Philip and Celia just stared at him. "A cat fancier!" Joseph threw up his hands in exasperation. "I'm surrounded by simpletons." He stalked into the house.

Celia rolled her eyes at Philip. "My husband is the linguistic consultant for the branch. Now you know why."

"I can see he's going to be an education in more ways than one," said Philip.

Dinner with the Haaf family was a cacophony of competing agendas that oscillated wildly between moments of brilliant, if perfervid, conversation dominated by Joseph and stretches of childish nonsense from the girls during which Joseph appeared to retreat helplessly behind a wall of stoic indifference. In the moments when the adults could be heard above the kids, Philip learned that the Haafs had met at a Bob's Big Boy at 3:00 a.m. after a Grateful Dead concert. Stoned concert-goers filled the restaurant trying to sober up with pitchers of coffee before beginning the drive home. Joseph and Celia wound up crammed in a booth with a half dozen other Deadheads. The first words Celia spoke to her future husband were "What are you doing you little shit" when a thoroughly inebriated Joseph ground out his cigarette on her left arm. She still had the scar to prove it.

When she showed it to Philip, the girls squealed with delight, "Daddy why did you burn mommy?"

Joseph replied, "Daddy was in a happy place."

As a peace offering of sorts, Joseph had suggested on the spot that he marry her, or at least that's what Celia mouthed in exaggerated pantomime for the benefit of the girls.

"I offered to know her in the biblical sense," Joseph said with a shrug and glance at the girls.

For reasons Celia still couldn't clearly articulate, she had moved in with him the next day. All she offered to Philip was that Joseph had the most amazing record collection she'd ever seen. "Still does," she said with a nod toward the back door, an allusion which Philip wouldn't understand until after dinner.

Five years later, now with two children and Joseph back in college, where he proved to be somewhat of an adept, Celia converted to Christianity. With the girls down for their nap, she and a friend put on a Tim Buckley album and took a hit of acid. At this point she asked Philip if the story was "weirding him out." Philip replied that as a matter of fact he was really enjoying it and that he'd been surprised by at least one person every day since he arrived. "Well Joseph said we should tell you our story. We really haven't told it in too much detail to very many other folks in the mission." At that Joseph fixed him with the look that Philip was beginning to recognize. But Philip didn't have time to ponder the implications of Celia's remark for long. She was engrossed in the memory of her conversion.

The first thing she remembered after kicking off her slippers and lying flat on her back on the rug was the smell of warm earth and the sound of the most beautiful male voice singing somewhere just out of sight. She sat up and saw she was in a meadow on the side of a hill under a hibiscus bush. "I'm sure it was a tropical hibiscus, because the flower was salmon and about eight inches across."

Joseph groaned. "Just tell him the story Celia!"

Celia stared him down. "It's my story and the details are important."

Joseph sighed. "I don't think it matters what kind of hibiscus it was. That's not the point."

"Well I thought it was important enough at the time to notice, so I'm telling Philip about it. You never know what details are important in a vision."

Philip interrupted. "I take it you're a flower buff. I wouldn't have known what kind of flower it was."

"Oh yes," Celia said. "And I've got a salmon colored tropical hibiscus planted by the front porch. It reminds me every day who I am."

"Can we please?!" Joseph was starting to fidget.

Celia returned to her story. She remembered sitting under the bush for a long luxurious moment soaking in the sunshine. It was the kind of light you only get in dream, like basking in a Monet painting. Gradually the singing voice had pressed more and more upon her consciousness. It seemed to demand that she attend. She stood up and began to follow. She went down the hill, crossed a bridge over a weedy ditch, then entered a field of tall wildflowers. Some were waist high; others reached over her head. The colors swirling in a light breeze made her giddy. The first words of the song that she actually understood were "once I was your lover." The voice seemed both distant and right in front of her. She pressed forward but it was always just out of reach. "Once I was your lover . . . and I searched behind your eyes for you . . . and soon there'll be another . . . to tell you I was just a lie." She recognized the words from the Buckley song, but this voice was even more beautiful than Buckley's. She began to run, but the light reflected into her eyes making it difficult to see. Several times she caught glimpses of a figure before her; she begged him to wait, but he kept just out of reach. Finally, spent and exasperated, she threw herself on the ground and began to weep. "Please," she said, "please." At this point in the telling, Celia blinked back tears. Joseph's arms were crossed on his chest. He was staring at his wife. Philip couldn't tell if he was disgusted or enthralled.

As soon as she said "please" for the second time she found herself sitting on a stone bench on a hill overlooking a valley with a river far below. Just to her left were some stone ruins. It looked like an ancient watch tower. The singing man stepped through the crumbling walls and approached her. "And at that moment," said Celia, "I knew he was Jesus. I don't know how I knew. A lot of the guys looked like Jesus back then. But I just knew like you always know in dreams or visions. I think it was the way he looked at me."

Jesus stopped about twenty feet from her and continued to sing. "And sometimes I wonder . . . just for awhile . . . will you remember me?" He sang that line several times. "Will you remember me . . . will you remember me?" Celia said that while music continued to emerge from somewhere, it seemed like from the stones, Jesus stopped singing. He gazed at her with a troubled expression and she heard the following words in her head. "Though you have forgotten all of your rubbish dreams . . . I find myself searching through the ashes of these ruins . . . for the days when you smiled." She remembered thinking the phrase "I love the silence of your words." Then the man turned, began singing again, and walked back into the ruins. She heard his song trailing after him. "And sometimes I wonder . . . just for awhile . . . will you remember me?"

"And then I woke up," Celia said. "And I vowed to myself that I would remember him. I took a hit of acid, lay down, had a cool trip, and woke up a Christian. And I've been a Christian ever since."

Philip's mind boggled. Celia was inverting all of his familiar categories. You were supposed to see the devil on drugs, not Jesus. "So what did you do? How did you become a Christian?" He was waiting for the prayer. She must have prayed the prayer. But no, Celia had simply accepted the fact that from that point on she was a follower of Jesus. She started reading her Bible, found a local Calvary Chapel filled with Jesus people like her, and dramatically changed her life.

At this point Joseph burst in. "My turn," he said. Anticipating the story he was about to tell he began to laugh and rub his hands together. "All right, you'll love this."

Joseph had initially tolerated his wife's conversion and had even begun attending Calvary Chapel with her. But very quickly the constant proselytizing and what Joseph considered the morbid and at times downright inconsiderate emphasis in the church on the stark choices between God and devil, good and evil, saved and unsaved, heaven and hell, began to irritate him. Out of pure orneriness he undertook an intense program of Bible study. Soon his fecund mind began to conjure a host of theological conundrums that hoisted the pastor and his epigones on an entire forest of petards. The good folks at Calvary had simply never crossed a mind like Joseph's. Before long Joseph had become the pastor's personal *bête noire* and the good man ordered the church members to have nothing to do with him. When Joseph showed up at church with Celia, he found his way blocked by a two hundred eighty five pound ex-defensive tackle for the Cal football team. He was politely informed that, like the poor sap in Saint Paul's first letter to the Corinthians, he was being delivered over to Satan for the destruction of his flesh so that his spirit might be saved in the day of the Lord Jesus. Joseph had simply laughed, told Celia to carry on without him, and retired to a local breakfast spot with the Sunday paper.

But over the next several months Joseph continued to study the Bible. He was deeply impressed by the person of Jesus and by the mind of Saint Paul. He recognized a hunger within himself for some sort of spiritual experience. And, especially when drunk or high, the pastor's imprecations and the threat of being delivered over to Satan gnawed at his self confidence. Although he wasn't sleeping with his stepmother like Saint Paul's whipping boy in Corinth, he felt that the force of the Apostle's logic somehow applied to him as well. "Shows you what smoking too much weed does to your faculties," Joseph admonished Philip in an aside. One night, while driving home from school, Joseph stopped by the side of the road to smoke a joint. One joint turned into two then three before their combined effects settled him into a lengthy nap.

"What's a joint?" asked one of the girls.

"Joseph," Celia exclaimed, "use a euphemism."

"What's a oophamism?" chimed in another daughter.

"I figured joint was oophamism enough," growled Joseph. He addressed the girls. "A joint is a marijuana cigarette." Celia threw up her hands and went into the kitchen to get dessert. "Marijuana is a weed," Joseph continued, "kind of like those dandelions in the yard. Daddy and

Mommy used to smoke it in cigarettes, especially Mommy. But we don't do it anymore. We know smoking is bad now."

"I'm sure that little lecture will keep them out of trouble when they get to high school," Celia called from the kitchen.

"They won't remember any of this in two days," yelled Joseph. "Now can I get back to my story?"

"Be sure to tell the girls you had sex with lots of strange women when you smoked your dandelions," Celia called.

It was Joseph's turn to be put out. "The only strange woman I ever slept with was you," he said.

Philip decided to chime in. He didn't know if conversation like this was par for the course or whether fisticuffs might break out. Whatever, he didn't want to find out. His view of marriage tended to be idyllic, probably hopelessly naïve. Arguing couples made him nervous. "How come missionaries like you guys never came to my church when I was a kid? All we ever got were the boring ones with missionary barrel clothes and really bad slides. I might have wanted to be a missionary if someone like you had dropped by."

Celia poked her head out of the kitchen. "We're a little out of the ordinary I think."

"I don't know," Philip said. "I think too many missionaries hide these sides of themselves when they visit churches back home. All we get are the sanitized perfect prayer letter Christians. A plague of rats might have devoured everything they owned, but they're still praising God for their trial by rat. You just know that they're really pissed off, but they'll never admit it."

"Philip, the girls!" Celia exclaimed.

Philip clapped his hand over his mouth. "Oh crap. Sorry. Oops, sorry again."

Joseph had heard enough. "Can we please get back to my story? This is all very nice, but we can discuss this another time. I had the floor here until I was rudely interrupted."

"Sorry," Celia said. She withdrew into the kitchen.

"Do you mean it gets more interesting than smoking three dandelions?" Philip asked.

"I'm just getting started," said Joseph. "You haven't even begun to plumb the depths of my madness."

It was dusk and fog had rolled in off the water before Joseph pulled back onto the road. He'd been driving several miles when a glance in his rearview mirror revealed a motorcycle with sidecar gaining on him. The cyclist was dressed all in black. He wore a black helmet. The bike and the empty sidecar were a deep black as well. Joseph blinked and looked again, but the cyclist vanished, swallowed in the fog.

"Now this is bizarre, I know," he said to Philip, "but I immediately knew that the guy on the cycle was Death and the empty sidecar was for me. I was utterly convinced of this. The pastor's threat was coming true. And I panicked to say the least."

Joseph kept glancing in his mirror, hoping he had been mistaken, but the cyclist was there again, wisps of cloud streaming from his visor. And he was gaining rapidly. Joseph stomped on the gas and his car surged forward. The bike disappeared behind a curve, then there was a stretch of fog through which Joseph drove dangerously fast, but emerging from the fog in the gloom of early evening Joseph saw that the biker continued to gain. He was going perversely fast. Joseph began to sweat and pray. He begged his car to go faster, but Death kept gaining. Another stretch of fog which both vehicles hit at over eighty miles per hour.

"I really shouldn't have survived that," Joseph acknowledged, "but fortunately we were on a straightaway."

When he emerged from the fog again, the motorcycle filled his mirror. The needle on Joseph's speedometer registered over ninety when the bike swung into the oncoming lane and pulled alongside. Joseph's eyes were riveted on the road ahead. His hands were frozen on the wheel. He expected at any moment to feel a clawed hand yank him screaming from his seat and hurl him into the sidecar. He saw a sharp turn around a cliff face rapidly approaching. He assumed that once Death had him secure in his sidecar he would steer straight off the road into space where with a sulfurous bang they would hurtle into another dimension. The bike was directly alongside when Joseph risked a glance. The motorcycle was dark blue, not black. The sidecar had a bumper sticker that read "Honk If You Love Jesus." The biker gave Joseph a thumbs-up before roaring on by. Joseph immediately took his foot off the accelerator but still took the curve at over seventy miles per hour. The biker seemed impervious to the turn. It was only as the motorcycle disappeared in the distance that Joseph thought to honk. He honked three times. "And I decided I better become a Christian," he told Philip.

"You see, now if I was the head of your mission, I'd have the two of you plastered on every brochure we had," said Philip. "It'd be Joseph next to Satan in a sidecar and Celia's acid dream. And the tagline would be something like 'God can use anyone on the mission field.'"

"Well thanks. I'll take that as a compliment," said Joseph.

"So did you join Celia at Calvary Chapel?"

"No, I couldn't give that pastor the satisfaction. I attended a Presbyterian church. They had a much more sensible theological system. We've never attended the same church until we got to the field. And you've seen what I have to put up with here."

Philip heard Celia groan from the kitchen. But she didn't say anything, apparently deciding her husband's latest remark wasn't a battle worth fighting.

"And what turned you into missionaries?"

Celia emerged from the kitchen to answer this. She was carrying a large bowl of chocolate pudding in one hand and a wooden spoon in the other. "Well first we had to get married. But then it just seemed like that was how God was leading us. Joseph's professors said he was great with languages, and we wanted to serve. A mission that desperately needed linguists seemed like the right place for us. But we couldn't be Bible translators because Joseph couldn't handle the jungle and I didn't want to be separated from the girls. So Joseph became a linguistic consultant. He only has to go out to the jungle for brief visits. Most of the translators consult with him here. And we get to live on the base and be with the girls."

This sparked a question that had been bothering Philip. "So all those little kids in the children's homes are the kids of translators? Why don't they take correspondence courses? Sending first graders away from their parents for long stretches seems like something people wouldn't be happy to do."

"That's not the missionary ethic," said Joseph. "It's God first, work second, family third. If the kids stayed with their parents in the jungle that would take one parent away from the work pretty much full time." He shrugged. "Most kids survive the children's homes just fine."

The idea of sending her girls off to boarding school clearly disturbed Celia and she began to weigh in on the topic. As she did she waved her serving spoon around. Philip noticed that flecks of chocolate flew off as she gestured. He looked closer. The flecks of chocolate were moving on the spoon. The eldest Haaf daughter exclaimed, "Mom!"

Philip glanced at her. She was staring in horror at her mother. Philip looked closer. Just as he realized that Celia's spoon was covered with ants, she plunged the spoon into the bowl of dessert and began stirring. The little girl shrieked. Philip said, "Celia, I think," but it was too late. Celia looked at her daughter, felt something move on her hands, looked into the bowl, and abruptly dropped everything on the floor.

Joseph jumped up. "What are you doing?!" Everyone gathered around the bowl. The pudding was teeming with large black ants. "Dump it outside quick," said Joseph. "Didn't you cover it up or put it in the 'frig?"

"I got distracted and left it out." One of the girls began to cry. "Don't worry honey, Mommy will make some more. It won't take long." Celia picked up the bowl and exited out back through the kitchen.

"Follow me," Joseph said to Philip. "You might as well continue your education." Philip complied. "Never leave food out or this is what you get." The counter around where the bowl of pudding had been was swarming with ants. The trail came through the window across the stove and onto the counter. "It's an absolute mystery how they get on the scent, but get on the scent they do and very quickly. And where there's one there's thousands." Joseph was disgusted. "I warn Celia about this all the time, but she's a bit scatterbrained." He got out a can of Raid and began spraying the counter. He sprayed the line all the way to the window, then leaned out the window and sprayed down the outside of the house as far as he could reach. When Celia returned he and Philip were wiping up the dead ants. The smell of Raid filled the room.

"I'm sorry Philip," said Celia. "Dessert will be delayed. But dessert there will be."

"Don't make it on my account."

"Yes, make it on his account," said Joseph. "In the meantime I'll take Philip out to my study and have a little man-to-man talk."

"I'm sure Philip is really looking forward to that," said Celia.

Joseph gave his wife the look. "Hon, Philip needs help. Half the people here probably think he's a bad seed. It's my duty to take him aside, like Aquila for Apollos, and give him some instruction."

Celia stopped washing out the pudding bowl and gaped at Joseph in utter exasperation. "Joseph, nobody thinks Philip is a bad seed. Philip, nobody thinks you're a bad seed. Joseph is being ridiculous."

"Weren't you listening the other night?  The man gets up in front of the assembly and asks to be introduced to our eunuchs. If that monkey hadn't saved him, he'd probably still be waxing eloquent on the benefits of being a member of the castrati. And look at his hair. He looks like a bad seed to me. I need to straighten him out." With that Joseph opened the back door. "After you," he said to Philip.

Philip grinned at Celia, shook his head, and stepped onto the porch. The Haafs' back porch ran the length of their house and looked down through a stand of trees to the far end of the swimming pool where it emptied into the creek. "Wow," said Philip. "Who did you kill to get this house?"

"Yes, it's nice." But Joseph's mind was clearly on other things. At the far end of the porch stood a small room. It was Joseph's office. The door was padlocked. "Got to keep the women out," Joseph whispered as he fumbled for his keys.

The room into which Philip was ushered might have been the last stand of a mad professor or a very sick bibliophile or, more probably, both. There appeared to be a desk by a window, a chair or maybe two, some other indiscriminate lumpy objects, and in one corner a stereo and a pile of something under a blanket. But it was hard to tell exactly what things were because everything was covered with books. Book shelves had been crudely built into every available inch of wall space, and books were double and triple stacked with no regard for proper bookshelf etiquette. Piles of books and scattered papers covered the floors. The path from the door to the desk was not entirely clear, and Joseph had to spend almost five minutes rearranging and restacking before Philip had a place to sit. After Philip was seated, Joseph smiled in triumph, moved a pile of books, opened a small refrigerator which magically appeared, and removed two orange sodas. Philip noticed that orange soda appeared to be the refrigerator's sole occupant. The tall glass bottles immediately began to sweat in the heat. The soda was delicious, ice cold, very sweet and sharp.

"One more thing before I sit down," said Joseph. He turned to Philip. "You are sworn to secrecy. Do I have your word?"

"You do."

"O.k. You see this stereo. Nobody else in Ilusan has anything like this. And if they did, they'd be playing 'The 101 Strings Does Blue Hawaii' or 'George Beverly Shea's Gospel Favorites.' But here at the Haaf household in the Joseph Haaf stronghold you get . . ." here Joseph threw back the blanket . . . "voila, Bob Dylan and friends."

"You've got to be kidding." Philip found himself staring at stacks of records. It appeared to be the entire Dylan corpus, and that was just for starters. He couldn't stay in his seat. Soon he was flipping through stacks of CCN, Janice, the Band, the Dead and hosts of other luminaries from the counterculture. "I really don't believe this. How do you get away with it?"

"Well for starters I have a very good set of headphones. And most important I keep the door padlocked. I don't even let Celia in here. I think some of the eighth grade boys whose parents either turn a blind eye or are simply remarkably unobservant might have a Chicago record, maybe some Beatles and Elton John, but nothing else. This is the mother lode." Philip could see Joseph was hugely proud of his collection. It must have been terribly frustrating to have nobody to share it with. Before they sat down Joseph put on "Highway 61" at a very low volume. "Can't be too careful," he said.

They listened in silence, enjoying the music and the orange sodas. Philip noticed that the cicadas had begun to sing in the trees outside. He looked over Joseph's massively disorganized book collection. There were technical linguistic books, but also numerous novels, as well as works of history, theology, and philosophy. A number of books were in German and French.

"How do you find anything?"

Joseph glared at him. "I can put my fingers on anything I want at a moment's notice. But please, can we just listen? This is Bob."

Philip didn't see how anyone could possibly find anything at a moment's notice in this particular room, but he didn't press the issue. He waited respectfully for a few more songs before finally asking the other question that was begging to be asked. "You know, the Christians I grew up with and went to school with would have considered a collection like this a sign of worldliness. How do you know I won't think the same thing? How do you know I won't tell tales? If what you say is accurate, I'm the only person outside of Celia that knows about this. I've been here, what, three days?! And clearly you already think me an accomplice in worldliness."

Joseph was quiet for a few more minutes. Philip began to speak again, but Joseph held up his hand. Philip realized he was just waiting for "Ballad of a Thin Man" to end. "Well first of all," Joseph finally said, "let's get one thing clear. Just because somebody else says something is worldly doesn't mean it is. Didn't the Reformation teach you anything? Let conscience rule. So the only accomplice I consider you to be is an accomplice in appreciating good music." He fixed Philip with the look and reluctantly turned the music down even further. "However I did tell Celia that we should be candid with you about our past, and I did show you my room for a reason. Let's say I'm throwing my cards on the table in the hope that you will reciprocate. That story you told Sunday night struck me as only half right. How did you wind up over here? Wait, we'll get to that. Start earlier. You said your Dad was a preacher. Tell me about your Dad."

Philip groaned. "You really want to hear this?" Joseph just looked at him. "All right." He leaned back and propped his feet on a pile of books. He rolled the sweating glass of orange soda on his temple. "You want to know about my father." Philip sighed and said the words under his breath a few more times like an incantation. Finally he took a long drink and said, "My relationship with my father can be summed up in his dying words to me, the very last words I heard him speak. He was practically in a coma; this was just last summer by the way. He hadn't said anything for at least a day and a half. Hadn't even opened his eyes I don't think. I was staying at the house to help my stepmother care for him. I got up in the morning to check on him. I remember I touched his arm and leaned over and said, 'How are you Dad?' He never opened his eyes, but he very clearly said, 'Your breath stinks.' And that was it. He died the next day. Those were the last words he spoke to anybody as far as I know." Philip stopped because Joseph had burst out laughing. "I can see you're going to be a very sympathetic listener."

"I'm sorry, but that is very funny."

"Yes I know it is. I thought it was funny at the time. My father was a humble man, but he was also a hard man. He was never pleased with himself or his own abilities, but he was absolutely convinced that he understood God and what God was trying to do in the world. And he was feverishly determined to be a godly man. He loved God I suppose, but had little patience for God's creatures who never seemed to measure up to either God's or his ideals. And so, of necessity, he had little patience with me."

Joseph's eyes were closed. For a moment Philip thought he might have dozed off. But then he said, "Go on."

"I did repair my relationship with my father in his last few years. Or at least circumstances led to their repair. My mother died and eventually my dad fell in love and remarried. Just one catch! He married a divorced woman. And the church he'd given his life to for almost twenty years fired him on the spot. Unbelievable!"

"Actually that's not hard to believe at all." Joseph held up his hands. "I don't mean to be cruel, but divorce is one of the big ones."

"Yea, I know." Philip did know. "And what's more, my dad knew. I stopped by for a visit the week it all came down. My stepmom was devastated, but my father was curiously impassive. I think the event served as some sort of epiphany for him. You know what he said to me? He said, 'I taught them to love righteousness more than they loved each other. They were just doing what I taught them.' Can you believe that?"

"That is impressive."

"Our relationship improved after that. He only had a few more years, but it was like he flipped one hundred eighty degrees. All of a sudden he was all about grace and forgiveness. I actually felt like he genuinely cared about me."

Joseph abruptly changed the subject. "You know with that background I'm surprised you didn't end up at a Bible college somewhere. Didn't you say you went to some state school?"

Philip was startled. Out of the frying pan into the fire. He couldn't imagine a more dangerous topic to discuss with someone from the mission he had recently joined. This was the one story he hoped to keep quiet, to forever expunge from his record. His turmoil must have showed on his face, because Joseph immediately said, "Ah, got you didn't I? I knew there was some aspect of your story that didn't sit right. What happened at Bible college? Out with it."

Philip was silent for a moment, then asked, "So how far is this story going?"

Joseph smiled. He pointed to his records. "You could cast public aspersions on my character. I won't even tell Celia."

"O.k." Philip decided he might be able to finesse the issue by using oblique language. Besides, Joseph seemed genuinely interested in his story. If he had sinister intentions, he was hiding them very well.

"I did attend the Bible College of San Diego for a brief period, a semester and a half to be exact. But let's just say it was a bad fit." Philip winced at the memory. "You know, they had an ad that they put in all the Christian magazines. The ad was a picture of a spring bubbling up in a beautiful oasis. And the text, which was very minimal, simply said '100 percent pure,' and then under that tag line was the name of the school, the Bible College of San Diego. So here I was, a pretty drifting kid at that point, attending a Bible college that advertised itself as one hundred percent pure." Joseph was already laughing again, but Philip went on. "So let's just say that as soon as they discovered that student Andrews remained cussedly impure, they flicked me away like I was a fly crawling on their white shirt."

"But you must have done one of the biggies." Joseph's voice remained easy and conspiratorial.

Philip gave up. "The biggest."

"Oh-oh, not good," said Joseph.

"Yep, and she was the daughter of one of the school's board members, an evangelist pretty high up in one of the supporting denominations, I forget which one. Anyway, she had her fun, and don't get me wrong, this isn't an excuse, but she took a back seat to no one in the fun department, but, eventually at one of her Daddy's meetings, her conscience got the better of her and she confessed her sin to her old man." Philip was surprised at the bitterness that suddenly welled up in him. "And of course as part of her confession she felt it her duty to finger me. So I get hauled in to the Dean's office. And they had me right where they wanted me. Our pleasure, what there was of it, was already mixed with mutual recriminations, guilt, and fear. I probably would have flipped and repented and whatever. But the Dean listened quietly to my confession and then very publically booted me out anyway. She was oddly honest. Their constituency would expect them to act, she said. I don't know, maybe she was just trying to tell me that her hand was being forced. But I'm afraid I lost it and said some fairly regrettable things. And I got the boot. Off to San Diego State for me."

"What happened to the girl?"

"Nothing was ever made public about her. She had to leave the dorm and live with the campus chaplain, which if I know her, was probably punishment enough. And then I get a call from her the fall of the following school year. She wants to see me, needs to 'get away and have a good time.' Well I knew her well enough to know what that was code for. And, guess what, I took her up on it. I've never been good at saying 'no.' I hate to disappoint people."

"Better learn quick if you're going to survive as an evangelical. But you probably won't have to say it much here." Joseph didn't seem too disconcerted by Philip's story. "So how *did* you wind up here?"

"Well, to be honest, I think I'm a family reclamation project. I suspect that after my dad died, my stepmom and my uncle got together and hatched this scheme. I haven't exactly been a great Christian for quite a few years. I think they think, and they're probably right, that by getting me away from my friends and into this new setting that I'll come back around. I owe a lot to my uncle. He obviously cooked the books a bit to get me here. But I had to promise to be on my best behavior." Philip saw Joseph's eyebrows go up. He thought he might have said too much. "But it's not like I'm a rank heathen or anything. I'm still a Christian. Or at least I've believed all my life. I can't stop believing. I'm still evangelical I guess. I'm just not very sure about anything anymore."

Joseph chuckled. "Then you're definitely not evangelical. Evangelicals have answers, not questions. What do you think brings them to the jungle? Would you live out there for thirty years if you had doubts?"

"No, I probably wouldn't. I see your point."

Their conversation was interrupted by Celia knocking on the door. "Time for dessert," she said.

"We'll be there in a few minutes," said Joseph.

But the two of them sat in silence, neither particularly eager to return to the company of the family.

Finally Philip said, "So am I, as you claimed, a bad seed?"

"The answer to that question my friend is blowing in the wind. Only time will tell."

Joseph stood to go. But Philip had a question. "What about you? You seem to have an interesting perspective on all this. Why are you here?"

Joseph picked up their bottles and put them in a case already half full of empties. "Because the foibles and follies of evangelicalism aren't the sum total of the gospel. What these folks do is great work. And they're the only ones doing it. Only evangelicals and fundamentalists, like your Dad for instance, care enough to do this kind of thing. So I support their work, I support them, and, most of the time, I keep my opinions to myself."

"When have you ever kept an opinion to yourself?"

"All the time, well some of the time, well maybe not all that often. But I'm also on my best behavior. Celia makes sure I stay there. Although every now and then I ask a question or two to help sharpen their thinking." He shut down the stereo, lovingly placed the Dylan record back in its sleeve, moved to the door, gave one long glance back around his private kingdom and said, "We better rejoin the women."

# Chapter Five

ON WEDNESDAY, THE FIRST day of school, Philip was out of bed before 5:00 a.m. "I bet Bobby Sorenson hasn't even thought about that wretched piano yet," he grumbled. Mr. Bumbles certainly wasn't ready to get up. He gave Philip a puzzled look, then gratefully commandeered the half of the pillow he hadn't already usurped, stretched out luxuriously, and went back to sleep. "Lucky bastard," muttered Philip. But he really had no choice. He had to get up. He had slept fitfully all night. He dreamed of racing through school hallways desperately searching for his homeroom. Once he found the room, he realized he either hadn't prepared at all or had brought the wrong lesson plan. The hostile glares of his dream students woke him up with a feeling of dread. Once awake he turned the first day's lessons over and over in his head. It didn't help that Bumbles' raucous snores indicated his bedmate was resting easy with a clear conscience.

He tried to have devotions on his porch, but found himself staring at the sunrise over Capistrano. It was the time of morning that simply demanded attention, a gift from God to early risers. The cool early morning light retreated grudgingly before the warm rays of the emerging sun which clung to the grass as they crept under the barbwire toward Philip's yard. Above this quiet drama the waking birds played their sleepy whispering chords like the high lost melody of a violin trembling over the advancing rush of the full orchestra.

Philip sat on his steps, sipping coffee and taking deep breaths of the cool moist air. There was no air like this in California. Nothing this moist, nothing this clean. He was grateful for the quiet. There were moments in his life when his loneliness came with a keen accent of pleasure so sharp it brought tears to his eyes, and he felt that now. No matter what happened later in the day, he would have these few solitary minutes. And he knew this experience would be waiting for him any day he chose to rise early enough to embrace it. He lifted his coffee in a salute to God.

"You've outdone yourself this morning old man, you really have." And with that introduction he began to pray. And his prayer was uncluttered with bitterness, fear, or regret. In a few words he gave thanks for an opportunity to begin again.

The school day began at 7:30, but Philip wanted to be there at least by 7:00. He had a keen sense that the school was the kids' turf, and he knew it would take some time to make it his own. But at least if he was there when the first child arrived he might start the day with the upper hand. "Are you coming Bumbles?" he asked the cat as he climbed on his bicycle. Mr. Bumbles, who had made his first appearance on the porch about 6:15, looked up from the saucer of water Philip kept for him next to the door. He was a vigorous drinker and his long whiskers glistened with droplets. He blinked once at Philip, then trotted down the stairs and with two bounds was in the basket, facing forward, ready to ride. "You are one weird cat," said Philip. He carefully guided the heavy bike around the corner of the house.

As they took off down the hill, he heard an old woman's voice wail "Jesus!" He turned just enough to glimpse Dorothy peering from her bedroom window. He waved and formed his left hand into Spock's Vulcan salute. "That was dumb," he panted to Bumbles as he peddled hard to pick up speed. "I probably should have done that weird thing Robert Powell did with his hand when he performed miracles." The cat looked at him over his shoulder. "He played Jesus in Zeffirelli's movie last year on TV. You wouldn't have seen it. He did something like this when he was feeling supernatural." Keeping a tight grip on the handlebar with his right hand, with his left Philip showed Mr. Bumbles Powell's signature miracle move. The cat seemed satisfied. He turned back around and licked his whiskers as Philip pedaled across the road by the post office and headed toward the plaza in front of the Haaf house. Two women stepped out of the path to let him go by. They greeted him warmly and laughed to see the cat so comfortably in his basket. Philip pedaled hard past the Haaf house because he knew what awaited him. The hill in front of the school buildings was steep and, despite his speed, Philip didn't make it to the top. He had to push the bike the last twenty feet. He walked his monstrous conveyance between the school buildings and parked it in the bike rack. Mr. Bumbles jumped out and followed him up the stairs into his homeroom.

Philip really didn't have that much to do. He was ready for day one. After a few minutes of idle desk straightening, he began to cast about for the proper posture to assume as the children entered. Should he greet them at the door? Should he be sitting behind his desk? Perhaps a casual posture on top of the desk? That might communicate more who he really was. Or maybe a grand fun-filled gesture like hiding in the closet and springing out at the last minute? He quickly discarded that idea. He really wasn't a bold stroke kind of guy. A vigorous yawn from Mr. Bumbles drew his attention. Bumbles was sitting like a feline Buddha in one of the windows that lined both sides of the room. Philip went to the window closest to his desk. It looked out over the hill and the school buildings.

"I think you've got just the right idea," he said to the cat. None of the windows were screened, and they turned out to be the perfect size for sitting in, although he had to curl his right leg and leave his left on the floor. The library was directly across from his room, and he looked to see if Kari had arrived yet. She hadn't. He noticed two small boys walking up the hill, arms thrown over each other's shoulders. A group of girls, two of them holding hands and skipping, called out to the boys. A few bike riders laboriously stood on their peddles and attempted the hill. Most made it in much better shape than Philip.

Philip heard his name being called. Jerry Van Kleek was on the steps to their shared building. He had spotted Philip in the window. "You look ready for the big day," Jerry said.

Philip wasn't sure. "I suppose the proper response if we were in a really bad action movie would be 'I was born ready,' but somehow I don't think that applies to me in this case."

Jerry laughed. "You'll surprise yourself." On the way into his room he said, "I'll see you at recess. If you don't show, I'll send out a search party."

At 7:15 Sally bounced up the steps. Philip had noticed her almost running up the hill. She was the first of his students to arrive. She was wearing pink culottes, a white blouse, and tennis shoes. An empty book bag hung artfully over her shoulder. Her long hair was neatly tied back in a pony tail. Upon entering the room she slowed down visibly and greeted him formally. "Good morning, Mr. Andrews." Then she spotted the cat. "Mr. Bumbles," she cried as she ran to the window and gave the cat a tight hug, which he endured with admirable equanimity. "I can't believe you brought Mr. Bumbles."

"I didn't bring him; he brung himself. He appears to enjoy bike rides." Philip watched her pet the cat. "I haven't seen you since Sunday. What have you been up to?"

She continued to stroke and murmur over the cat. "My mother told me to leave you alone."

"Ah." Philip considered that a moment. "And why do you suppose she said that?"

"She said I shouldn't bother you. Adults always think kids are a bother." The last was said as both exclamation and question. She was looking at him again.

"I see," he said. "Well let's think about this. Why did I come to Ilusan?"

"To teach our class."

"Very good. And who is in our class?"

Sally started to name the other seventh and eighth graders.

"No, I mean as a group. Who makes up our class?"

The light went on. "Kids," she said.

"Very good again. Now what would be a logical deduction from the fact that I traveled over five thousand miles for the express purpose of teaching kids?"

The girl's smile could be incandescent at times. "Maybe that you don't think kids are a bother."

"Right. It probably means that I actually like kids." The words were a revelation to him even as they came out of his mouth. He couldn't be certain whether he spoke the truth, not having much experience where kids were concerned, but the logic of the conversation had led him there and he thought it both the clever and the Christian thing to say under the circumstances. As the other students trickled in he determined that at least for one year it would be true.

Philip was thirty minutes into Bible period when he realized he had made his first serious tactical error. Admittedly there had been a few minor flubs already. It had required vigorous miming from Sally to remind him to open the day with prayer and the pledge of allegiance. From her seat near the door she was taking both her roles seriously, that of student and cultural coach. Her eyes rarely left him as he moved about the room, and he had already learned to shoot her a glance from time to time at key moments to make sure he was on track. During introductions he had followed Bobby Sorenson's remarks by cracking, "So you're the one who makes that infernal racket at 6:00 every morning." He thought he might have gone too far, but Sally smiled and the other kids all laughed, and Bobby had simply asked if Philip could really hear him all the way up at his house.

But now halfway through Bible period Philip was trying to figure out how to end a game he had started without embarrassing himself further. He had thought it might be fun to begin with a contest to see how many Bible characters the kids could name. The game was a round. When your turn came, if you couldn't come up with an as yet unnamed Bible character you were out. There were just two problems. Although Timmy Mullen and Elaine Pauley had both exited before the class had even made it through the twelve apostles, and Charlie Pilarski and Donny Meyer were gone a few rounds later, the rest of the kids were engaged in a struggle that seemed destined to outlast the period, if not the week. Worse, Philip was expected to be the judge. With Mary Michaels and Bobby Sorenson locked in a personal duel to see who could name the most obscure biblical character, Philip's concordance was getting a furious workout. He was growing increasingly befuddled trying to keep up with them. It was soon apparent to the entire class that most of the kids knew the Bible a whole lot better than the teacher did, and they hadn't even reached recess yet.

It was Bobby's turn. He leaned back in his chair, his eyes turned to the ceiling. Philip groaned. He knew all the theatrics weren't because Bobby was stumped. He was merely trying to come up with an entry to top Mary's last trivia twister. "Belteshazzar," she said with a demurely wicked glint in her eye. Philip had momentarily relaxed. He remembered a Babylonian king whose dream Daniel had interpreted. But no, "Belteshazzar," she gloated, "not Belshazzar!" Only after she told him it was Daniel's Babylonian name had he been able to find it in the Bible to confirm her answer. Now Bobby was determined to top it.

"Eglon," he finally said.

Philip stared at the class. They were clearly as stumped as he was. "You guys are unbelievable. I give up. Who is he?"

Bobby was relishing the moment. "He was a king of Moab. A judge named Ehud made a dagger. He told the king he had a private message for him from God, so all the king's servants left the room." Here Bobby couldn't contain himself. He stood and mimed the action. "Ehud was left handed. He grabbed his dagger and shoved it in Eglon's stomach. And the Bible says that Eglon was so fat that the dagger went all the way in and disappeared." Some of the girls made faces. Mary said "yuck." But Bobby wasn't done. "The handle also went in after the blade, and the fat closed over the hilt, for he did not draw the sword out of his belly; and the dirt came out." The way Bobby said it, Philip could tell he had memorized the passage. Bobby noted Philip's raised eyebrow and shrugged. "It's the coolest verse in the Bible." The boys gave him an ovation.

"Lovely story," said Philip. "Thank you Bobby." Bobby sat back down. "If Bobby ever tells any of you that he has a message from God for you, well, let's just say I wouldn't get caught alone with him."

Bobby's brother piped up. "Bobby would never get away with it. As soon as he stabbed someone, he'd faint from the sight of blood." They were the first uncoerced words Drew Sorenson had spoken in front of the class. He was a small boy, chubby where Bobby was lean, with close cropped blond hair.

Bobby just looked at his brother. He held up his left hand, fingers splayed wide apart. "Five," he said.

Drew started from his seat. "You're dead." The other boys were laughing.

Philip held up his hands. "All right you two. Save it for recess. You can beat each other up then. I don't like the sight of blood either, especially in my classroom." He looked at Bobby and held up his left hand, fingers splayed. "Five? Family secret code? Do I just have to do this to set you guys off?"

Donny Meyer, a preternaturally muscled boy who was probably already shaving, was delighted by this turn of events. In what was clearly a practiced gesture, he shook his hands in front of his face and emitted a high pitched exclamation. "Reee!" The entire class laughed.

"Excitable fellow," said Philip. "So how does that go?" Philip shook his hands in front of his face and came out with a squeal of his own. "Reee!" This really got the class going and Donny spent the next five minutes demonstrating the many variations on his favorite exclamation. Other boys chimed in. Apparently the degree of excitement registered according to the volume, vigor applied to the hand shaking, and the length of the Reee. "And do any of you girls do the Reee?" asked Philip.

"No!" they exclaimed in unison. They appeared horrified at the thought of engaging in such a boy activity.

"O.k. Just checking. I want to make sure I understand how things are done here."

The clock showed only five minutes left in the period. Philip said, "Why don't we do this? We'll call the game a tie between everyone still in it. That appears to be most of you. And instead of studying Matthew like we're supposed to, I'm going to let you pick the book you want to study first."

For a moment the class stared at him. Then they looked at each other. Sally appeared a bit concerned.

"No?" said Philip.

"Let's do Judges," said Charlie Pilarski. "It sounds like it'll have some good stuff."

Timmy Mullen said, "That's the first good idea you've ever had."

"Shut up," said Charlie. He drew out his words in a petulant Southern twang.

"O.k.," interrupted Philip. "How many want to study Judges?" All the boys raised their hands. "That's six out of eleven. So we'll start with Judges. But the girls get to pick next. What would you women like to study?"

The desks of the eighth grade girls were clustered together, although Sally's was a bit apart and behind. They ignored Marcia Proud sitting on the other side of the room with the two seventh grade boys. The older girls quickly decided on Esther. The boys groaned.

"Hey don't knock it," said Philip. "Esther, as I'm sure you Bible experts remember, has a guy getting hung in it. That's pretty cool stuff."

The boys agreed that might be o.k. Philip told everyone to write a two page report on their favorite judge. The recess bell rang. Philip said, "All right. Scram. Have a fun break."

Both Philip and the children recognized that a certain tension had broken. The year could proceed with a sense of anticipation. This might be fun for all concerned. The kids leapt for the door. Philip sat on his desk looking after them. He noticed Bobby and Donny looking back at him and talking as they went down the stairs. Sally was the last out the door. "I wonder where Mr. Bumbles went," she said. It was the first Philip had noticed the cat was gone.

"He's probably on recess too. Which is where you need to be."

Sally smiled. "That was fun," she said.

$\approx\approx\approx$

True to his word, Jerry came looking for Philip during recess. Philip was leaning on a window sill on the back side of his classroom watching the kids play. There were two tetherball poles, a swing set, and a cement foursquare court directly behind the building. Most of the older kids from Philip and Jerry's classes swarmed the foursquare court. The waiting line was almost ten deep. When Jerry joined Philip, Donny Meyer and Madeline Broderick occupied the first and second square. They were hitting the ball gently back and forth while staring into each other's eyes. The other kids were restless and shouted abuse.

"Let me guess," said Philip. "This is Ilusan's version of going on a date."

"It's a daily rite of recess amour," said Jerry. "It really gets fun when they finally give up the ball."

Philip decided to prod the action. "This is boring to watch," he called to the kids.

"Don't worry, we'll take care of it." Timmy Mullen was in the fourth square. When he glanced up at Philip, Donny deftly placed a spinner in the corner of his square. Timmy lunged at it, but the ball was already back in Donny's hands. "Get him out," he spat with disgust to Bobby, who was next in line. Rather than go to the end of the line, he wandered towards the tetherball courts.

"Do you ever have to police this?" Philip lowered his voice so only Jerry could hear him.

"Every now and then if the yelling gets too loud, but fights are few and far between. It's all in good fun, as much as competition can remain in the fun category among the callow folk."

The obvious choice for the threatened couple was for Donny to serve the ball to Madeline, who would then gently set him up for a kill on Bobby. But Philip had already observed that there was a tight friendship between the two boys, and sure enough Donny served the ball to Bobby. Bobby passed the ball to the sixth grade boy in square three who promptly slammed out Madeline. Some of the kids cheered. The boy sheepishly moved into the second square where he immediately received his comeuppance. Donny again served to Bobby, this time across to square three. Bobby returned a high ball to Donny who spiked out the sixth grade boy so hard the ball bounced clear over his head. "Come on

Bobby," he complained as he left the court, "I thought I was doing you a favor."

"You did," said Bobby. "And now I did you the favor of returning you to the end of the line."

With Madeline now removed from the court, the game settled into a fast paced, every person for themselves battle. Spinners, corner shots, body shots, and all manner of slams ensued. The two eighth grade boys, although not overtly colluding, concentrated their firepower on squares three and four, and a succession of children paraded onto and off of the court. When Madeline returned from the line to square four, Philip thought he detected a visible deflation in Donny. Despite Madeline's presence, he served the ball to Bobby who shot a ball across to Madeline's corner. It wasn't an obvious kill shot, but Madeline could only get a hand on it and knock it off the square.

"Sorry Madeline," Bobby said, but his look was to Donny. The boys clearly knew the code. Donny served a corner shot to Bobby. It wasn't particularly vicious, and Philip thought he had an easy play, but the boy fumbled the ball out of bounds.

"Geez Donny," he said as he left, but the look the two exchanged did not appear at all unfriendly. Philip thought he read Bobby's lips when he got to the back of the line next to Madeline. "He got me for you Mad." Madeline beamed.

"Hmm," said Philip. "Methinks I just witnessed some sort of tribal ritual. Am I correct?"

"You are correct sir," said Jerry.

When everyone returned from recess, Mr. Bumbles was sitting nonchalantly on Philip's desk. The children had been introduced earlier, and now several stopped to rub his head on the way to their seats. Bumbles accepted their obeisance with good humor. Philip sat beside the cat as he instructed both grades to take their math books out of their desks. Several kids groaned. "I don't know what you're groaning about," said Philip. "Mr. Bumbles appears to like math. He's purring like a bear."

"Maybe he should teach it," said Timmy.

"You should be so lucky," Philip shot back before the girls, always concerned about classroom decorum, could even register their consternation at Timmy's effrontery. "Besides, I hear Mary and Bobby are good at math. They can help us if we get stuck."

Mary beamed. Donny punched Bobby and said, "That's why I sit by him."

"Great, where does that leave me?" said Charlie Pilarski. "Stuck between these two morons." The other two seventh graders glared at him.

"Still in the seventh grade," said Philip, "where I think I'll leave you next year as well if you don't open your book to chapter one and start reading it. I'm going to get the eighth graders going first and then I'll be over to help you guys."

Math class went smoothly enough. After math came P. E. for the fifth through eighth grades, which was always right before lunch so the kids could cool off with a swim on the way home. P. E. was primarily Fossia's bailiwick. There was a large field between the three school houses and the hangar and airstrips. The field wasn't ideal for outdoor sports because it sloped from the hangar toward the school and radio shack. But it was large enough for most sports and everyone made do. Fossia barked orders. The girls would begin the semester with volleyball while the boys played flag football. Philip quickly realized the other teachers were simply there to do Fossia's bidding. Jerry was shanghaied to referee football with Fossia. The principal had already ascertained that Philip played volleyball in California, so she assigned him to teach that sport to the girls. "Kari will help you," she said.

Philip started at the mention of the librarian. He had completely forgotten about her in the exhilaration of the first hours of teaching. He turned to see her standing by the bike rack. She was wearing white shorts, a sleeveless blue top, and a Pittsburgh Pirates ball cap. She waved.

"O. k.," said Philip, "that sounds good." It was a plum assignment indeed. He would teach his favorite sport while hobnobbing with the woman who twisted his stomach in knots. It was the perfect excuse to spend more time with her. And if he could slip in a little showing off on the court, so much the better.

There were no volleyball courts at the school. They were down on the central plaza in front of the meeting hall. "Take your watch," said Fossia. "Let them out at 11:45."

The twelve girls had already started walking down the hill. Those who had bikes rode. Only Sally lagged behind. She lingered by a guava tree next to the bike rack trying to look inconspicuous. As he walked toward Kari, the librarian pulled her bike out of the rack. "Are you ready to teach some volleyball?" she said. "I'll ride down with you."

The charge that went through him at that moment was immediately offset by the realization that a bike ride with Kari would leave Sally walking alone. The girl was twisting by the tree. She heard Kari's invitation and appeared to suddenly decide to begin walking. Philip watched her go. "Great," he said to Kari.

But then he couldn't do it. It wasn't a rational thought process. He just couldn't do it. And for the first time in a very long while he rejected his self interest for what was necessary and good. Later it would seem like a small thing, but he would always remember the moment with great personal satisfaction.

"Sally," he called. "Aren't we forgetting something?"

The girl turned. The anticipation on her face was palpable. "What?" she said.

"Mr. Bumbles! We can't leave our friend here. Why don't you bring my bike over to the classroom and I'll see if I can find him. Then you can ride my bike down to the courts. If you and Miss Trainor go slow enough I can keep up." Without waiting for an answer he walked toward his classroom. He was gratified to notice Sally running for his bike.

They didn't have to search far for Mr. Bumbles. He was sitting on the porch. Although he looked puzzled for a moment to see Sally on Philip's bicycle, he quickly ensconced himself in his basket, much to Sally and Kari's delight. They fawned over the purring cat as the four of them made their way slowly down the hill to the volleyball courts under the merciless noonday sun—two adults, one walking, one riding, and a cat perched in the basket of a very ugly bicycle ridden by a slip of a girl, her toes stretching to reach the pedals.

That afternoon Kari brought homemade chocolate chip cookies to school. She made her rounds with them during recess. Philip was sitting on a swing next to Annabel when he saw the librarian in the middle of the foursquare line sharing something with the obviously delighted kids. Jerry must have noticed too, because he leaned out his window and helped himself from Kari's upraised plate.

Philip had seen Annabel sitting on a swing by herself watching some of her first and second graders jump rope on the grass. He joined her, thinking she might like company, but now he wasn't sure. Their conversation advanced in fits and starts. She rarely looked at him, keeping her eyes fixed on the children playing. She seemed almost embarrassed to be sitting next to him. When they did converse, Philip had a difficult time keeping the conversation on comfortable ground. Even when Jesus wasn't front and center in Annabel's speech, he lurked just around the corner of every sentence. When Philip asked how she liked her class so far, Annabel's voice trembled as she remarked how desperately she just wanted to make Jesus real to her students. When Philip noted that the kids seemed to enjoy their game of jump rope, she glanced at the older children around the foursquare court, and hoped that her charges wouldn't learn any uncharitable behavior from the older kids. Philip didn't feel that, after only one day in class, he should take that as personal reproof, but he couldn't be sure. He thought he'd try humor. "I blame their behavior on Jerry," he said.

At this Annabel looked at him reproachfully and said, "We must all work together to teach them to love each other."

Philip noticed Kari looking at them. She seemed undecided. He called to her, "We want some of whatever that is you're passing out." Kari smiled and joined them. Annabel seemed even more uncomfortable. She got up. Kari offered her a cookie. Annabel shook her head.

"Well I certainly want one, maybe two or three," said Philip.

As soon as he took one, the children skipping rope shouted, "Miss Trainor can we have some?"

"You certainly can," Kari said.

As she joined the children, Philip said to Annabel, "I can't believe you turned down homemade chocolate chip cookies."

Annabel glanced at him. Her expression seemed sad. Just as quickly she looked away. "As soon as I find myself wishing for something I renounce it," she said. She briefly steadied her swing, paused, then walked away.

Philip looked after her. He muttered "Wow" to himself. He noticed that Kari had a couple of cookies left on her plate. "Hey Miss Trainor," he called, "can I have another one?"

Philip was heating water to do his dinner dishes that evening when Lillian Troyer called "maayo" in his back yard. He was proud of himself for remembering the proper response, "dayon," but when he got to the door Lillian was in too much of a hurry to come in.

"I don't know if anyone told you," she said, "but tonight is prayer meeting. I'm heading for the meeting hall right now. Evelyn is staying home with mother."

Philip had been told by several about prayer meeting, but, although he knew he would eventually have to attend, he hoped to put it off as long as possible.  It had been many years since he had comfortably prayed in public, and the thought that he might somehow be forced to do so at prayer meeting filled him with dread. But he didn't know how he could turn down such a direct invitation without appearing unspiritual, and besides, there was always the possibility that the librarian might be there. He thanked Lillian, told her to go ahead because he had to finish a few tasks in the kitchen, but that he would be down.

Ten minutes later he was standing in the meeting hall beside an elderly man who was making it very difficult to follow the responsive reading from the Psalms. The man was tall, taller than Philip. His gray hair was plastered against his skull with some sort of pomade. He wore a short sleeve yellow button-up shirt. His arms were scrawny and splotched with age. He hitched his brown pants high, the black belt cinched tight around his gaunt belly. The belt was old, and the extra length was cracked and curled. Too much black sock showed between his pants and his immaculately polished black shoes.

The man had warmly greeted Philip when he slid into the pew and immediately handed him his own hymn book opened to the song the congregation was singing. Philip noted that his pew mate had a good singing voice, but his responsive reading technique was idiosyncratic in the extreme. The man possessed the text as if he were an actor on the Elizabethan stage, accenting words of personal import, pausing, speeding up, "hmmming" to himself, even gesturing with his free arm, so that Philip was soon hopelessly lost. Before long the man was a half line behind everyone else, and he eventually finished a full five seconds after the congregation. "Boy that was a great reading," he whispered to Philip as they sat down. "I've got to remember to memorize that passage."

Philip's fears were realized a few minutes later when the leader, after writing numerous prayer requests from the crowd on a large chalkboard, divided the congregation into groups of five or six and assigned them each a handful of the public requests. Philip's group was tasked to pray for two translation projects, a sick chief from one of the local tribal groups, an intestinal outbreak in another tribe ("sounds like diarrhea to me," confided an elderly woman next to him), the visa application process (speed and the request for bribes seemed to be the issue), Tom Jacobson's sister-in-law in Oregon with pleurisy, someone's sister in Idaho whose eldest daughter was rebellious, the friend of someone's cousin who was upset with God because he had received an expensive speeding ticket, and two unspoken requests.

Philip was assigned the rebellious daughter (because he "knew that age group") and one of the unspokens. His mind boggled. Fortunately the prayer circle began on the opposite side from him and the old man, so he had time to collect his thoughts. It was bad enough that he had to pray out loud in front of strangers, but how was one supposed to pray for requests that people didn't even have the courage to mention? Were they that personal? How personal was personal? And who was this idiot girl anyway? He had no clue. His mind began to furiously speculate. What was there to rebel against in Idaho? Was she refusing to shuck corn? By the time his turn came, he realized he had forgotten which unspoken request he was supposed to take. He glanced at the board. There were actually three unspokens up there, and his group had been assigned two. Would it be terribly outside normal protocol to ask his group before he started praying, or should he just pray a generic unspoken prayer, or should he take a shot? He had a one in three chance of getting the right one. He didn't like those odds. He wished he'd been listening more closely to the other prayers. Someone must have already prayed for at least one of them. But his time was up. He had to start.

Philip took a deep breath and prayed, "Father, thank you for this beautiful day." How lame was that? But he *had* been genuinely thankful at several points throughout the day. But he wasn't very thankful now. Still, the line garnered a few mmmms. "Father we just ask for Donna's sister's daughter Janice." He couldn't believe it. He had uttered the most useless prayer word in the evangelical lexicon. Just. Just?! Like this is all we're going to ask for? Or that the request was so slight it was almost a throw-away? It was an evangelical prayer tick, almost as ubiquitous as "Dear Lord," and Philip remembered how he and his friends used to mock users of that word in Bible college. He was utterly chagrined. But he had to slow his mind and keep going. "Janice is at that age when young people struggle with rebellion." For whose benefit had he said that? Did God need this information? Or was he trying to sound empathetic and knowing for the benefit of those in the group? It was filler and he knew it. "Please help Janice to . . ." To what? He was stumped. To not be rebellious? To get over it? To stop acting like a child? To get back on that tractor? He had a brainstorm. His group was made up of older folk, most of them probably parents. Why not side with them? "Please help Janice to understand that her parents only want what's best for her." This got several loud mmmms. Philip began to feel better. "Help her turn to you when she's frustrated. Please be with her." Another lame line. Hadn't the Bible promised that God would always be with them? It was like asking water to be wet. Oh well, Janice's fate was now between her, God, and her poor mother. Better tackle the unspoken. Whose did he have? He decided to finesse the issue. "Father there have been several unspoken requests tonight and, in fact, there might be many more. Only you know our hearts, our deepest needs, the things we can't even say to each other. Please meet all of us in a special way tonight. In your name, Amen."

Philip held his breath. But he needn't have worried. The groans and amens were hearty. There would be time later to castigate himself for the fallback penultimate line. Meet us in a special way indeed! Was God going to show up at the door in an ice cream truck? Was he dispensing massages? Wouldn't any meet with God by definition be special? Philip realized his prayer had been much shorter than the others. But he had survived. As the lady next to him began to pray, he noticed that his shirt was soaking wet.

"My name is Gordon Lundy." The old man who had so thrown Philip off rhythm during the responsive reading had both of his hands wrapped around Philip's right. "It's so good to have you young people here on the center." He spoke with unselfconscious warmth. "I would be honored if you'd come by my house for tea and cake. In fact, let's invite a few more young folk." He scanned the auditorium. They both spotted Kari at the same time. "Kari, come, come," he called. Kari practically skipped over and Gordon enveloped her in a huge hug. "Hi pumpkin," he said. "Philip have you met my favorite girl? Of course you have. You two work together." He winked at Philip.

Kari was delighted to join them for dessert. "Who else shall we ask?" Gordon was already scanning the room again, one arm around

Kari. "Matt, are you and Julia free for tea and cake?" Philip didn't think of Matt St. Clair as particularly young, he had a teenage son after all, but he supposed most anyone was young where Gordon was concerned. The St. Clairs quickly agreed to join them.

Both Kari and the St. Clairs needed to stop by their houses before coming over. "Great," effused Gordon, "that will give Philip and I time to prepare." Philip decided that meant he had to accompany Gordon directly. On the way to Gordon's house, the old man told Philip that he had spent most of his missionary career in Ecuador. He administered the jungle base there for more than thirty years. Ten years ago, when his wife died of cancer, he decided to retire. But life back in the States didn't suit him. He tried to return to Ecuador, but they didn't have a position for him. When the Philippine branch posted a notice looking for someone with experience in the printing business to run their Ilusan publishing office, Gordon had immediately volunteered. He admitted to Philip with a sheepish grin that he had fudged his résumé a bit. He had no experience running a press. He just desperately wanted to get back to the field. A friend in North Carolina let him work in his shop for two months before he left, so that when he arrived at Ilusan he at least knew more than anybody else about the printing business. He had been at Ilusan for the past eight years. "I've never taken a furlough," he said to Philip. "Why would anyone want to leave this place?"

Gordon's house was one of the oldest and smallest on the center. It seemed to be on stilts, it sat so high on rough hewn posts. The roof was made of tightly woven leaves. Windows hinged at their peak and opened out; they were propped open with yard-long sticks. The house had the weathered look of a ship too long at sea. Indeed, upon entering, Philip thought it listed slightly to starboard. Nevertheless it was bright and cozy inside. Gordon was a natural homemaker. Shelves filled with knickknacks, mementos of a life spent in curious places. Pictures covered vast stretches of the walls. A spear and some nasty looking arrows hung above the dining room windows. There was a rocking chair by one lamp. A couch accented with a carelessly, but immaculately, placed crimson throw. A thick rug of indigenous design. Gordon appeared to have planned the dessert before prayer meeting, because five place settings were already carefully arranged around the dining room table. Philip noticed that the settings matched the throw. Gordon continued to tell Philip his story while he bustled about the kitchen. In short order a teapot armed with a thick cotton cozy made its appearance on the table. Then five generous slices of chocolate cake.

When Gordon finished setting the table, he glanced out the window. "It looks like we still have a few minutes," he reported. "I don't see our guests yet. No flashlights moving around out there." He turned suddenly to Philip. "Let's pray together brother." Without waiting for a response the old man threw himself full length on the rug.

Alarms began to scream in Philip's head. "What about the others," he began, but Gordon cut him short.

"We'll hear them coming. Don't worry about them." Gordon looked up at him with a huge grin. "Come on down brother. This is the only way to pray. Face first before God."

Philip didn't see any way out. He sank to his knees, then stretched out beside his host. The rug smelled lightly of vanilla. Gordon's prayer was a bursting dam of longing and supplication, and Philip felt himself first overwhelmed and then buoyed up by the flood of his words. Where Philip's prayers were halting and monosyllabic, Gordon's were fluent and operatic. For five minutes the words never stopped and they were primarily words spoken on Philip's behalf. Philip felt adopted by the old man's prayer, and, as embarrassed as he was and as fearful of discovery by the object of his infatuation, he found himself equally as fascinated and warmed. He wasn't sure he recognized this Philip for whom Gordon so passionately prayed, for his new friend clearly believed that Philip was fully one of them, that he longed for God with naked desire, that he rose every day with one goal, to do God's will. But somewhere in the midst of Gordon's words, Philip felt kindled an infinitesimal flame. Perhaps it was possible to live up to Gordon's prayer; perhaps there lingered deep within his own better self the person that Gordon seemed to believe existed.

Philip was spared any attempt at matching Gordon's outpouring by the sound of approaching conversation. He heard Matt say something and Kari laugh. Gordon quickly ended with a brief blessing on the upcoming gathering, and they both stood. "God bless you brother," and with that his host bounded to the door and greeted the other guests with an exuberance utterly unfeigned. Philip just shook his head and smiled wanly at Kari as she entered.

She immediately crossed to him and whispered, "He's something isn't he? Did you pray?" Philip's raised eyebrows were answer enough.

"You've got a little carpet fuzz on your shirt," and she laughed as she brushed him off.

Gordon seated everyone, Philip by Kari, and then said another prayer. Before anyone could begin eating, he said with a nod towards Julia, "I hesitate to serve cake to present company, but I wanted to try this new recipe."

Julia, a tall dark-haired woman, was sure the dessert was wonderful, but everyone rushed to inform Philip that Julia had the reputation for making the best cake on the center. She enjoyed serving the center's children, and on baking day, usually Thursdays she told Philip, many of the kids found an excuse to stop by the St. Clair home.

"Are teachers allowed to follow the kids in?" asked Philip.

"I'll send you some," Julia assured him. "We're worried about you cooking for yourself."

For a few minutes the conversation swirled around Philip's early attempts at cooking, but then quickly moved to his first day of teaching. In response to Matt's question about how things went, he replied, "Well I found out who Ehud and Eglon were," and from there he kept them entertained for some time with self-deprecating observations of his teaching prowess. He was gratified that Kari chimed in with compliments for his volleyball skills and was even more pleased when she said that the kids seemed to enjoy him. He couldn't be certain yet that was true, but it wouldn't hurt to get such rumors started. The truth would out one way or the other soon enough.

At the end of the evening Philip surprised himself by offering to help Gordon clean up. He supposed it must have been the intoxication of sitting so close to Kari for an hour. He hoped that Kari would offer to stay and help as well, which might lead to a walk home together in the dark, and in fact thought he saw her begin to voice such a thought, but Matt cut it off with his own offer to see her home. It was only slightly out of the way for them. Julia gave Philip a commiserating look, or at least that's how he interpreted it. He placed equal interpretive weight on Kari's face, which in his imagination fell in unprecedented disappointment. Gordon, at any rate, didn't seem to mind doing the dishes with Philip and he chattered on happily, interrupted only by instructions as to where various newly scrubbed items belonged. Afterward he insisted Philip stay for one last cup of tea. They took the cup on Gordon's small porch with only the light from the kitchen spilling across the doorway and over Gordon's feet.

"I love evenings here," Gordon said, but then was quiet for a long time. The two men sat enjoying the night noise and the sweet warm tea.

"You've never been married I guess," Gordon finally said.

Philip smiled in the darkness. "No, I'm afraid not."

"I love marriage." Philip sensed Gordon sizing him up. "My wife has been dead for ten years. I truly miss her. Intimacy with a woman is the most beautiful thing. When you get married Philip never forget that it's more blessed to give than to receive."

Philip thought that was a sound idea. "It would probably make a good wedding sermon," he said. "I suppose you would have a great marriage if you really focused more on your wife's needs than your own."

Gordon enthusiastically agreed. "Yes," he said. "Yes." He leaned forward. "When you're concentrating on her, on giving to her, she just blossoms, and you find yourself growing stronger and then she just blows." He made a gesture with his hands and smiled. It struck Philip then that they were talking about two different things. He prepared himself for an extremely awkward silence, but Gordon would have none of it. "I'll never forget when I first realized how much pleasure I could give my wife if I just took a little time and care when I made love to her."

Easy Gordon, Philip thought. He hoped voices didn't carry well in humid air. But Gordon had the lack of discretion earned by seventy years of absorbing life's tough knocks. He didn't want Philip to miss his point. "Don't ever let anyone tell you that a married couple, even Christian couples, can't do anything they want to in bed. And it's up to the husband to make sure his wife thoroughly enjoys herself." He went on to describe a technique he'd learned from an Ecuadorian friend. Listening, Philip was so tense he thought his back might snap. Apparently it had an entirely different effect on Gordon's wife. "Beth almost passed out the first time I tried it," the old man said with a conspiratorial giggle. "My wife and I used to love making love in the outdoors. We kept a mattress on the back porch for those perfect summer evenings. On our twenty-fifth anniversary in Ecuador we went for a drive, lost ourselves in a deserted spot (we thought), climbed in the back seat, then just when I got my pants down, a German on a motorcycle drove up and asked what we were doing in his driveway. We were on his coffee plantation and didn't know it." Gordon leaned back and laughed and laughed. "Oh my," he said. "Oh my." He lingered with his memories for a few minutes, then said, "I've been alone for ten years now. You don't lose those desires when you're seventy. I wish you did."

Philip had no clue as to what to say and no real notion to say anything, but he was drawn to Gordon's honesty. The man must be immensely lonely at times. Despite his piety he was a rampantly, pantingly sexual creature. Or perhaps "despite" had nothing to do with it. Perhaps the two went hand in hand. Gordon certainly embraced both aspects of his life without shame. "I'm sure you were a wonderful husband," Philip finally said. "I hope I can be a good husband someday too."

"Your day is coming," Gordon said. "And mark my words, it will be wonderful."

That night Philip tossed and turned for a long time. Gordon's tales, while humorous, were hard to shake. His mind flitted around the librarian, but he desperately didn't want to go there. He wanted, he needed, this relationship to be different, if in fact there was to be a relationship. He wanted to be fully present with this young woman, and he knew that if he allowed himself to be overwhelmed by the erotic that it would only bring guilt, and would more than likely cost him the relationship. And who knows what harm it might do her. There was an innocence about her that he didn't want to damage.

He remembered his past lovers. Several of them had cared for him deeply, but he had rarely been fully attentive. Once they began making love, there was simply too much conflict behind his eyes, too much guilt and shame, to embrace them with an open heart. He had always been waiting for the other shoe to drop, convinced that God would find a way to disfigure or maim him as punishment for his sexual activity. Death was too good for a son who had squandered such a birthright. He was a preacher's kid after all. Only life as a paraplegic, or some equally nightmarish fate, would suffice. Martin Luther suggested that if a Christian decided to sin, he should at least sin boldly, knowing that God's grace was bolder yet. But Philip had been a squeamish sinner, never jumping in with both feet, always pretending that his lovers were at fault. He felt regret now when he thought of them, those lovely girls. They deserved better than a guilt-ridden fundamentalist.

Unfortunately memories of exuberant young lovers were charged with eroticism, and Philip, despite the altruistic trend of his thoughts, soon had a fierce erection. Mr. Bumbles, disturbed by Philip's restlessness, decided to shift sides of the bed. He placed his front paws on Philip's stomach, but then paused and regarded the tent pole in Philip's shorts with skepticism. "It's locked and loaded Bumbles," Philip said. "I think we should both get as far away from it as possible." He untucked the mosquito net, climbed out, grabbed an orange soda from the refrigerator and went outside. He sat on his porch and listened to the night.

He was a grown man and knew, of course, a simple way to relieve the desire in his body. Kleenex from the commissary, while a bit rough, would do the trick almost as well as Kleenex back home. But he couldn't bring himself to do it. For one thing, he didn't want to disgrace himself in front of the cat. It just didn't seem right somehow. Mr. Bumbles had followed him outside. He sat at the head of the steps, staring into the darkness, his ears riveted on a world Philip couldn't begin to comprehend with the cat's insight. "You'll keep me pure, Bumbles. But I bet you're out there getting your share." He took a long pull from his soda. "But I don't begrudge you. Just make sure you're always in the moment."

But the cat wasn't the main reason for his tentative self control. With every passing day his resolve to use his time at Ilusan to start over grew stronger. He wasn't sure what he would look like coming out the other end of this year abroad. In fact he was quite sure he wouldn't return to the fundamentalism of his youth. Maybe he wouldn't return to anything; maybe he would go forward, find an entirely new way of being Christian. But whatever path he ultimately chose, for the moment it was hard to shake the nagging sense that sexual indulgence was somehow at the root of all evil. He knew he would need to rethink this aspect of his upbringing, but didn't know quite how to begin. The conversation with Gordon had certainly provided a jumpstart, but Philip needed time to process. He needed time to think. And if it meant being a monk for awhile, he would do his best to oblige.

Ultimately, however, it was the snuffling of a large animal just outside his yard that cost him his erection. Mr. Bumbles leapt to the railing and Philip lunged toward his door when a voice with a Filipino accent said, "It's o.k. Just the night watchman. I'm making my rounds." A flashlight came on, and Philip was grateful that the man didn't shine it directly on him, although a quick check assured that the surge of adrenalin had saved him any potential embarrassment. The pool of light revealed an enormous German Shepherd tugging at a chain held by the tallest Filipino Philip had yet seen. He was almost as tall as Philip. "My name is Ben. I'm sorry if I startled you. Not many still up this time of night." His English, despite the accent, was flawless. He stood between the trees at the edge of the yard, careful not to enter.

Philip introduced himself, but stayed on the porch. "Is your dog friendly?" Mr. Bumbles seemed to think so, as he was settled comfortably on the rail. But he kept one eye on the panting beast.

"Oh yes Mr. Andrews," said Ben. "He won't hurt you." Philip invited the watchman into his yard and came off the porch to give the dog's head a good scratch.

"His name is Lechón, because he'll make a lechón out of any bad guys." Ben laughed, but Philip didn't know what lechón was. The night watchman had just begun an explanation of how lechón was prepared, when Philip interrupted.

"Why don't I get you a cold drink and you can sit awhile on my porch and chat."

"Oh no." The Filipino man seemed startled. "I should make my rounds."

"Rounds can wait for ten minutes. I'll get you a drink." Philip started up the stairs.

"Oh no thank you," the man said again. "Mr. St. Clair would not want that."

"I know Mr. St. Clair, and I know he wouldn't mind if you had a drink with me. Besides you're educating me about Filipino customs. These are things I need to learn. He should pay you extra." Without waiting for a reply, Philip went inside. He threw on pants and a shirt, grabbed another orange soda and came back outside. The watchman was still there.

"O. k. Mr. Andrews," he said. "Maybe just a few minutes." Philip indicated a chair and Ben sat down on its edge. He seemed nervous. He took a drink. He thanked Philip profusely, but remained on the edge of the chair. The dog lay down at the foot of the stairs. He seemed never to have noticed Mr. Bumbles.

"So finish telling me about the lechón."

Ben carefully described how the pig was spitted and baked over charcoal. "You have to brush the skin with leaves dipped in water and the pig's fat. This makes the skin very crunchy." By the time Ben finished describing all the dishes typically included in a good lechón, twenty minutes had passed and he had relaxed in his chair. When he finished his drink he thanked Philip and insisted it was time to go.

"I often sit out here late at night," said Philip. "I can't get used to going to bed at 9:30. I'll have a drink waiting for you whenever you come by. You can tell me more about the Philippines."

Ben's shy laugh seemed odd coming from a man his size. "Oh no Mr. Andrews, you should be sleeping."

That night Philip had a dream about his father. He found himself standing on his block in his hometown. A young family emerged from a house three doors away. It was his family. His father and mother were intoxicatingly young. Philip would wonder the next day why he hadn't been more interested in seeing himself and his two brothers, but it was his father that held his attention. "Dad," he called. The man turned. "Dad, it's me, Philip." He walked urgently toward his father. He hugged him. "You're so young." But then he remembered that his father was dead. He reminded his father of this. He reminded him twice. Then he said, "Tell me about heaven. Tell me about God." He was clutching his father's arms, desperately trying to hold himself in the dream. "Tell me," he insisted. But his father seemed reluctant to speak, and when he did it was in nonsense syllables. Philip woke up to crushing disappointment.

When the final bell rang on Friday and the kids had exploded out of the room for the weekend, Philip collapsed behind his desk. It had been a hot day. Fortunately, being at the highest elevation on the center, and with windows up and down both sides of the room, the schoolchildren were often gifted with a light breeze, and Friday had been no exception. Still, Philip had noticed papers sticking to student arms as they wrote. The kids scarcely seemed to notice. When too much sweat accumulated on their arms, they simply wiped them front and back on the edge of their desk and then flipped the gathered water onto the floor. But Philip was ready for a cold drink. Even Mr. Bumbles seemed lethargic. He lay on his side on Philip's desk. When Philip asked him how he was doing, the cat just grunted. "I guess you're too hot to move. But how about we go home and get a cold drink? Shall I carry you to the bike rack or can you be troubled to walk?"

When Philip left his room with his books and papers, Bumbles trotted out behind him and easily beat him to their bicycle. He was already in the basket when Philip got there, and Philip had to wedge his homework in around him, an action which didn't seem to discomfit the cat. His nose was already pointed downhill. Sally was nowhere to be seen. "Looks like we'll be able to rip right along today," said Philip.

The past two days Sally had lingered to walk home with them. Philip's chat with her the first morning of school seemed to have persuaded her she could safely ignore her mother's direction. The girl lived in a cluster of houses at the southern end of the base, and, while Philip's house wasn't exactly on the way for her, no place was really all that out of the way at Ilusan. It simply meant she swung down the eastern edge of the center rather than walk home through Ilusan's heart. She didn't seem to have a bike, and had refused to ride while Philip walked, so Philip pedaled slowly and kept the girl company. Yesterday he had invited her to share a cold pop with him on his porch before she went home. As they walked and talked and drank cold orange soda, Philip began to learn more about her.

Sally's family had spent the past year in the United States on furlough. It had been a tough year for the young girl. Her parents had no extra money, so she had been forced to attend a public school. Walking the halls in her second-hand clothes from her church's missionary barrel, she had for the first time in her life found herself utterly alone. The solitude she seemed to crave at Ilusan had become a terrifying twenty-four hour reality.

"No friends?" Philip had asked. "No," the girl had replied. "I couldn't talk to them." It was a refrain Philip was beginning to understand. Her innocence, so free here to gambol unselfconsciously, had been assaulted on a daily basis. The other kids had used words like hammers, hoping to shatter the quiet girl's façade into a thousand delicate pieces. "I never cried," she said, "at least not in front of them. They were just stupid kids." But she had begged her mother every day not to make her go to school. But every day the yellow bus waited at the bottom of the hill. Entering it each morning had been a monumental test of will.

Church life had not been much better. She found herself embarrassed by her father, and then ashamed for her embarrassment. Her father was a shy man. He loved words, but he loved them written on note cards, where he could arrange and rearrange them, study them like butterflies pinned to a wall, hear the voice of his native informant unlock their delicate susurrant sounds, chase down their often tantalizingly hidden meanings. But to speak words, to stand in front of other human beings and permit the words in his chest to bubble out into the atmosphere to be claimed by others? No, that was profligate. It risked imprecision. It was even dangerous. On note cards, he felt he owned the words. They were captured. Every letter served its purpose. But abroad in the atmosphere, like popping soap bubbles they were magical for a moment, but then they vanished and released mysterious energies that might land on their hearers like a moist kiss or a mortar shell. No, to set words free was to unhinge a Pandora's Box of possibility. Words must be confined and rigidly controlled.

Sally's father was a remarkable, if frustratingly unproductive, linguist. He gave up new chapters of translation work to his superiors like an oyster gives up a pearl. His masterpieces required years of oleaginous polish, the mastication of a mind fixated on bestowing the honor on the words which they deserved. "Just one more week," he would tell his superiors, and when enough "one more weeks" had passed, an assistant director would be dispatched to pry Robert Fraser's jewels from his locked fingers. But however good a linguist, he was a terrible public speaker. And unfortunately when missionaries went on furlough, they were required to do a lot of public speaking. Money had to be raised. Supporters required appeasement with exciting missionary tales. And a young girl suffered through her father's every public humiliation and took it personally. "Mommy was better in churches than Daddy," she said.

Philip was remembering his conversations with Sally when he began the climb toward his house. Halfway up the hill he saw Bobby and Donny in a mango tree. He stopped below them. "What are you guys up to?"

"We're just hanging around waiting for the volleyball bell to ring." Philip remembered that every Friday and Saturday afternoons the missionaries gathered to play their favorite sport. The first one to the courts rang the bell. The eighth grade kids were permitted to play in the first game. After that it was an adult affair.

"Why don't you come up to my house? I'll treat you to a Coke. If I can hear Bobby playing the piano up there, we'll be able to hear the bell from my back porch." The boys immediately began climbing down the tree. A few minutes later they were all on the porch, Bobby on the steps with a Pepsi, Donny on the railing with a Coke, Philip in his chair with an Orange, and Mr. Bumbles face first in his bowl inhaling water like a Great Dane.

"So Donny is Madeline your girlfriend?" Philip was discovering that when he talked to kids he liked to approach things directly. No outflanking, no sneaking about, just a straight-ahead daylight assault. Let's see what you've got kid. He especially enjoyed seeing how children responded to questions that required a measure of self reflection. It certainly kept the kids on their toes in his classroom.

Donny looked at Bobby in astonishment. Then he looked out at the corn field and said, "Oh gash." He turned a little red, looked at Bobby again, but Bobby was watching Mr. Bumbles drink. "Yeah, I guess she is. Sort of."

"So what does that mean at Ilusan that you and Madeline are boyfriend and girlfriend? Do you go on dates?" Both of the boys laughed at this notion.

"Yeah right," said Bobby. "Where would they go?"

"Exactly," said Philip. "So do you just stare at each other and hit the ball back and forth when you play foursquare? Do you try to spend a lot of time with her? I see you with Bobby all the time, but I've never seen you with Madeline."

"Donny and I are best friends." Bobby interjected the statement of fact and went back to watching Bumbles, who now came over and sniffed the boy's face.

Donny said, "Actually I hardly ever talk to Madeline at all. I talk a lot more to the other girls. I like Madeline, but I don't talk to her. It's hard to talk to someone you like."

"I know what you mean," said Philip.

"It's kind of a pain really," said Donny. "When everybody knows you like a girl, then you have to defend her all the time. If someone gets her out in foursquare, you've got to get them out. If someone pushes her down, you've got to push them down. And if they start crying . . . then what do you do?"

"Indeed," said Philip.

"Bobby likes Sarah. She's in sixth grade."

"Bobby? Your turn." Philip and Donny laughed.

"She's really pretty," said Bobby. "She lives next door to me. So if we're going home we have to stare at each other all the way up the stairs. Then we stand on the porch staring at each other until our parents make us come in."

"Bobby once walked backwards all the way to the pool so he could keep staring at Sarah on her porch." Both boys were now laughing at the absurdity of it all.

"Sometimes when Donny and I are in my house, and we want to go outside, we'll peek out the windows first to make sure Sarah isn't there. It makes it easier to get where we want to go. But at least Sarah isn't in my classroom, so I don't have to see her all the time."

The boys asked Philip how kids who liked each other acted in the States. "Well I'm no expert boys," said Philip. "You don't see a Mrs. Andrews around do you?" He went on to explain that parents sometimes drove couples to events at their school.

Bobby suddenly said, "You're lucky to have your hair so long."

"Well that was a quick change of topic," said Philip.

"Yeah, Bobby's Dad buzzes him off all the time," said Donny. Both boys were looking at Philip's hair.

"It's really not all that long compared to other young guys in the States," said Philip. "I was worried some people here might have a problem with it."

"Yea." Bobby began to rub Mr. Bumbles.

Donny said, "Bobby's Dad thinks it's womanly."

"Long hair in general?" asked Philip. "Or has he said something about me?"

Donny looked at Bobby who was focused on the cat. "He said you shouldn't be teaching us. He said you're a bad example. He said no good Christian man would have hair like yours. He said it shows you're rebellious."

And there it was. One minute you're enjoying a stroll through a golden wheat field and the next there's a tornado on the horizon. Both boys were staring at him, embarrassed, astonished at their own frankness, but waiting.

"I see," said Philip. "And yet you said I was lucky to have long hair. Interesting. I haven't met your father yet have I Bobby?" He put his feet up on the railing, took a long drink of his soda, and let the moment drag out. He had always wanted to see a tornado up close. "What do you guys think?" he finally said. "Does long hair make me a bad teacher?"

"No." The boys spoke in unison.

"But that isn't exactly what your Dad said, is it?" Philip looked at the boys. "He said I was a bad example, and that my hair shows that I'm probably not a good Christian, that I'm rebellious. Let's think about that for a minute." Philip found that he was enjoying himself. "How might I defend myself against that charge?"

"I don't know," Bobby began. "I suppose you could cut your hair."

"Right, that would be the easiest thing to do wouldn't it. But would that prove anything about my real character, about what's inside me? Because your Dad's comment is about what's inside isn't it?"

The boys were catching on. "You really can't defend yourself at all," said Donny. "I mean you could say I'm a good Christian, but that doesn't prove anything."

"You're absolutely right. Good point. So what should I do? You boys tell me."

There was a long silence. Mr. Bumbles sauntered down the stairs, stretched, then turned and went under the house. Finally Bobby said, "I don't think you can do anything right now. You just have to be here awhile and let people make up their minds when they get to know you."

"Do you agree Donny?"

Donny shook his head yes. "Then that's what I'll do," said Philip. "Thanks boys." Just then the bell rang. They walked down to the volleyball courts together, one boy on each side of their teacher with the cool hair.

Philip had always loved playing volleyball, really most team sports. He had never enjoyed individual sports, because he didn't like seeing anyone lose. In grade school his tennis coach had called his father one afternoon to complain that he thought Philip was throwing matches. "I feel so bad for them when I beat them," the young boy told his father. "I can handle losing, but I'm not sure they can." "But don't you feel bad when you lose?" his father had asked. "No," the boy replied. His father had decided that as a minister he could hardly condemn such depth of feeling, so the next day he pulled his son out of tennis and put him in basketball. And

Philip had never looked back. He excelled in basketball and volleyball in high school. He enjoyed the camaraderie of team sports. He enjoyed celebrating with teammates after a victory and commiserating after a defeat. And when the other team walked off the court, their heads hanging in dejection, Philip told himself that at least they had each other.

More than thirty people showed up for Friday afternoon volleyball. All the school teachers were there. Philip saw Matt St. Clair talking with several of the pilots. All of the eighth grade boys were in a circle passing the ball back and forth. Gordon Lundy was there, pontificating from a folding chair to several missionary ladies. He clearly had no intention of playing, but Philip had a hunch he'd probably enjoy himself immensely as a spectator. Celia Haaf was there, but Philip didn't see Joseph.

Fossia took it upon herself to organize teams. "Which eighth graders are going to play in the first game?" she asked. All the boys raised their hands. Madeline raised her hand. And then Sally said, "I want to play."

Fossia was surprised. "Sally you've never wanted to play before." The girl didn't reply.

"She's been doing very well in P. E.," said Philip. Philip had immediately recognized that the girl was not a natural athlete. But she had sucked up his instruction with almost comical intensity. "Put her on my team. She'll be a good little setter for me."

"O.k.," said Fossia. "You two go stand in that court." By the time Fossia finished placing the teams, she had two six-on-six matches going. In addition all of the teams had at least two people waiting to rotate in. Philip was surprised at the level of play. There were plenty of carries and throws, but each team had at least three people on it who knew what they were doing. He thought that he could have some fun here.

The only people on his team that he knew right away were Sally and Peggy Margaret Mitchell, the third and fourth grade teacher. But a lanky pilot named George Donahoe proved to be an asset, and Philip's team won their first game. He was gratified to see the adults take the moment to praise Sally for how well she had done. She hadn't said a word the entire game, but had played with fierce concentration. Peggy Margaret had turned out to be quite a ham, curtseying to Gordon Lundy after every good play, much to Gordon's delight, and shooting barbs across the net at the other team in her best Scarlet O'Hara manner. "You're feisty," Philip said to her at one point.

"You bet. Now get your britches up to the net and start pulling your weight," she replied. "We didn't bring you all the way over here to lose volleyball games."

Although the kids were supposed to sit down now, everyone was having such a good time, and the kids begged so hard, that Fossia announced the kids could play one more game. "Winners play winners; losers play losers," she announced.

"You ready to go again?" Philip asked Sally.

The girl's face never lost its focus. "Yes," she said.

Philip was delighted to see their new opponents. In the first place, Kari was on the team. "They won with you on their team?" he said to her under the net. She laughed and stuck out her tongue. He had snuck glances at her as she played on the next court over and had noticed that she handled herself as well playing with adults as she did with the kids in P. E. The team also included Jerry and two eighth grade boys, Bobby and Timmy Mullen. "You guys better not beat us," Philip said to the boys. "Remember I've got the power of the grade book."

"Don't listen to him," said Jerry. "He's all sound and fury."

That was when Philip recognized the man preparing to serve the ball. It was the lean gray-haired man who had so vigorously opposed Joseph in Sunday school and who had observed Philip so carefully after the Sunday evening service. Philip felt a momentary catch in his stomach, but then the man served the ball, hard, and the game was on.

The match was memorable for two moments, one light-hearted, one fraught with tension, both of which would be remembered in their own way for months to come. And both involved Philip.

The first came after Philip leapt to block a ball at the net that Bobby Sorenson deftly dumped around his outstretched arms into the open space right behind him. Philip whirled on the boy and, grasping for faux outrage, sputtered, "I'm going to crush you like . . . like a flower." Both Bobby and Timmy immediately picked up the phrase and began using it on each other when one made a mistake. The phrase quickly became part of the standard lexicon for the children of Ilusan. It was still in use in Philip's classroom, by both the students and Philip, when Christmas decorations began to appear.

The second occurred late in the game. The gray-haired man had proven to be a fierce competitor. He contested each point as if some aspect of truth or justice lay at stake with every bounce of the ball. And he expected serious play from his teammates. Although he had not spoken, it was clear he despised the frivolity frequently displayed by the two boys. Even Jerry and Kari seemed affected by his mood. Then, with the score tied at thirteen, a ball passed from the back row hung tantalizingly between the gray-haired man and Bobby playing next to him. Both went for the ball. But the man leapt through the boy, knocking him hard to the grass, before spiking the ball outside Philip's block into an unreachable corner. When Philip saw Bobby lying on the ground, he immediately leaned under the net to see if he was all right.

"He'll be all right." The gray-haired man's words were spoken with unexpected authority.

"I'm sure he will," said Philip. "Let's just make certain."

"He'll be all right." The man's voice had a strong edge of warning. Philip caught the man's tone this time. He stood and looked at him. "He needs to be tougher," the man said. They looked at each other for another moment. Then, when Philip turned back to check on Bobby, the man said in a voice as soft as a serpent's, "He's my son."

Philip felt a cold nerve begin to jangle away back in his brain. Bobby was sitting up. Philip noticed that he was now standing on the opposite side of the net from his own team. Sally was staring at him with what seemed like terror. He turned back to the man. "I'm not sure I understand what difference that makes," he said. Then he bent down, grabbed Bobby's arm, pulled him to his feet and helped him off the court.

Moments later the game resumed. After one brief rally, Philip's team lost fifteen to thirteen. The eighth graders joined Bobby on the sidelines, but the adults played for another hour. Philip enjoyed himself immensely, although his exchange with Mr. Sorenson was never far from his mind. As they had lined up across the net from each other awaiting the serve for the last point of their match, Philip glimpsed conflicting inchoate impulses in Mr. Sorenson's eyes. One was simply cold anger. But the other was the thrill of rising to the chase, the challenge ahead to crush the outsider, to crush him like a flower.

It was very early Saturday morning, just after 6:30. Philip was sitting with Jerry having a cup of coffee at the Van Kleeks' dining room table. Jerry's golf clubs were cleaned and ready to go by the door. Jerry had just finished warning Philip about clashing with Bobby Sorenson's father.

"Carnley Sorenson is one of God's Myrmidons," said Jerry. "He's a nice enough man, but he has an edge to him. Where principle is concerned, he won't bend. And when he thinks God's honor is involved, well let's just say he shoots first and questions later."

At this point Mary, Jerry's diminutive wife, popped out of the kitchen with three slices of coffee cake. She arranged the dessert in front of the two men, then sat down with a piece herself. Mary wore her hair long. The gray tresses hung thickly on her shoulders and tumbled over her back. "Well I think Philip did the right thing," she said. "Carnley is entirely too hard on his boys."

"That may be true," said Jerry. "I'm just trying to help Philip see the lay of the land."

The Van Kleek home was one of the newer homes on the center, a two-story affair with a wide veranda around the entire second floor. The home was part of a cluster of houses on the northern end of Ilusan. On its eastern side the home overlooked the north-south airstrip. From the southern balcony you could see the road out to the highway and, just across it, the row of trees and houses that culminated at the water tower. You could just make out a corner of Philip's roof through the trees. Philip was asking a question about the Sorenson family, when Mary said, "Who's that on the airstrip?"

They all stood and looked out the window. Jerry had earlier pointed out to Philip that the swipe of paint on the runway about fifty yards from his balcony marked the first tee box of his manufactured golf course. Now a young girl loitered there. From time to time she cast a glance toward the Van Kleek home. It was Sally. "That girl follows Philip around like a puppy dog," said Jerry. "She must have heard us talking about golfing today."

"Yep," said Philip. He sipped his coffee and remained staring down at Sally. He wasn't sure what to feel. But Mary had no ambivalence in the matter. She stepped out onto the veranda and called to Sally. She invited her up for some coffee cake. The girl ran toward the house.

Mary stepped back inside and eyed the two men. "That girl needs an adult in her life. It seems like every time I see her she's alone."

Jerry said, "Well she's not the only girl in Philip's life. He also seems to have taken a shine to a certain fetching young librarian."

Philip almost spit out his coffee. "Jerry, where do you come up with that?"

Jerry shrugged and went back to his cake. "I merely offer it as an observation."

Mary had a different reaction to Jerry's revelation. "Well Philip this is a gift. Sally is the sweetest kid, and if she's taken a shine to you, you need to take that responsibility very seriously. You can chase the librarian on your own time, but when you're teaching you attend fully to our kids."

Both men were now startled. Jerry said, "Mary that seems like a rather stern lecture for our young charge."

"No, she's absolutely right," said Philip.

"Philip knows how I intend it," said Mary. "I think he and Kari would make a nice enough couple, but I love these kids, and when one of them reaches out to you, well that's a big step for a kid to take. So you reach back. I hope you two intend to take her golfing with you."

"Yes, that's exactly what we intended," said Jerry. He winked at Philip. Sally's footsteps on the stairs cut the conversation short. Mary welcomed the girl and seated her at the end of the table next to Philip. Philip observed over the next few minutes how the girl glowed at being included in the adult ritual of early morning coffee and conversation. When Mary was in the kitchen Jerry gave Sally a sip of his coffee. "Mine's better," whispered Philip. "It's sweeter." And when next Mary entered the kitchen, Sally was treated to a sip of the sweeter coffee. She decided she liked Philip's better, and the three of them all smiled at Mary when she re-entered the room.

"All right, what's going on?" asked Mary.

"Absolutely nothing," said Jerry. "We're just heading for the links."

"Sally is going to be my caddy," said Philip.

Mary laughed. Her laugh was one of the most musical Philip had ever heard. It was as if someone was squeezing an accordion in short staccato bursts. "Well you all better get started. The hangar will get busy pretty soon."

The two adults and the girl stood on the first tee scanning the airstrip. Jerry outlined the only ground rule at his exclusive club. "You have to do due diligence hunting for every ball. There's never a foursome behind us and golf balls aren't exactly a common commodity in central Mindanao.

I get a shipment from my brother twice a year, but that's no reason to waste balls."

"Then I probably better not use driver too often," said Philip. "Standing on this tee, I'd be apt to hook one and ding one of the airplanes. And I imagine on other tees, I'd end up in the corn. But maybe after I get warmed up."

The two runways formed a large plus sign in the middle of surrounding corn fields, although the southwestern quadrant opened onto the hangar and the school buildings and the cluster of homes around Jerry's house. Most of Jerry's holes therefore were either straight or sharp doglegs. Jerry teed off first. He crouched over the ball for what seemed an eternity, every muscle in his legs twitching. Then he hit a gentle fade that started out down the left side of the runway and wound up pretty much right in the middle. Philip was to learn that virtually all of Jerry's shots were gentle fades. "Did you see how big Mr. Van Kleek's leg muscles are?" Philip said to Sally.

"No," the girl smiled.

"I'll thank you not to be looking at my legs Mr. Andrews," said Jerry. They addressed each other formally in the presence of the girl.

"Well check them out next time Sally. They're quite something."

Philip teed off with Jerry's three wood. He took two huge practice swings, then settled into his stance bouncing up and down lightly on his toes. He hit the ball hard down the left side of the fairway. When it landed it clung to the side of the runway for a few bounces, but then rolled down onto the empty hangar tarmac. "I trust I get a free drop from there," he said.

"Did you see how Mr. Andrews bounced up and down Sally?" asked Jerry.

"I think he needs to go to the bathroom," said Sally.

"That's the spirit," said Jerry.

The first green was right in the middle where the two runways bisected each other. "I think I'll need an eight-iron from down there," said Philip. "Is that o.k. with you Mr. Van Kleek?" Jerry thought he could part with his eight-iron. He handed it to Philip who handed it to Sally. "Let's go Sally. If you're my caddy you have to carry my club and then give me advice before I swing."

An hour and a half later the three stood on the sixth tee. Philip was thoroughly enjoying himself. Jerry was a delight to golf with, all dry wit and intense focus. Sally took her role very seriously. She ran around with boundless energy hunting for lost balls, running ahead of Philip after every shot to find where his ball landed, giving him advice when he asked along the lines of "Try to keep it out of the corn." When they got to Jerry's spray painted greens, she pretended to help him read them, and after a few holes was actually able to warn him of bumps and spots where the grass was long or mushy. After he putted, Philip always let Sally hit the ball from the same spot. "We're a team," he said, and he played whichever one of their putts was closer to the hole. She had even taken some swings with the shorter clubs. Scores were high as the greens were impossible to putt with any accuracy, but, as golf scores are all relative anyway, nobody seemed to mind.

The sixth tee stood at the extreme western end of the east-west runway. A right-handed golfer standing on the tee faced down the hill toward the school buildings. Just off the tee to the right at the edge of the runway the ground dropped sharply down a six foot slope to the hangar. One of the planes was taking off. It taxied directly toward them then spun around right on top of the tee box. Tom Jacobson was the pilot and he waved to the golfers standing at the side of the runway. The plane was the familiar Helio, a tail-dragger with wide overhead wings, the best airplane ever made for short takeoffs and landings. Tom ran up the engine a few times, then with one last wave, powered forward down the strip. He was in the air within what seemed like one hundred fifty yards. They watched him bank sharply to the left and head north. "It was a lot of fun flying in that airplane," said Philip. "I can't wait to do it again."

"All things in their time," said Jerry. "The time now is for a long par five." He showed Philip on his crudely drawn map how the sixth hole laid out. The hole ran down the east-west runway to the intersection and then took off all the way down to the northern end of the north-south runway.

"A long sharp dog indeed," said Philip. "Mr. Van Kleek I think it's time I take your driver on a shakedown cruise. Even if I do hook it a bit I can probably just shoot the dog." He turned to Sally. "That's golfer talk for cutting across the corn and landing safely in the other runway."

"O.k. Mr. Andrews," said Jerry, "we haven't lost any balls yet, so I suppose we can spare one here."

Philip laughed. "Oh ye of little faith." He teed up a ball, took a few practice swings with Jerry's driver, then swung hard. The ball leapt off the club. Sally said "Wow" as it shot down the left side of the runway. But glory was not to be his. About one hundred yards out, as if glancing off an invisible airplane, the ball bit hard north and took off across the corn field. "The duck hook," Philip groused. "Keep an eye on it Sally." They all watched the ball sail deep into the corn.

"The only person who'll ever see that ball again is a Filipino farmer," said Jerry. But Philip disagreed. He thought he had a good line on it.

"I'll just take one quick look. Sally you wait with Mr. Van Kleek. I don't want you getting lost in there." He jogged toward the corn. He lined himself up with the row approximately where he thought the ball left the runway, waved to Jerry and Sally who were slowly walking toward him, and entered the corn field. The corn was tall, well over his head, so all he could do was proceed down the row he had entered and hope he got lucky. He hurried because he didn't want to keep Jerry waiting. When he thought he was about where the ball might have landed he slowed and began to look around. Although only just after 8:30, the day was already warming up and he began to sweat. It was close in the corn. But then he felt a slight breeze. He had just looked up to see what was ahead when he stepped out of the corn into a recently plowed field. His ball lay cleanly on top of a furrow about thirty yards in front of him.

And standing beside the ball was the largest animal Philip had ever seen. He had seen bulls in pictures, but never in the flesh, and certainly never face to face with no intervening fence. The animal's skin had the gray weathered look of an ancient cement foundation. Rising from its shoulders was a massive hump that looked to be solid muscle and gristle. The bull was looking down the field, but now it swung its head toward Philip. There was something wrong with its face. That was when Philip noticed the angry red welt between the bull's eyes and the thin trickle of blood running down its nose. "Bulls-eye," he said. "You can keep the ball."

He would remember the next few moments like a dream. As he stepped slowly backward toward the corn, he happened to glance down to check his footing. He noticed he was wearing an Ohio State tee shirt. Ohio State colors were scarlet and gray. "I've stepped into a cliché," he thought. The bull began to paw the ground with its right front foot. Not a good sign. He walked backward until he was about five feet inside the corn. Then he turned and began to trot back the way he had come. He didn't break into a run because he had the absurd notion that he didn't want to look foolish in front of Jerry and Sally. The bull would undoubtedly do nothing.

That was when he heard the crash of a large animal entering the corn. He wasn't sure what gland was responsible for the release of adrenalin, but he could tell it had done its job well. His feet began to fly. The crashing behind him grew louder. "The farmer's going to be pissed," he thought. He remembered how he used to have nightmares when he was a kid in which large animals chased him and devoured him. His mother had taught him to rebuke his attackers in the name of Jesus. In his dreams the technique had invariably worked, at least when he remembered to employ it. Sometimes you just forgot that sort of thing even in dreams. He half turned over his left shoulder and shouted, "I rebuke you in the name of Jesus." Whether Jesus heard his cry or not he couldn't be sure, but the bull was clearly unimpressed. Although he couldn't see it yet, it sounded like it was right behind him. "I guess that makes me a son of Sceva," he thought. He had a sudden sense of light in front of him. He burst out onto the airstrip.

Sally and Jerry had clearly heard something coming because they were already edging back toward the hangar. "Run," Philip shouted. They both turned and ran for the corner of the building. Philip had only a fleeting moment to wonder whether that was all the faster Jerry could run, when the bull burst from the corn behind him. He had half the width of the airstrip between them. He sprinted toward the hangar. He begged God for a miracle. He saw only one door on this side of the building. It had to be open. It would be open. He almost fell down the slope on the other side of the runway. He slammed hard against the door. It was locked. Without looking behind him he sprinted toward the corner of the building around which Jerry and Sally had disappeared.

And then a miracle. The bull stumbled at the edge of the runway. It hurtled down the bank, its forelegs buckling. An eye blink later it crashed head first into the side of the hangar. The building rocked on its foundation. Glass shattered in every office. Joseph Haaf, Kari Trainor, Fossia Gertrudes, Mary Van Kleek and everyone else on the northern end of the base thought one thing. A plane had gone down. They streamed from their houses and ran toward the airstrip. Philip careened around the end of the building, heard the crash, saw glass spray in front of him, stopped, listened, and then peeked back around the corner. The bull lay in a crumpled heap against the wall. Philip leapt into the air and pumped his fists. "Down goes Frazier," he screamed, "down goes Frazier."

But Frazier might get back up. Philip watched the bull intently. He could hear Sally crying hysterically. Hearing the sonic crash from the other side of the building, they must have imagined Philip crushed between the bull and the wall. "Jerry, Sally, come look at this!" he called. They peeked around the corner. "It's all right," he said. "You've got to see this."

As the first startled missionaries arrived at the scene, the bull was just staggering to its feet. George Donahoe, who was fueling an airplane on the tarmac and had seen the last moments of the chase, and Fossia were busy keeping everyone well away from the groggy animal. Sally, tears still bright on her cheeks, breathlessly recounted the story to anyone who would listen. Several, including Joseph Haaf, ran back home to get their cameras. Mary Van Kleek was telling Philip and Jerry that from now on any ball hit deep into the corn belonged to the farmers. She got no argument from Philip.

The bull made its way to the middle of the airstrip, where for the first time it managed to raise its head fully erect and look around to get its bearings. It glanced back toward the assembled missionaries and the hangar, knew that wasn't the correct direction, then gazed at the corn field. "That bull's going to have one monster headache," said Joseph as he snapped pictures.

"It's lucky it didn't snap its neck," said Philip.

"You're lucky it didn't snap your neck," said Kari.

"I was praying so hard," said Sally. "I thought it was going to catch Mr. Andrews."

"You *were* praying weren't you!" said Jerry. "I thought I heard you praying."

"Thank you Sally," said Philip. "I needed someone like you praying for me." He squeezed the girl's shoulder.

Just then the bull made up its mind. It lumbered toward the corn field and was gone. The group gazed after it for a few moments then decided to inspect the damage to the building. More than half the windows on the lower floor had blown out. The oil-stained siding where the bull crashed next to the door was stove in for a five yard radius. On the other side of the wall two filing cabinets had toppled.

When Philip emerged from inside after helping to right the cabinets, the crowd had grown to more than forty people. Boys on bicycles had spread the news throughout the center. Matt and Julia St. Clair roared up on his motorcycle. Gordon Lundy was there and the Troyer sisters. Philip saw every one of his students. It took another half hour to tell the story to all the newcomers. Philip shared the stage with Sally, letting her take over the story once he and the bull emerged from the corn.

Later, after Matt sped off on his motorcycle to find his chief carpenter, and Philip had been patted on the back more times than he could count and had heard innumerable jokes about how the repairs would be taken out of his salary, he and Joseph walked back toward the center of the base. "What a morning," he said.

"Your morning is a perfect illustration of my most deeply held belief about life," said Joseph. He paused dramatically, forcing Philip to ask the obvious question.

"O.k. if you insist, I'll tell you," said Joseph. "Never expect things to go smoothly. Never expect good to happen. Never even expect the laws of the universe to function normally. Because just when you relax and let down your guard, in fact just when you're having a really good time, the inexplicable will jump up and skewer you to a wall."

Philip raised his eyebrow.

"You think I kid. Let me tell you a story. When I was a boy a friend of mine got a new bike. It was a great bike, a really cool off-road racer. We had this course all set up through the woods. I ask him if I can try out his bike. He says sure. So I take off. I'm flying down this hill and I come to a place where we had a little jump. And I decided to use the bump to pop a wheelie. So I pop this wheelie and I see something odd in the road ahead. And I realize with horror that it's the front tire. I've popped, and it's kept right on rolling. So there I am riding a wheelie at good speed without a front tire thinking, 'How is this possible?' Turns out my buddy had been working on his bike and simply had neglected to put the nuts back on the front axle. 'I didn't know you were going to pop a wheelie,' he says. Now that, my friend, is a perfect model for what the universe is like. Just when you get comfortable enough to pop a wheelie, just when you begin to believe that tires will always be where they're supposed to be, boom, the inexplicable jumps up and punches you in the face. And thirty stitches later you hope you've learned your lesson. Don't say I didn't warn you."

That night Philip had dinner with Fossia and Kari and the other teachers. Fossia had invited the entire staff over for a year-opening dinner party. Everyone was there, Jerry and Mary, Annabel, Peggy Margaret, Philip and the two hosts. Fossia's home was a lovely two-story two doors down from the Van Kleeks' and just across the road and down about fifty yards from Philip. The lower floor was only half finished, but provided plenty of room for Kari. Fossia had the upstairs, and the two women shared the kitchen and dining room on the second floor.

Conversation at dinner returned naturally to the adventure of the morning, and the story was told and retold. "I was sure we had lost a pilot," said Fossia.

Much was made of Philip's prowess with animals. He'd been at the center for a week and already made intimate acquaintance with a monkey, cat, and now a bull. "Don't forget the mosquitoes," said Philip.

After dinner Fossia brought out a Monopoly game. Everyone played, and, as games of Monopoly are wont to do, this one went long. After the lights went out at 9:30 Fossia and Kari lit lamps and the game continued. On the screens the lizards and bugs played their deadly game, but no one inside noticed. Even Annabel seemed to enjoy herself. Nevertheless she was the first out, leaving the game at 9:50. Although she owned Boardwalk and Park Place, she never had the heart to charge full price and forgave too many debts. But she graciously consented to be the banker, and, in fact, focused on that task with great scrupulosity. Philip had actually had the first opportunity to drive Annabel into bankruptcy, but hadn't had the heart. He had fudged how much she owed him several times to keep her playing. Peggy Margaret had no such scruples and took a firm grip on the game when she drove Annabel from the board and gained the two premium properties. Philip was the next out, then Mary, then Kari and Jerry in rapid succession. But it was after midnight before Peggy Margaret finally wrested control from Fossia. Everyone stayed to view the conclusion, so Fossia served another round of dessert before the teachers finally left for home.

Philip was the last out the door. He paused in the doorway, caught Kari's eye and motioned with his head, the smallest suggestion that she step outside with him. She nodded. He waited for her at the bottom of the stairs. He was about to go where he had rarely gone before. He was about to initiate a relationship. He wasn't good with this kind of tension. He was suddenly gripped with the need to find a bathroom.

"It's a beautiful night," he said when she joined him. "I thought I'd walk up to the school and sit on the swings for a bit and look at the stars. Care to join me?" It was one of those questions around which the fate of the world seemed to swing. A yes or a no, like the proverbial butterfly wing, would set in motion two entirely different futures, certainly for these two, but also for countless others whose lives might later intersect with them. If you were inclined to believe in faeries, you would have noticed that they paused in their nightly routines to bend an ear to the girl's response. It was just that kind of question.

Kari didn't say "Yes," or "I'd like that," or "Love to." She simply said, "Let me tell Fossia that I'll be out for a bit." The butterfly soared deep in the Amazon. One faerie winked at another. And the currents that carried these two lives in their immense depths nosed their way into a new channel.

Philip wasn't sure what he intended. He just knew that he didn't want the day to end, and that it was time to roll the dice. They scarcely talked as they walked across the hangar road toward the school. Kari glanced once toward the airstrip and said, "It gives me the creeps to think that bull's out there somewhere."

"Let's hope he's asleep," said Philip.

When they reached the swing set behind the school they sat next to each other and began to swing. Several of the swings had been designed for the older children, and the adults worked them comfortably. "Put your head back and stare at the sky." The librarian's voice was soft. With just a little effort, and with their eyes fixed above them, they soon felt as if they were spinning through a vast sea of stars. Philip thought that if he jumped off the swing he would simply float into a warm eternity of soft light. He could hear Kari keeping pace beside him, could hear her soft intake of breath as she pulled on the chains, straining to kick higher. Then they both lay back and drifted slowly to earth.

To break the silence Philip said, "That is so cool." You're a naturally suave guy, he thought to himself.

"Hush," she said. "Don't mess it up by talking." Then, maybe to make sure she hadn't hurt his feelings, she reached across the space between them and placed her hand for just a second on his where it gripped the chain, before sliding her fingers quickly below him.

When they stopped swinging and had been silent for a few minutes, Kari said, "I come over here quite a bit on nights like this."

"I bet," said Philip. "I just sit on my porch for an hour or two after lights out. I can't go to bed at 9:30. I could light a lamp and read, but there's something about being out in these evenings. It clears the head, helps you think."

"What do you think about?"

"Oh, life, this place, the future, you."

She laughed. "And what do you think about me?"

"I wonder how in the world to ask you on a date when there's no place to go. And nobody has a car."

"I thought we were on a date right now. Aren't we?"

"I'd like to think so." Her fingers still rested lightly on the chain next to his hand. It felt like an invitation. He slid his hand down to hers and lightly traced her thumb with his forefinger.

"You've been here much longer than I have," he said. "So tell me. How can I spend more time with you? How can we be alone?"

"You just have to be creative."

They spent the next ten minutes coming up with ideas. They decided that several times a week they would bring their lunches to school, and instead of going home to eat they would spend the hour together there. "We both have bikes," Kari said. "There are places we can ride to. We can ride out to the end of the airstrip and be out of sight of everybody."

"Kind of where the bull hangs out?"

"Yes, but we'll have bikes. And we can ride down along the river into the banana orchard at the other end of the base. And there are some paths off the base. Fossia doesn't like me riding alone out there, but if you're with me . . . ."

"You could sneak over some night and sit with me on my porch. I'll treat you to a cold soda."

She was silent for a long moment. Finally she said, "I'd like to, but that would be risky here Philip." He loved to hear her say his name. "People will talk as it is, but if they see us too much alone after dark, the talk won't be good. Especially after lights out." She tugged on his hand and squeezed it. "Do you know what I mean? This isn't the States." He could hear the earnestness in her voice.

"I know what you mean."

They were silent for a few minutes longer and then Kari said, "We should probably go. Fossia knows I'm out so she'll be listening for me." As they walked back toward her home, she reached over and tugged on his shirt sleeve. "Next time we just can't make it so obvious we're going out. If Fossia doesn't know I'm gone, she won't be listening up."

When Philip got home he grabbed a cold orange soda and sat for a few minutes on his porch. Mr. Bumbles, purring like Philip had been gone for weeks, jumped into his lap and rammed his chest hard. Philip pet the cat vigorously for a few minutes, and eventually Bumbles jumped onto the railing and cased the darkness. "I've had quite an evening Bumbles."

He had wanted to kiss Kari good night, but the old fear had returned. She might think he was out of line. He didn't want to do anything to jeopardize her affection. But she had lingered for a moment, seeming to expect him to do something. She spent four years in the States in college, so she must have been waiting for a kiss. He began to chide himself, but then gave it up. "It's a long year my friend," he said to the cat. "I'll figure it out."

He ran his fingers slowly over the cold bottle, then reached out and gripped the railing by the cat. His fingers were alive. It was like a new nerve had been created in his hands, a nerve that pulsed with the deep veins of life that ran through everything around him. He felt that if he gripped hard enough he could slow down time. He stood, took a deep breath, leaned on the railing and was exquisitely alive to the moment.

## Chapter Six

PHILIP WAS HALFWAY THROUGH his fourth week of teaching, the calendar had turned to August and the rains had come, when it struck him early one morning, as he sat in his classroom window watching the children gather to their respective buildings, just how much fun he was having. He had heard teaching described as a noble profession. Four weeks in he was beginning to agree. Or at least he felt ennobled every day as he stood in front of his students. Here were children at an impressionable moment, and he had been entrusted as the primary impression-making adult in their lives, outside of their parents. Certainly the good folks at Ilusan might have been foolish to place him in such a position, but Philip found he no longer worried about that. Whether they were correct in their judgment of him or not, and to be honest very few of them had been consulted, he wanted to be there. Furthermore, and this was a thought he found exhilarating, he sensed that the kids wanted him there. More and more they arrived early, stayed late, invited him to join in foursquare at recess, enlisted him after school in games of tag at the pool (of which they had endless varieties, including the aptly named mud tag which involved pulling up seaweed to create water so thick and brown you couldn't see an inch), and came calling on Friday nights to drag him out for hours of kick the can, bulldog, and capture the flag.

Although the best part of his job was the interaction with the children in their daily lives and the relationships he was building, Philip found he even looked forward to the actual classroom instruction. There was a certain freedom in knowing he would only be there one year. He could do whatever crazy thing came into his head. The kids had never known anything like his freewheeling style before, his easy dismissal of accepted pedagogies with which on the spur of the moment he decided he didn't agree, his banter that made him seem almost one of them, if just a little more knowledgeable and with a bit more authority.

The boys took to his style immediately. The girls were concerned at first, but gradually warmed to him as well. Mary Michaels had been the hardest to convince. She preferred the kind of classroom activities that exalted the natural edge she had over the other students in sheer brain power. She wanted to proudly hand in quizzes and tests on which she knew she would earn perfect scores. And when the class discussed a story they had read, she wanted to know the correct answers to Philip's questions. There had to be a reason why Bartleby said "I prefer not to." She grew exasperated when, in response to her persistent questioning, Philip said, "I prefer not to offer an opinion on this issue." She sulked while the rest of the class laughed. But eventually even Mary came around. Philip made sure to defer to her in math period, frequently asking her to explain difficult problems to the class. And when discussing literature or history or the Bible, he always asked one or two esoteric factual questions that usually only Mary or Bobby could answer. But when he insisted the children form an opinion for themselves and present their arguments for it, Mary was usually quiet.

And every now and then, when the class was quiet, Sally raised her hand. She seemed astonished at first to hear her own voice speaking from the back of the room, almost as astonished as the rest of the class. But as Philip found ways to affirm her insights, she spoke more and more, once even interrupting Bobby in her rush to share her thoughts. And, observing her growth, that teacher part of Philip's heart that had probably always been there but had never been nurtured, grew, until at times he felt almost strangled with joy at the privilege given him, the privilege of participating in leading children into young adulthood.

Ever since he had picked Bobby off the ground at the volleyball court the boys had been all over him. They were the ones insisting he join in their recess and Friday night games. Several times a week he found them waiting on his back porch when he got home from school, where they could always count on a soft drink and rambling conversation. Philip enjoyed the boys, especially Bobby and Donny. With Carnley Sorenson being who he was, Philip knew there had to be tension between Bobby and his father, and he sensed the young man longed for positive adult input. But Bobby had a best friend in Donny, and, in fact, the entire group of eighth grade boys was pretty tight, so Philip knew Bobby had plenty of support.

But Sally was another matter entirely. Everyone seemed to agree that she spent a lot of time alone. And with a virtually inarticulate father, Philip worried about her home life, although her mother seemed nice enough. But perhaps of most significance was the fact that Sally, through the serendipitous placement of her favorite tree, seemed to have chosen him as the adult with whom she valued interaction. Philip had decided he had to take that charge very seriously. In addition, virtually every Saturday morning before golf, Mary quizzed him about Sally's progress, and Philip knew his balance sheet between Kari-time and Sally-time had better not lean too heavily toward Kari if he wanted to keep on Mary's good side.

But with the boys now demanding so much of his time, Philip found himself struggling to carve out time for Sally. Fortunately the more he played children's games, the more Sally hung around and even began to participate. Her typical recess activity, he learned from Jerry, had been to walk the fence line behind the school staring into the distance, or to climb the guava tree behind the seventh and eighth grade classroom and from a perch high in that tree again stare into the distance. But a week ago she had suddenly shown up in the foursquare line at recess. She had been there ever since. The only time she missed was when Philip asked her to play tetherball with him. And the past Friday night, there she was, along with Philip and a dozen other children, playing bulldog on the plaza in front of the meeting hall. When Timmy Mullen, standing alone next to the meeting hall bell yelled "Bulldog," she ran across the plaza with her hair flying behind her, armed with her typical intense look, trying to avoid Timmy's tag. Philip was never sure she actually enjoyed the games, but he was delighted to see her participating. Still, whenever the boys waited for Philip after school or gathered on his porch, she would linger indecisively for a moment, before walking home alone. Consequently, on the days when Sally escorted him and Mr. Bumbles home, Philip made sure she always felt welcome to stay and chat. They had even begun doing some of her homework together. At times dusk found them both quietly reading on his porch. At least now she usually said "Goodbye" before dashing around the corner of his house heading home for dinner.

All this had made it difficult to spend much time with Kari. They packed a lunch virtually every day now. They usually ate together in Philip's classroom or outside on the steps. Every now and then they sat in the swings. They talked about Philip's burgeoning relationship with the kids, and Kari insisted that he reserve afternoons and Friday nights for them. So Saturday, after golf with Jerry and Sally, became their date day. They took their bicycles on several long rides off the base where they discovered a few favorite spots along the river. They managed to spend a few Sunday afternoons together and once even cut Wednesday night prayer meeting in order to take an evening walk.

Word, of course, was beginning to get around the center of their interest in each other, and several astute and friendly observers had invited the two of them over for dinner. Gordon Lundy was their chief cheerleader. He managed to get a group together at least once a week, and always included Kari and Philip. Once, as the three of them cleaned the kitchen together, he suddenly excused himself with a wink to take a late night stroll. "You two don't need me to tell you how to do dishes," he said. They knew that Gordon had gifted them with time alone in a house after dark, something of which no one on the base would approve. They carried Gordon's couch onto the porch, where they sat holding hands and enjoying the night. Philip kissed Kari for the first time that evening. He would always be grateful to Gordon for the gift of that moment.

On a breezy Thursday afternoon in August that promised rain later in the evening, the students demonstrated their science projects. The seventh graders presented as a group of three. They were germinating durian seeds. The eighth graders were only mildly interested. Mary and Madeline were up next. They carried a cage to the front of the room and set it on Philip's desk. Madeline opened the door and two white mice nosed out onto Philip's papers. Philip motioned for the rest of the class to crowd around. "Our project is to raise two white mice and carefully observe their eating habits, how they spend their time, and how they get along," said Madeline.

"What are their names?" Elaine Pauley seemed genuinely interested.

"That's David," said Mary pointing to the larger of the two mice. "And that's Jonathan."

"How do you know they're boys?" asked Charlie Pilarski. "Maybe they're Ruth and Naomi."

"They can't be Ruth and Naomi even if they *are* girls," said Mary. "David and Jonathan are almost the same age, and Naomi was much older than Ruth."

"O.k. maybe they're Rahab and Ruth," said Donny Meyer.

"Or Miriam and Deborah." Taking his cue from Donny, Bobby was getting in the spirit of the moment.

"Or the whore of Babylon and the woman riding the scarlet dragon." Sally spoke softly without a trace of humor in her voice.

The boys burst out laughing. They looked admiringly in her direction. "Sally shoots, she scores," said Bobby. Philip caught Sally's eye and raised his eyebrows and nodded. Only then did Sally smile.

Mary was flustered. "They're two boys. That's David and that's Jonathan."

"Or it could be a boy and a girl." Philip winked at Bobby. "Don't forget that possibility."

"The man in Malaybalay told us they were two boys," insisted Mary.

Just then David, using his teeth, grabbed Jonathan by the scruff of his neck and mounted him. Mary squealed. Even the boys looked a little embarrassed.

"Stop it David. You're hurting Jonathan," cried Mary.

"Maybe what we have here is David and Bathsheba," said Philip.

Mary was horrified at the suggestion. "If they *are* a boy and a girl," she said, "they're Zacharias and Elizabeth."

"Or Mary and Joseph," said Charlie.

Mary turned redder than she already was. "Don't be sacrilegious," she hissed at Charlie. "Besides Mary and Joseph didn't do that." She pointed at the two mice. "At least not until after Jesus was born."

"Maybe they're Ananias and Sapphira," said Donny. Coming up with those two was clearly a reach, and Philip could tell Donny was proud of himself.

"Judah and Tamar," said Bobby.

The class seemed ready to begin another round of biblical esoterica, when they were interrupted by two sudden movements. David rose up, let go of Jonathan's neck, shook himself, dismounted and wandered back toward the cage. And a large gray form sprang from behind Elaine Pauley, landed lightly on the desk, seized Jonathan in its teeth and bolted for the door. Everyone had forgotten Mr. Bumbles. Mary and Madeline shrieked and ran after the cat. The boys looked at Philip. "I guess we better follow," said Philip.

"Reeee," yelped Donny, and a stream of children chased the girls and the cat out the door. Bumbles led the screaming girls and whooping boys on a merry chase around the corner of the building, across the foursquare court, under the swing set and finally, just when the children had him surrounded, he shot between Charlie and Madeline and raced up a tree, where he settled with a smug look on a branch just out of everyone's reach. Jonathan's tail dangled out of his mouth. The tail twitched twice, setting off another round of screams from the girls. By now Jerry's fifth and sixth graders crowded the windows of their classroom. "We might as well join the fun," said Jerry, and the fifth and sixth grade boys leapt from the windows, while the girls ran out the door, down the stairs, and around the building to join the crowd.

"Et tu Jerry?" said Philip when Jerry joined him.

Jerry surveyed the scene for a moment. "More like touché Charles Darwin," he said.

"I'm not sure what Bumbles has in mind," said Philip.

Indeed the cat was gazing down at the crowd of agitated children with an air of serene indifference. Some of the girls were now crying. Bumbles eased his hold on the mouse. The children clearly saw the mouse struggling as the cat's cheeks bulged first on one side, then the other. Suddenly a pair of pink paws protruded through Bumbles' teeth and grasped his lower lip. A second later Jonathan's head appeared. The mouse shook himself, gasped for breath a few times with tongue lolling, looked down at the children, then began polishing its ears. "Doesn't look particularly put out," said Jerry.

Mary stomped her foot. "Mr. Bumbles, you release Jonathan this instant." Other girls took up the cry.

"Eat him Bumbles," said Charlie.

"Shut up Charlie," said Madeline.

"Do something Mr. Andrews," pleaded Mary.

"Well Mary, Mr. Bumbles and I are friends, but he has a very independent mind. But I'll see what I can do." Philip saw Sally smiling at him. "Mr. Bumbles, you have Mary and Madeline's science experiment in your mouth. They're going to get a bad grade if you eat him." The girls gasped. "Just kidding. Now Mr. Bumbles I think you should let Jonathan go."

"Or Ruth," said Bobby.

"Or Miriam," said Donny.

"Or the whore of Babylon," said Sally.

"Interesting class you're running here," Jerry said to Philip.

"It's a long story," said Philip.

Mr. Bumbles stood on the branch and stretched. Jonathan let out a little squawk. The children held their breath. The cat took one last long look at the children then spit Jonathan out. The mouse, legs splayed like a flying squirrel, sailed down toward Mary. The girl screamed and jumped out of the way. Jonathan landed on the grass, apparently decided he'd had enough of being a science experiment, and made a dash for freedom. Twenty-five fifth, sixth, seventh, and eighth grade children gave chase. "I wash my hands of this entire affair," Philip said to Jerry. The two men watched the children disappear around the corner of the building after the mouse.

"I don't know," said Jerry. "It was a very innovative lesson plan. Interesting mix of science and religion. Perhaps you'd be so kind as to return my class once they've corralled the little rodent."

Philip was discovering that there were basically two seasons in the Philippines, dry and wet, which corresponded roughly to what he knew as the usual calendar dates for summer and winter. When Philip arrived at Ilusan in July, the center had only seen sporadic rainfall since March. The grass everywhere was brown and the pool was relatively low. Rain barrels were only half full. Roads were deep with dust.

But the rains came early that year, first appearing in any serious manner in early August. Rain was rarely monotonous in the Philippines. It came in many varieties. There were the sprinkles that seemed to spray from cloudless skies. The sun remained out, and the warm pellucid drops through which the children, and at times even the adults, skipped and ran, were like wet sunbursts against their skin. There were the passing showers. They appeared in the afternoons in the shape of a dark cloud or two. They announced their arrival with a rumble of thunder, doused the center for fifteen minutes or so, then wandered on down the river. There were the vicious storms that skirted the base, but set off spectacular displays of horizon to horizon heat lightning that drew people out of their houses to watch, sometimes for hours at a time.

Some of these spectacular storms, of course, scored a direct hit on Ilusan. Then the missionaries huddled indoors as the lightning cut loose its utterly undisciplined fire, and thunder threatened to crush their homes, homes that suddenly seemed insignificant before nature's raw energy. Rain from such storms pelted down in a deluge of drops so large they smacked and stung when they struck human skin. Water sheeted off roofs in torrents. Rain barrels filled in minutes. Plazas reached saturation levels in less than half an hour, and, if the danger from lightning seemed remote, the children appeared to run and slide in the inches of standing water, or to tube down the raging drainage ditches. Afterward the barefoot children enjoyed the warm squish of mud between their toes. Mothers made them clean their spattered legs at the rain barrel before coming inside.

If such rain continued for half a day or longer, low stretches of the center filled with standing water, the basketball court disappeared, and passage to the southern end of Ilusan grew difficult. The water and mud brought out hibernating creatures of every shape and size, and the evenings now filled with a chorus of ecstatic bullfrogs belting out their joy at receiving the gift of water and willing females. No matter how fiercely the water fell, Philip found that he loved such rain, a rain that made no bones about what it was up to. These were no gelid downpours leaving their recipients chilled and morose. Philippine rains brought life, a cool break from the heat, and cocoons of reflection. He would sit on his porch for as long as it rained, feeling comfortably entombed by the sheets of water pouring from his roof, listening to the drumming on the tin overhead and the singing of the frogs. He shouted out his pleasure and nobody heard him. At times he found himself wishing the rain would never stop.

On a Saturday afternoon shortly after the Bumbles-Jonathan tête-à-tête, Philip and Kari sat on their bicycles at the north end of the north-south runway and watched a storm approach across the plateau. They had been for a long bike ride and had stopped to catch their breath and to enjoy a few more minutes together before returning to the center. The sheet of rain to the north looked like a child had colored with a dark gray crayon against the blue sky.

"I wonder how fast the rain is moving," said Kari.

"I don't know," said Philip, "but I feel like gambling. What do you say?"

"O.k." She looked at him expectantly.

"We wait here until the last possible minute, then see if we can beat it home without getting wet. I'll let you call it. Let's see how gutsy you are."

"Deal." She turned her bike around and pointed it south down the runway. Then she dismounted and watched the rain approach. Philip did the same. After turning his bike, he moved behind her and put his arms around her.

"Is this o.k.?" he said.

"It's nice." She leaned back against him. The approaching rain announced itself with a long low rumble of thunder. This was going to be a local downpour. The sun still shone brightly over the western mountains. Philip inhaled deeply, memorizing the smell of her hair, which now began to stir against his neck and chin as the first exhalation of the oncoming storm breathed down the length of the airstrip. With his next breath he smelled it, that invigorating scent of fresh water and damp earth carried along on an as yet dry breeze. He wondered if that was what a cloud smelled like.

"Maybe one more minute," said Kari. She placed her hands on his arms, preparing to force her release.

"What are you worried about? You've got a much better bike than I do."

She laughed. "I can't believe you're still riding that thing."

"It's very durable. And Mr. Bumbles would never let me get rid of it unless I brought his basket along."

"Wait," said Kari. She tensed. "Can you hear it?"

He could. The sound was hard to describe. A hiss. A low moan. A giant with finger to its lips saying "Shhhhhhhh." The sound of an army of large drops of water striking grass, weeds, stalks of corn, burying themselves in rich earth. "It's time to go," she said.

As they leapt for their bicycles there was another rumble of thunder, much louder this time. They both began peddling as fast as they could down the runway. Philip had to work hard to stay even with Kari. "You kept us too long," she yelled. "I think we're going to get very very wet."

"Shut up and drive," Philip yelled back.

As they burst from between the ranks of corn into the open by the hangar where the two strips intersected, Philip looked first to his right then to his left. He could distinctly see the wall of advancing water already almost parallel with them. "Look," he yelled to Kari. But she was working too hard to look. They flew across the empty tarmac. Philip thought Kari might take shelter in the hangar but she never slowed down. They plunged down the short but steep hill between the hangar and the northernmost cluster of houses. That was where the rain caught them. Philip just had time to register the roar from half a dozen tin roofs before the stinging drops began pelting his back and shoulders. He saw water bounce off Kari's head in front of him. As they rushed by the Van Kleeks', Philip heard Jerry yell from a window something about mothers and a warning about rain. Without looking up he waved.

With the grass immediately slickening, they slowed to make the turn by Kari's house. Philip drew alongside and said, "I guess I'll see you later."

"No way," she said. "We're already soaked. I'm coming with you."

There was no easy way to dart across to Philip's house. The intervening fence meant they had to go through the ditch to the road that connected to the highway, travel down that road to where a gate barred their way, go through the ditch on the other side to get around the gate, then swing around the fence and bike back up the hill along the tree line to Philip's house. The trees gave them some protection, but as wet as they were it really didn't matter. They both dumped their bikes unceremoniously in Philip's yard and dashed for his porch. Mr. Bumbles sat in the doorway regarding them with an expression that said "Well at least I knew enough to beat the rain home." They were both breathing hard. Kari was exhilarated. "Just listen to that rain," she said.

"I'll get us some towels," said Philip. He shook as much water off as he could, gave Mr. Bumbles a quick pat, then went inside. He only had two towels. He grabbed the clean one from a shelf by his bed and threw it through the door to Kari. Then he retrieved his towel from the bathroom. On his way back out he paused in the living room and looked through the doorway at Kari. She was sitting on the porch railing, one leg thrown over the rail, the other resting on the porch. Her head leaned to one side as she observed the rain cascading off the roof just a few feet from her. With her hands she slowly toweled her hair that hung down in front of her right shoulder.

Ever since he had taken Kari in his arms at the end of the airstrip, Philip had been aware of the erotically charged nature of the moment. Indeed the entire frantic flight from the rain had been soaked with eroticism. Watching her now he felt flooded, overwhelmed, entirely over-come. It hurt to look at her, as if all the beauty of the universe was raging through a gaping hole in his chest. He wanted desperately to touch her, but it wasn't particularly sex he craved. The erotic impulse that surged through him was the overwhelming longing to possess beauty. Watching the rain surge across the fields held an erotic charge all its own. But rain could not give itself to the beholder. The potential of this moment was that beauty might turn and yield herself to him. Beauty is truth, and truth beauty. Isn't that what the poet had said? He was drowning in truth.

He stood in the doorway breathing with difficulty. When she turned and looked at him, she seemed made of a material too fragile for this world. He blinked hard, afraid he might tear up, and smiled at her wanly. His head was too full. All he could think of was the lamest line from one of the lamest jokes he'd ever heard. "If I said you had a beautiful body would you hold it against me?"

It took her a moment, but then she laughed delightedly. "That's very clever," she said.

He was momentarily astonished. "It's not original with me. It's an old joke."

She wasn't disappointed. "It's still very clever." He thought that he must be in the Garden of Eden. There was innocence here so pure it made him wince. But then the thought crossed his mind—Am I Adam or the serpent?

He looked at her for a long moment. "I'm desperately attracted to you," he finally said. "Is that a bad thing?"

She returned his gaze for a minute, then got up, crossed the porch, looked around, pushed him just inside his doorway, put her arms around his neck and hugged him with all her strength. She was still soaking wet. Her slender body seemed almost diaphanous. It melted into him. "No," she said. "It's a very good thing." She pulled his face down and kissed him hard. He felt her teeth through her thin lips mash against his mouth. Then she opened her mouth and he tasted the warmth from the interior of her body.

After a moment she collapsed back against him breathing hard. Then she turned in his arms away from him and together they watched the rain. "I wish we could float away," she said. But then something shook her. Was it the inner voice of practicality? Was it the echo of twenty-four years of Christian training? Was it the voice of God? She released herself from him and returned to her seat on the rail. "You're only here a year Philip." It was a statement, a question, a suggestion. "I'm not ready to leave here. Not yet."

"I understand," said Philip. "I don't blame you."

Then her mood changed again. She jumped off the rail and hugged him right out on the porch. "But we've got a year to figure something out."

Later, after the rain stopped, and he had watched her slowly bicycle away he wondered if the ache he felt was the special province of youth. Gordon Lundy had told him as much the other night. They were walking together and Gordon had said that there was a certain quality of life that young people had that he thought he was losing. "It's a zest, an enthusiasm, or what have you. You still have the opportunity for it," he said, grabbing Philip's shoulder. "I'm fighting a rearguard action. And I'll fight it mostly alone. But don't you let one day pass."

Philip wondered if an old man like Gordon still felt what he felt right now. That zest that Gordon spoke of was usually connected with youthful love and its concomitant passions. But Philip knew that he had never experienced that love as it should be experienced. His loves had always been trapped in a turtle shell of guilt and fear, the knowledge that an all-seeing eye was upon him and that it disapproved. But this love felt unencumbered by guilt.  Surely God could not disapprove. He thought this must be what the newly germinated plant feels when, rising above the mud for the first time, it glimpses the sun above. How it must relish the sight! How it must leap toward that warmth! Philip felt as if he were seeing the world clearly for the first time. Nothing could taint this love. It had the stamp of divinity upon it. He knew he was making a memory that would haunt him for a lifetime, and he longed to be possessed by that ghost.

The next day was Sunday. As so often happened after a storm, the following day dawned hot and sticky. When the community gathered for church, not a breath of air stirred in the meeting hall. Women fanned themselves vigorously. Men sat erect endeavoring to honor the service for what it was. Children counted the minutes until they were free. Philip was miserable. He watched sweat drip off the earlobe of the hefty man sitting directly in front of him. He noted that it took a full minute and twenty seconds for the sweat to gather from around the ear, pool its resources into a drop large enough to dislodge from the slick lobe, and then land softly on a beefy shoulder where it mingled with the stain that soon covered the entire upper half of the man's body. When the man bent forward to grab a hymnal the creases in the back of his neck parted to reveal oil slicks. Tough conditions for a preacher, Philip thought.

Philip's mood didn't improve when he saw who that preacher was destined to be. He had heard some fairly decent sermons from various missionaries the past few weeks, but today was Carnley Sorenson's turn and he mounted the pulpit with an eagerness that seemed unseemly on such a hot desultory day. Despite the suffocating damp, Carnley's body snapped and crackled in the pulpit like heat lightning. His text was Matthew 7: 13 – 14. Jesus said, "Enter through the narrow gate; for the gate is wide and the way is broad that leads to destruction, and there are many who enter through it. For the gate is small and the way is narrow that leads to life, and there are few who find it."

Philip thought it an interesting text for this crowd, but he was quickly disappointed. Carnley had little imagination. Or maybe it was simply a lack of desire to see anything other in the text than an affirmation of his chosen way of life. Philip held his breath as Bobby's father ranted against all who ignored the call of Christ and paraded down the broad way to their doom. Carnley's catalog of heedless hell-bound miscreants included Catholics, drunkards, homosexuals, people who had sex of any kind outside of marriage, children who were disobedient to parents, secular humanists, jungle tribes who had never heard the good news, liars, and then, yes there it was, Philip had known he wouldn't be able to resist it, effeminate hippies and drug users. At least he hadn't said long-haired hippies. Philip thought he had a little wiggle room there. But still he winced.

He glanced around the room. Surely the assembled missionaries had heard this all before. Surely they had all made their choice for the narrow way. But then he thought that such sermons were probably somehow important to evangelical faith. By reaffirming over and over the simple truths, you defined your community over against what was perceived to be a hostile world. Philip supposed that might be comforting. And if he somehow managed to shut out the messenger, the twitching sizzling man in the pulpit, he thought that maybe after all it was all right. These people *had* discovered the narrow way. They *were* the insiders. You could feel at peace here. No matter what happened out there, here at Ilusan you were with the protected chosen. I could be worse places, Philip thought.

Afterward Joseph Haaf corralled him. Joseph was streaming with sweat. The long strands of his comb-over draped like lank seaweed across the empty spaces on his skull. He was clearly irritated. "Good day to think about hell," he groused.

"But hell is a dry heat," said Philip.

Joseph wasn't amused. "Name one person here who needed to hear that sermon. Outside of maybe you and other effeminate hippies. You're not a drug user are you?" He glared around the auditorium as if he longed for someone to pick a fight with him. But folks were caught up in their own conversations.

"Don't hold back," said Philip. "Go tell Carnley what you think of his little pep talk."

"You'd like that wouldn't you." Joseph eyed Philip quizzically. "I've heard you two have issues."

"Come on. We had one little exchange on the volleyball court. How do such things get around so quickly?"

"Celia was on the next court over. If there are human beings within a square mile of her, she knows their most intimate secrets. She's got antennae like My Favorite Martian."

Just then Sally joined them. She was holding a small poster. "Look Mr. Andrews," she said, "next Saturday is movie night. They're showing a movie about the rapture."

Philip took the poster from her. He and Joseph looked it over. The film was called "A Thief in the Night."

"Great," said Joseph. "Just what we need. A showing of the worst film ever made in the western world. A bunch of idiot Christian kids who can't act and who clearly never washed their hair running around trying to save the world. All that and the rapture and the longest dullest chase scene in movie history."

"Clearly you've seen this masterpiece," said Philip. "Well Sally and I haven't. And we're going to have a good time, aren't we Sally? I'll bring the sodas. What do you think?"

"I'll make popcorn," Sally said.

But before the good residents of Ilusan gathered at the meeting hall for movie night, another drama played out in the same building, a silly drama in Philip's opinion, but nevertheless a drama which led to a good bit of tension in the community between those who listened to the voice of Carnley Sorenson and those who trusted the youthful instincts of the long-haired seventh and eighth grade teacher. By the time the lights darkened on Saturday night and the first scenes of the evangelical block-buster flickered to life on the screen, a fault line in the community had opened up, a fault line that would remain buried for the most part over the next few months, despite some unsettling and very public shocks, until it erupted in the earthquake that would forever mark all in the community for good or ill.

It began that Friday afternoon with a practical joke. When Philip got home from school, Timmy Mullen, Bobby Sorenson, and Donny Meyer were hard at work on Philip's porch injecting red pepper juice into a cube of Tarzan bubble gum. "Look Mr. Andrews," said Donny, "we're gonna play a joke on Danny." Danny, Donny's twin brother, and Charlie Pilarski were the two most picked on boys in Philip's class. But where Charlie relished his notoriety and seemed to feed off the relatively good natured abuse, Danny took it more to heart. More than once, Philip had urged the boys to ease off the kid. He couldn't do much about the fact that the other kids so frequently ditched him, but when he was around, Philip tried to include the boy as much as possible. He didn't say anything about this prank, however, because it looked fairly harmless.

The boys had half a dozen shiny red, orange, and yellow peppers laid out on Philip's steps. The peppers were the size of a couple of large vitamins. Philip could tell by the oil content of the skin that they were fiercely hot. The boys inserted a syringe into each pepper and drew out what liquid content they could. They then unwrapped a piece of Tarzan bubble gum, the local gum that was perfect for such an experiment because it had the thickness of a Tootsie Roll. The boys injected the content of the peppers into the heart of the gum, then wrapped it carefully back up. All that remained was to casually offer a stick of gum to an unsus-pecting brother.

As they worked the boys told Philip that they, along with most of the rest of the older boys, were planning a campout by the pool for that evening. They had already pitched several tents by the spillway. Philip noted that it had rained the past few nights and that it looked threatening again. Had they made contingency plans in case they got flooded out? Bobby thought they'd probably have to all go home in that event. Philip suggested that if they wanted to continue the campout they could always grab their sleeping bags and make for the one building that was fairly close and large enough to offer shelter to all of them, the meeting hall. The boys thought that a good idea. And the conversation moved on.

It did indeed begin to rain hard about dusk. Philip thought of the boys several times that evening as he read, first by the electric light and then, after 9:30, beside the Coleman lantern he had purchased from the commissary. "I bet our boys are getting pretty damp," he observed several times to Mr. Bumbles. About 11:30 he turned off his lamp and went out and sat on the porch. Bumbles followed and together they sat listening to the rain and the frogs. Sometime after midnight, or so Philip estimated the next day, he heard the familiar panting of Lechón coming up the path by the fence. Ben's flashlight illuminated the entrance to the yard. "Good evening Ben," Philip called. Mr. Bumbles sprang for the porch rail.

Philip had gotten to know the night watchman quite well. At least twice a week, sometimes three or four nights in a row, they engaged in late night conversations. Ben always made it by Philip's corner of the base sometime between 11:30 and 12:30. If Philip was up and on his porch, he called the man in for a visit. Philip noted that Lechón automatically turned into his yard now even before he said anything. Their routine was the same. Ben would stop with the dog at the foot of his stairs. Philip would invite him to rest a moment and have a drink. Ben would suggest that tonight he should be going on about his rounds. For the first several weeks, it took Philip three invitations to get the man onto his porch, but last week Philip noted with pleasure that it had only required two. He thought by Christmas Ben might just walk straight in and sit down. But he knew that as polite as Filipinos were, his nightly invitations might never get below two per visit. Still, once seated on his porch, the night watchman invariably relaxed and appeared to genuinely enjoy the company. Philip was learning a good bit about Filipino history and culture from the man.

But on this night Philip noticed immediately that Ben was agitated. Despite the pelting rain he stood at the foot of the stairs and appeared reluctant to come onto the porch. Finally he stepped up just enough to be out of the worst of the rain. He was wearing a heavy raincoat. "Mr. Andrews," he said, "maybe you could come with me."

Philip was surprised. The thought of going out in the rain wasn't appealing. "What's up Ben?"

Ben was clearly uncomfortable. "The boys are in the meeting hall."

"Oh," Philip laughed. "It's o.k. They were going to camp out by the spillway, but I'm sure they got too wet down there and decided to take cover. They should be all right."

But Ben wasn't convinced. "They are noisy. Someone might see them."

"I'm sure you're the only one out in this. And the rain will cover up any noise they make, won't it?"

Finally Ben came out with it. "Mr. Andrews. They have taken off their clothes."

Philip gaped at the man for a moment, then put his head in his hands and groaned. He was beginning to get the picture.

"I thought I should go to Mr. St. Clair, but I know that you know the children well, and I didn't want to cause problems. Perhaps if you spoke to them."

Philip was already heading inside. "I'll get an umbrella."

As they walked together to the meeting hall, Philip thanked Ben for coming to him first. "You did the right thing. I'm sure they're just boys being boys, but you're right, if someone happened to come by, it could be quite a scene."

Philip had armed himself with a powerful flashlight, but he followed Ben's lead and turned it off as they approached the hall. Might as well get the lay of the land before ruining the boys' party. Ben looped the dog's chain around the stair railing. "I'll stay outside," he told Philip. When Philip protested, he said, "It will be better."

Philip climbed the stairs and stood quietly in the back of the hall. He could hear boyish laughter. Someone called someone an anus-eye. Philip thought he recognized Donny's voice. As his eyes adjusted Philip saw at least four boys standing in the meeting hall windows. They were urinating into the rain. Other boys were moving around the stage. He cut his light onto the urinating quartet. There were gasps and the boys all dove for cover. One peed all over his neighbor as he whipped around in surprise. Philip's light next caught naked boys diving for their sleeping bags on the stage. He walked down the center aisle. When he reached the pulpit he said, "It's me fellows. Mr. Andrews."

"Mr. Andrews?!" Philip recognized Donny for sure this time. "What are you doing here?"

The four boys who had been in the windows were hiding in the pews. "Why don't you guys come on up and get in your bags," said Philip. "I'll turn off the light for a second." The boys scrambled for their bags.

"Timmy peed on me!" It was Drew, Bobby's brother. Everyone laughed, including Philip.

"On that note," Philip said, "I suppose it's about time for everybody to get their clothes back on and settle down for the night. Drew, if you have to, go outside and wash off in the rain barrel."

"Are we in trouble?" someone asked.

"No you're not in trouble," said Philip. "There's nothing particularly wrong with running around the meeting hall naked. But, and this is a big but, I want you guys to think about something for a second. I know it's late and it's raining, but what if one of the girls had walked by? Or one of the ladies on the center? Or, and this is the real question, didn't anybody think about Ben? You guys know he's out every night. You can be thankful he came and got me. I want you to imagine some of the other people he could have chosen to go to. What conversation might you be having right now? And what would your parents say tomorrow?"

"Yep, that wouldn't have been good," said Bobby.

"How come nobody thought about Ben?" asked Donny.

"It was Timmy's idea," said Charlie.

"It doesn't matter whose idea it was," said Philip. "Like I said, you're not in trouble. I'm not even sure you'd have been in trouble with someone else. Just think things through before you go running around naked."

"Are you going to tell our parents?" It was Bobby.

"I'm heading for your house right now," said Philip. "I'm going to bang on the door, wake up your mother, and tell her that her sons don't have any clothes. And would she please come get them to spare us all that sight." A few boys snickered uncertainly.

"My parents would kill us," said Bobby. He had sobered right up at the mention of parents.

"Can I go to my sleeping bag?" asked Donny. Donny had hidden behind a curtain on the stage. When he went for his bag, Philip flicked his light on him. Donny raised his hands, made peace signs, and said,

"Peace friends!" Then he flexed his muscles and boomed, "I am Thor." Finally he did a three hundred sixty degree rotating moon just to make sure he didn't miss anybody. The boys busted up. Philip had to laugh too.

"Very nice Thor," he said. "Thank you for that show. I'm sure none of us will ever forget it. I'll be having nightmares for months."

"Is Ben outside?" Bobby asked.

"Yes he is," said Philip.

The thought of Ben observing their shenanigans quieted the boys a bit.

"Sorry about getting you out of bed Mr. Andrews," said Bobby.

"Oh, I wasn't in bed. I was reading and then Mr. Bumbles and I were just sitting on the porch enjoying the rain when I was summoned. But now I would like to go to bed." He flashed his light around on the group of pensive faces, asked the boys if they were o.k., then, upon receiving their nods and assurances, he went outside to join Ben.

"They'll be all right," he told the watchman, "especially now that they've been reminded that you're up and about. But after this little adventure, you and Lechón really must come by for a soft drink."

Ben smiled. "Come on big dog," he said, "let's go have a drink with Mr. Andrews." The German Shepherd fell in silently beside them as they walked back up the hill through the pouring rain.

About 11:00 the next morning, Philip was relaxing on his porch. He was tired and was thinking of taking a nap. After his visit to the meeting hall and conversation with Ben, he hadn't managed to get to bed until after 2:00. Then he'd had to rise at 6:00 to golf with Jerry and Sally. After golf he had taken a long swim. Now he just wanted to rest until seeing Kari later in the day. But it was not to be. Matt St. Clair pulled into his yard on his motorcycle. When he saw Philip on the porch, he kept the bike running. He politely asked if Philip would accompany him to the office.

"What's up?" asked Philip. "I was thinking of taking a nap."

"We're just trying to clear up what happened in the meeting hall last night."

Philip sat up and groaned. "So Ben said something after all."

"No, Ben didn't mention anything, although I'm curious to find out what role he played. One of the boys told their parents."

"So what do you need me for? I just went down and told them to cool it."

"The parents and dorm parents are at the office. As are the boys. We just want to get all the facts straight."

Philip could see that he wasn't going to get his nap. "All right." He climbed onto the back of the motorcycle. Matt didn't say anything during their brief trip. As Philip followed Matt into the low office complex next to the meeting hall he noticed the boys sitting around a table in the room just inside the door. They were all bent over writing something.

Philip supposed the boys might be in trouble for camping in the building that was used as a church and that some of the parents might be mildly upset because they were running around naked. When he entered the room full of parents and dorm parents, he quickly realized he was swimming in a far deeper pool. All the boys' names were on a chalkboard. The group appeared to have been attempting to categorize the level of their involvement. Category A was titled "Leaders." Philip noticed Donny's name. Category B was for "Followers/Participants/Without Clothes." Most of the boys' names were in this group. Category C was titled "Followers/Observers/Clothed." The names in this category were primarily the younger boys, the fifth and sixth graders. Philip observed that the Sorenson boys and Timmy Mullen had not yet been placed. Carnley Sorenson's face was red and he appeared to have been arguing with Don Barker, the dorm parent for the older kids, about how to properly categorize his sons. A and B, thought Philip. William Mullen, Timmy's father, was also standing and pointing. Philip smiled to himself. Definitely A. Everyone stopped and stared at him as he entered. Their gazes were nervous, suspicious. "This looks like a rational response," Philip muttered as he sat down.

Matt took over the meeting. "Now that Philip's here, I suggest he tell us exactly what happened last night."

Philip took another look around the room. It was crowded and hot. "Can I ask first what exactly is going on here? Do I need legal counsel?" Humor was always a good fallback. He felt his back stiffening at the scene before him. He desperately wanted to be polite. Matt and Don Barker smiled. Everyone else just looked at him.

Matt said, "We're just trying to get to the bottom of what happened last night."

"What is that?" Philip pointed at the board.

Ruth Sorenson spoke. Philip had never heard Bobby's mother speak. She always deferred to Carnley. But now her lips quivered with revulsion. "We must find out who the leaders in this homosexual activity were and what part you played in guiding our boys down this path."

Philip was so stunned all he could say was, "What?!" Then the second part of the sentence hit him. "What?! Are you out of your mind?" He felt a cold finger crawling deep in his belly. He'd seen faces like this before. "Look folks. This was boys being boys. Nothing more. Do you have any evidence to make a leap from a bunch of boys horsing around to homosexual activity? Did any of the boys suggest anything like that?"

"Maybe where you're from boys being together late at night naked is called horsing around." Carnley looked at him with undisguised disgust. "But we protect our children here from such influences, and I don't think they would have thought of doing such a thing if someone from outside hadn't put the idea in their minds."

"And just how did I do that?" Philip could feel himself being drawn into a conversation he didn't want to have.

"Was it your idea for the boys to go into the meeting hall?" Carnley spoke softly.

Philip began to say "Of course not," but then he remembered the conversation on his porch the day before. "Yes, I told them that if the rain got too hard they might think about seeking shelter in the meeting hall. It was the only nearby building that I knew of that would be big enough for them all. What of it?"

"When did you tell them that?" asked Matt.

"They were on my porch yesterday afternoon. They were talking about their campout. It seemed a logical idea to me."

"What were they doing on your porch?" asked Carnley.

"What they always do. They stop by to talk. I'm their teacher. I build relationships with students. That's what teachers do."

"Do you regularly have the boys over to your house with no other adults present?" It was Ruth Sorenson again. As it hit Philip where the conversation was going, his anger overwhelmed his caution. He didn't often lose his temper, but it had happened enough that he knew the symptoms. He could feel it race to fill him, like a storm boiling up suddenly on a summer afternoon. He wished Jerry, or Joseph, or Gordon, or Fossia, or Kari, or any of the other teachers were present. He needed an ally, someone who would see how ludicrous this all was. He remembered the dean's voice and face at Bible college. He took a deep breath.

"Look folks. You are about to make accusations that you will regret. I have been here barely a month, but I have grown to care deeply for your children. I spend a great deal of time with them. They are in my classroom all day long. At their invitation I play games with them after school and on Friday nights. My home is open to them any time they want to stop by. Now if you are going to accuse me of hurting these kids, you had better have hard evidence. Bring them in and ask them. But if anyone accuses me of anything like that again, I'm walking out of this room. No that's not right. If you want to talk about last night, fine. But if any of you suggest anything again like what the Sorensons have just insinuated, man or woman, I'll . . . ." He wanted to say "I'll tear your heart out," but he wrenched the words out of his mouth before he could verbalize them. He tried desperately to dial down the pounding in his chest and the heat in his mind.

Even without his final threat, the missionaries were astonished. They gaped at Philip like he was a Gila monster that had just dropped through the ceiling. They weren't sure if he was dangerous, but they wanted desperately to stay out of range. Philip and Carnley stared each other down. Don Barker finally said, "Philip's right. I've said from the beginning that this is ridiculous. Carnley, you and Ruth are way out of line. Now I want to hear from Philip exactly what happened last night and that's it. Nobody is accusing Philip of anything. Nobody is accusing the boys of anything. We just want to know what happened." He looked at Philip. "I'm sorry Philip. Please tell us what happened last night."

Philip repeated his story of the afternoon. Then he cut to the evening. He told about Ben coming to fetch him.

Matt interrupted. "I'm sorry Philip. Like Don said I'm not accusing you of anything. But why did Ben come to you and not to me?"

Philip thought quickly. He didn't want to get Ben in trouble. "Ben and I have gotten to know each other quite well. He knows that I'm often up late at night. I can't get used to going to bed at 9:30." A few in the room chuckled. "We've had quite a few late night conversations when he passes my house on his rounds. I think Ben just thought that rather than wake you on a rainy night, he'd see if I was already up. He knows I know the kids and thought maybe I could get them to settle down."

Carnley muttered loud enough for all to hear, "What I want to know is what he's doing every night up so late."

Philip whirled on him. "What business is it of yours what I do at night? I turn into a werewolf and howl at the moon. I've been devouring local peasants by the score. What do you think I do at night? I read, grade papers, sit with my cat and enjoy the outdoors. You ought to try it sometime. Reading. Books. It's called an education."

Carnley was fiercely red and began to rise from his seat. Don slammed his hand on the table. "Enough! Let me remind all of us that we are Christians. And we're supposed to be adults." He glared at both Carnley and Philip.

Philip held up his hands as a mea culpa. He continued the story. He decided not to mention the boys urinating out the window. He simply said that he observed them running around naked. The next time one of the parents spoke, it was William Mullen. "Did you tell the boys that they wouldn't get in trouble, that you wouldn't tell their parents?"

"Not in so many words, but yes, I had no plans to tell anybody."

Ruth Sorenson couldn't control herself. "You didn't think we would want to know that our children were involved in something like this?! Why would you ever decide not to tell us?"

Philip was deliberately patronizing. He found he had no patience for the couple. "Mrs. Sorenson perhaps you'd look around this room right now. Look at what is going on here. Look at those ridiculous categories on the chalk board. And you wonder why I didn't want to tell anyone?! Maybe because I knew you'd do exactly what you're doing. I knew you'd blow this all out of proportion and turn a fun night out for your boys into a witch hunt. It frightens me to even think of what's going on in that other room where your kids are right now. What are they doing? Writing out confessions?!"

The people in the room had a hard time meeting his eye. Philip was suddenly tired. "Actually what I just said isn't even true. I had no idea what direction this would go. If I'd thought for even one second that such a scene as this one might materialize I certainly wouldn't have said anything. But the truth is I simply didn't think it was that big a deal. I tried to use it as a teaching moment, to help the boys think through the implications of what might have happened if a woman or girl had walked by and seen them. Sometimes you just have to get children to slow down and think a bit. Who knows, I very well might have mentioned the incident to Matt or one of the other adults later. I don't know. But if I had mentioned it, it certainly wouldn't have been to make a big deal out of it. I just would have wondered if I'd done the right thing."

The room was quiet. "I'll say one more thing." He looked slowly around the room. "Your children are the most wonderful kids I've ever met. Not one of those boys did anything mean-spirited or abnormal for their age last night. Kids that age in the States right now are doing drugs, drinking, smoking, having sex, getting in trouble with the police. And you're in a twist because your boys took their clothes off on a campout. And please trust me, none of them are homosexual. They're barely sexual at all. But they are boys. Does anybody remember what that was like? It's a volatile condition and it's frustratingly incurable. The only prescription is time."

After a moment, Matt said, "Thank you Philip. Unless there are any more questions, I think you can go." There were no more questions. At least none that anyone was willing to voice just then.

Philip's afternoon with Kari didn't go quite as planned. They had just begun their bike ride when he told her about what had transpired over the past twenty-four hours. She insisted they go back to the house immediately and tell Fossia. "She's our boss, she's smart, she knows this community, and she needs to know what they're saying about her teacher."

Philip spent the rest of the afternoon with the two women. Fossia was furious. She paced up and down the living room. Philip had a hard time convincing her not to immediately convene a meeting with everyone involved. "You should have insisted that I be there," she kept saying. Philip argued that he'd had no idea what he was getting into and, once in, events moved much too quickly to get out. But he had to admit he appreciated Fossia's fury. Finally she decided she would meet with Matt St. Clair on Monday and let her position on the matter be known. Later, over a dinner of sandwiches which the two women threw together before they all went to movie night, Fossia said, "You know the problem is Philip that you're a single man and you live alone. That was probably a mistake. They never should have let you live alone. You've left yourself open to suspicion."

Philip protested. "But what about all the single women? There are single women all over the center."

"Two things," said Fossia. "One, we all live with a partner. And two, and this is the main thing, we're women. You're a man. Everyone knows that men are more prone to sexual temptation." Kari and Philip stared at her astonished. The principal glared back for a moment and then grimaced. "O.k. maybe that's a bit of an overstatement, but don't think for a minute that an awful lot of our folks don't harbor those kinds of thoughts." She thought for a minute. "Here's what needs to happen. It's time for the two of you to start being seen together in public. Sorry Philip, Kari doesn't tell me everything, but I do know that your bike rides aren't just bike rides. You two have a yen for each other. Well your yen has to go public. That means sitting together tonight at the movies. That means sitting together at church and prayer meeting. Folks have to see that Philip is a normal man and that he's chosen a normal young woman. That should quiet the kind of talk you heard today."

Kari looked at Philip. "I think she's right."

"You don't mind?" he asked.

"Nope. It's time."

Fossia was appraising Philip. "And I wish you'd cut your hair," she said. "It makes people suspicious."

"Don't do that," said Kari. "I like your hair."

"Well another thing then," said Fossia. "What about you and that girl Sally? She's always hanging around. If they're talking about you and the boys, they'll be talking next about you and that girl. You better never be alone with that girl in your house."

Philip explained that while Sally had never been in his house, she spent a lot of time on his porch. "And she's always alone," he said. "She doesn't move in a pack like the boys. And she resists stopping by when anybody else is there."

They discussed the situation for awhile, finally agreeing that Philip should keep reaching out to Sally as long as she remained only on his porch. But Fossia also insisted that Philip let her parents know that she was spending time there. Philip agreed to talk to them as soon as possible.

"Can Kari visit me on my porch?" Philip thought he'd take a shot.

"Only on your porch and never at night," said Fossia. She didn't smile when she said it.

Movie night was a big deal at Ilusan. It ranked right up there with skit nights. The films shown at the center were sent down from one of the western embassies in Manila. Most of the missionaries had not been film goers back home; in fact many felt quite strongly that attending even so-called good movies was a sin in as much as it lent support to Hollywood. You might as well pull a twenty-spot out of your wallet and place it directly in Lucifer's incendiary hands. It was pretty much the same thing. Consequently the powers that be were particular about the films they ordered for the center. Typical fare was a travelogue or two, maybe a Perry Mason episode, a Billy Graham film, and cartoons. Everyone at Ilusan remembered the scandal of '75, when someone, exactly who had placed the order was still under dispute three years later, had decided to show "Fiddler on the Roof." There were old ladies who still hadn't recovered from the scene where ghosts visited the sleeping Tevye and Golde. Carnley had fulminated about demons being the only real ghosts for weeks. What would the Filipinos think if they knew the missionaries were viewing films that made light of demonic activity? The center had not risked a Hollywood movie since. Tonight promised to be a big deal. A genuine Christian epic was something to be celebrated.

As Philip, Kari and Fossia drew near the meeting hall, Philip suddenly remembered his aside to Sally the previous Sunday. "I promised Sally I'd bring sodas tonight," he told the women. "She might show up with popcorn." He asked Kari to sit with Sally if she was already there and to tell the girl he'd be there momentarily.

"Bring me a Pepsi," Kari called after him as he ran for his house.

When he arrived back at the meeting hall, he realized his trip had been a waste of time. Celia Haaf had opened up the back room and was selling drinks and candy from the commissary through the window. "Yea, but she doesn't have fresh popcorn," Kari said when he sat next to her. Sally had indeed made a huge bowl of popcorn. The girl filled a small bowl and handed it across Kari to Philip. He reciprocated with a Coke. He glanced around the room. The Sorensons were nowhere to be seen. But Fossia's plan still seemed to work. He and Kari were noticed. There were nudges, whispers, turned heads, nods. Gordon Lundy slid into the seat in front of them. "Hello kids," he said. He squeezed Sally's knee. Sally smiled and then politely asked Uncle Gordon if he would scoot over a bit so she could see better.

The evening began with a travelogue from the Canadian embassy. As soon as the title appeared the kids all cheered. Clearly "Tejon" was a familiar favorite. In this film, Tejon, a chubby young man, found himself on a one-person open railway car traveling across Canada. His adventures were slapstick and sophomoric, involving tunnels, trains, rain, mud, bird droppings, all the usual suspects, but Philip found himself enjoying the film along with everyone else. He shot frequent glances at Sally. The girl followed the film intently, but the only time Philip saw her laugh was when the runaway rail car plowed through a hayloft and Tejon hurtled toward a lake with a large gray cat wrapped around his head. "It's Mr. Bumbles," Philip whispered to Sally. He was rewarded with one of her rare luminous smiles.

Philip initially enjoyed the main feature as well. Joseph had been right. "A Thief in the Night" was a train wreck, but fun in that "I can't believe what I'm seeing" sort of way. Several lightly groomed Christian teenagers lamely attempted to convince a group of equally homely heathen teens that Jesus was about to return and they'd better get right or they'd get left. Philip would have left the entire lot of them. Their hair will get grease on the heavenly sofas, he thought. It was easy to tell the soon-to-be-saved heathens from the soon-to-be-left-behind heathens. The good heathens listened to the speaker's tedious lecture about the end times with intense looks on their faces, while the bad heathens just wanted sex. The heathen boys leered indiscriminately at girls both righteous and unrighteous, while the Christian boys had clearly been neutered.

The most unconscionable scene in Philip's opinion was when a little girl woke up in a seemingly empty house and, freaked out by all the rapture talk to which she'd been exposed, began to shriek, thinking she'd been left behind. When her parents rushed in they capitalized on their daughter's terror to lead her in the sinner's prayer. Now there's a genuine conversion, Philip thought. She'll be a bitter hooker by the time she's seventeen.

Eventually, and not nearly soon enough for Philip's taste (after twenty minutes or so the comic appeal had worn off), a white cloud appeared, some jangly music played, and a guy who had been mowing his lawn was no longer there. Thank you Jesus for ridding the film of that character! From there the film regressed into a series of long shots of the moping heroine meandering city streets filled with leering left-behinders. Tragically she had neglected to invite Jesus into her heart before the cloud wandered by. The trick, if you were left behind, was not to get stamped with the mark of the beast, the dreaded 666. Once branded there was no hope for you. Pitchforks, caves, and uncomfortable heat were in your future. The heroine gamely avoided the mark and eventually was chased into a remote area by the Antichrist's police force. The Antichrist did not appear to be well funded, as his forces consisted of about five people driving second-hand vans. When cornered on a bridge, the heroine leapt to her death rather than take the mark, only to suddenly wake up in her bed. It had all been a dream. Rats, thought Philip, and I was all ready to repent.

As the film progressed and Philip's internal dialog changed from humor to something approaching disgust, he was stunned to realize that the majority of the audience did not share his sentiments. Clearly he and Joseph were in the minority. He tried to engage Kari in whispered mockery, but she shushed him. After his third shushing, he realized she was enrapt. He peered at Sally. The girl's expression was typically intense, but she had stopped eating popcorn. When the little girl screamed upon waking from her nap, Kari stiffened beside him, and Sally looked pale. As her parents led her in prayer, Philip saw tears on Kari's cheeks. Sally looked terrified. The entire audience was deathly quiet. He looked for Joseph. Joseph was asleep in the back row, or maybe he was praying. It was hard to tell. But if he'd had to put money on it, he would have guessed sleeping.

When the film ended, Philip noticed many red eyes. Men smiled at each other and shook their heads. That was intense, he heard several say. More than one child was crying. He tried to say something to Sally, but she thanked him for the soda and left immediately. He walked Kari home in silence.

When Philip arrived at church the next morning Kari was waiting for him outside by the bell. "We've got to put the plan into action," she said. She had seemingly recovered from the film-induced melancholy of the evening before. She even mentioned it. "Sorry about last night," she said. "Those kinds of movies freak me out." Her hand flitted around his arm. She seemed to be thinking of taking his hand as they entered, but must have decided such a gesture might be overkill. But they walked in side-by-side and sat together.

The service was led by Joe Washington. He was the dorm parent for kids in the middle grades, roughly fourth through sixth. He was a slender earnest man with thinning blond hair. At the conclusion of his competent sermon on the woman at the well, he stepped from behind the pulpit and was joined at the front by several other men. "Last night," he began, "our community was witness to an extraordinary film." He paused and appeared to have difficulty maintaining control. He took his glasses off and wiped them with his shirt tail. "When Candace and I got back home we found several of our kids in a very emotional state. They were very receptive to the gospel and we prayed with them for quite some time. We thought that this morning there might be others who would like prayer, especially among our children. As we close the service, I'd like to invite any who were affected by the movie last night and who want to make sure that they are right with God to come forward and receive prayer. We don't want anybody to be left behind when Jesus returns. Parents, dorm parents, and teachers are welcome to accompany their children to the front."

Philip held his breath as from here and there kids began to go forward. He wanted to feel good about what was happening. After all, what could be wrong with children going forward to dedicate their lives to God? Maybe Jesus wouldn't have jumped out from behind a wall with a Halloween mask on to get them moving, but could the end result be bad? Philip found it hard to seriously think so. They were kids. Their lives wouldn't be settled here. They had a long way to go and many roads to follow. After all he had done something similar when he begged Jesus to come into his heart every night of his young life.  He knew he had been motivated by precisely this sort of fear. And he hadn't turned out so terribly bad. Carnley Sorenson might disagree, and he'd certainly been down some unapproved roads, but he was still a Christian. At least he thought he was. He wanted to be. He just didn't want to be Carnley.

He was yanked from his reverie when Kari got up. He couldn't help himself. He grabbed her arm. There was no way she was going down there. "Philip!" She was astonished. She sat back down. "Rebecca Stanton just went forward. She's the sweetest girl. She talks to me in the library all the time. Joe said teachers should come down to pray for their kids. I'm going to pray with her."

"Oh, sorry." Philip just shook his head. "I'm sorry." Kari looked hard at him again, then went down to join Rebecca. Philip looked around to see if anyone had noticed him grab her. He hoped they hadn't. He supposed forcibly preventing someone from going forward in a meeting would be an unpardonable sin. Probably one of the millstone ones. Put the millstone around his neck and throw him overboard mateys. He tried to stop someone from gettin' saved. Philip couldn't believe what he'd just done.

It suddenly occurred to him that some of his kids might have gone forward. He checked. The Meyer twins went home every weekend. Their father was the doctor in Malaybalay. Not much chance one of them would have bolted for the front anyway. The Sorensons hadn't even attended movie night. Probably a punishment of some sort. Old Carnley would probably be pissed that his boys had missed the rapture fright. He saw the family now. Bobby was staring straight ahead. So was Carnley. Drew was reading a hymnal. Ruth was praying. Then Philip saw her. Mary Michaels stood right in the middle down front. She had adopted a sweet angelic pose. She was being prayed for by a woman Philip didn't recognize. The girl practically had the Bible memorized. If she wasn't going up, there wasn't much hope for any of the rest of them. He was not about to go down to pray with her.

Truth was nothing could have gotten him down front. He had been in these sorts of meetings all his life and had never gone forward. Too self conscious. Of course the fact that he'd never gone forward was one of the primary reasons he'd agonized in prayer during so many late dark nights. Somewhere in the Gospels Jesus said that he would be ashamed of any person who was ashamed of him. And the primary way in Philip's community of demonstrating that you weren't ashamed of Jesus was to march down front. Either that or pass tracts to strangers. Philip left his in public restrooms, usually on the urinals. Philip tried to explain to Jesus during his late night pleadings that it wasn't him he was ashamed of. He was just too embarrassed to go down front. But he had always doubted that explanation would wash on judgment day. His father certainly didn't think so.

Philip watched Kari pray for her little friend. When they were done, Rebecca hugged her. It was an indescribably sweet scene. Watching her, he loved her. It was as simple as that. He noticed Annabel praying with about four of her tiny charges. As Kari came back to her seat, Philip wondered about Sally. He looked for her. She was sitting by her mother and father on the far side of the room. She was frozen in her seat, staring down at her lap. Philip wondered what she was thinking of all this. He determined to ask her at some point.

After church Gordon corralled Philip and Kari. "I'm so glad to see you two together in public," he beamed. "You must come over for lunch. Who else should we invite?"

As they walked together to Gordon's, Kari slipped her hand into Philip's. "So you didn't want me getting saved?" she said. "What was that all about?" Then she started laughing. "It doesn't matter," she said. "I think it was a sweet gesture. Horrible maybe in one way. But sweet nonetheless."

Philip finally thought of something to say. "You're the only person on this earth that I care about enough to try to stop her from getting saved."

Kari shrieked with laughter, then tried to stifle it. "Don't you dare look at me at Gordon's," she finally said. "I'll lose it, and I don't want to have to explain this to him."

Sunday afternoons were prime nap time as far as Philip was concerned. His only regret was that there was no Sunday paper. The Sunday paper was the best nap inducer ever invented. He grabbed some student book reports. They would be adequately soporific. During the month he had been at Ilusan more and more of his furniture had migrated onto the porch until now four chairs and a couch were scattered haphazardly along the rail. He brought a pillow from inside and stretched out on the couch. Mr. Bumbles soon discovered him and climbed onto his chest. Philip idly rubbed the cat's shoulders. Whenever he drifted off, Bumbles reached up and tapped his cheek with his paw. Apparently he wasn't going to get much of a nap, at least until Bumbles was tired of his shoulder rub. If the cheek tap didn't rouse him, the cat hooked his lower lip with a claw, drug it open, then let it snap back shut. Philip decided no sleep was worth the lip snap. That was humiliating. Worse, he didn't know where that paw had been, or rather, he could guess where it had been and he didn't care for the image. "All right Bumbles," he said, "I'll rub you until you're sated."

He thought about his conversation with Matt St. Clair after church. The man had been abjectly apologetic for the proceedings of the day before. His strong face was twisted into a squint of shame. He admitted to Philip that although he was the base administrator, sometimes men like Carnley tied him into knots. He didn't know how to assert a contrary opinion when someone invoked God or the Bible or sin. "My brain just shuts down," he said. "How can you argue against that? Later I might think of a different spin to put on things, but I'm just not smart enough to argue with those fellows who really know the Bible. Once Carnley started talking about homosexuality I just started having these terrible thoughts and I didn't know what to say."

Philip had always liked the man, and he assured Matt that he understood. "I don't always know what to say either. Sometimes it's best just to lose your temper. That shuts them up long enough to let you think of an escape route."

Matt smiled. "I almost did later after you left," he admitted. Apparently one of the boys, in his written confession, gave an account of Donny's perp walk when he had flexed and mooned everybody. Philip groaned. "Yea," said Matt, "that really set Carnley and Ruth off. They wanted Donny kicked out of school. And of course they drew all sorts of conclusions about you, because you flashed your light on him."

"I bet they did," said Philip.

The only thing that had quieted them down was when Don Barker and then Matt had put their feet down. They reminded Carnley that if he wanted to kick Donny out, it would require bringing Fossia in on the decision. She would want to talk to her teacher, which would mean dragging Philip back in. And then there were Donny's parents to consider. If the Sorensons thought any member of that party would go along with their half-cocked suspension, they had another think coming. The meeting had broken up with considerable acrimony. Carnley had vowed that his boys would not be associating with Donny in the future. Matt reminded him that Bobby was in the A category along with Donny. In fact they were the only two boys to wind up in that category. At that Carnley had said, "I'll deal with my son," and stormed out of the building, dragging Bobby behind him. Philip shuddered at the thought of Carnley and Bobby alone in a room.

Philip was torn from his thoughts by the voice of a young girl calling, "Mr. Andrews come quick." He sat up as Sally rushed into his yard. "There's a bird by the fence. I think it's hurt."

Sally had been walking the long fence that ran in front of Philip's house, slowly making her way his direction, when she had literally stumbled over the bird. It was the color of velvet. It had yellow eyes, a strong beak, perhaps slightly larger than a robin. It was sitting in the grass by the fence. Philip and Sally walked right up to it. It never moved. Philip prodded it with a stick. He turned the bird on its side. Still it made no move. At times its eyes closed. Sally began to cry. The bird had no visible injuries. Philip realized it was probably just old. "Sally," he said, "I don't think this bird is injured. I think it's just time for it to die." For some reason he found himself deeply moved. He didn't want the bird to spend its last moments being savaged by a predator, so he picked it up and carried it back to the house. He and Sally sat on his steps taking turns stroking the bird's soft feathers.

"Maybe we should put it in a nest," said Sally. Philip agreed that might be a comforting place. He remembered seeing an abandoned nest in a tree next to the rain barrel. But when he placed the bird gently in the nest, they watched for only a few minutes before it suddenly lurched off the nest and wedged itself between several small branches. Its head hung down, its eyes were shut, but it continued to breath.

"Maybe it recognizes that it's the wrong kind of nest," Philip said. He told Sally to keep an eye on it while he ran back inside and found a small box. It was an avocado container, about the size of a shoe box. He grabbed one of his tee shirts and lined the box with it. The bird struggled a bit as he pulled it out from between the branches. When he wrapped it in his shirt, its head was bent so far down that it couldn't raise it. It lay on its side, face buried in the shirt, breathing slowly. Philip and Sally sat on the steps watching the bird take its shallow breaths. Neither said anything. Philip found himself praying that its dying memories would be of flight, high and effortless, far above the trees.

After about fifteen minutes the bird's breathing became heavy and labored. Sally immediately began talking to it. Philip was entranced as he listened. The girl was telling stories. She went through fairy tale after fairy tale, all having to do with animals. She was halfway through the tortoise and the hare when the bird opened its eyes wide. Its tail flexed spasmodically. Its feet clenched and it tucked its legs tight up against its body. They both realized the bird was in its last moments.

Sally began to softly pray. Philip was mesmerized by this death that was bringing tears to his eyes. It was a scene he knew was repeated by animals and humans countless times every day around the world, yet this time it was being enacted right in front of his eyes. He found himself more affected than by his own father's passing. The bird breathed hard a few more times, then simply stopped. Its wings twitched, then its body relaxed back into the shirt. Philip closed its wide-open eyes and the bird was gone. Tears were streaming down Sally's face. Oh death where is thy sting? Well, Philip thought as he looked at the weeping girl, despite what the Apostle wrote, death for us on this old planet still packs a powerful sting. He felt that if resurrection did not come for innocent sufferers like this bird, it should not come for anybody. He put his arm around Sally and hugged her. "Let's bury him," he said, "and you can say some final words."

They buried the bird wrapped in Philip's tee shirt in the avocado box under Sally's favorite tree. Sally placed a few rocks over the grave as markers. "Will it be in heaven?" she asked Philip.

"I think it will. I'm sure it will. And so will Mr. Bumbles and all our animal friends. God loves them too right?"

Sally smoothed the dirt over the simple grave. "We'll see you in heaven," she said.

They sat on Philip's steps again in the warm sun. They each drank a cold soda. Sally looked pensive. She was looking across the field toward Capistrano when she suddenly said, "I'm haunted by the thought that I should have gone forward in the meeting this morning." Philip was stunned anew, as he so often had been, by the adult phrases that from time to time came out of the girl's mouth. He knew he had to address her statement. He couldn't let this moment pass. But he felt at a loss.

"Why do you think you should have gone forward?" he finally asked.

"I'm a sleeping bridesmaid," she said. "If Jesus came back today he'd leave me behind."

"But you're a Christian Sally. Isn't Jesus going to take all the Christians with him? He won't leave you behind."

"But I'm not like those Christians in the movie. I'm not a bold disciple."

What could he say? The girl might have been him. She was feeling the same things he had felt all his young life. Not good enough. Not really loved. He wanted to be angry at a tradition that left kids in such despair. But he just felt utterly weary. Then he remembered the emotion they had both felt for the bird and how easily he had assured the girl that God loved the bird and would take it to heaven. This is ridiculous, he thought. We naturally dispense grace to an animal that we won't dispense to ourselves. Why do we care so much about a dying bird? Why are we so prone to fits of absurd love? Because we're made in the image of a God who is damn well supposed to know a whole lot more about love than we do.

"Sally," he finally said, "I know this is crazy, and I don't want to be sacrilegious, but I want you to imagine for a moment that I was Jesus. Would I leave you behind?"

The girl answered immediately. "No, you wouldn't leave me behind."

"How do you know that so certainly?"

"Because you like me." She thought for a moment. "And you wouldn't leave Mr. Bumbles behind. And you wouldn't leave that bird behind."

"Right," said Philip. "You're exactly right. And do you think Jesus likes you less than I do?"

The girl looked troubled. She gathered some dirt in her hands and let it sift through her fingers. Philip could tell she was pondering the notion in the serious way she thought about most things. Philip tried another example. "Or put yourself in the place of Jesus. Would you leave Mr. Bumbles behind? Would you leave that bird behind? Think of the people you love. Would you leave them behind?"

"No." Her voice was barely audible.

"Every time you think about Jesus leaving you behind, I want you to remember how you felt about that bird. And how you feel about someone you really love. And I want you to say out loud that that way I feel about someone I love is how Jesus feels about me."

The girl threw the last of her dirt onto the ground. She smiled at Philip. "I think I can do that," she said.

❧❧❧

Late that night Philip sat on his porch. He was feeling bloated. The Troyer sisters had invited him for Sunday dinner, as they frequently did. In fact they often insisted he drop by several times a week. They couldn't permit this single young man living just two doors down to starve. They were wonderful cooks and Philip always ate as if he was stocking up for the next few days. This week they had two of their language helpers in from their allocation. The two extra women made for a full house, but it was a house full of the chatter of a language Philip had never heard and the smell of strange herbs which the women sprinkled liberally on their food. The table was loaded with both Filipino and tribal cuisine. Philip tried everything. Now he was paying the price. He laughed as he remembered the Troyer sisters' attempt to define his relationship with Dorothy to their language helpers. The shy women wrapped in their thin full-length skirts had placed their hands over their mouths, which they always did when they smiled, and giggled and giggled as Lillian pointed to Philip's hair and then to a picture of Jesus in a children's Bible.

The sisters had explained to Philip one day that they were not going to disabuse their mother about Philip's identity. It would require immense effort, an effort which might ultimately be fruitless anyway. Besides, they considered his presence a gift to the old woman. If she wanted to believe that Jesus stopped by regularly for dinner, so be it. Philip had learned after his first night with the Troyers that the best way to keep their mother calm was to immediately bless her whenever he entered the house. He would take both her hands in his, greet her, then tell her over and over how much God loved her. By the time he was finished the old woman's lined face would be streaming with tears. She would spend the rest of the evening staring rapturously at Philip. They had learned to seat her on the opposite side of the table from him, both to allow her free gazing rights and to keep her from suddenly grabbing him. She tended to lock on and repeat his name over and over, or rather the name of their Lord and Savior. It could be disconcerting. Then, after the sisters had tucked their mother in for the night, Philip would once again hold her hand and whisper whatever blessings came to mind. Lillian swore that Dorothy slept through the night like a baby whenever Philip came to dinner.

Mr. Bumbles suddenly bounded up the stairs and leapt to the rail. Philip hadn't seen the cat since early in the afternoon. "Where have you been buddy? You missed quite an afternoon with your favorite girl."

He had probably talked with Sally for another half hour after their discussion about the rapture. At one point she had suddenly asked, "Are you a Christian?" He had not been able to hide his astonishment.

"Of course I am," he stammered. "Why would you ask that?"

"I don't know. You're not like us." Unpacking that remark was an unnerving prospect, but he had to try.

"What do you mean?" He held his breath.

"I don't know." She said that several times. "It's like you're from out there somewhere." She waved her hand in the general direction of the other side of the fence. "You're not afraid of out there." She was silent. Philip decided to wait her out. "And in class, or whenever, it's like you're not afraid of the Bible. You'll joke about the stories. But then when we ask questions, sometimes you won't even answer them out of the Bible. You'll just talk about things. Aren't you afraid to just talk about things?"

Philip thought he understood the girl. "No I'm not afraid. I used to be afraid of a lot of things. I used to be afraid of talking about things, or reading things. I used to be afraid of out there. But you know what Sally? You know what I learned? God's out there. And he wants us to talk about what's out there. In fact, and this is something you'll learn as you get older, you need to go out there and then look back in here. You can't really understand in here until you've been out there." Philip found he was talking to himself as much as to the girl. He'd never really thought about any of this until just now. In fact, he wasn't even sure he was talking about the same thing as Sally. Regardless he needed time to think about what he was saying. It sounded right somehow.

The girl had said one more intriguing thing before she dashed off to meet her mother for some errand or another. "I want to change," she said. "I need to stop being a kid."

Philip had thought to mouth some platitude about not rushing into adulthood too fast, enjoy being a child while you can, blah, blah, blah. Fortunately he had just shut up. All he said was "So do I kiddo. So do I." And he'd been rewarded with a smile.

Ben and Lechón stopped by later that night. Philip and the night watchman reviewed the weekend's events together. Matt had spoken to Ben, but, according to Ben, had told him that he'd done the right thing. Philip blessed Matt inwardly. As Ben and the dog left the yard, the watchman called back over his shoulder, "The next time you become a werewolf please don't eat my daughters. Well, maybe you can have Lorena. She's in a mood." Philip heard him laughing to himself as he ducked through the fence to cross the road and head toward the hangar.

It could only have been Matt who shared that story with him. Philip thought to himself that things just might work out well for him at Ilusan. He just had to keep downwind of Carnley.

Philip woke up Monday morning when the first hint of light raised the outlines of his mosquito net and of the sleeping cat wedged up against his chest. He was wide awake and eager to get up. One of the biggest surprises about his life at Ilusan was that no matter how late he stayed up at night, at least three times a week he came fully awake at first light. He had always been a late sleeper. If most doctors said humans needed eight hours of sleep per night, Philip figured ten would be even better. But he regularly got by on five or six at Ilusan. Although in his more spiritual moments Philip fancied that God woke him early to call him outside to read and pray, he couldn't really convince himself that the Almighty was that personally involved with his sleep patterns. But it was a lovely thought. He greeted his host every morning with "Good morning Father. Thanks for waking me up. I wouldn't want to miss one of your mornings." And indeed Philip thought that therein lay the real reason he woke up. He had simply fallen in love with dawn at Ilusan. It beat the hell out of dawn in the city. He had mentioned that to God as well. He thought God agreed.

Philip's pattern had been to throw on a pot of coffee, rush through a quick and freezing shower, then grab his Bible and coffee and head for the porch. Mr. Bumbles always joined him. The cat either leapt to the rail or sat on the top step. He lazily cleaned himself, but always with his ears radiantly alert tracking the birdsong and other sounds Philip could only imagine. From time to time Bumbles' head snapped up and he stared into a tree for a moment, before resuming his morning constitutional. As the sun crept over the mountain, both Philip and the cat grew silent and watched, sometimes for as long as fifteen minutes. When the first rays reached the porch, Mr. Bumbles' pattern was to raise himself to his tiptoes, stretch luxuriously, look at Philip, then trot down the steps and head under the house. He always went under the house first. From there Philip had no idea where he went until he turned up later with bits of bloody breakfast. Sometimes he didn't show back up until time to leave for school. Then inevitably he appeared, loping from as far away as the fence to leap into his basket. He had yet to miss a day of class.

Philip always took Bumbles' departure as his signal to open his Bible and read. True to his word he had followed no set devotional pattern. He read wherever he wanted, as much as he wanted, as fast or as slow as he wanted. It was liberating to discard all the rules. He had stopped by Joseph Haaf's house one afternoon and found Joseph in his study reading the Bible with his headphones on. Even with the headphones clamped to Joseph's head, Philip had heard Dylan singing "Rainy Day Women #12 & 35." He figured if Joseph could read his Bible while listening to a rock star sing about getting stoned, then there really were no rules left worth worrying about. It had been a profoundly liberating moment.

Mostly Philip had been reading the Gospels. He found himself deeply impressed with the artifice of the Gospel writers. He forced himself to use that word, because he knew it would keep his saintly observers at bay. When he threw out all the interpretational grids that had been hammered into him as a young man, he thought it pretty obvious that the authors were not writing history, at least the kind of history he had studied in school. They weren't trying to tell the story exactly as it happened. They were creating a masterful painting of an extraordinary life, a life that had impacted them deeply. They took bits from here and there and arranged it, hoping that the readers would get their point. Philip was beginning to.

He was stunned by Jesus. He remembered distinctly the morning when it struck him with utter clarity that if this man that he was reading about walked into his yard and challenged him "Follow me," he would be helpless to resist. You'd have to be nuts to say "no." Everything Jesus said was said with such authority and made such profound sense once you caught on to what he was all about. It was like he knew something about how things really were that you didn't. But he wasn't just going to lay it out for you. He teased you with bits and pieces, just enough to make you dissatisfied with yourself and your life. Morning after morning Philip thought "I can't believe I was afraid of this man." The Jesus of his youth had been angry. This man was intense, yes, but the intensity was all about getting people to see with better eyes, that God wasn't about rules and slapping people down nearly as much as he was about a life lived from the heart, lived passionately, and driven by love.

On this particular Monday morning, Philip followed what was becoming his practice, as much as he practiced anything. When he shut his Bible he remained in silence for long minutes thinking about what he had just read. Then he prayed. He prayed without rules. His practice of prayer had become more and more simple. On this morning, he prayed, "God, help me love people. Help me love my students. Help me love Kari." And then he got up. More often than not that was all he said. Somehow it seemed enough.

As the students straggled in that morning the boys clearly had something on their minds. They looked at Philip with expectant faces. There were smirks and grins. Philip thought even the girls appeared to anticipate hearing something about the weekend. Clearly word had gotten around. When all the kids were seated and the morning prayer, offered by Mary, and the pledge of allegiance were out of the way, Philip sat casually on his desk, took out the children's book reports, glanced through them, then said, "So Thor, how was your weekend?"

Donny burst out with a transcendent "reeee," and it took five minutes to quiet everybody down. Clearly the boys thought the entire event a great lark. Donny asked if Philip had really told Mr. Sorenson that he turned into a werewolf at night. Philip pled the fifth, which led to a brief discussion about the nature and meaning of pleading the fifth. There was some discussion about the identity of the nark. Most thought it was one of the sixth grade boys. Meanwhile Madeline, who had probably had the whole story from Donny, was busy whispering to Mary, filling her in on the entire sordid affair. The nark discussion was interrupted by Mary's exclamation, "You boys are so stupid. I hope you got in trouble."

"I didn't," said Donny. Danny nodded in agreement.

"I didn't," said Timmy.

"I'm grounded for three days," said Charlie.

That left the Sorenson boys. They were quiet. Philip thought Bobby was moving rather gingerly. He looked at the boy and raised his eyebrows. "Well?"

"Bobby's parents went way overboard as usual," said Donny. "Tell him Bobby."

It turns out that Bobby and Drew were grounded for a month. "But they'll probably forget about it pretty soon," Bobby said. They weren't allowed to see Donny anywhere except at school, a rule that clearly distressed the boys. Bobby hoped his parents would forget that one soon as well. They weren't allowed to check out any library books without first clearing their choices with their parents. Apparently Carnley and Ruth thought the boys might have imbibed some of their scandalous ideas at the library. Maybe "National Geographic," Philip thought. He doubted volumes of D. H. Lawrence or Charles Bukowski were available. "Oh," said Bobby, "we also had to miss movie night, and I had to stay in all day on Saturday and read the Bible."

"You had to stay in on Saturday and were required to read the Bible all day?" Philip wanted to make sure he had heard correctly. "Huh!" He looked slowly around at the class. He knew he should leave it alone, but the whole situation was simply too absurd. He might have made the excuse that he couldn't help himself, but he really wanted to pick this scab. He set the papers down, settled even more comfortably on his desk, and went ahead and made a show of it.

"Bible reading as punishment," he said. "O.k. class, let's think. You are a Christian parent. Do you want your kid to want to read the Bible?"

"Yes." They all agreed. Sally saw where he was going. She shook her head furiously from side to side and mouthed, "No, no, no." But he was already into it, and he didn't feel like stopping.

"So, you want your kid to actually want to read the Bible on his own. Now your kid does something wrong, or at least you think he does, and you decide to punish him by making him stay inside all day on a Saturday and read the Bible. Is this a good way to reach your goal of making your kid want to read the Bible?"

Some of the students were laughing. Some looked embarrassed. Bobby grinned sheepishly. Sally's eyes were wide open. She had both hands on her cheeks as if she were witnessing the crash of the Hindenburg.

"Well is it?" said Philip.

"No," said several.

"It's pretty stupid," said Charlie, "really stupid."

Philip went on. "Do you think if I went to the library and checked out a book on parenting tips for Christian parents that I'd find that idea in there?"

"No, probably not."

He saw he had their absolute attention. "Here's the good thing about it though. You're all kids. Everything that happens to you is an opportunity to learn, so you don't repeat the same mistakes when you're a parent someday. Every parent makes mistakes, or so I've heard. What do I really know?" The class laughed. "So, let's use this and learn something. You're a parent. You want your kid to want to read the Bible on his or her own. How do you encourage this?"

The class actually had some pretty good ideas. Philip thought it turned into a nice teachable moment. He was quite impressed with himself. But by recess he found he tended to agree with Sally. If word got back to Carnley, the man could make even more trouble for him. Philip didn't know for sure, but he imagined that somewhere in the teachers' playbook was a rule about not messing with parental authority.

What Philip didn't know at recess was that, in addition to all the other punishments, Bobby had taken a savage beating. Philip wasn't aware of the extent of the boy's injuries until later that afternoon, but when he saw them it put a dark spin on the whole affair that began to make him question just what his role might be at Ilusan.

Philip had two sets of visitors that afternoon. He had assigned a research paper of sorts in history class. He spent the period teaching the eighth graders how to make note cards. He had arranged with Kari to hold a session immediately after school in which she showed the students the best library resources for history topics. The library was small. The tour lasted five minutes. The students had to have at least three note cards by Wednesday, so most of them stayed late at the library. Philip and Mr. Bumbles bicycled home alone.

He had been reading his mail on his porch for about twenty minutes when Bobby and Donny appeared between the trees at the side of his yard. They called his name but hesitated to approach.

"I thought you guys weren't supposed to be together except at school," he said when he looked up.

"We're not." Bobby stepped into the yard. "There's something else I didn't tell you. I'm also not supposed to ever come over to your house again." Both of the boys looked at him expectantly.

"Well you better come here and sit down and we'll discuss it," said Philip. The boys looked around as if they expected Carnley to leap out of a tree or from a hole under the house. Maybe Ruth had a mask and snorkel and was lurking in the rain barrel. Philip wondered what Ruth would look like in a bathing suit, mask and snorkel. He started to laugh as the boys gingerly sat on his steps. "Sorry, just a crazy thought," he said when the boys looked at him.

Before they could talk about their predicament, Philip said, "Actually Bobby I think there's still another punishment you didn't tell me about. You move like you're kind of tender."

"Show him Bobby," said Donny.

Bobby was clearly reluctant to go there. "I got a pretty good licking I guess."

"Uncle Carnley has a belt and a board," said Donny. "When he's really mad he uses the board."

"My Dad used to spank me pretty good too," said Philip. "I've had a bruise or two."

Donny pushed Bobby in the shoulder. "Show him," he insisted.

Bobby reluctantly stood up. He had on long shorts that almost reached his knees. He turned around and pulled the legs of the shorts up. He held them for a moment, then released them and pulled up his shirt. Philip felt sick. The boy was black and blue from the middle of his back almost to his knees. Philip didn't know how he had even walked to school, let alone sat in a chair. "My mom had to soak my pants off on Saturday," Bobby said. He slowly sat back down.

Philip didn't say anything for several minutes. He didn't trust himself to speak. He went inside and came back out with three soft drinks. Finally he said, "Did he do that to Drew too?"

"No," Bobby said. "I was the ringleader and besides he was too tired after me."

"Gash," Donny muttered.

"O.k. boys what are we going to do about all this?" Philip thought it best to put the ball in their court. He needed time to think.

"Well Mr. Andrews," said Bobby, "please don't say anything about the spanking. It would only make it worse."

Philip nodded. "How often does it happen?"

"Oh, not too often. Only when he gets really mad."

"Yeah, like once a month," said Donny.

"So what are you going to do about the other stuff?" Philip asked.

"That's what we wanted to ask you about," said Donny. "We'd like to still come over here if that's o.k. with you."

"You realize you're asking me to lie for you," said Philip.

"I don't know, maybe," said Donny. "Is it a lie if you just don't tell anybody?"

"Maybe not. Maybe it doesn't matter. Maybe you try to do what's right before you worry about whether or not that involves a lie. I'm no expert on these matters boys." Philip felt immensely sad. His pristine garden had been invaded by something ugly. He'd thought the only evil he might have to confront here would be in himself. But now there was something else crawling around that nobody wanted to look at. And it had crawled right up onto his porch.

The boys were silent, waiting. "O.k. fellows here's what we're going to do. Let's do what's right, but let's try not to give anybody an excuse to kick me out of here. I happen to like being your teacher. It's a great gig and I don't want to screw it up, and messing with parents is a quick way to screw it up. You understand me?"

They both nodded. "He'd beat me to death before I'd tell," said Bobby.

"Let's hope it doesn't come to that," Philip said. He couldn't believe what he was about to say. "Bobby you said things might blow over after awhile with your parents. So, you stay away from each other and from my house for a week. Then, if you honestly think that it's the right thing to do and that it's worth the risk, you can start coming back over here. But I don't want to see you getting beat up again over this. Deal?"

"Deal." They both nodded.

Philip relaxed a bit. "We may have to post guards mind you, but at least my house is in a great location. We're pretty much up here by ourselves."

They chatted for a few more minutes, before Bobby decided he'd better get home. He was supposed to be grounded after all. "I'll tell him I was at the library," he said. "I've got note cards to prove it."

"O.k.," Donny said. He patted Bobby on the shoulder. "I'll see you in a week."

"I'll keep the sodas cold for you," said Philip.

The boys had only been gone for about ten minutes when Beverly and Robert Fraser walked into the yard. Beverly was carrying a tray covered with tin foil. Robert looked like he'd been drug along by his ear. The man scarcely glanced Philip's way during the brief conversation, although he did shake his hand when Philip stepped off the porch to greet them. But Philip didn't think Sally's father was mean spirited. He just didn't care for the human species. Beverly began the conversation by handing Philip the tray, which turned out to be filled with brownies. "We just wanted to stop by and thank you for the attention you've been paying to Sally," she said. "I hope she hasn't been a bother."

"Not at all," said Philip. "Your daughter is the coolest kid I've ever met. In fact I've wanted to talk to you. I think you're aware of this, but I have to make sure that you know Sally stops by my house quite often." He suddenly felt embarrassed, and felt dirty for feeling that way. "We always just sit on the porch and talk, or I help her with her homework. She's not a bother. I enjoy helping her. But I wanted to make sure you knew where she was." He trailed off.

Beverly smiled. "We've never really known where Sally was, so this is actually a relief to know she's here. I love my daughter," Philip thought it odd that she hadn't said "we love our daughter," "but I know she's different. She's always been a wanderer. She's never had close friends her own age. We moved our work from our allocation to the center here because we felt she needed more of my attention." Philip noted again that she hadn't said "our" attention. "We've had her repeatedly tested at school, because she's always done poorly. But now she comes home and does her homework. She even asks me for help sometimes. And she's shown me papers with A's on them. So we're very grateful."

Robert looked up and nodded. "Yes." That was all he said, but he seemed to mean it.

"Well," said Philip, "I can guarantee you one thing. Your daughter is very bright. I'm not a teacher with any vast experience, but my guess is that she just hasn't found school interesting in the past. Maybe she's finally arrived at the right age, maybe I've been able to do something, intrigue her somehow, but whatever, the light bulb has gone off. She's a very savvy thinker. When she's challenged to think outside the box, outside the lines, she really lights up. You can see her mind working. It's a wonderful thing to see as a teacher."

"She never did like to color inside the lines," said Beverly. "Remember Robert?"

"Yes," said Robert. He squeezed the word out like he was giving birth.

As the couple walked away, Philip tried a brownie. They were very moist. He had two more. Then two more after that.

Philip had a difficult time getting to sleep that night. He felt like his brain was on spin cycle. Twice Mr. Bumbles raised his head from where it lay on Philip's shoulder and chattered at him. It was a rapid "ack ack ack" sound, a cross between a meow and an outraged squirrel, and Philip knew what it meant. It meant "You're disturbing my rest buddy. Settle down or get swatted."

"Sorry," he mumbled. But it didn't help him get to sleep. As if there wasn't enough to worry about, his stepmother had added to his unease with the letter he'd received that afternoon. His stepmom was a big believer in dreams. She seemed to know the difference between indigestion dreams and portent dreams, or dreams from God as she preferred to think of them. And she'd had a doozy about her stepson. Of course she'd had it over three weeks ago, but Philip knew what she would say about that. "God knows the speed of the mail dear. That's why he gave me the dream when he did."

In her dream Philip's family and other friends were relaxing by a river. A group of young people gathered around Philip on the bank close to the water. "You always have so many friends," she had written, and Philip could feel her glow. Someone pointed downstream and everyone turned to look. Just then his stepmother saw the head of an enormous crocodile emerge from the water at midstream. Slowly, cautiously. Like a commando on a raid. The croc fixed its eyes on Philip as it drifted closer to the bank. It ignored everyone else. She had wanted to scream a warning, but couldn't. Then with terrifying speed it exploded from the water, charged up the bank, seized Philip in its jaws, yanked him into the river, rolled violently two or three times, then carried him downstream. His stepmom ran screaming along the bank next to the retreating beast for a few yards and then plunged into the water. That was when she woke up crying.

"Now honey," she wrote, "I know you don't think much of my dreams, but try to humor me on this one. I'm praying every day, and I believe God will protect you. But I'm afraid Satan might be targeting you. Or maybe it's someone or something else. Just be careful. And plead the blood of Christ."

Philip had never been quite sure what that last phrase meant. It was Christianeze, that language peculiar to saintly women and preachers. He'd never been comfortable speaking it, although he had memorized the phrase book. And there were moments in his life when it comforted him to hear his mother, and now his stepmother, speak it. And this was one of those moments. A giant crocodile! Good grief! Probably a metaphor. But for what? He began to plead the blood of Christ. Mr. Bumbles swatted him.

That night Philip had a doozy of a dream himself. In fact it was the dooziest dream he'd ever had in his life. It was a rapture dream, although Philip didn't know it at first because, as the dream opened, he was standing at a urinal in the boys' bathroom at his old Christian high school. He was concentrating on the tiles on the wall in front of him as men always did at such moments. Out of the corner of his eye he saw a man enter a stall behind him and to his left. The door clicked shut. Then a rich leather jacket appeared, casually thrown over the door. Philip could tell the man was settling in for an extended session. From the sound of things he needed it. Philip had always wanted a soft leather jacket. He finished up his own business and stood for a moment pondering the opportunity. The man was in no position to give immediate chase. You could clean up after hurricanes quicker than he'd be shipshape again. Philip's breathing was quick. He took two steps, grabbed the jacket, and bolted for the door. "Hey," the man said, but Philip was already hurrying down the hall. He carried his prize under his arm.

He banged through the door at the end of the hall and emerged into bright sunlight. That's when he knew that the dream was about something else entirely. Things began to move in an eerie slow motion. Arranged in tableau before him around the courtyard were clusters of people, everyone in his high school that he had disliked the most. The principal who had suspended him for a week for flipping off his shop teacher was talking to a classmate who had become Pentecostal and insisted that speaking in tongues made him more sanctified than the rest of them. Just beyond them a half dozen of Miss Sandalo's super spiritual groupies beamed and touched each other knowingly on their arms. They all carried Bibles. To his right three or four popular jocks and their gorgeous girlfriends held hands and postured like they were on a catalog photo shoot. Next to them stood the basketball coach who had cut him even though Philip thought he was better than several boys on the team. He just hadn't run with the right crowd.

And then he saw him. Lounging against the flag pole like he didn't have a care in the world was Carnley Sorenson. Carnley had a long piece of straw dangling out of his mouth. He was wearing a cowboy hat. He looked like Paul Newman as Butch Cassidy. Philip stared at him. Was he wearing a sheriff's badge? What are you doing here, Philip wanted to say. But then he noticed that everyone was looking at him. They were looking at the jacket. He felt naked. Carnley mouthed a single word. "Nice."

Just then the sky turned a vivid purple. Everything slowed down even more. A brilliant cloud appeared. Then a musical instrument sounded a high clear call. It was infinitely far away and yet it filled the courtyard. Philip recognized the signs. His heart began to pound.

"Was that the last trump?" he asked.

His portly sweating band teacher suddenly appeared beside him. He hooked his thumbs under his red suspenders. "I don't believe it's a trumpet," he said. "Possibly something in the woodwind family. Perhaps a piccolo. Yes, it's the last piccolo."

"But it's supposed to be a trumpet," Philip said. Those were his final words. Everyone in the courtyard had turned and was gazing into the sky. And then Philip knew with sickening clarity that the tableau of personal enemies before him had been arranged deliberately. It was a divine in-your-face moment. They would go and he would be left. Even as the thought passed through his mind everyone disappeared. He was alone in the courtyard with the stolen jacket.

And then came the voice. It was haunting, unearthly, majestic, rich. It said two simple sentences. "You fucked up son. You missed the rapture."

Philip jerked awake. He was pouring sweat. He took several deep breaths and shook his head to clear it. Mr. Bumbles sat up and looked at him. "That was unexpected," he said to the cat.

The next morning Philip sat on the porch with Mr. Bumbles. They both watched the rising sun. Philip couldn't get the events of the past few days out of his mind. He remembered his mother's dream. Then his dream. The thought idly crossed his mind that maybe he should go home. Maybe his attempt at transformation wouldn't work. Maybe things here would turn out badly. But then he thought of the kids and Kari. He thought of Sally. He looked around at the morning. No, this was all much too good to pass up.

He glanced toward the sky. He was glad to see there were no clouds. "You wouldn't leave Bumbles and I behind, would you God?"

Then he heard a voice. It wasn't an audible voice. It was a voice deep within him. In his mind or in his spirit. The voice said, "Hell no. I love Mr. Bumbles. I'd never leave him behind."

Philip wasn't far enough along in his Christian walk to know for sure whether what he heard was the inner voice of God or merely his own voice. "Regardless," he said to God, "one of us has a really cool sense of humor."

# Chapter Seven

On a cool early September morning deep in the mountains south of Ilusan, three men carrying long wooden spears stepped out of the jungle onto a newly created logging road. Their faces from the nose up were painted black. They were short. The tallest was just over five feet. The only article of clothing they wore was a brown and red gourd into which they had shoved, or more probably, carefully inserted, their genitals. The men stared up the road, listening intently. They were still standing there when the logging truck appeared around the bend.

The first Philip heard of these events was when Joseph Haaf ran into his yard. Joseph had the most unique run Philip had ever seen. He was actually pretty fast, but he ran with his arms held stiffly at each side as if to raise and pump them risked some sort of upper body failure. Joseph didn't typically hurry anywhere, so Philip had only seen the odd gait once before when Joseph got the news of a package at the post office. He took off like an erect sprinting gorilla, shouting over his shoulder, "That might be my Dylan bootlegs." Philip had watched him for a few seconds, then turned to Celia and asked, "What the heck is that?" Celia had replied, "It gets him from here to there."

He had to smile again as Joseph loped toward his porch. When Joseph entered Philip's yard, he bent over and put his hands on his knees. He gasped for breath. His comb-over reached for the ground. It appeared he'd been running all the way from his house. "You've got to come with me" was all Philip could get out of him for the first minute and a half. Finally, when he was able to stand, he gasped, "They want me to go to the jungle. There's no way I'm going unless somebody's got my back."

It turned out that the logging truck driver, after very cautiously approaching the three men, had picked them up and dropped them off near a jungle path about three miles further down the road. He had pointed them toward the trail, and for some reason the men took it. Two hours later they showed up in the yard of Samuel and Virginia Clayton. The

Claytons were missionaries with the Bible Translation Mission who had been living in that part of the jungle for almost twenty years. When the startled Claytons attempted to communicate with the men, they quickly realized that the strange dialect they spoke was not related to any of the surrounding tribes. "I think we've discovered a brand new tribe," Samuel told his wife.

She responded, "Or they've discovered us." Samuel immediately put in a radio call to Ilusan requesting that Joseph Haaf be flown out to help him analyze the new tongue to confirm whether the men were indeed from a heretofore undiscovered indigenous group. They wanted him as soon as possible. No telling how long the men would stick around.

Although fascinated intellectually, Joseph was undergoing his usual jungle freak out. He wanted Philip to come with him. "The Claytons have gone native," he gasped. "They're liable to do just about anything. I want someone with a bit of sanity to cover me."

The earliest the pilots could fly Joseph in was Friday. It was Wednesday afternoon. Philip was more excited than Joseph, although for different reasons. He really wanted to get out there. "I'll see if Fossia can cover for me on Friday," he said. Ten minutes later, Fossia agreed that the experience was worth Philip's missing a day of school. She and Kari would take his classes.

Philip had a hard time concentrating on Thursday. All he could think about was flying in one of the mission's small planes again and experiencing the real jungle. He spent the bulk of the morning discussing with the kids what their various allocations were like. Almost all of them had lived with their parents in the jungle and they had a lot of good stories to tell.

At the end of the day he checked on the eighth graders' note cards. They had been working on their research projects for several weeks now. Donny had ten cards. Elaine had six. Mary had fifty-two. The class groaned. Bobby had seventy-seven. Donny shoved him. Mary flushed. Madeline had thirteen. Philip knew how many Sally had because he'd been working with her. She had thirty-four. He gave her a slight nod. She returned a slight smile. Danny and Timmy forgot to bring theirs. Philip asked Timmy to estimate how many he might have. The boy adjusted his glasses, looked at his classmates, and said, "Maybe four." Danny said, "I think I have somewhere around one hundred and twenty-five." The class hooted him down.

"Thank you Danny," said Philip, "I'll expect to see all of those on Monday."

"Maybe if he put one word on each," said Donny.

"At least I can spell more than one word," said Danny.

Philip held up his hands. "All right." Then he picked up a notebook from his desk and pretended to write in it. "Note to self. Next time check more regularly on progress of student note cards. Set deadlines for students who have a hard time keeping on task." The class laughed.

"You'll be a really good teacher by the time you leave us," said Timmy.

Sally was teaching him how to skate his floor when Bobby, Donny and Timmy showed up on his porch that afternoon. Philip had found half a dried coconut husk in the closet of the bedroom he wasn't using. He was going to throw it away but showed it first to Sally. "That's a skate," she said. When he looked puzzled, she took it from him, dropped it on the floor, put her right foot on the rounded top and began to whisk it back and forth, hopping alongside with her left foot as she progressed across the porch. "You probably really wouldn't use it out here," she gasped between hops. "But inside it'll make your floor shine. You sweep first and then skate. And then sweep again." When the boys arrived they all went inside and took turns skating the living room. Philip was exhausted after just a few planks. But he had to admit the floor looked a lot better.

Afterwards they sat on the porch, drank cold drinks, and tried to teach Bobby how to burp. Donny and Timmy were in championship form and even Sally let out a tiny bleat. The boys applauded her and were rewarded with a fleeting smile. Philip was gratified to see that she stuck around after the boys arrived. Usually she quickly made an excuse and left. But today she seemed determined not to be driven off. Now even Sally tried to coach Bobby, but he couldn't make a sound. They made him drink half a Coke in one swig and still he opened his mouth to nothing. He looked like a fish out of water, methodically popping his mouth open searching for something that just wasn't there. Timmy asked Philip if he had any baking soda. "We could mix it with the Coke," he said. "If that doesn't make him burp, he might throw up, which would be pretty cool too." Philip didn't have any baking soda. Eventually they all gave up.

Philip agreed that Bobby must be some sort of scientific oddity. Freak of nature is how Timmy put it.

The Sorensons had relaxed their boys' grounding. A week and a half after the incident and after Bobby and Drew officially apologized to their parents at the supper table, the grounding had ended. Bobby sheepishly told the story of his apology and their official release. "They rescinded his punishment," Sally said and beamed at Philip.

The boys all said, "They what?"

"They rescinded Bobby's grounding," said Sally. And that's all she said.

For the past several weeks Philip had been giving Sally a new word every time she stopped by. It was a game they started after Philip said something she didn't understand. "My Daddy would be really happy if I talked like that," she said. So they had decided to give her new words every now and then that she could practice and try to work into her speech. Philip thought that if nothing else it might encourage her to talk to somebody besides himself and her mother. Her favorite word so far was pedant. Whenever Mary sat up straight in her chair with her hands curled demurely in her lap and began a lengthy recitation in response to one of Philip's questions, Philip knew he dare not look at Sally or they'd both start giggling. Neither of them needed to say it. Words had that kind of power. Her other favorite word was apocalyptic.

"You boys should be able to figure out what rescinded means from how Sally used it," said Philip. After a brief discussion they did indeed figure it out and the conversation moved on.

"But I'm still not supposed to be with Donny after school and I'm still not supposed to be here," said Bobby.

"That's why I'm sitting like this keeping my eye down the path," said Donny.

"But there are other directions someone could come from," said Philip. This started an animated conversation among the boys about how best to cover all angles of approach. Timmy even got down and peered under the house.

"You can see anyone coming to the front of the house from here," he reported. Philip saw Sally looking at him with a puzzled expression. He supposed she was wondering about the propriety of her teacher apparently endorsing the disobedience of one of his students. He decided to let her wonder about it. It would be good for her to puzzle over. Besides he had no idea himself whether or not he was doing the right thing. He probably wasn't. He worried that he might be letting himself be carried along by the desires of other people as he had so often in the past. But there was nothing to do about that now. He wasn't about to deprive the two best buddies of a meeting place. And if it meant tweaking Carnley's nose in the process, so be it. The man was way out of line with his boys anyway. Philip had seen enough evidence of that.

Philip tuned back in to the conversation when Bobby suddenly said, "I really hate my Dad. I wish they'd go back out to the tribe and put me in the dorm." Philip knew the Sorensons had decided to live permanently at Ilusan because they hadn't wanted to leave their boys in the care of dorm parents. The thought occurred to Philip that Carnley and Ruth either really loved their boys or didn't trust them or maybe both. And, having gone through similar moods as Bobby was feeling with his own father and later reconciled and seen his father change dramatically, he thought he maybe understood both sides of the Sorenson family.

"Hate is a strong word Bobby," he said. "There must be something you like about your Dad. Think about it. He does something you like. What is it?"

Bobby thought for a minute or two. He appeared ready to say something, but then shot a look at Sally. Then he shrugged and said, "He's really funny when he poots."

"Oh gash," said Donny and he and Timmy lay back on the porch and laughed and laughed.

"Sorry Sally," said Bobby. Sally looked bemused.

"He thinks he's being real sneaky about it," Bobby went on. "We'll all be reading in the living room. He'll start peeking around over his glasses with this really funny look on his face. Then my Mom will say 'Oh dear,' and she'll pull her shirt up over her nose. Then Drew will yell and leave the room. And my Dad will shake his head and go 'Woof.' Sometimes it's so bad we all have to leave the room. Mom will say, 'Carnley, what if someone comes to the door?' And he'll just sit there laughing."

"So," said Philip, "we've established that he's funny when he poots. That's good to know. Give us another example of when you like him."

"He was better out in the tribe. He wouldn't get mad nearly as often. He would take us swimming in the river. There was one place where the rapids were real fast. He'd go downstream and wait for us. We'd swing into the rapids on a vine like Tarzan. We'd hold onto the vine as long as we could and we'd bounce on top of the water. Then we'd let go and zoom down toward him and he'd catch us as we shot by. It got rocky a little further down." Bobby mentioned a few other moments in the tribe where he'd enjoyed his father, including long mountain hikes, but then he trailed off. "But here at Ilusan he mostly just says no. And gets mad."

Everyone was silent for a while. Finally Philip said, "Well we all know your Dad doesn't really like me, but I'll defend him for one minute anyway. One thing you learn as you grow up is that there are reasons everybody acts the way they do. That doesn't make what they do right, and it doesn't mean you don't have a right to be angry with them. But something happened to your Dad when he was younger that makes him get mad easily. I don't know what it is, but it's something you should try to figure out when you get older. But for now just try to keep out of trouble. We don't want you getting hurt."

"It's hard to stay out of trouble when he wants us to be perfect. You never know what might make him mad."

"I know," said Philip. "My dad was kind of like that too." For the next few minutes he told them stories about his own father. He made sure to let the kids know that his father had eventually changed. "But," he concluded, "your Dad probably won't change for a long time. So just lie low for the rest of the year. Remember next year you'll all go away to Faith Academy for high school. Then you'll at least be a bit freer. And pretty soon you'll be bigger than he is."

"Yeah," said Donny, "you just need to start growing you runt."

Donny's comment turned the conversation a new direction. Philip idly followed along. He knew Bobby felt locked in a universe he couldn't change. The hardest thing for kids to fully comprehend was the gift of time. Before the boy knew it, his relationship with his father would transform forever, whether through absence, physical growth and maturity, or simply through grace. Philip hoped the boy could avoid serious injury until that time came.

The boys decided to go for a swim. As she watched them disappear around the corner of the house, Sally said, "Technically, and speaking strictly as an outsider, Bobby's Daddy is a very poor father." Philip was about to burst out laughing at her wonderfully odd and adult sentence, when he saw her face tremble. She put her chin in her hand. He thought she must be wondering about her own father. He waited for her to say something. He thought she might, but the arrival of Mr. Bumbles from inside the house distracted her. The cat walked up to her and sniffed her face. She hugged him.

"That reminds me," said Philip. "Can you stop by every day this weekend and make sure Mr. Bumbles has food and water?"

"Can I sit with him on the porch?"

"I'm sure he would appreciate that. You can hang out as much as you want." The girl buried her face in Bumbles' back. She hugged him hard again.

"I'd like that," she said.

Philip was sitting on his porch about 9:00 that night thinking about the next day's great adventure, when he heard a rustle in the bushes beside the house. Then, "Philip!" Kari was crouched down almost under the porch. All he could see was her eyes and the top of her head. "Turn off your lights, so I can come up." Philip leapt to obey. Kari made hardly a sound as she whispered onto the porch, grabbed his arm, and pulled him onto the couch. He felt her warmth more than heard her movements. "Shhh, we have to be quiet. I snuck out of the house." Then she threw her arms around him and they kissed for a few long minutes.

Kari kissed like it was an athletic competition. Philip worried she might bruise her lips. Or his. His heart pounded. He wondered if she had any idea the effect she had on him. Over the past few weeks when they were alone she had taken to hugging and kissing him with an innocent exuberance that seemed naïve to the possible repercussions. There was almost no hint of a broader sexuality about it. It was like she needed to reestablish their bond every time she was alone with him, and the bond was created through the strength of slender arms and the crushing of mouths. Although she had never yet used the word, she appeared to love him with an open-faced honesty that was exhilarating to experience. His own feelings for her began to feel oceanic.

When they finally relaxed, Philip said, "My, my, to what do I owe the pleasure of this late night visit?" She had never before been to his house after dark except for a game night he had hosted several weeks before, when they had been joined by Fossia, Joseph and Celia, Gordon, and Jerry and Mary.

"I wanted to see you before you left. You're running out on at least two dates we were planning this weekend remember." Indeed that was the only regret Philip had about his sudden trip. He and Kari had planned a picnic at one of their favorite spots along the river for Saturday afternoon. Then on Sunday afternoon they were going to bike a new trail they had spotted on a ride the week before. Philip had been working toward the L word. He thought he might tell Kari he loved her this weekend. He wanted to try the word on for size, to feel its heft, to say it once when it felt like it actually meant something, to gauge her reaction. Now that would have to be postponed.

"Let's always be happy," she whispered into his ear. Her breath tickled, she had brought her mouth so close. Philip thought that no woman he had ever met deserved happiness more, and he realized that with no woman was it so in his power to grant it.

"I'll always be happy," he said, "if we're always together."

And just like that the mood changed. She kissed his cheek gently, her arm slipped down his, she withdrew and seemed to struggle to speak. Then she drew her knees up to her chest and rocked ever so slightly. It was too dark to tell exactly where she was looking, but it wasn't at him. He became aware that she was crying. Philip was astonished. He put his hand on her back. "Did I say something wrong?"

"No," she said softly. But she held her posture.

Philip had always found women's tears utterly disconcerting. How to respond? It occurred to him at that moment that he experienced women's tears as rejection. And it struck him that whether or not that was an accurate interpretation, as it very well might be at times, it was an utterly selfish response. It was antithetical to everything he was struggling to change about his life. If he was going to be something other than the old Philip, intimate moments such as this one could no longer be just about him. They had to be about his lover. He couldn't casually try the word on for size. He had to embody it. And so he reached across the gulf and gently, but insistently, drew her to him. And instead of her tears falling on her own knees, they ran down his shoulder.

"I'm sorry," she finally said. "I have to tell you something. And I'm afraid that you won't love me after I tell you." And there it was. She had dropped the word so casually that Philip knew she hadn't really even thought about it. She just accepted it as an honest description of the state of things between them. And he thought that no official declaration could ever be as moving as that unwitting slip.

"Try me."

She took a deep breath. "I'm not what you think I am. I'm not a very good person." Philip understood intuitively that she could only be talking about some sort of sexual indiscretion. Nothing else he could think of would cause such bitter tears. No other confession would make a tender-hearted life-long evangelical fear the destruction of a relationship. He wanted to immediately assure her that it didn't matter, that he certainly had no call to judge anybody for such things. But he knew she needed to tell the story. She needed to confess. So he said, "Tell me why you're not a good person."

She told him the story. He would later realize how much courage it took for her to open her mouth and begin. She had lived in fear ever since meeting him. Every moment they were together the thought lurked just behind her consciousness that when he finds out, he'll leave. And so her physical passion had been driven as much by fear as by love. She was literally reconnecting every time she touched him, reassuring herself that he was still there. But all the while she was certain he was just a mirage.

Although she had completed her degree in literature at the Christian college, by the end she was living a double life. "I was a backslider," she said. It was evangelicalism's most pejorative term. The sexuality of American culture had simply overwhelmed her. At the pizza parlor where she worked, although her boss treated her with relative respect, other employees, both male and female, had aggressively propositioned her. She had been handed the keys to a motel room by a married man who informed her that he had just left his wife; he would love for Kari to stop by. She had been backed into a corner by another young man on a late night shift while he begged for a kiss. She had been invited on ski trips, offered rides home, treated to meals, all the while recognizing that the attention came loaded with the desires of the man making the offer.

What horrified her most was her own speechlessness in the face of the onslaught. She simply had never dealt with such things on the mission field. She had gone in the space of a few months from a girl who had never been kissed and never seen a movie to being offered oral sex by a female co-worker. As she gaped at the girl, both comprehending and uncomprehending, the girl shrugged and said, "What! Everybody's doing it." Kari's conscience had been doubly seared. First by what she witnessed and second by her inability to respond in what she considered a Christian manner. She should have said something; she should have challenged their worldview, told them about her faith. But she found all her years of Christian training had failed to provide her a voice. She imagined her parents and Christian friends rebuking her; her own conscience condemned her; but despite all her knowledge she had no faith to call her own. And so, although she kept herself technically pure for several years, she remained so out of fear of God's anger, not from a positive embrace of Christian values.

But such a defense could not be continued for long. Eventually, in her senior year of college, when the proffered intimacies came from a man to whom she was genuinely attracted, the fear of hell could not overcome her passion. As her lover undressed her, she had surrendered both to his tenderness and to the now certain endless torments of hell, a psychologically untenable position that turned each act of human intimacy into a hammer blow on her psyche. As she walked to the podium to receive her college diploma, the echoing silence mandated by the college to ensure that no senior received more applause than the others acted upon her as an affirmation of her alienation from God, family, and friends. She imagined them all in league against her, their eyes observing with cold disdain her forever sullied body, now the muddy, bruised playground of Satan. Believing herself exiled forever from God and the community she loved so deeply, she collapsed into her seat and sobbed.

It had taken her parents a week to get the story out of her, but eventually she told the truth. And her mother, as she held her and stroked her hair, had simply said over and over, "Who ever taught you that we would stop loving you?" And her father had taken her for long silent walks, and his silence and the hand around her shoulders had been an affirmation. And somewhere through the response of her parents she began to hope that God might forgive her as well. Although of this she was never entirely convinced.

But that God and her parents might forgive her was no assurance that a Christian man ever would. She'd heard enough sermons to suspect otherwise. After all didn't you carry every sexual relationship you'd ever had into the marriage bed? You had become one flesh outside the marriage bond and those bodily stains could never be washed off. Philip had heard the same sermons his entire life. Some evangelists made their living touting such things, essentially affirming for young Christians that there was no forgiveness for sexual sin. Philip was nonplussed, faced now with such tender bruised feeling. But he understood it. He had felt it himself. His arm was still around her. He rubbed her shoulder for a minute then withdrew his arm and rubbed his hands together. "Well I'm sorry sweetie," he said. "I'm just going to have to dump you."

They were both astonished. Philip was horrified that he'd resorted to humor at such a moment. And she scarcely registered what he intended. But then it worked and they were saved.

"No you're not," she said. She grabbed his arm. "No you're not." In the tone of her voice was the realization that had blessedly come to her from somewhere deep in the sticky-sweet God-haunted night. She had already known it. She had betrayed it when she slipped the word "love" into her speech just a few minutes prior. She just didn't know that she knew it. She balled up her little fist and punched him hard in the shoulder.

"Ow," he yelped.

"Shhh," she hissed, and they both collapsed helplessly against each other and as silently as possible laughed themselves silly. She stayed another two hours, long after the generator eased its way into silence and the night noise crescendoed in response. He, of course, told her his story. Before he walked her home they had both used that word they'd been longing to hear numerous times. And she had kissed him so hard he thought he might have chipped a tooth. As he very quietly said good-bye at her door below where Fossia slept, she murmured, "Good night my precious damaged goods," and then clamped her hand hard over his mouth to muffle his spasm of laughter. "You'll wake up Fossia," she whispered in his ear.

Philip thought at the time that their laughter and intimacy had freed Kari from the shame and fear that cloaked her past. He flattered himself with the power of his redemptive love. But he would later come to realize that it wasn't nearly as easy as that.

Philip arrived at the hangar at 6:30 the next morning. Their flight was scheduled for 7:00. Oscar Platt, the chief mechanic at Ilusan, took Philip's bag. Oscar was built like a bull, but he was an extraordinarily gentle man. His tight crew cut accented the thickness of his head and neck. He should have been a football coach, Philip thought. "It looks like it'll just be a formality, but I've got to weigh your bag," he said. "I'll stow it in the airplane."

Tom Jacobson and George Donahoe were just pushing the Helio out onto the tarmac. While one leaned on a front strut, the other pulled a grip from the airplane's side immediately in front of the tail and used the tail wheel to steer the craft. The early morning sun glinted off its broad wings. Philip felt his excitement building.

Over the next half hour over twenty people showed up to see them off. The news of the possible new tribe had excited the entire center, but most who came now had personal reasons for seeing the travelers off. Joseph and Celia were there of course, Joseph talking rapidly and constantly to cover his nerves. "I'm just going along to drive Joseph crazy," Philip told Celia.

"That's a short trip," she replied as she watched her husband yammering away with the pilots. Joseph was worried about thunderheads over Katanglad.

Jerry and Mary ambled up from their home nursing steaming cups of coffee. "Have fun spending a weekend arguing with Joseph," said Jerry. "It's like doing isometrics in a doorway. You won't budge the door, but the effort does enhance your muscles."

They watched Joseph discuss with Oscar about whether the airplane would be carrying too much weight with four adults. Philip thought he heard Oscar say, "Not to worry Joseph. When Helios go down they go down easy. If you can survive in the jungle, you'll make it out alive."

Sally was the first of Philip's students to arrive, but most of them were there by the time the flight left. "I can't believe you're spending an entire weekend with Uncle Joseph," said Sally. "I'd go crazy."

Joseph was now arguing with Oscar about whether the left front tire was inflated properly. Timmy had picked up a small frog on the way over from the school building. Donny pointed to Joseph's bag sitting on the far side of the airplane unattended. None of the adults except Philip noticed as Timmy slipped the frog into the bag. "Nice work," said Philip.

"Be sure to tell us what happens when you get back," said the boys.

Philip thanked Sally for looking after Mr. Bumbles. He had walked to the hangar, leaving a puzzled Bumbles sitting by the front tire of the monster bicycle preparing to leap into his basket. The cat had long since figured out the difference between weekends and school days. Philip's early morning routine made that obvious. Philip was sure the cat was thinking, "Where are you going? This is Friday." Philip knew Sally would probably spend every available minute with Bumbles on his porch. He said quietly, so only she would hear, "I've stocked the refrigerator with cold drinks. You have permission to go into the kitchen and get one whenever you want. It'll be your pay."

Gordon Lundy gave Philip a big hug. "Have fun in the jungle brother! I'll be praying for you." Then he turned to hug Joseph. Joseph bleated something that sounded like "ak" and jumped back. They shook hands. When Philip turned to greet the Troyer sisters, Joseph was pointing out to Gordon a spot on the wing where a rock had kicked up and left a deep gouge.

"I think they should have fixed that," he fretted. "Wings are key to proper aerodynamics."

"I'll pray for you brother," said Gordon.

"No airplane will ever crash with Jesus in it," whispered Lillian, and Philip shared a private laugh with the sisters. They were joined by Matt and Julia, then Don Barker, then Peggy Margaret ("You're going to fly in that flimsy thing?" she taunted Joseph, "the cannibals are going to find you mighty tasty," this last with a poke at his soft belly), even Annabel. Annabel promised to pray every day that God would use their trip to open up the new tribe to the gospel. When Fossia and Kari arrived, Philip managed to grab a few minutes of whispered conversation with his now more public girlfriend.

"I wish I could hug you," he said.

"You got enough of that last night. No public displays of affection. It'll freak people out."

"O.k." He pinched her elbow instead. She looked for a minute like she was going to punch him again. "That little fist of yours is a deadly weapon," he said.

"You remember that."

At five minutes before seven Oscar announced that it was time to load up. He helped Philip and Joseph get into the back seat and showed them how to fasten their seat belts. He checked to make sure they were snug, snapping Joseph's shoulder strap across his chest perhaps a trifle tighter than necessary. Then he checked the baggage net behind their seat one more time, tugging on it to make sure there was little play between it and the luggage. "We'll see you on Monday," he said as he closed and locked the door.

"Did you inflate that tire?" Joseph asked through the window, but Oscar was gone.

Tom Jacobson climbed into the pilot's seat. On a typical flight Joseph or Philip would have had the privilege of sitting up front with him, but George Donahoe had never been to the Clayton allocation. Mission policy dictated that no pilot flew alone into an airstrip upon which he had not previously been checked out by a more experienced flyer. The Claytons' strip was one of the most unique in the mission, "cut right into the side of the mountain," Tom said. George was as excited as Philip to make the flight. "We're all going to die," muttered Joseph.

Tom kept his window propped open. After a few minutes spent reading from a checklist and flipping switches, he looked around, called "Clear" through his window, and the engine spluttered to life. Within seconds its roar drowned out all other noise. The onlookers backed away into the shadow of the hangar. Philip waved. Sally was shading her eyes from the sun. She raised her free hand and held it motionless toward the plane.

"Sally must never have learned how to wave," Joseph shouted in his ear. Philip could feel his seatmate shaking with laughter. Kari glanced around, then mouthed a kiss his direction. It was just the slightest pucker. He only caught it because he was staring right at her. He wanted to mouth "I love you," but knew Kari wouldn't want him to risk it. So he simply nodded and tried to communicate with his eyes. It must have worked because she was blinking back tears. But maybe the propeller had just blown sand in her eyes.

The airplane whipped around in a tight half circle and Philip was on the side facing away from the hangar. Joseph only had time for a quick wave before the Helio rumbled toward the runway. Philip watched the left wheel turning through the grass. It kicked up spray from the early morning dew. Grasshoppers leapt out of its path. He felt choked with excitement. There was little wind, so Tom had decided to take off heading north on the north-south runway. All things being equal he preferred to take off away from the center. Just in case. He taxied south for a minute then spun the airplane around right on top of Jerry's first tee box. He ran up the engine to a fierce roar twice before throttling it back down. He said something into his radio, closed his window which cut the sound significantly, turned around to give a thumbs-up to his passengers, then opened the throttle all the way.

The Helio surged down the strip. Within seconds the tail wheel came up bringing Philip and Joseph level with the pilots for the first time. They were only three quarters of the way to Jerry's first green and even with the hangar when Philip felt them lose touch with the ground. The front tires canted inward. Everyone at the hangar was waving. Philip waved back searching for Kari in the crowd. Joseph leaned across him and pointed. "Look at Sally." She had raised both hands now. They were motionless in the air above her as if she were imparting a blessing. "That girl will never be a cheerleader," Joseph said. But as he gazed down on the girl and the small knot of friends at the hangar, Philip found himself deeply moved. He felt like he was leaving home.

Philip quickly realized that Joseph was even more terrified of flying than he was of entering the jungle. He rarely glanced out the window, preferring to stare straight ahead while talking Philip's ear off, something Philip found mildly irritating, as he was desperate to keep his eyes glued on the terrain below. He tried to make a joke, urging Joseph to calm down and pray for journeying mercies. "Think about the angels under our wings," he said.

But Joseph wouldn't shut up. Philip found if he didn't respond, Joseph kept on talking and Philip could remain looking out his window. Joseph was a conversational omnivore. He could argue at length about virtually any topic. For some reason this morning's rant was about bats. His homily spanned space, time and species to such an extent that Philip rarely knew which bats he was referring to or even which continent he was on at the time. But it really didn't matter. It was tension release for Joseph and background noise for Philip.

"Have you ever tried to get information about bat attacks? Nobody ever tells you anything useful. Some numbskull kid in Indiana got rabies from a bat bite. The authorities informed us that the kid would be treated. Really?! I thought they had a policy of letting people die! Then we get this little mysterious insult to the inquisitive public. The paper said, 'The Kosciusko County health department declined to describe the circumstances of the bite.' You've got to be kidding! The absolute single piece of useful information that could come out of this story, an actual fact that might help people avoid bat bites, and thus rabies, and they 'decline to describe'! Wonderful. Oh, right, I forgot, the people really have no right to know about such things. I wonder if there isn't a chance this will backfire. Conspiracy theories tend to thrive on ignorance of the facts. Might the rumor-mill begin churning out stories that

Indiana bats are unusually aggressive, and that the health department is suppressing the facts for economic reasons, a la 'Jaws'? Here's hoping. Then, at the other end of the spectrum from the speak-no-evil health department, you have the chuckle-headed bat-huggers, whom you come across whenever you do some real research trying to find the facts surrounding the circumstances of bat bites. I remember reading in one article, 'Unprovoked bat attacks on humans are extremely rare, despite exaggerated stories to the contrary.' Really? How rare? Not in absolute terms, of course, but what are the chances if you have a bat in the room with you? If it's rabid? Etc.? 'Bites usually are defensive, occurring when people handle sick or moribund bats,' they said. Do tell. With statistics, please. If you have them, that is. Assuming you aren't just making this up, of course. 'Effective ways to minimize potential human-bat contact are, one, cautioning the general public not to handle wildlife and, two, exercising care in handling suspected sick wildlife. Inexperienced people should never touch any wild animal with bare hands.' Really?! I mean, I would have assumed that, whenever encountering wildlife, we were supposed to stick our fingers in their mouths! Thanks for setting me straight, oh all-knowing animal-expert! Glad all that education is being used to illuminate the public with arcane information normally only available to scientists! 'Bats can be picked up with gloves, forceps, or a stick.' Right. Honey, have you seen my bat-forceps anywhere? But first, how about telling us how you get them to hold still. Good grief.'"

Philip nodded at what he hoped were appropriate times, but soon tuned Joseph out completely. They were still over the central plateau flying southwest, but he could see mountains approaching. As he gazed at the landscape unfolding beneath him, Philip's thoughts were scattered, jumpy. He remembered his first days in the country, in Manila. As the 747 descended he had been glued to its window as he was to the Helio's now. The land was so green! The rivers winding through the steep mountain gorges. The little brown houses precariously clinging to the mountainside. Finally, Manila, a sea of houses, smoky vehicles, the downtown skyline, the smog. It was not yet 8:00 a.m., but the wet heat was more impressive and oppressive than he ever imagined. Outside the large jet, an instant cloying stickiness. A taxi took him across town through an ever moving phalanx of other taxis, jeepneys, and buses, every vehicle an explosion of idiosyncratic color. Herds of motorcycles with sidecars darted between the larger vehicles. The entire city seemed to consist of drivers and passengers. The Virgin of Guadalupe hung from every mirror, silently blessing the sweating occupants. It seemed every vehicle had its signature horn, and drivers sounded them constantly, a cacophonous Morse code announcing their every intention. Traffic signs and lane markers were utterly disdained. Philip imagined a Coliseum chariot race. Every driver sought his own lane, his own advantage. Vehicles needed all nine of their lives.

He had purchased a book on cock fighting which pronounced all who dislike the "noble sport of cock fighting" sissies. Saint Peter was the first cock fighter, because his cock crowed three times before he denied Christ.

Late one night he played two hours of outdoor basketball at a local college. A crowd gathered because of the gringo. He hadn't sweat like that in his entire life.

The mission arranged an introductory lecture covering Filipino history and culture by Professor Boy Bautista from the same college. Tall, skinny as a rail (a woman next to him wondered if the professor were on a hunger strike), with a minute voice, he read his lecture with nervous glances at the Americans. Very boring, but very Filipino, or so he had been assured by his mission host. Then a slide show, during which the volume ranged from a whisper to a thunderous roar. Afterwards their host remarked, "You've just experienced the difficulties inherent in a third world presentation."

He'd been given a tour of Manila. Wealthy areas with broken bottles cemented to the tops of high stone fences to keep the poor out. Poor areas with heavy rocks balanced on the tin sheets over the shacks. "Keeps their roof from flying away during typhoons," a man on the bus told him. Some of the shacks had a television antenna protruding from a window. No broken bottles needed to keep the rich out. Smokey Mountain garbage dump. He had felt like an ass taking pictures of people and their hovels built on a mountain of refuse, but the more pictures he took, the more they smiled and waved. An air-conditioned bus moving through scenes of smelly heartbreaking squalor.

Magnolia ice cream. Different flavors like sweet corn, durian, mango. "Would you like playbor ub da montd?" his waitress asked. Playbor ub da montd was sweet potato. He ordered a blueberry parfait. That first bite of nuts, cream, and vanilla ice cream. Best ice cream in the world. He wondered if he could take some back to the States with him.

He snapped out of his reverie when Tom turned around and shouted, "Here comes the jungle." Below them the plateau was increasingly riven with steep gorges. Philip noted a spectacular tumble of water and was briefly reminded of Bridal Veil. Then, with a line of demarcation so clear it was like an invisible fence, the landscape turned a dark green.

"This is where your options narrow if that engine quits," muttered Joseph in his ear. Everywhere the ground surged up toward the small airplane, and everywhere the uneven slopes were covered with trees. Trees, trees, and more trees. The Helio began to bounce.

Tom turned around and said, "It'll be a bit bumpy close to the mountains. Air going every which direction." He shook his hand in a rapid up and down motion.

"This is fun," Philip said to Joseph.

"You're a sick man." Joseph leaned back in his seat and closed his eyes. He was finally blessedly silent.

They flew for another thirty minutes. Philip thought Tom was following a series of narrow valleys. He kept pointing out landmarks to George. Philip wished he were in the front seat. Except for the rivers, the jungle never broke. He strained his eyes, searching for clearings, signs of human life, but saw none. If there were natives, or missionaries, down there, they were well hidden. He couldn't imagine what life under that monotonous canopy must be like.

Tom turned around again. "O.k. We're getting close. I'm going to get in next to the side of this next mountain. I'll do a flyby past their strip. They radioed this morning that it was clear, but we always have to take a look. If they've had a recent downpour it could be too muddy. Or there could be a pig on the strip. You never know. And this is one you can't take chances with."

He reached over his head and cranked a handle on the ceiling. The flaps that dropped from the wing over Philip's head slowed the craft noticeably, and it hadn't been going particularly fast to begin with. As promised they settled in next to a high forested ridge. Philip was so close he looked for monkeys in the trees. Tom tapped his window, and there it was. A narrow strip cut directly into the side of the mountain. It looked about fifty feet long. Philip saw a group of people standing at the edge under the trees. They waved. Tom banked abruptly away, flew for a minute or so toward the next ridge, then banked hard back around. Philip could tell he was lining up for the landing. Philip read his lips as he shouted at George, "You only get one shot at this. You do it right or you're into the side of the mountain below or above. Take your pick." George grinned and nodded his head. Joseph's eyes were closed. His hands were folded on his lap. They were clenched so tightly that his fingers were turning red.

Now Tom was all concentration. He throttled the Helio back and cranked the flaps even lower. He sat ramrod straight and stared fixedly over the dash. Philip could tell George was on fire. He gripped the crash rod over his head and looked bug-eyed at the approaching strip, a clown smile plastered on his face. The airplane seemed suspended over the precipitous valley. Philip craned his head, but all he could see in front of him was mountain. He took a deep breath and breathed, "Well God, I may soon find out if it's all true." The trees rushed toward him. Then the jungle gapped, grass appeared so suddenly it seemed to sprout from the wheels, and they were down. They couldn't have rolled more than fifty yards. Tom spun the plane around and cut the engine. Philip looked behind him. The tail rested less than ten feet from thick underbrush. Before he could register anything else, the Helio was surrounded by naked brown people. They smiled with wide open mouths. He could hear them laughing through Tom's open window.

Five minutes later Philip was standing in the middle of a crowd of shy but curious Tagobos. He learned that name from Joseph, who was already deep in conversation with Samuel Clayton. Philip didn't know where to put his eyes. He'd never seen so many naked people. They all had some sort of band around their waists, and the women had cloth protection in a jungle version of a string bikini, but the men had simply folded their scrotums up over their penises and somehow fastened the loose skin to something so that Philip, when he dared glance that direction, had the impression of hairless ball sacks tucked tight into their belts.

And the women! He had no idea breasts came in so many shapes and sizes. They came tight and perky, long and stringy like deflated balloons, huge and full, pointed up, pointed down, pointed left, pointed right, pointed in opposite directions like spastic eyes, lopsided, uneven, and everything in between. He saw one woman with enormous suckling breasts that hung so low her nipple, navel, nipple made a picket fence across her midsection. He saw tiny bump nipples and nipples that had to be two inches long. He saw areolas of a pigment so faded they seemed invisible and others dark and big as saucers. He thought he understood why there weren't many single male missionaries. He wasn't particularly aroused, but he was definitely distracted.

He was grateful when the pilots climbed back into the Helio and he could tear himself away to watch the takeoff. Samuel told him to go to the far end of the strip. "You'll insist on hiking out after you see this," he said. Joseph refused to accompany him, so Philip went with a crowd of children to the edge of the precipice. Two boys clung to his arms. They were giggling almost hysterically.

But when Tom revved the Helio's engine to an earsplitting roar, the children hushed. Their eyes said they were in the presence of unknowable magic. Tom had told him what to expect, but it was still heart stopping to watch. There was no way to reach takeoff speed on that short strip. The Helio's tail wheel had just lifted from the grass when the airplane plunged off the side of the mountain. With its nose pointed directly at the river far below, it hurtled toward self destruction. But then just as suddenly its broad wings and screaming engine pulled it level and then into a steep climb against the far green wall. Tom banked sharply, waggled his wings at the onlookers, and disappeared down the valley. Only then did the children begin to leap about, tug on his arms, and chatter to each other their renewed faith in the white man's extraordinary powers. On the far side of the strip, Samuel, Joseph, and the crowd of naked adults were already disappearing up a narrow trail. The children pulled him across the grass in a half-jog. He scooped up his bag and followed them into the jungle.

Philip hurried to catch up with Samuel and Joseph. Samuel had the look of a nineteenth century explorer. He had a thick gray beard. His skin was deeply tanned and weathered. He looked older than he probably was, but he moved with surprising alacrity and his eyes and voice sparked with humor. He had a PhD in anthropology and he had lived in the jungle for twenty years. Philip would find him to be a man of cool passion and deep understanding, but also a prankster and exhilarating conversationalist. And if he ever slept, Philip was unaware of it. Every night when, exhausted, Philip crawled under his mosquito net desperately searching for sleep, Samuel was still on his porch quietly smoking his pipe ("I stay in the jungle because it's the only place I can smoke," he informed them, then, with a nod at Philip, "With hair like that you better join me in the jungle") and talking either to Joseph, his wife Virginia, any Tagobo who happened to wander by, or himself if he had worn everybody else out. And Philip woke up every morning to Samuel's deliberately loud complaint that "They just don't make missionaries like they used to, why, look at this young fellow sleeping half the morning away." If 5:00 a.m. was half the morning, Philip thought Samuel had a very narrow definition of morning indeed.

When he caught up with Samuel, Philip asked about the Tagobos. He wondered if the entire village had met them at the airstrip. "There's no village out here," said Samuel. "The Tagobos live scattered all over this mountain. But they stay in touch. You mention to one that the great bee (you flew in on it) is coming on such and such a day, and by three in the morning I'll have twenty families sitting on their haunches in my yard. We're going to have to feed them all when we get home. I'll let you prepare the monkey."

They had only talked for about five minutes when the trail suddenly opened up into a clearing. A rail fence enclosed what Philip supposed was a large house by jungle standards. It was up quite high on posts. Philip saw chickens scratching in the dirt beneath a long porch that ran the length of the house and then kept going to an additional small room at its end. There were no stairs. Only a notched log fastened to the porch. The house was sided with split and woven bamboo. The roof appeared to be constructed of tightly woven leaves. A large water tank sat on a stone foundation next to the house. A series of pipes fed from the peak of the roof to the tank. A short white woman, surrounded by Tagobo children, waved from the yard. On the far side of the yard, crouched next to an open fire, three men with painted faces warily watched the crowd approach. Long spears leaned against the fence next to them. Philip realized he was looking at the mysterious visitors. He determined to keep someone between him and the spears until he was certain the men were friendly.

The front gate consisted of two long horizontal poles which Samuel now lifted from their cradles in the fence and set aside. A three-legged brown dog leapt with surprising agility from the porch and ran barking toward the crowd. "This is Pete," said Samuel as he rubbed the dog's head. The dog was missing its left rear leg. "We call him slippery Pete, because if you don't catch him before he urinates, he gets slippery. Unfortunately that leg he lost was his plant leg. So now when he goes to do his business he lifts his right leg, tips over and sprays whatever's in range, sometimes his own head." Samuel grabbed Pete's tail and lifted his hind quarters off the ground. "If you see him looking like he needs to empty his bladder, just grab his tail and lift him like this. That way he'll shoot straight down. Oh, and if you see any Tagobos carrying him out of the yard, grab him back will you. They've had their eye on him for their fiesta for some time now."

Virginia was the next to be introduced. "My wife is sassy," said Samuel, "so be careful with her. That tongue of hers will shred you like a cheese grater."

Philip quickly decided that sassy would not have been the word his friends would have used. Smart ass was more akin to her personality. But Philip had always enjoyed a smart ass if the smart side of the equation was as prominent as the ass side. And Virginia was definitely smart. Now she snapped something in Tagobo to her husband and made an exaggerated hand gesture that set all the women in the group to laughing. The men smiled sheepishly and looked at Samuel. Samuel just threw up his hands and pointed Joseph toward the three men by the fire. Virginia clasped her hands in front of her and said sweetly, "Be careful Joseph. I watched those men practice with their spears yesterday. They were splitting bamboo trunks from fifty feet." Joseph stopped in his tracks and looked at her. "Oh go on," she added. "But remember, they can smell fear."

Then she turned to Philip. She adopted a coquettish pose as she looked him over. She had short cropped brown hair and sharp features. Her eyes constantly searched for a sparring partner. A few freckles around her nose and scattered primarily across her pale right cheek made her look both lopsided and endearing. "Welcome to our humble abode," she said. Then, dragging out the words in deliberately accented tones, "Sorry to disappoint you, but the white women in lovely Tagobo land wear clothes. But you're free to go naked if you wish. I've tried to get Samuel to adopt local customs, but he's such a prude. And the women have voted and the consensus is that they'd prefer Joseph keep his knickers on. But," and here she gestured to the smiling uncomprehending women standing around, "they've decided they wouldn't mind if you went native. When in Rome . . . ." She turned to the women, motioned to Philip's hair, and said something in Tagobo. The women all chimed in and a brief discussion ensued. "They've decided they like your hair,"

Virginia finally said. "They've never seen a white man with hair, how did they put it, like a grandmother's."

Philip laughed. "I see." He bowed slightly to the women.

"Well done," said Virginia. "You just agreed to marry the buyog there, the old woman you bowed to. She says you'll do quite well."

Two hours later Philip sat on the porch leaning against a rail. His leg dangled over the side. He was drowsy and enjoying the warm sun, but also keeping an eye on Joseph's animated conversation with the three strange men. That Joseph could have a conversation at all was a sign of some genius. Even Virginia stopped her work to watch. She raised an eyebrow at Philip. "As much as I tease him, when it comes to language, he's Houdini."

Joseph had begun slowly, pointing, gathering words. In their responses he picked up verbs and their tenses, and his mind cataloged and instantly memorized everything he heard. Within twenty minutes he was responding, asking questions in their language, building exponentially on the foundation he had laid. The Tagobos squatting in the yard were equally transfixed. Philip had little idea what was being said, but it was mesmerizing to watch.

Samuel hadn't been joking about feeding the assembled guests. Virginia had been working all morning, along with the older women, to prepare a feast. Food was served on long green leaves. The leaves had a waxy coating which prevented moisture from leaking through. They made excellent plates. Samuel also hadn't been joking about the monkey. A large gob of white rice, a green vegetable that looked like spinach, and a strip of lean dark meat lay neatly on each leaf. Philip helped hand the portions to the Tagobos, then took a leaf himself. His meat strip looked disconcertingly like an upper arm. Samuel said a prayer in Tagobo and everyone fell to. The men and children squatted on their haunches, while the women sat on the ground. Everyone ate with their fingers. Philip looked for silverware, saw none, and tentatively dug in with his fingers as well. That's when he caught Virginia and Samuel looking at him. "What do you think honey?" she said. "Philip's decided to go native, but I'm not sure I want to see him eating with his fingers." She handed him a fork and tin cup full of water.

After the meal, half of the Tagobos wandered off, presumably back home. Others lounged under a papaya tree. Although they were still resting on their haunches, Philip thought they had fallen asleep. Some had gone under the house to rest in the shade. The floors were strips of narrow bamboo with a quarter inch gap between each one. Philip could look through the floor and see several women resting in the dirt. When Virginia cleaned the kitchen she just swept crumbs through the floor to the waiting chickens. Nice system, Philip thought.

He roused himself from his lethargy and asked Virginia if it was safe to take a walk in the jungle. It looked like Joseph and Samuel would be working for some time. "Well," she said, "if you take the path back to the airstrip, just on the other side it forks. The right fork goes down the mountain to a logging road. I'd give you a thirty percent chance of reaching the road in one piece. The left fork goes along the ridge and then up and over the top. If you take the trail the other way, you'll be in thick jungle in about one hundred feet. If you stay on the trail, you should be o.k., although it sort of disappears at times. Things grow so fast here. Just step aside for the snakes."

Philip was considering his options when four men emerged from the far side of the house. They were carrying bows and arrows and long reed tubes that Philip soon learned were blowguns. Virginia called to the men and an animated conversation ensued. They looked frequently at Philip and laughed and nodded. Finally Virginia said, "I'll go you one better. I've just arranged for you to accompany Totog and his friends on a hunting trip. They're going after monkey. They've promised to carry you back if you fall off the mountain."

"Really?" said Philip. "Are you serious?"

"Yes, and so are they."

The men stood by the gate waiting for him.

"Wow," Philip said. "This could be really cool."

"That's one way of looking at it," said Virginia.

When Joseph spotted Philip heading for the gate, he said, "Where are you going?" He stared dubiously into the jungle. "I don't like the sound of this Virginia. I'm sort of responsible for bringing him along. Snakes, spiders, there are bound to be jaguars. Who's going to teach the seventh and eighth grades if he gets eaten by a jaguar or carried off by a gorilla?"

"They let this guy teach our kids?!" asked Samuel. "No wonder they're not learning anything. Philip probably reads them Walt Whitman and Margaret Mead. I know these young fellows. Let him go hunting. He'll learn something useful. Besides the snakes won't bother you if you don't bother them, the spiders are mostly cleared off the trails, and the jaguars will be busy eating monkeys or boas or some such thing."

"Jaguars don't discriminate when they're hungry," said Joseph. "If you happen along when they need a snack, you become the snack. They look at a boa and they think sharp teeth. They look at Philip and they think soft dessert."

"Nonsense," said Samuel. "Look at him. He's much too stringy. Just keep eyes in the back of your head young man in case Joseph is right."

Ten minutes later Philip was walking in third position in a single file line along a path just broad enough to see. He kept his eyes on the trail and the naked bottom in front of him. The trail was made for small people and Philip frequently had to duck under a branch. There was little ambient sound other than the breathing of the men and the padding of their feet. Philip wasn't sure what he had expected, bird calls, animal grunts, something. But the trees and brush closed in so thick that most sound was blotted out. Every now and then he heard the dripping of water. Often around the next bend a small stream, scarcely larger than a running faucet would make, spattered down moss-covered rocks and across the trail. At times an insect buzzed around his ears. But other than that the jungle was a vast quiet place. All he felt was breath and sweat.

It was the smell, more than the sound, which let him know he was in an exotic land. He remembered walking along a country lane one October while visiting family in Ohio. The fallen leaves smelled like pre-incarnate smoke. There was no such smell here. Here was only a vast damp vegetable smell. It smelled like roots in mud, like mineral-saturated water, like growth, like decay. He imagined that if he fell, the worms and bugs would turn him to dirt overnight, but as fast as he crumbled, new bushes and trees would take root in his body and surge upward. It was creation run amok.

The men pushed on at a steady pace for forty-five minutes. Philip's clothes soaked through with sweat and his shoes blackened with mud. But he was determined to keep up. Totog seemed solicitous of his welfare. He turned every five minutes or so to check on him. He smiled, Philip smiled back, and the line kept moving.

Shortly after crossing a small creek the men left the trail and began climbing a steep ridge. Totog made a "tss, tss, tss" sound through his teeth, which Philip took to be their version of shushing someone. They were quiet and moved slowly. Totog held up his hand. Philip heard it now, a distant chattering, a far off shriek. How in the world had the men known exactly where the monkeys would be? Two of the men took small darts out of a cane case toted by the last man in line. They dipped the darts into a gourd. They came out coated with black. The other men readied their bows. Totog shifted his machete from his hip to his hand. Then silently, except for Totog's "tss, tss, tss," they moved forward. Philip tried to stifle his breathing. It sounded too loud in his head. The ground leveled a bit and the calls of the monkeys increased. All the men stopped so suddenly that Philip ran into the man in front of him. They crouched. Philip looked up. He would never have seen them if they hadn't moved. But then a large monkey leapt from one branch to another and three more followed.

The men ignored Philip now, caught up in the hunt. Two disappeared into the jungle on his left. Totog vanished in front of him. Philip, bent over nearly on all fours, tried to keep one of the men with a blowgun in sight. He was painfully aware that he could not move silently. But he was desperate to see what happened. For a moment he was alone. He crawled forward, keeping the monkeys in sight. Then, just ten feet away, one of the men stood erect from under the bush where he had been crouching. He raised the long tube to his lips. Philip heard a sound like a compressed air gun releasing. Then from somewhere off to his left a similar sound. He snapped his head up to look for the monkeys just as the trees thrashed above him and a painful shrieking filled the air. With a burst the monkeys fled.

But one stayed behind. It held onto a branch with its left hand while with its right it swatted at its side. It looked after its fleeing comrades. It called to them. It seemed to want to follow, but Philip could see that its life was moving now in a dreamlike slow motion. It called again. But there were no answering calls. The gray monkey was alone with its death. It gathered itself to leap to the next branch, but when it released its hold, it reeled and fell. It dropped silently. Philip watched it all the way down. It struck a branch about thirty feet up which broke its fall enough that when it hit the ground it was not yet dead. Philip instinctively moved toward it, although he had no desire to see what he knew must follow.

The monkey lay gasping for breath in a weedy thicket. It struggled to a sitting position. The men closed in around it. They talked happily to each other. One tugged at Philip and pointed. They were wreathed in smiles. The monkey blinked its eyes at the men as if it was struggling to see what had attacked it. It did not appear able to focus. Then it looked again up into the trees. It tried to call, but no sound came out of its mouth. Philip could see bone sticking out of one leg. Then Totog stepped from the trees behind it. He raised his machete. The monkey died without seeing its killer, without understanding from where its pain originated.

As Philip walked home with the happy men, the monkey dangling from a branch between two of them, he thought of that logging road at the base of the trail beyond the airstrip. Go past the airstrip and turn right. An hour or so down the hill and you could hitch a ride on the twentieth century. For that matter, the great bee was already bringing the modern world to these jungle trails. He knew that nothing would stop the inexorable advance of those roads. Soon they would comb these mountains. Would flatland villagers be far behind? Would the Tagobos see their enemies approaching? Would they know that they were enemies? Or, like the monkey, would they and their culture perish without ever understanding the dart to their heart?

The Coleman lantern hissed happily above the dining room table. The hens made contented night noises to their chicks beneath the house. Samuel had called them half an hour earlier. The yard had been empty at the time, but after Samuel's loud and rapid "Bwock, bock, bock, bock, bock," the hens and their chicks scurried out of the brush from all corners of the compass to gather under the large basket that kept night predators away. A heavy stone held the basket down. The Claytons' two roosters had too much pride to spend the night in hiding. They were enormous birds with thick flopping red combs that hung over their right eye like an Elvis pompadour, the largest chickens Philip had ever seen, and from the look in their eye he could tell they could take care of themselves. Even the dog slunk away when the roosters took an interest. They perched next to each other in a tree just outside the dining room window. "Yes, they will crow right outside that window an hour before dawn," said Samuel. "If you can sleep when those two get started, you're a better man than I am." Slippery Pete lay in the doorway hoping for table scraps. He had bounded up the log stairway with stunning agility. "Looks like he survived another day out of a Tagobo stew pot," said Samuel.

Virginia was in the middle of relating a story at her husband's expense. It seems Samuel had been observing a young mother caring for three children, all of them barely walking, when he got a notion to teach the Tagobos birth control. "I told him it would never work," said Virginia, "but no he had to try." Samuel constructed an ingenious pedagogical device. He dug twenty-eight holes in a circle around the outer rim of a piece of wood. Into each hole he placed a bead. Red beads marked a woman's menstrual period. Black beads marked her most fertile days. Green beads marked the days during which a couple could safely engage in sex. "Copulate like rabbits" was how Virginia put it. Finally he mounted a spinner in the middle of the board. The idea was the couple would point the spinner at the first red bead when the woman began her period. Then, simply by moving the spinner one notch every day, they would know when it was safe to have sex.

"That's a terrific idea," said Philip.

"Thank you," said Samuel. "I thought so."

"You're going to listen to Philip," scoffed Virginia, "the one unmarried person in the crowd. What does he know?" She fixed him with a look.

"All right," said Joseph, "Did it work or not?"

"Would she be gloating like this if it had worked?" groused Samuel.

"Did you see any lack of kids today?" exclaimed Virginia. She went on with obvious relish. "Just two problems. They always waited until they went to bed to check the color of that day's bead. And it seems they couldn't tell what color it was in the dark or by firelight." She was laughing and miming the action. "But wait, it gets better. Samuel couldn't get the men to understand that the board and the silly beads weren't magic. They don't know science from sunshine. So even when they could tell the colors, the men, it's always the men, just turned the spinner to a green bead, figured that protected them, and had a jolly good romp. So now it's back to the drawing board for Samuel. And back to churning out babies for the Tagobos."

"Tell Philip how Samuel convinced them a demon didn't live in their spring," said Joseph. He began to laugh to himself at the story he clearly already knew.

"My husband is a very sensitive anthropologist," said Virginia sarcastically.

Samuel returned from their first furlough with a ghoulish Halloween mask carefully packed in their luggage. Knowing the Tagobos feared the spirit living near their primary water source, Samuel hid there one day with the mask on. "I was just having a little fun with them," shrugged Samuel. "I was young and full of beans."

The first unsuspecting Tagobo who saw the apparition bob up from behind a rock fled shrieking back to her home. Soon two men approached. The result was the same. The next day a dozen men rendezvoused at the Claytons' home before setting off for the spring with all their most powerful amulets. Samuel beat them there, only this time as they began to flee, he called to them and showed them the mask. "Now you'd think they'd be traumatized and humiliated," continued Virginia, "but they loved it. They begged Samuel to help them set up all their friends. One after the other Samuel had to play his joke on every single Tagobo in the region. One day when a man from a nearby family group arrived for a visit, they insisted Samuel hide with the mask again. Only this time Samuel came back to the house with the mask on. The man kept yelling and pointing at Samuel, but all the Tagobos insisted they couldn't see a thing. They had this poor guy so worked up, he almost passed out, before they let him in on the joke."

"Tell our young impressionable school teacher the end result," said Samuel.

"Well," said Virginia, "as odd as it sounds, we've heard much less talk since then about spirits lurking here and there. Of course the fact that a few are now Christians might have something to do with it."

Virginia was still chuckling at her story when a terrified squeak sounded from the rafters. They all looked up to see a rat sprint across a crude ceiling beam. "Probably a snake after him," said Samuel. Sure enough, a second later, a long green snake wound its way around the beam in hot pursuit.

"My money's on the snake," said Virginia.

Several hours later the four Americans sat on the porch with the three-legged dog and stared into the dark jungle that surrounded them. The chickens were quiet. Every now and then the light from the lamp reflected off a pair of yellow eyes staring curiously, Philip thought hungrily, back from the surrounding brush. The fire in the corner of the yard around which the three naked visitors slept had died down to embers. Joseph had convinced them to stay one more day.

"If, as I suspect," he said, "they are from an as yet unknown tribe, we're going to have to notify the government. It's interesting why they came out when they did. If I understood them correctly, and I usually do," he said with a satisfied glance at Philip, "they've been having a harder and harder time finding food. These three guys were sent out to scout ahead. The entire tribe might be thinking of moving. They watched that logging road for three days before they dared step onto it. Amazing that the driver knew you guys were here and sent them up. They're going to need your help negotiating the outside world."

Samuel puffed his pipe and shook his head in agreement. Virginia sat beside him, her head on his shoulder. After a long silence Philip asked a question he'd been trying to phrase unsuccessfully all day. He wasn't convinced he expressed it well now.

"So are many of these people really Christians? And how have their lives changed? And what happens when that logging road arrives on top of the ridge?"

Joseph shot him a look but remained quiet. Samuel puffed on his pipe for a few more minutes. Finally he looked at Philip and said, "If you could see what I've seen through these old eyes." He tapped his pipe on the arm of his chair. Then he resumed smoking for what seemed to Philip an inordinately long time if he actually intended to answer the question. Virginia never stirred on his shoulder. She might have been asleep. When Samuel began speaking again, he spoke for over an hour. One by one he introduced Philip to every adult Tagobo who had greeted them at the airstrip that morning and eaten with them at the house. He named them and then described them as "the man who ate under the papaya tree," or "our friend with the scar on his face," even "the woman with the lopsided breasts." That last brought Virginia awake enough to grunt and cuff her husband on the shoulder. But she quickly lay her head back down and kept listening or sleeping.

After each introduction he told a story about the man or woman. They were not all Christians by any means, but each had a tale of a life affected in significant ways by the coming of the missionaries. Scarcely a family had not seen a child rescued from death by Virginia's nursing. Adults with severe injuries had been flown to the Malaybalay clinic from where they returned with a new lease on life. New and better tools made life easier. But perhaps the most profound change was in worldview. Lives that had been bound by fatalism and fear of witchcraft and spirits had been introduced to an even more powerful spirit with an even more powerful magic, a white magic that seemed to banish the darkness and the fearsome spirits of the deep woods. And the cycle of violence stemming from reprisals over suspected witchcraft had been broken, so that at least this small group of Tagobos no longer lay down each night in terror of enemies both physical and spiritual. As Samuel's stories wafted over Philip they seemed a comfort in this strange, wild, far-off place.

"There are times," said Samuel, "when I think that God has left the West and settled here in the jungle. And why shouldn't he? These people need him, and brother, they believe in that other dimension like you do in your books and science."

It was quiet on the porch for a long time. Finally Samuel said, "By the time that logging road gets here, we'll be ready. We'll be ready."

As Philip watched Tom bank hard against the adjoining mountain to approach the tiny airstrip early on Monday morning, he thought that the three days had certainly been a weekend of firsts. First time in the jungle, first time on a monkey hunt, first time eating several strange things, first time holding a dog in the air by its tail while it urinated, first time washing dog pee off his leg when he didn't check to see which way Pete's pecker was pointed, first time skinny dipping in a jungle river with a crowd of laughing Tagobo men and boys, first time gashing his leg while leaping over rocks to get out of the way of the boa that broke up the aforementioned swimming session, first time having his leg cleaned up by a cheeky missionary lady who insisted on using the phrase "big baby" over and over. Samuel had sat smoking his pipe, shaking his head, and saying, "Like I said, they just don't make missionaries like they used to. Back in my day we were a lot tougher. I knew a missionary who hacked his finger off with a machete and walked for thirty hours out of the jungle with his finger in his pocket."

To which his wife had replied, "It still is your day dear, although it won't be for long if you don't hand me that tincture of Merthiolate."

The weekend had also included his first trips to an outhouse. The Claytons' outhouse was about twenty-five yards outside their perimeter. Nobody wanted to walk the path after dark, so there was always a rush for the back gate around dusk. "After dark the boys just whizz through the fence," said Samuel. "The room at the end of the porch has a little nighttime facility for Virginia."

The outhouse itself was a lonely perch surrounded by barbwire in the middle of the jungle. "Take a flashlight even at noon," Samuel advised, "and check carefully under the seat. If one of those spiders bites you, you're going to be real embarrassed while Virginia cleans you up." Philip had completed his business in record time.

"He's back before he left," mocked Virginia.

"Like I said," said Samuel, "they don't make missionaries like they used to. I like to read my Bible out there. Exercise both body and soul."

"Now there's an image I'm sure Philip and Joseph want to take home with them," said Virginia.

"All boys here," replied Samuel, "accepting you of course my dear. We do like to watch our mouths around a lady of your breeding."

On Sunday they had attended a Tagobo church service. Twelve Tagobo families arrived at the Claytons' early on Sunday morning. Very early. The roosters hadn't even woken yet. When Philip asked when the service was scheduled to begin, Samuel replied, "When it starts. Out here nobody watches clocks." Sometime between 10:00 and 10:30 most of the Tagobos found their way to one of the folding chairs that Samuel and Philip had set up the night before. Samuel had left a clear aisle down the middle, and now the men sat on the right, the women on the left. The children played around the yard. The service roughly followed a typical Sunday back home, except that nobody watched clocks. It was after 3:00 before the last prayer was said. The Tagobos appeared to figure that if they'd hiked this far to attend church, they might as well get their money's worth.

The singing was the worst Philip had ever heard. Virginia had carefully translated American hymns into Tagobo, but at least on that Sunday they bore no resemblance to their western models. Philip thought a dozen cats might have carried the tune better. The Tagobos mouthed, spoke, chanted, or sang the words according to whatever tuneful notion struck them at the moment. Most puzzling to Philip, nobody seemed thrown off stride by what their neighbor was doing, least of all Samuel or Virginia. The couple sang the hymns at the top of their voices. "You have to drown them out," Virginia told Philip later.

Prayers were like nothing Philip had ever heard either. Various Tagobo men took part. Sometimes they closed their eyes, but only if they happened to be stationary. Otherwise they paced the yard, looking up to heaven, or at the gathered crowd. They gestured, argued, turned this way and that, and kept at it for as long as twenty minutes. Then another man would rise and repeat the performance. Watching them, Philip realized he had a lot to learn about prayer. The Tagobos appeared to believe that God was a real person who wanted to help them with their daily lives, but he just needed convincing about a thing or two. So convince him they did.

Finally the sermon. Samuel was the primary orator. But he was flanked by two Tagobo men. After he spoke for a minute or two, the Tagobo elders each took a turn. Since Samuel spoke Tagobo, Philip didn't think they were translating. They appeared to be riffing on what he said, like Phil Lesh and Jerry Garcia trading licks. They usually carried on twice as long as Samuel. After the hour-long sermon, there were more prayers and more singing. Through it all people came and went at will. Virginia spent at least a third of the service in the house with several women preparing a meal. She made a point of leaving shortly after Samuel stood up to preach. "I've heard it all before," she whispered to Philip, "but you be sure not to miss a word." Bathroom breaks were taken whenever needed. A man would simply rise, walk to the fence, urinate vigorously through it, repackage his genitals, and return to his seat. If he didn't walk far enough away, the splattering of his urine on the broad leaves threatened to drown out the speaker. The women, when faced with similar need, used the outhouse.

"I'll never complain about an hour and a half long Sunday morning again," Philip said to Joseph when the service finally ended and the eating began.

As they loaded the Helio on Monday morning, Joseph noticed some odd artifacts stuffed into the sides of Philip's bag. "I did a little bartering," said Philip. "I'm out all my tee shirts, but I'm going home with three genital gourds."

"You sent those men home naked?" exclaimed Joseph.

"Samuel didn't think it would do any harm. They knew how to do the tuck. And they're the only jungle Indians in the world with Star Wars tee shirts. And just think of the conversations these will start. Maybe, just for laughs, I'll offer these to guests as drinking cups from a newly discovered Stone Age tribe."

"You're an anthropologist's worst nightmare," said Joseph. "Not to mention a very sick puppy."

A few minutes later they were buckled into the airplane and waving to the Claytons and the Tagobos. Tom turned around and gave a thumbs-up. "Over the falls we go," he shouted. Philip couldn't wait. Joseph's eyes were closed and he was muttering something that sounded suspiciously like a plea for journeying mercies.

# Chapter Eight

IN LATE SEPTEMBER, ON the Friday before fall break when the entire center was buzzing with the anticipation of the arrival of their high school kids from Faith Academy in Manila, Philip found Bobby in the boy's bathroom before school trying to cover up his newly shorn scalp with rubber bands. He was stretching them one by one around his head. When Philip arrived he had managed to get half a dozen in place just above his ears, but he was having trouble getting them to stay where his head started to narrow toward the crown. They would hold for a second, clinging to the stubs of his fresh crew cut, but then snap off into the mirror or wall. Bobby's face was contorted in frustration. "You're a really smart kid," Philip said before Bobby noticed him, "but you don't have a lot of common sense do you?"

It turned out that just the night before, Carnley had ordered both Bobby and Drew into the chair, thrown a sheet around them, plugged in the clippers, and summarily buzzed their hair off. He ignored the tears trickling down Drew's cheeks and the look of anger on Bobby's face. Both boys knew better than to complain. Whether Carnley was trying to deliberately humiliate his sons before the Faith kids arrived, including their older brother and sister, or whether it was just Carnley being Carnley, Philip would never know. Perhaps he wanted to send a message to Derek, his son in senior high, about the fate that awaited him. But what was very clear was that the boys were deeply humiliated. Drew's round little face would stare glumly at Philip the entire day. Bobby's long lean face was accented even more by the close-cropped hair. He had a prominent knob on the back of his head that Philip hadn't noticed before. "My Dad shaves my head and then calls me hammerhead," Bobby complained bitterly. "I look stupid."

"Looks to me like you've got a lot of extra brains packed in back there," said Philip. But he understood the boy's mood. Bobby had been nurturing a bit of a wave for the last month, carefully applying pomade before he left the house in the morning, hoping his father wouldn't notice that his hair was creeping down toward his ears. Bobby worshiped his older brother, and Philip knew the boy wanted desperately to look more adult when his brother and sister returned from high school. He tried to cheer him up. "I can just see you in about ten months. You'll be walking the halls at Faith Academy and your hair will be hanging onto your ears and almost to your collar. And all the girls will be looking at you."

Unfortunately, as with most young people, Bobby had a difficult time projecting his life into the future. The here and now reigned with brutal tyranny. "Everyone will make fun of me," he said.

"Will Donny make fun of you?"

"No he won't," agreed Bobby.

"Well who else matters? You're not going to lose any friends over a haircut. And the Faith kids won't even know you got it cut. They haven't seen you in months. I bet the last time they saw you, you had pretty short hair. You'll just look like their friend Bobby to them."

"Maybe," Bobby said dubiously. "I'm going to punch anyone who laughs at me."

That was when Philip remembered one of his favorite stories from his own life. He related it now to the boy. Shortly after he had been kicked out of college, he had been sitting on the back porch of his parents' house. All he told Bobby was that he'd been suspended from school for awhile. "I haven't always been as good a guy as I am now," he said. Bobby was clearly impressed.

"Everyone was talking about me," Philip told the boy. "Everywhere I went I could tell people were whispering. They would look at me and I knew what they were thinking, about how bad I was." As Philip sat on that porch that afternoon feeling his failure, totally miserable, he noticed a cat walking across the field behind his parents' house. Suddenly four large dogs charged from the back of the house next door just twenty yards from the cat. They barked ferociously. The cat froze. But there was a fence between the two parties, and very quickly the cat, "always smarter than dogs" Philip winked at Bobby, realized the dogs couldn't touch it. It refused to run. In fact it made a show of luxuriously moving its bowels and then methodically covering it up. Then it polished its face for long minutes as the dogs howled their fury at this display of feline chutzpah. When it finally finished its face wash, it raised its tail high overhead and sauntered slowly away in what was clearly meant as a "kiss my ass" moment.

"That afternoon I really loved that cat," said Philip. "And I learned that there's always a fence between me and other people that they can't cross. They can howl, they can hate, they can laugh, they can make fun, they can despise, but ultimately they can't touch me. And if I really understand this, I can be completely calm no matter what is going on around me. You've just got to be smarter than them, like that cat. Friends matter. The howlers don't. They can't get over the fence." Philip didn't know if his little pep talk helped the boy, but at the very least it distracted him. For a few minutes he forgot his haircut. "Let's go to class," said Philip.

When they exited the boys' room they ran into Peggy Margaret. Philip knew immediately it was a day to avoid the third and fourth grade teacher. "Nice haircut Bobby," she snapped. "As for you Philip, where I come from some good ol' boy might just take a pop at you and mess up that pretty little face of yours. We don't like girly men in South Carolina. You should let Carnley make you into a man like he did to Bobby here."

"Now, now, be nice," said Philip. "You seem a bit out of sorts this morning."

Peggy Margaret stopped walking and glared at him. She put both hands on her hips. Philip glanced around for help, but no other teachers were in sight. He was on his own.

"Am I out of sorts? Am I just a tad put out this morning?" At some level, Philip thought, Peggy Margaret must enjoy her own shows. She was working up to a curtain call. "Well let's see. Why am I just a tad put out? Maybe because I'm a beautiful thirty-two year old woman and I don't have a husband. And I'm stuck on a mission base in the middle of Nowheresville with no prospects in sight." She wagged her finger. "And the only eligible man within a thousand miles has hair longer than mine. He's at least seven years younger than me. And he has a crush on the librarian."

Philip thought she might break into tears. But she was tougher than that. "And the husband I did have fell off an oil rig into the Gulf of Mexico and by the time they pulled him out the sharks had taken several chunks out of his backside. We had to have a closed casket funeral because some squid ate the top of his head off. And before he fell in or jumped in or whatever he did, he might have been in love with a man. And every now and then that bothers me. So you best stay out of my way today with your shaggy hair and Kewpie doll moping-for-the-librarian face. Or I just might crush you like a flower, as your little camp followers delight in putting it." She whirled and stomped toward her classroom. "Nobody around here appreciates class," she shot back over her shoulder.

Philip and Bobby stood silently until she disappeared around the corner of her building. "What's a Kewpie doll?" asked Bobby.

"Beats me."

"Will a squid really eat your head?"

"Beats me again. I've never known it to happen before. But then I've never seen a squid before. I think as long as we stay out of the ocean we're o.k."

"What did she mean that her husband was in love with a man?"

"I think she just meant that her husband had a best friend. Sometimes women get jealous of a man's best friend."

"You mean like a dog?"

"No more like you and Donny. Like Madeline might wish she could be with Donny as much as you are."

"Maybe Miss Mitchell's on the rag."

Philip was so astonished all he could do for several seconds was stare at Bobby. The boy was quickly embarrassed. "Do you know what that means kiddo?"

Bobby admitted he didn't. He had heard one of his older brother's friends say it last summer.

"Let me give you some advice. Never say that about women. Always be extra nice to girls. It'll pay off down the line. And one day you'll discover that girls are pretty cool. In fact I'd venture the theorem that girls are the key to human happiness."

"Even Miss Mitchell?"

"Even Miss Mitchell."

Over the past few weeks since returning from the jungle with Joseph, Philip had had some good moments with both women in his life, as he now thought of Kari and Sally. On a roasting afternoon earlier in the week, Philip and Sally had worked on her math homework for over an hour. The girl had made real strides in the reading and writing subjects, but math still turned her brains into pansit, as she put it.

"I like pansit," Philip said.

"It's good on your plate," Sally said, "but not in your head."

"I don't know, a few noodles behind your ears and coming out of your nose would look pretty cool."

Sally laughed, but then said in her most serious voice, "Mr. Andrews I really need to figure this out." And so they had left their discussion of Filipino cuisine and returned to fractions. Philip hated fractions. But he tried gamely not to let on.

After they finished her math homework, Sally decided she wanted to learn another new vocabulary word. "I want something I can say when I'm mad at someone. But they can't know what I'm saying."

There were moments when Philip thought he really rose to the occasion. This was one of them. "I've got it," he said after just a few minutes thought. "Porcine. It's perfect." He wrote it out in Sally's notebook. "Now it's important that you pronounce it correctly. That way they'll never know that you're really saying they're like a pig." They had laughed over the word for ten minutes while Sally practiced using it in sentences.

"You have a lovely porcine face."

"Has anyone ever told you how porcine you are?"

"You're not fat, you're just porcine."

"You have porcine eating habits."

Philip chimed in with "Maybe you should rescind your porcine habits." Sally was impressed. She spent the next few minutes trying to work two of her new words together into one sentence. "Why settle for two?" asked Philip. Challenged, Sally went for three, then four. Her final effort was a triumph, a semantic smack down of truly epic proportions.

"If you keep derogating me, I'm going to descant at great length on the pedantic nature of your porcine mind."

"I'm not exactly sure how a porcine mind would be pedantic," said Philip, "but I'm going to give you four stars anyway."

When she finally got up to leave she paused at the foot of his steps. She was holding her books in her arms. She said, "Mr. Andrews, you're the best teacher I've ever had." Philip teared up so fast he had no time to find cover. He blinked rapidly to hold the measure of his emotion in check. But the girl was gazing at him with her typical intent expression. There was no cover to be had. He almost said something lame that he would have instantly regretted such as "You must not have had very many good teachers," but he knew such a flip remark would cheapen what was a sincere declaration on her part. Not that he could ever remember her saying anything insincere.

Instead he said, "Thank you Sally. You have been a very good friend to me."

He was rewarded with one of those smiles, the kind that lingered in the air for hours like the grin of the Cheshire cat. "Goodbye," she said. He couldn't remember when she'd started saying goodbye. The word and her smile trailed after her as she dashed for home.

His good moment with Kari, or his especially good moment, they all seemed wonderful to Philip, occurred on the same night Ben discovered them alone together on Philip's porch. It was the Monday of his return from the jungle. Kari arrived on his porch shortly after lights out. She careened into his arms with the pent-up energy of the weekend apart. After mugging his lips she sat on his lap listening to his tales of the Claytons and the Tagobos. "I always liked them," she said of the Claytons. She moaned at his story of the monkey hunt, laughed at much of the rest, and tsked when he mentioned acquiring his gourds. When he finished, she waited only a moment before saying, "We need to make plans for the future."

"Really?!" said Philip. "Like me and you?"

"No, me and Mr. Bumbles. Of course me and you."

Mr. Bumbles regarded them coolly from the rail.

"Really?!" Philip said again.

"Don't repeat yourself. What happens when this year is up and Miss Morgan returns from furlough? What are you going to do? What are we going to do?"

"I don't know. I thought we'd just say goodbye and never see each other again? Isn't that what you had planned?"

"Very funny."

"O.k. The truth. I guess I've tried not to think about it. I have learned that I really like teaching. Maybe I should go back to the States, get a real teaching certificate, and then maybe the mission would want me full time. If there are no openings here there might be somewhere else. And somewhere else might need a librarian."

"I like that," she said. "But I've been doing my homework, and I've got an even better idea. Jerry and Mary are going on furlough next year." She let the sentence hang there. Philip couldn't escape the implication.

"You think?" he said.

"Don't get mad at me." She suddenly sat up straight on his lap. Even in the dark he could tell she was searching his face eagerly. "I did more than think. I've already asked Fossia about it." She seemed to hold her breath. Philip's brain was abuzz.

"Really," he said. It was less question this time than exclamation. "And pray tell what did our good principal say?"

"She said," and here Kari started pounding her hands on his chest, "that if you spent time with Jerry next semester going over his lesson plans, that she didn't see why you couldn't teach fifth and sixth just as well as you're teaching seventh and eighth. And by the way she thinks you're wonderful with seventh and eighth." She breathed "wonderful" into his ear like a world class seductress.

"Really."

"Yes, really." She was still all seductress. "And we'd be together for another year. And then . . . ." She trailed off.

"And then?"

She squirmed in his lap. As if it wasn't difficult enough to keep control with her sitting and whispering, when she squirmed the outline of her legs and hips ground against him with intoxicating energy. He knew she didn't intend to drive him wild with desire, or he thought she didn't—Christian girls were sometimes clueless that way (they basically thought boys were childish girls)—but regardless he could feel himself surging to attention.

"I haven't told you yet, but my parents are coming in November for a visit." He instantly felt the return of a gratifying limpness. Thank you God, he thought.

"Really?" he said.

"You're hopeless. Yes, really."

"Cool." Then a thought wormed its way into his head. "Are they coming to check me out?"

She leaned in close again, all innocent Delilah, and whispered, "Yes." She drew out the single syllable in a dreamy sigh. If sound could transfer to paint it would have been a Wyeth, all gently blowing lace and cool naked skin. Indian summer where summer never sleeps.

He was just about to say "really" yet again, when they both clearly heard Lechón snuffling his way in their direction. Philip had of course informed Kari about his late night discussions with the night watchman, but in the intensity of the moment they were caught off guard. Kari froze for a brief second, then leapt for the doorway. He heard her hiding behind the couch inside. Philip was torn, but there was no time to make a clearheaded decision. It was probably fortunate that Ben took the decision out of their hands. He paused at the edge of the yard as he did every night. "Do you have a guest Philip?" he asked politely. Kari would say later it was the first time she had ever heard a Filipino at Ilusan address a westerner by their first name.

Philip paused. His brain raced furiously. Then he couldn't quite see the point of maintaining the charade. "Yes I do. Come on out Kari."

Philip was glad for the darkness as he imagined Kari was blushing from head to toe. The night watchman greeted her formally. "Good evening Miss Trainor."

Philip decided truth was the best policy. "Miss Trainor and I have been dating for several months. It's hard to get any time by ourselves here at Ilusan, so sometimes she comes over to my house after lights out. We sit on the porch and talk, like you and I do. But Miss Trainor is embarrassed to let anybody know, because she's afraid they'll assume bad things."

"Philip!" Kari's voice was soft, but alarmed, maybe irritated.

But they needn't have worried. Philip thought he could hear Ben smiling. The man was always unfailingly polite. "I'm sorry if I startled you Miss Trainor. Mr. St. Clair told me of your interest in each other. It's a good thing for Philip to meet someone so good for him. My wife and I used to sit together on the porch in the evenings when we were courting. It is not your fault that they turn out the lights here at 9:30." It took about three extra invitations, but eventually Ben joined them on the porch for fifteen minutes and told them about courting his wife. And after that Kari no longer hid when the watchman and his dog came by. And Philip suspected that within a few more weeks, Ben might address them as Philip and Kari instead of Philip and Miss Trainor.

Since that evening they had continued to talk about the future, sometimes explicitly, sometimes in veiled terms. And Kari visited his porch after lights out more frequently. Some evenings she was fiercely physical; at other times, seemingly checked by some internal watchdog, she seemed shy. On those nights, when she touched him it was with the tenderness of a falling leaf. Regardless, Philip tried to be in the moment. He kept no guard up behind his eyes. He loved her with an open face. His future filled with promise.

Philip's life seemed topped off with such moments. His friendship with Mr. Bumbles had also grown more intimate. When Philip approached the porch on the Monday of his return from the jungle, Mr. Bumbles had run from the house, tail erect, bouncing on his pads. Philip said, "I think you missed me Bumbles," and he clapped his hands in greeting. The cat appeared to take this as some sort of invitation, or maybe he'd just seen dogs welcome their friends and decided to have a canine moment, but he had abruptly launched himself from the porch toward Philip's shoulder. Philip managed to get his hands up to catch the flying cat, but even so, in the process of securing his footing Mr. Bumbles left some nasty scratches on Philip's shoulder and chest. But Philip forgave all as the cat rubbed cheeks and purred like a tractor. That night Mr. Bumbles took extra time to settle down. He kept ramming Philip with his head, purring, rolling. Eventually he got up and scratched at the mosquito net. Philip let him out. Ten minutes later the cat returned. When Philip let him back in, he proudly lay a bloody mouse on the pillow.

Philip was sensitive enough not to reject the gift outright. "Thank you Bumbles," he said. "I don't think I'll eat that right now." He got up and wrapped the mouse in wax paper. But he kept it in bed that night next to the pillow. He didn't want to hurt the cat's feelings. "I'm only changing the pillowcase so we'll have a clean one to start the week. It has nothing to do with the blood and guts you spilled on the last one." Mr. Bumbles thanked him by licking his forehead raw with his sandpaper tongue. The cat's chest rumbled with content long past the time Philip wished he were asleep.

Although Philip couldn't be sure, as he found it difficult to be certain about much of anything where religion was concerned, he thought his relationship with God was improving as well. He had finished reading through the Gospels and begun with the Epistles of Paul. But he had quickly tired of Paul's lecturing and had been utterly bewildered by the letter to the Romans. So were the Jews in or out, up or down, saved or damned, toast now but good in the future, good now but toast in the future? He didn't know and found he didn't care. He had enough trouble figuring out his own life. So he returned to the Gospels. He started over at the beginning. He couldn't get enough of Jesus. He read some of the stories over and over. As he did so he found his internal life adjusting to some sort of new reality. Maybe that was too pretentious. But he thought his conscience was changing. His holiness neuron was losing its interest in being a watchdog over the superficial silliness of human ideas of perfection. It decided it didn't want to simply be a quick response to human slipups. If Philip said damn when the morning shower was frigid, it didn't seem to care. Instead it had served notice that it had bigger fish to fry. And Philip found this version of his conscience much more of a nuisance. It had taken to giving off a deep throbbing ache wherever it found a lack of charity in Philip's life. It had taken to buzzing over Carnley of all people. Philip thought he had every right to dislike, despise, even hate the man, but whenever he entertained such thoughts, his holiness neuron threatened to turn into an entire central nervous system of rebuke.

"Are you saying I have to somehow love Carnley?" Philip asked God one morning.

And the thought came back to him, "Do you expect me to pat you on the back for loving Kari? Let me grab some angels and dance a jig on the head of a pin. Whoopee! Philip loves Kari, the prettiest girl within a thousand miles. What a great guy he is! Stack those jewels on his crown. He's really learned some hard lessons."

"When I was a kid I never heard a sermon about how sarcastic you could be," Philip grumbled.

The bus transporting the Faith Academy contingent from Cagayan to Ilusan pulled through the gate and stopped in front of the meeting hall with horn blaring and high school kids leaning out the windows yelling and pounding its dusty sides. They had flown in the very early morning from Manila to Cagayan, and now had driven all day over a jarring pothole-filled dirt road to the mission base. It was cheaper to rent one bus than to make half a dozen Helio flights. Children and adults poured from their homes and ran toward the vehicle as it disgorged its cargo from every window. It was 4:00 on Saturday afternoon. Philip watched from a distance. He felt disconnected from the scene unfolding before him. He had begun to feel an integral part of Ilusan, as if his story and the story of the center were melding, but now with the influx of true insiders, he felt on the outside once again. Everybody, even Kari and Jerry and the other teachers were there greeting their favorites. Gordon Lundy was there, the Troyer sisters, and Celia Haaf, although none of them had any children or former students on the bus. Fall break was a celebration for the entire center. Long hugs, long kisses. Tears. Even Carnley and Ruth seemed caught up in the emotion of the moment. Carnley sported a huge smile as he shook hands with his son and daughter. Ruth clung to them both for long minutes.

Finally Kari saw Philip hanging back. She ran to him and pulled him into the crowd. Over the next half hour he was introduced to Benjamin St. Clair (handsome, thick and dark like his father), Derek and Elizabeth Sorenson (Derek with tight curls and boisterous manner, so unlike the rest of his family; Lizzie with a tall, fair, Nordic look, but wary eyes), James Montgomery (with Derek, the only seniors and clearly the leaders of the pack), three Platts (John, Jenny, and Joby . . . Oscar liked J's), two more Meyers (Delbert and Debby . . . another alliterative set of parents), and half a dozen others whose names Philip would never remember. Only Sally among his students didn't have an older sibling returning for the week. Bobby and Donny went out of their way to introduce Philip to their siblings. Derek pulled James Montgomery over. "Check out my brothers' teacher." It was obvious they were impressed with his hair. "You could never teach at Faith looking like that," said Derek, "but you can teach at Ilusan. That's pretty cool." Then he lowered his voice and grinned at Philip. "But I bet my Dad doesn't like you much."

"I can't speak for him," said Philip, "but I'm just trying to get along."

"I'll let you know what he says about you." Derek led the others in knowing laughter. There was an ease about the young man, a natural leadership. Philip thought he'd make a good politician someday.

"Hey Derek, let's go swimming." It was Drew pulling on his brother's sleeve.

"Let's all go swimming," said Derek, and families disbursed to their homes led by children eager to gather at the pool.

"The entire base will be down there," Kari said to Philip. "Let's go too."

"Why not? I've only been twice already today. Third times a charm."

"It might cool you down from that beating you took on the golf course this morning," said Jerry, as he and Mary ambled by.

"I think it was something Mary put in my coffee," said Philip. "I haven't had the yips that bad since I nailed that bull."

The week passed in a haze of parties, water fights, volleyball almost every afternoon, Frisbee golf, basketball, late night card games, seeing how many frogs could be stuffed into Oscar Platt's desk at the hangar, shooting chickens out of bamboo cannons, an all-base softball game on the school field (Philip hit a homerun over the radio shack roof that earned him big-time points with the Faith kids), egging Charlie Pilarski into peddling his bicycle off the high dive (the boy was desperately eager to please and thereby made an easy target for the older kids), flying Charlie to the hospital in Malaybalay, teasing Charlie over his broken nose, crashing Matt St. Clair's hovercraft into a banana tree (Matt had been working on it for months so he could unveil it with the Faith kids present), and always, after every adventure, a swim in the cold waters of Ilusan springs.

The kids quickly decided they liked Philip, and he was included in everything. He got very little sleep. His house became command central for lazy afternoons and late nights, especially after Keith Vaughan, a friend of Derek's who was supposed to spend the week with the Sorensons, was forced to change his residence to Philip's house. Philip spent a fortune on soft drinks, but felt repaid with an abundance of good will. Mr. Bumbles enjoyed a surfeit of attention, and was fawned over and indulged to an egregious degree, especially after he swished his tail through a candle during a late night card game and went up like a Chinese rocket. Bumbles never realized what all the fuss was about. His fur was so thick he could have blazed for ten minutes before feeling a thing. Nevertheless the smell of singed cat hair drove everyone outside, and Bumbles was smothered with well wishes. He decided he liked girls and there was rarely a moment without an available lap. With all the days lazily active and filled with good feeling, it was difficult to separate one from the other. Nevertheless a few would stand out in Philip's mind for weeks to come, some for many years.

The Sunday after the Faith kids arrived, Matt St. Clair was in charge of the service. Philip knew Matt wasn't looking forward to the event. He didn't consider himself a preacher. But he thought he'd found a way out of his dilemma. His sister back home regularly sent him tapes of her pastor.

His sister attended a Southern California megachurch, and her preacher was famous in evangelical circles. He was known far and wide for his books on Christian living and for his collection of hot sports cars. At any rate, Matt figured he'd found the perfect sermon for the occasion. It was aimed directly at young people. After the hymns and announcements, Matt propped his tape recorder on a stool at the front of the meeting hall, bent a mike stand next to the speaker, and flipped the switch. It was an odd moment, but no odder than having a service interrupted by a monkey. The audience didn't seem to think it was unusual.

Philip had to admit the man, or at least the recorded voice, was a good speaker. He told lots of stories and had a good sense of humor. His theme was God's will for the life of every young person. God's will had three points. What a surprise, Philip thought. Every sermon he'd ever heard had three points. Weren't there ever four important things to say, or only two? The points were even alliterated. Philip imagined God writing down his message to young folk on a slip of paper, searching for how to boil down his will for every kid into three snappy subjects all starting with S. If you couldn't find an S-word you discarded the argument. The S was the most important criteria.

As the sermon unfolded, Philip realized that God sounded an awful lot like every preacher he'd ever heard. Which, he charitably supposed, proved that evangelicals had really caught the Almighty's wavelength. If he were inclined to be uncharitable, which he had to admit was really closer to his natural disposition where such things were concerned, he thought it proved that evangelicals had created a God for themselves that resembled a worried parent.

Regardless, God's will for kids was pretty clear according to the disembodied voice echoing from the front of the room. Kids were supposed to, one, get Saved, two, remain Sexually pure, and, three, Submit to their parents. Philip wondered if those were really God's top three priorities. He imagined number one made good sense, although if Saving everyone's aSS from the Savage fire of hell was really God's number one priority, he thought it might be easier to just do away with hell. Wait, why not Scuttle hell? That fit better. But he decided to be charitable. Perhaps there was more to Salvation than just Saving one's Skin. The preacher didn't mention it, but he probably just couldn't figure out how to express a larger vision for Salvation that started with an S.

But God's next two priorities Seemed Skewed as far as Philip was concerned. He had been reading the Gospels for months now, and had yet to find Jesus warning young people not to have Sex. Not that he was encouraging them to hop in the Sack, but there Seemed to be a lot more important things on the Savior's plate. And God's third agenda item, well that was just wacked. Important maybe, but hardly top three. Philip was reminded of how preachers in the South before the Civil War Spent their valuable Sermon time exhorting the Slaves to Submit to their masters. And that, he knew full well, was an idea full of Shit. Philip thought most of this megaman's ideas deserved a Similar fate, despite his funny Stories and Snappy outline.

After the service he and Joseph met in the back of the room. It had become standard operating procedure for them to debrief after every sermon. Joseph looked grumpy. Of course he always looked grumpy, so Philip couldn't be sure, but he doubted Joseph cared much for the tape-recorded message.

"So what did you think?" Philip asked.

Joseph glared at him. "I thought it Stunk."

It took Philip a long time to explain why he couldn't stop laughing. And even then Joseph didn't think it was funny.

On Tuesday Keith Vaughan moved out of the Sorensons' house and joined Philip for the rest of the week. It was either that or fly home to Leyte where his parents worked. The move caused quite a stir and it came about in this fashion.

The provoking incident occurred during a basketball game. It was a typical hot afternoon. There was a large crowd of kids at the court. Just last week it had been under water after three days of unrelenting rain, and the high school boys set the eighth grade boys to sweeping the worms and the largest deposits of mud off the playing surface. "If you guys want to play in our game, you sweep," said Derek. And the boys, desperate to join their brothers, swept. They had enough for five on five full court with several subs for each team. Whenever someone tired, they raised their hand and an eager sub took their place. Two of the high school girls played, although most of them were artfully arranged around the court. They only watched the game when they thought the boys were watching them. Most of Philip's students were there. There were even some sixth graders. Philip was the only adult.

The game was shirts vs. skins. In the heat everyone wanted to be skins. Philip was a shirt and it was soaked through in five minutes. He was panting hard in less time than that. It was embarrassing to see what poor shape he was in. But the kids seemed able to run forever. The game was fiercely contested, but mostly good natured.

Keith Vaughan was a skin. He was a tall gangly kid with a Beatles' mop top. His nose hooked like a prize fighter's. He was tall enough to be a good rebounder, but his shots tended to rattle hard off the rim. That didn't stop him from putting up a lot of them. Philip was on the court but wheezing at the far end when Keith took a long pass from John Platt and pounded his way hard to the rim. His shot slammed out and, frustrated, he went up for the rebound between James Montgomery and Donny Meyer. Donny was much shorter than either of the high school boys, but he was already as thick as a high school senior. He leapt into Keith's body, knocking him off the ball. James came down with it and whipped it out to Philip who had just now reached half court.

That's when the action stopped. "Quit fouling me you little fuck!" That was Keith's loud commentary on the preceding play. He gave Donny a shove. No fight ensued because Donny didn't react. But the damage had been done. The word, that word, was out there. And that word didn't tend to float around and land softly. Especially at Ilusan where even much tamer words were never heard. Even Philip, who had been known to use the word in his past, felt clubbed by it in this setting. It bruised.

"Easy Keith," said Derek.

Keith laughed. "We're good." He grabbed Donny and gave his head a Dutch rub. Philip glanced quickly around. The players were all fine. The spectators, although momentarily hushed, seemed fine too. He relaxed. But then he saw Mary Michaels standing under the berry tree next to the court with Madeline. Mary said something to Madeline and walked quickly away. By the time she reached the path by the banana trees she was running. Philip bent over with his hands on his knees. He felt depressed. The incident on the court was already over. But he knew what was coming. Or at least he had a good idea. The repercussions off the court were just beginning.

As Philip surmised, the situation metastasized with frightening speed. Already at Defcon Two, Philip thought as he walked slowly to the hastily arranged meeting in that familiar room in the office. As the only adult at the court, his presence was once again required. He wondered how he got into these situations. Maybe it was time he started hanging out with adults instead of kids. But he liked kids. He could be himself with kids. This whole adult thing had him a bit buffaloed.

At least at this disciplinary hearing he wasn't front and center. The usual suspects were gathered around the table. Parents, dorm parents, and poor Matt St. Clair, always drug into these moments because he was base superintendent. Matt said, "Well Philip, sorry to pull you into this, but once again you were the only adult there."

"Yep, I was there."

Matt looked like he didn't know how to phrase the question. He seemed to want Philip to just come out with it. Philip waited him out. "We have reports that Keith Vaughan used extremely bad language in the presence of children while playing basketball. Is that true?"

Philip would always regret that he didn't have the guts to say, "Yes. Keith said fuck." He thought that might have brought the house down. But he wasn't really in the mood to bring the house down. He could not, however, resist a needle. "Are folks upset that he said that word or that he said it in front of children? Would it have been o.k. if only the Faith kids had been present?"

"Of course not." Carnley exploded. He'd been fidgeting ever since Philip walked in. He probably resented the fact there was no way to pin this one on Philip's influence. "I want that boy out of my house and off the base. I want him on a plane home now."

Don Barker reminded Carnley that it was his son who invited Keith to spend the week with them. "The Vaughans are with Far Tribes Mission in Leyte. That's a long expensive trip. And it won't do much for intermission relations to send Keith home."

Carnley's face said all that needed to be said about what he thought of intermission relations. It was rumored that Far Tribes personnel considered themselves more spiritual than the Bible Translation Mission members. Certainly they were more on the fundamentalist end of the spectrum. The BTM folks responded privately that the Far Tribes people were not very educated. Although Carnley didn't say it, to send a Far Tribes kid home from a BTM base for saying that word would be to score big points in the undercurrents of battle between the two large mission boards. All Carnley said now was, "We can charge the trip to the Vaughans. Certainly we can't be expected to pay for it."

"It's already Tuesday," said Matt. "Maybe we should just have a talk with Keith and then ride it out through the end of the week."

"I want that boy out of my house now," Carnley insisted. "I've already told him as much. If we harbor him here we're opening our doors to an unclean thing. And there's enough in the Bible to warn us against doing that. I won't have it."

A new voice spoke. "I don't like the idea of consigning a high school boy to the realm of the unclean thing." Philip hadn't seen Robert Fraser sitting alone in the corner. He supposed he was present because Sally had been at the basketball court. He was astounded now to see the man speaking in a public setting. "He isn't a perfect Christian, but that hardly makes him worth casting away."

The man stared down at his hands, never looking at anyone. He spoke so softly the room was forced to hush to hear him. "Why not call forth the good in the boy, like Lazarus from the tomb, rather than consigning him so quickly to the side of evil? Why reinforce the rot, which is all such drastic punishment will do? What is there to fear? Might the dark in this case overcome the light? I don't remember too many biblical writers expressing much concern about that eventuality."

Sally's father slumped back into his chair, as if desperately seeking a return to anonymity. But then he leaned forward once more. "Someone once gave me a second chance." His eyes lifted. He seemed to want to continue. But having now looked on the faces all staring at him, he froze. His mouth worked, but nothing came out. His eyes registered the knowledge that he was finished.

The room was silent. Philip felt as if the normally mute man had spoken an essential poetry from the cornerstone of creation. "I'll take him," he said. Every face turned his way. "He can spend the rest of the week with me. That gets him out of Carnley's house. I'll talk to him. I'll supervise him the rest of the week. I'll guarantee his good behavior." He looked hard at everyone around the table. "I'll guarantee it."

Don and Matt immediately wanted to see the wisdom in that course of action. "He's probably a good kid," said Don. "He just needs firm guidelines."

Philip locked eyes with Carnley. He knew there was much Carnley wanted to say against his idea, against the idea that someone like Philip could be a sound guide for anybody. The man's eyes flickered with anger. But he simply wasn't sharp enough to come up with an adequate rejoinder in so little time. If Carnley had been a larger than life character, his nastiness might have been tempered with the keen argument and wit that makes for stimulating opposition. But in fact he was a smaller than life character, which made his meanness more intolerable.

"Keep him away from my kids," he snapped at the room. After the meeting broke up, Philip stepped outside looking for Robert Fraser, but Carnley was standing at the edge of the cement walk. Philip thought he might have been waiting for him.

"I'll send him right up," Carnley said. Then he added, "The blind leading the blind."

Philip kept his voice even. His holiness neuron began a slow throb. "You know Carnley, you are convinced the world is evil and you know God is good. So you work hard to keep the two apart. I suppose that's admirable in its own way. But I think Robert is on to something more important. Jesus lived with sinners. And he never worried that such contact would pollute or disgrace him. What harm would it do to love that kid?"

"Love without law is compromise." Carnley said compromise like historians said Nazis.

"And which side should we err on do you think?"

"I know which side you err on. And I see compromise written all over you." And then Carnley tipped his hand. Even as Carnley spoke, Philip could see in his eyes that he knew he was playing his cards too early. "I've put out feelers back home. I'm checking your story. I don't believe you are who you say you are."

Philip felt a twinge of panic. He saw in Carnley's face that the man comprehended his discomfort. What had been concern about overplaying his hand flamed to cold victory in the man's metal-hard eyes. Desperate to turn the tables Philip lashed out. In so doing he ignored the pleadings of his conscience. "My past is of no concern to you. What you should be worried about is a house full of children growing up hating you."

Carnley's face flushed. He looked wound like steel cable. His mouth worked. He searched desperately for a response, but there was nothing there but raw anger. Hatred clouded his thinking. He spun on his heel and walked away. But Philip felt no triumph. His conscience made sure of that.

∾∾∾

Twenty minutes later Keith arrived with Derek Sorenson and James Montgomery. Keith had a blue Faith Academy Vanguards bag over his shoulder. He looked embarrassed.

"Have a seat guys." Philip pointed them to the chairs on the porch. "What would you like to drink?" He brought out their choice of soft drinks. "So we find ourselves in an interesting position."

Derek spoke first. "I'm real sorry about this Philip. My Dad is . . . I don't know . . . a real jerk."

Philip didn't want to talk about Carnley. "Don't worry about it. Keith, you're not putting me out at all. I'll enjoy your company. I've got lots of questions about life up at Faith. And there's no better place to sit and shoot the breeze in all of Ilusan than this porch. Everybody's welcome. Keith won't be lonely."

The boys seemed to relax. Mr. Bumbles jumped into Keith's lap, looked him over for a second, then leapt to the rail and settled into his Buddha pose.

James said to Philip, "I hope you have a big bar of soap in case you have to wash Keith's mouth out."

"I do." Philip smiled. "But I better not have to use it. The only way we kept Keith from getting shipped home was that I had to promise, actually guarantee, his good behavior. If at any time during the rest of this week Keith chooses to expand his vocabulary beyond the accepted words, we're both in trouble." Philip eyed Keith quizzically. "So my friend what'll it be?"

"I'll keep my mouth shut," said Keith. "And thanks for helping me out. My parents would have killed me."

"You're welcome." And then before he had time to think it through carefully, Philip said, "Most Christians just don't appreciate what a good word that is that you used back there on the basketball court." The boys straightened and stared at him like he'd spontaneously combusted. Philip felt his own brain gaping at him. It said, You know I'm here if you ever want to use me. But then another little voice said, Come on let's have some fun. Philip listened to the second voice.

"Your problem Keith was that you cheapened what is really one of the most precious words in the English language. It's a word like son of a bitch, which personally I prefer, that was created to express the most profound outrage and anger. It's not a word to use when you get fouled on the basketball court. It's a word to use when the girl you love as much as your own life is betrayed by someone and all her hopes and dreams destroyed. Now you go to address that someone to let them know the depth of your anger and hurt. If you've been in the habit of casually using fuck and son of a bitch in your daily conversation, what vocabulary do you have left now when you desperately need it? But if this someone is approached by the boyfriend of this girl, and this boyfriend has the reputation of being a fine Christian gentleman who never loses control over minor matters, who chooses his words carefully, well when this boyfriend says to that someone with every ounce of passion he can muster, 'You son of a bitch' . . . well let's just say it's going to have its intended impact, maybe right before your fist has its own intended impact."

The boys laughed, astonished, bewildered. They even felt a bit guilty. They looked at each other. Derek said, "So you don't think it's a sin to use those words?"

"No I don't think it is," said Philip. "Look them up in the dictionary. They're all good English words. They're impolite, rude maybe, but there are times in this life when those are the only words that'll do. Imagine in the scenario I just described that the boyfriend approaches the betrayer and says 'you jerk.'" The boys grinned. "Personally I'm trying now to learn not to say them." He winked at Keith. "Like Keith, I used to use them too casually. So I'm trying to get them out of my head. If I ever use them again I want it to be a deliberate choice, not a kneejerk reaction."

"Unbelievable," said Derek. Then, "There have been times I wish I'd had the guts to use those words on my Dad. Like after he beats the crap out of my brothers. He doesn't dare touch me anymore."

Philip wanted to agree that there might come a time when Carnley would need to hear those words from his oldest son. Instead he just caught Derek's eye and nodded slightly. Then he said, "I had a dream once that ended with a pretty funny use of Keith's favorite word. I'll tell it to you if you promise not to share it with anyone else until you get back up to Faith."

The boys wanted to hear it. Two houses away the Troyer sisters wondered what the whooping and hollering was up at Philip's.

"Jesus is laughing," said Dorothy.

Wednesday was set aside for climbing Capistrano. Matt St. Clair and Oscar Platt, who enjoyed organizing outings for the kids, had given the Faith students the choice of climbing Capistrano or going down river. The girls wanted to go down river, but the boys talked them into the climbing expedition. Their logic was that with three more months of rainy season, the river would be higher when they all returned at Christmas. "The rapids will really be ripping then" was how James Montgomery put it. "But we should climb Capistrano now before it gets too muddy." The girls acquiesced.

Early Wednesday morning the Faith kids along with the seventh and eighth grade children, Matt, Oscar, Kari and Philip gathered at the shop. Kari didn't particularly enjoy climbing mountains, but she knew first aid. It was either her or the base nurse on every outing; mission policy required it. The weapons carrier (as an old WWII army surplus truck was affectionately dubbed) and a small Toyota pickup were serviced and ready to transport the group to the base of the mountain. The weapons carrier had board benches along the sides of its bed. Philip and Kari were the last in, so they sat across from each other in the premium seats at the rear. Sally sat directly beside him. Beverly Fraser, who had walked with Sally to the shop, had pulled Philip aside and asked him to look after her daughter. "It's her first time up the mountain," Beverly said. Philip had promised to hike with her.

"I'll keep her right in front of me," he said.

Philip felt a growing excitement as the two trucks drove through the gate and headed for the highway. "You know," he said to Kari and Sally, "except for my trip to the Claytons' allocation, this is the first time I've been off the base since I got here."

"Except for our bike rides," said Kari.

"Except for when the bull chased you," said Sally.

"You're right Sally, I guess I was ever so briefly off the base then." Still, although he had been out and about in Manila, he had never driven off the Ilusan center, had never seen a Filipino town, driven Filipino back roads. He had observed the Filipinos who worked on the center, Ben of course, but also the house girls and other laborers. He had found them to be unfailingly polite and gracious. The women were quick to smile and laugh, quick to cover their laughter with a hand over their mouth.

The men were hard workers. Almost all spoke good English. Someone had told him Filipinos were the friendliest people in Asia, and he had no reason to dispute that opinion.

He had, therefore, been surprised to observe the casual disregard with which the kids treated their hosts. While they all spoke with great affection of "our tribe's people," whichever jungle group their parents worked with, they referred to the lowland and city Filipinos disdainfully as "beaks," a reference which Philip had been unable to account for. They resented it whenever "the beaks" came to swim in "their" pool. The high school boys told stories of shooting beaks with peashooters out the school bus windows in Manila, of tricking cab drivers into carrying twice as many passengers as legally permitted, and of something they called "bawking," which amounted to quietly pulling up beside somebody on a busy street, say a man on a bicycle or someone urinating against a wall, and then screaming out the window at them (BAWK!) with the desired result a capsized bicycle or, their favorite, a man wetting himself. Philip supposed in one sense it was just boys being boys, but these boys were Americans in a third world country, and as such they got away with much that might have had serious repercussions back home. He doubted they fully understood that.  It wasn't naked prejudice or hate-fueled meanness that drove them. It was the casual cruelty of privilege. And when Philip thought of his friend Ben, it hurt.

The first thing Philip observed as the two-truck caravan left the center was that the highway was brutal on cars and human anatomies. Matt and Oscar weaved all over the road in an attempt to avoid the worst of the potholes, but the passengers still had to hold on tight or risk being thrown from the trucks. The dust billowed behind the vehicles in thick clouds. When the weapons carrier pulled briefly behind a logging truck everyone had to cover their noses and mouths. Kari closed her eyes.

The road was briefly paved, albeit still regularly cratered, through Bancud. The trucks slowed as traffic increased. "We'll stop here for cold drinks on the way back," Matt shouted over his shoulder. Philip gave Sally a thumbs-up. As soon as the Americans were spotted, children ran into the street. They chased the trucks waving, laughing, and shouting, "Hey Joe."

"We think it's from G. I. Joe during WWII," said Kari. She waved back. So did Philip.

Philip heard some of the high school boys shout "Pinoy," the local slang for Filipino. It was a lot better than beaks. Still, he thought there was a bit of an edge to their tone.

Shortly after leaving Bancud they pulled off the main highway onto a smaller road. It was essentially one lane. When they met cars coming the other way, both vehicles had to slow to a crawl and pull off the road. After about thirty minutes they turned onto an even smaller track, two parallel ruts with a grassy hump in the middle. Philip leaned out of the weapons carrier and saw the mountain looming. "We're getting close," he announced. Sure enough, ten more minutes and the trucks pulled off the road and killed their engines.

"Strap on your gear," Matt announced. Philip was impressed with how the high school kids checked on their younger brothers and sisters. He heard various ones telling their siblings to stay close as they hiked. All of his students save Sally were clustered with their older siblings; Donny however was with Bobby, Derek, Lizzie, Keith and James.

"You stay right in front of me," Philip said to Sally, "and Miss Trainor will be right in front of you."

Sally gravely fastened her canteen and fanny pack around her waist. She gazed up at the mountain. "I think this will be fun," she said. She sounded like she almost believed it.

Philip winked at Kari over Sally's head. "You'll work up a sweat, but it will definitely be fun. Just let me know whenever you need to rest. And I've got a surprise for you when we reach the top."

The mountain revealed itself in three stages. Stage one was a fairly easy ascent through the foothills, at least as easy as any climb can possibly be when the temperature at 9:30 in the morning was already approaching eighty-five degrees and the humidity percentage wasn't far behind. The trail wound its way through fields of tightly matted cogon grass. The long razor-edged spears, over six feet tall in places, trapped the wet heat along the trail. Not a breath of breeze stirred down the path. It was a relief to emerge from the grass field and begin serious climbing.

Stage two was a jungle trail up the side of the mountain that ranged in pitch from about thirty degrees to nasty runs that neared the vertical. Matt had brought ropes along for the steepest stretches. Several high school boys leapt ahead, eager for the honor of assisting the girls and younger children. Bracing themselves on the far sides of sturdy trees, they wrapped a length of rope around their waists and flung the remainder down the trail. Philip was amazed at the dexterity and strength of the girls and children. His seventh and eighth grade boys made an obvious show of ignoring the ropes, although Charlie, Danny, and Drew all at one time or another lost their footing and slid for fifteen to twenty feet before a timely grab at a root or branch halted their fall. If their ears burned with the laughter and good natured catcalls, they didn't show it, but immediately flopped back over on their bellies and resumed their climb. Even on the second try the ropes might as well not have been there.

Most of the girls used the ropes either because they genuinely needed them or because they wanted to demonstrate their pleasure at the chivalry of the boys. Still it was the rare girl who didn't scramble nimbly up even the steepest stretches. Kari, Sally and Philip did quite well, although Kari lost her grip once and carried herself, Sally and Philip for a twenty foot ride before they slammed into Oscar, taking him off his feet as well. They lay in a laughing heap, accepting the abuse of those above and below. It took Sally five minutes to stop giggling and she only stopped then because she needed her breath for more strenuous endeavors. By the end of stage two most everyone was covered in mud and it was the rare climber who didn't have at least one or two good scratches.

Stage three was less difficult and yielded itself at numerous points to breathtaking views. The party wound over and around enormous boulders in a gentle ascent to the top. Here again the boys proved their usefulness, reaching back and down to assist the girls to the most difficult handholds and across the widest chasms. Everyone was tired now and the going was a bit slower and quieter. But soon the breeze that swept up from the valley below recharged their spirits and the shouts and chatter increased. "Almost there," called Benjamin St. Clair from the front of the line where he and his father paused to let the others catch up. Fifteen minutes later Oscar appeared around the final bend and the last of the group arrived at the rocky peak. Everyone collapsed onto the rocks, reached for canteens and pulled out sandwiches. It wasn't Everest, or even Katanglad, but for what it was Capistrano's peak provided an exhilarating vantage point to view the plateau below. Derek, Bobby and Donny joined Philip, Kari and Sally where they perched, legs dangling over the side of an enormous boulder. Derek took binoculars out of his pack and pointed out the two trucks far below and the trail through the cogon grass.

"The views are quite vertiginous," said Sally.

On the way over, Sally had asked him for a new word. "Make it a mountain word," she said. He had heard her repeating it softly to herself until they began their climb. Now she enjoyed her moment of triumph as she explained its meaning to Bobby and Donny. Philip thought Derek might have needed an explanation as well, although he hadn't been as forthcoming with the question as had the two younger boys.

Philip suddenly remembered something. "What time is it?" he asked. Kari checked her watch.

"Almost two," she said.

"Then we're almost to my surprise. Where do you guys think Ilusan is?"

Derek scanned the plains below with his binoculars. "I think it's where that clump of trees is over there," he said pointing. "It makes sense that trees that thick would be around a water source." He handed the binoculars to Philip.

"I won't need these in about two minutes," said Philip. He handed them to Sally. He took something from his pack, but held it behind his back. "Keep looking out there," he said.

At exactly two o'clock a brilliant light stabbed from the trees that Derek had located. Even Philip, who had expected it, was startled. It seemed impossible that a light from that distance could reach them with such hard radiance. The boys called to the rest of the group and pointed. Soon everyone was standing and staring toward Ilusan. "Check this out," said Philip. He removed a mirror from behind his back, caught the sun, and shot it back across the plain from the mountain peak. Immediately he was answered from Ilusan.

"No kidding," said Derek. He called to the rest of the group. "It's a mirror."

"Who's doing that?" said James, scrambling to join them.

"You'll never guess. It's Aunt Lillian and Aunt Evelyn," said Philip, using the familiar Ilusan titles for the Troyer sisters. "Of course they're using a much bigger mirror than I am, but I bet they can still see ours. I told them to flash toward the mountain every hour beginning at one until I answered. I wasn't sure how long it would take us to get here. So they've already flashed once."

When Philip had stopped by early that morning, the sisters had been delighted to assist him in his little experiment. It was touching how much they enjoyed Ilusan's children. "The kids will love it," he said, and they had been immediately on board.  A great shame two women like that had never married, Philip thought.

"Philip is climbing the mountain today," Lillian had said to Dorothy as the old woman clung to Philip's arm.

"You're going there to pray," Dorothy said as she patted his shoulder.

"I will say a prayer for you," Philip said. "You'll know I'm praying for you when you see a light from the mountain." He imagined the old woman standing with her daughters in their yard. What he didn't know until Lillian told him later that night was that Dorothy had wept for ten minutes after. And she sat on the porch staring at the mountain for the rest of the afternoon. Evelyn found her there sleeping peacefully several hours later.

After the light show ended and the group returned to eating and resting on the rocks, Kari briefly slipped her hand into Philip's. "That was nice," she whispered.

Sally scoped the plain below with Derek's binoculars. "I think I see a porcine creature," she said.

"You're weird Sally," said Bobby. But his tone of voice said otherwise. Sally caught it and glanced at him. A brief smile and she was back in the binoculars. Bobby glanced at Philip. Philip grinned at him and nodded. He expected Bobby to blush and turn away. Instead the boy smiled back, looked at Sally, looked back at Philip and smiled again.

It was a lot easier going down the mountain than up, especially when everyone slid most of the middle stage. It was then Philip realized the wisdom of Matt's advice to wear a pair of sturdy shorts under his jeans. Almost everyone's jeans sported ragged muddy holes by the time they reached the cogon grass. But a trip that required over four hours going up only took forty-five minutes coming down.

True to his word Matt pulled into a parking lot next to a small grocery store when they reached Bancud. "Bathroom and drink break," he said. "We'll leave in one half hour and head straight for the pool."

Philip wanted to walk around the barrio a bit. He asked Kari to join him but she had to find a bathroom. Sally eagerly volunteered to come along. They hadn't walked half a block before they were trailed by a dozen kids calling "Hey Joe." Philip stopped and shook hands with every one of them, an endeavor which only gathered a larger crowd. Sally looked uncomfortable. "O.k. kids, my friend and I are going to keep walking now," said Philip. The children laughed and followed along.

After another block Philip spotted a Sari-Sari store on the opposite side of the street. "I'll buy you a drink," he said to Sally, and, shadowed by the children, they crossed the dusty central avenue. The store was a shallow walkup, doorless and open to the street, but blessedly cool in the shade. A counter ran almost the entire length of the small shop. A man and his wife stepped forward to serve them.

Three men lounged just inside nursing cold San Miguel beers. They wore tattered tee shirts, long pants, and sandals. They were all smoking Marlboro cigarettes. They smiled and nodded, immediately attracted to Sally. "Can I buy the two of you a beer?" one of them asked, and they all laughed. Sally blanched and stepped back outside. She might have walked a good distance away, but she was trapped by the crowding children. She glanced back at Philip looking miserable. The children shyly circled her, staring.

"I'll tell you what," said Philip. "How about you buy my friend and I an orange soda and I'll buy the three of you another beer?" The men were delighted. They shook hands and the orders were immediately given. Philip explained that they had just climbed Capistrano and pointed back down the street to where the rest of the Americans were lounging around the trucks drinking sodas. When the drinks arrived Philip looked for Sally. She had walked a quarter of a block away.

"She is afraid of us," one of the men said.

"I'll get her," said Philip. "She's just shy." He walked to Sally trailed by the children. "The men bought you an orange soda."

"They make me nervous," she said.

"Why?" Philip was puzzled anew by the way the missionary kids reacted to the nationals. Sally must have been around hundreds of Filipinos over the years.

"I don't like how they look at me. They aren't Christians. They say bad words. They scare me."

And there it was again, light versus dark, the fear of those outside, the taint of the world. Only here it shadowed the face of a sweet young girl. But how long before her innocent nervousness transformed into the quivering lip of Ruth Sorenson?

Philip gently took hold of Sally's arm. "Do you remember what we talked about awhile back when you said I seemed like I was from 'out there,' that I wasn't afraid of 'out there'? I think it was maybe the day the bird died. Do you remember you said you wanted to change, that you wanted to stop being a kid? Well guess where we are. We're 'out there.' And here's an opportunity for you to start changing, to take a step toward being an adult. These are good men. They want to do something nice for you. They don't see many Americans. I think you should let them buy you a drink and then talk to them."

She was silent for a moment, looking down at her feet. Then she turned and gazed at the men in the store. "What should I talk about?"

"It's always good just to ask people about themselves. What do they do? And I bet they'll want to know why you're all dirty and your pants all torn up? Do you think you can do that?"

"I think I can do that if you come with me."

"Don't worry. I'm coming with you. I want my orange soda too." Together they walked back into the small store.

Afterward, after Sally had bravely accepted her orange soda, thanked the men, and looked them directly in the eye as she narrated her Capistrano adventure, and after the men had purchased her a second orange soda and a piece of warm pandesal for the trip home, she walked beside Philip back to the trucks. "Did you buy them beer?" Her voice was a little shaky. He read the uncertainty on her face.

"Do you think that was wrong?"

"Beer is bad." She stopped in the street and looked up at him. "Isn't it?"

Philip decided to be indirect. "The people out here, Sally, are the ones we should be the nicest to. That's what Jesus would do don't you think? Do you think he'd be mad at me for buying them beer or happy with us for being nice to them, for making some new friends?"

She understood. "I think he'd be happy we made some new friends."

"And what about you?"

They started walking again. "I'm happy too," she said.

On Thursday afternoon Philip spent an hour at the Platts' with the Montgomerys and the St. Clairs. They were planning a progressive dinner to end the week on a high note for the Faith kids. They would gather Saturday afternoon at 4:00 at Philip's for drinks and hors d'oeuvres. Kari would help him make the snacks. From there they would all go to the Platts' for a salad, then the Montgomerys' for the main course, and finally to the St. Clairs' for Julia's famous chocolate cake and ice cream. Then they would all repair once again to the Platts' for games and a special slide show that Oscar and his wife, Rhoda, had put together documenting their children's lives growing up at Ilusan.

After leaving the planning meeting at the Platts' home, which was on the eastern end of the plaza in front of the meeting hall, Philip decided to walk down to the pool for a swim. He moved slowly, enjoying the hot sun on his skin. He wanted to be perfectly warm before the plunge into the pool instantly turned him perfectly cool. As he approached the Sorensons' two-story house, he was startled to hear the sounds of fierce argument and then a crash. Someone had been pushed into furniture. He heard Derek say, "You're never going to touch me again," then Carnley's angry, "You think you can lie to me and get away with it?!" Derek spat, "Stay away from me," and then the front door burst open and, his face suffused with rage, he clattered down the stairs, jumped on his bike, and pedaled furiously away.

Philip froze and then shrank into the shadow of the large hibiscus at the corner of the lot between the Sorensons and the Waltons. He thought he knew what had happened. On Tuesday when Derek and James brought Keith to his house, the boys had told Philip that Derek had been suspended for a week from Faith Academy. It was a silly offense. He had been walking on the road between the school buildings and his dorm when the late afternoon school bus drove by. Derek had rightly surmised that the bus was going to the two hill dorms, which meant it was filled with sophomore through senior boys. Derek being Derek, he decided to entertain them by dropping his shorts and exhibiting his bare hindquarters in their general direction. He was gratified to hear their cheers.

This, in itself, would not have constituted a suspending offense even at Faith Academy. What Derek didn't know, however, was that Mrs. Lonclear, the principal's wife, had been invited by his dorm mother to stop by for afternoon tea. She was driving directly behind the bus and got a clear and close-up view of parts of Derek she had never seen before. It was rare enough that she saw those parts on her husband. They usually only came out after lights out and even then she closed her eyes and tried not to focus on the details. After viewing Derek's youthful posterior in broad daylight, she promptly drove her car off the road into the ditch and Derek promptly got suspended for a week. The week's suspension occurred directly before fall break and the boys had been racing every day to the mail room to intercept the principal's letter before it reached Carnley. Philip figured they'd either gotten there too late today or someone else had ratted Derek out.

Philip saw Derek's path cross his sister's by the meeting hall. They spoke briefly and then both headed toward the pool. So the older kids were out of harm's way. He breathed a sigh of relief and was just about to continue his walk when he heard Carnley snarl, "You boys knew about this." Bobby and Drew were still inside.

Philip knew Carnley well enough to suspect what was coming next. What he had no way of preparing for, however, was the raw violence of the sound of the unseen beating. At least it was the belt, not the board, but the rapid stinging cracks and the moans of the boys made Philip clammy and sick. He looked wildly at the surrounding houses. Couldn't they hear this? Would they rush out to stop it? But windows were always open at Ilusan, and they'd heard it all before. Nobody came. For a long second Philip thought of running up the stairs and bursting in, but he hadn't the courage. He sagged into the hibiscus. When he heard Drew cry, "Stop, stop, stop," he'd had enough. He turned and fled in the opposite direction back to his house, to his safe porch, to where his cat was waiting to be picked up and hugged fiercely for a long choking moment. The taste of self-loathing and hatred was in his mouth. The memory of his own father was on his mind.

On Friday afternoon a number of the high school kids lounged on Philip's porch. Several of the eighth grade boys were there as well. They had just finished an hour of basketball in the hot sun and then a half hour of swimming. Everyone was lethargic. A few girls took chairs into the yard where the sun warmed their water-cooled bodies. They were content. Conversation drifted here and there.

Philip had a brief moment, when he and Derek raided his refrigerator for drinks, to bring up the events of yesterday. He had to know how Bobby and Drew made out. Derek accepted Philip's question as if he had a perfect right to ask it, although his eyes were briefly troubled. "They're bruised, but they'll survive. That's nothing new at our house." He looked sadly at Philip. "It was my fault. I shouldn't have left. But Lizzie and I survived him and so will Bobby and Drew. Another year and they'll both be up at Faith. And then they're almost free."

Philip didn't trust his voice. He simply nodded and briefly laid his hand on the boy's shoulder. "At least they have school and your class," said Derek. "They both love your class and your porch. You'll look after them." His eyes asked the obvious question.

Philip nodded again. "I'll do my best," he managed.

When they emerged back onto the porch the girls were planning a joke on the Montgomerys. With the progressive dinner scheduled to arrive at Bob and Loretta's for the main course on Saturday night, Jenny Platt and Lizzie Sorenson decided it would be funny to show up an evening early, all dressed and ready to go. "Loretta is so proper, she'll get totally flustered," said Jenny. They talked Debby Meyer and Jenny's sister, Joby, into joining them. The boys glanced at each other and said nothing.

After the girls left to put their plan into motion Derek, almost asleep on the couch, said to James, "We should go warn you parents." That woke the guys up.

"And when they come out we should nail them with water balloons," said Keith.

"Do your parents have a hose?" asked Philip.

The boys looked at each other. "This is too good," said James.

That night when the girls arrived, Bob Montgomery opened the door and said, "Hi. We've been waiting for you." They entered to find a table with four places neatly set and candles burning. Joby Platt, the youngest, squeaked with surprise while the older girls looked at each other desperate to figure out what was going on. They knew nothing else to do, so they sat obediently at the table. Loretta came out of the kitchen in a long blue dress. She laid dishes of cold peaches before them.

"We've been saving these for tonight," she said. Joby squeaked again and looked for cues from the older girls. Lizzie threatened a giggle fit, but managed to choke it off. They enjoyed their peaches and graceful conversation with the Montgomerys for the next forty-five minutes. From a room below the dining room, James, Derek, Keith and Philip listened quietly to the conversation above them and filled water balloons.

Outside, beneath the stairs the girls would have to descend, they had already hooked up a hose.

The boys were in place under the stairs and around the corners of the house when the girls said their goodbyes. Lizzie began to question Jenny in hushed tones as soon as Bob closed the door behind them. They had just stepped off the landing into the yard when the first balloons struck and exploded. Three of the girls screamed and ran into the plaza. Lizzie Sorenson ducked under the stairs yelling, "Ha, ha James you missed me!" She came face to face with Philip. "Oh," she said. Then she saw the hose. "Oh no you wouldn't." But Philip would.

Before the evening was over the water fight extended the length and breadth of the center and involved virtually every child Philip's age and under. Balloons, hoses, glasses, pitchers, buckets and rain barrels became weapons at various times, and blitzkrieg attacks from bicycles and even motorcycles were employed. Collateral damage included a direct hit on the back of Gordon Lundy's head as he took his evening stroll, loose pieces of water balloon on the Van Kleeks' verandah where Jerry and Mary had been enjoying the evening before being spotted by Philip, Bobby, and Sally (who had formed a water team of sorts), and Mr. Bumbles who had to clean himself for half an hour after catching most of a bucket intended for Philip as he ducked onto his porch.

After lights out that night Philip, Kari and Keith sat on his porch and told stories of the evening. They had worked for twenty minutes wiping down and mopping Philip's living room, which was thoroughly drenched after his house became the focus of an onslaught led by Derek, Lizzie, James, the Platt girls, and Kari herself. Philip, Keith, Bobby and Sally had eventually had to run up the white flag or risk the soaking of everything he owned. As it was he was down one lamp and an entire change of bedding.

"I can't believe you helped lead an attack on me," Philip said to Kari.

"We would have forced you to surrender even earlier if Keith hadn't switched sides."

"It was the honorable thing to do," said Keith, rubbing the welt on his arm inflicted when Derek threw his entire bucket at him as Keith changed sides in mid-battle. "It's my home now too."

"And despite the beating we took," said Philip, "I never heard Keith utter a prohibited word."

"Did anybody manage to nail Mr. Sorenson tonight?" mused Keith.

"No," said Kari, "which is probably a good thing. He would have melted, the wicked witch of the Far East."

Philip looked at Kari in mock astonishment. "Good for you girl! That's the first mean thing I've ever heard you say."

Kari covered her face with her hands. "I shouldn't have said that." Philip knew she meant it.

"The son of a bitch deserved it," said Keith.

The Saturday evening progressive dinner went off without a hitch. The Faith students dressed up. The boys wore long pants and button-up shirts. The girls wore summer dresses or slacks. Everyone looked well-scrubbed, tanned, and achingly young. The emotion that would build in Philip all evening first tugged at him as he and Kari served cold drinks and lumpia to the high schoolers as they sat on his porch or stood in his yard. In just one week he had been so thoroughly adopted by these kids that he felt not one hint of self-conscious tension as he moved among them. He was able for the first time to name what he had experienced that week, and indeed had been experiencing ever since arriving at this far-off place. It was the grace that flows between human beings when a community opens itself to welcome the outsider. He thought that perhaps it was one of the most powerful things a human could experience. He knew there were those who would still cast him out if they could, but he determined not to let the few ruin his friendship, his fellowship, with the many.

After the opening snack at Philip's, the group moved to the Platts' where Oscar and Rhoda had collected photo albums from all the parents as a teaser for the promised slide show later that evening. Then to the Montgomerys', where Bob and Loretta crammed tables into every available inch of their dining and living rooms so the group could have a sit-down dinner. Philip wound up between Jenny Platt and Lizzie Sorenson and, quite naturally, every detail of the evening before was hashed and rehashed. Jenny was a contagious giggler and enthusiastic story teller, and everyone in her vicinity wound up laughing more than eating. But the stories were difficult to contain. They spilled from table to table and at times various ones had the attention of the entire room as they recounted a particularly memorable moment during the week.

Afterward Bob Montgomery, who had given piano lessons to many of the center's children, entertained the group with a brief organ concert. The organ was a family heirloom which Bob had taken great pains to ship from his grandmother's home in Vermont. It was the best organ on the base, perhaps the best in Mindanao, and most of the young people had rarely heard one this nice played by someone who knew what they were doing. The applause was genuine. Moments later the applause at the St. Clairs' for Julia's chocolate cake was equally as genuine. She had baked an enormous cake decorated with a scene of kids playing by the swimming hole. Matt constructed a diving board from matchsticks and trees from bits of broom. Several cameras came out before the first slice of cake was served.

Everyone, including the St. Clairs and Montgomerys wound up back at the Platts' for the slide show. The room was packed. Every chair was occupied by two or three kids, including three beanbag chairs collected from various spots on the center. Philip wound up standing in a corner where he could both view the slides and watch the audience. It was there, with the lights dimmed, that the full force of his emotion swept over him. The slides were both poignant and hilarious. They chronicled the lives of a group of kids who had lived together on the center since before they entered grade school. Watching them now, the girls with arms around each other on the bean bags or the couches, the boys leaning against the girls or draped over the corners of chairs, he ached for what they so casually knew. He had never had one friend as close as these kids were to each other, and they had half a dozen or more within easy reach right in this room. Yes, he had been welcomed into this community, but he realized now the price he had paid for his estrangement from the community of his own youth. He was learning that grace could be exquisitely painful.

As he viewed the slides and laughed with the kids who had made him so quickly a part of their lives, regrets whispered around the edges of his consciousness. He thought that the beauty and unbearable sadness of life knew no bounds. He had experienced them both this week in the joy of a water fight and a mountain expedition, and in the terror of hearing children abused. He had a woman he loved now, but so many friends he had shortchanged in the past. He had been accepted into a community now, but could never be as tight with it as these kids were. Had he lost his opportunity to be part of something like this? He thought he probably had. Could adults ever know the unaffected passion of childhood friendships?

He hadn't realized that his face betrayed his feeling until he caught Kari's eye across the dim room. She was standing at the edge of the kitchen, leaning against the counter. Now she was looking at him with alarm. "Are you o.k.?" she mouthed. All he could do was smile weakly and shake his head. How could he explain that he was both o.k. and not o.k.?

Later that night, after Keith left the house for a late night swim with the older kids, and after he tried to explain to Kari what he had felt during the evening, they stood on his porch and hugged each other for a long time. With her face buried in his shirt, she took deep breaths as if memorizing his scent. She whispered, "I'll be your community." Later she pulled him onto the couch. "I love you," she said. "Most of the time I never let myself believe you really love me. Tonight I'm letting myself believe."

He thought it a statement that encapsulated the primary dilemma of human existence. "Believe it," he said.

There were two additional memorable moments for Philip before the Faith kids left on a bus for Cagayan early Monday morning. The first came at the center's outdoor potluck on Sunday afternoon. Tables were set up on the plaza in front of the meeting hall. By noon they were laden with food and the plaza filled with Ilusan's missionary families. It was a joyful gathering, albeit given a sense of urgency by dark clouds approaching from Katanglad. Philip was welcomed to a table lined with young people. Derek Sorenson and Jenny Platt insisted he sit between them, crowding against the friends sitting next to them to carve out a small space for Philip to squeeze in. He was absorbed with the conversation around him when he noticed Carnley standing with a plate of food, alone, casting about for a place to sit.

Uncertainty registered on his face. His children had warm spots, crushed between friends. His wife had found her place in a circle of women. But no welcoming seat opened for Carnley. Desperate not to stand out, the man made furtive glances, pretending to drink from his glass, scanning for a friendly face, a waving hand, a caller familiar with his name. But none came. Watching the man, Philip was touched with pity. But then he shook his head and turned abruptly back to the conversations and laughter around him.

Another moment that Philip would long remember came in the early dawn of Monday morning. Around the center alarms went off at 4:00 a.m. so that the young people could gather at the pool for one last swim before eating breakfast and boarding the bus that would launch their journey back to Manila and the completion of the fall term at Faith Academy. It was still dark when one by one they plunged into the icy waters to emerge with yelps of pain. It took Philip a long time to gather the fortitude to take the plunge and even then he had to be encouraged by the threat of a push from the high school boys. He then was equally encouraging of Kari.

After promising the kids they would see them off after breakfast, Kari walked with Philip back to his house. Before ducking through the fence and returning to her room, she opened the towel that was wrapped tightly around her and invited Philip in for a long kiss. Mr. Bumbles watched from the porch as the sun's first lengthy rays ventured across the lawn and fingered Kari's heels. As her wet chilled body, only thinly covered with the material of her swimsuit, pulsed against Philip's, the raw eroticism of the moment claimed his full attention. "This chastity bit is getting more and more difficult," he said.

Kari leaned away from him and smiled. "You know what to do about that," she said. "When you make that decision, I'll say yes."

# Chapter Nine

THE SATANISTS CAME TO Ilusan the first week of November. Well ex-Satanists to be exact. They were followed two weeks later by Satan himself. Well actually probably just a demon or two. Maybe three. Possibly four or more. There was some dispute over the actual numbers, and later the missionaries had to admit that none of them in the room that day thought to keep an exact count. Besides, one could never tell for sure when a demon gave its name whether it was referring to just itself or to an entire family group or kinship network. Demons were tricky that way. After all when Jesus asked the Gerasene demoniac to reveal his name, the demon replied, "My name is Legion," a pretty clever bit of wordplay which proved that, even when faced with annihilation, a demon could be irritatingly cheeky. Jesus seemed to find it clever too and he sent the devils into a heard of pigs instead of casting them immediately into hell, do not pass Go, do not collect $200. But at any rate the ex-Satanists came first.

Ilusan was abuzz for a week over the coming of the ex-Satanists, Joseph and Mary Salmon. That their names were Joseph and Mary was not a coincidence as it turned out; it was all part of the most exciting diabolical plot most evangelicals had ever been privileged to hear. And Salmon? Well a salmon was a fish, and the fish was the early symbol of the Christian church, so once again the devil was either being extremely clever in inverting Christian symbols, or he was just downright juvenile. The Salmons had first turned up on Bob Landers' television show in California. Landers made a splash, and a bundle of money, in the early 1970s with a book on the end times called *The End of the World as We Know It: Catch a Ride on the Rapture Express or Bleed Out and Burn at Armageddon*. The book sold more copies than the Bible for a few years. Philip read it during his aborted year at Bible college and had found it both hilarious and terrifying. Now, however, Landers was into Satan. He had his own television show on a prominent evangelical network, a gorgeous co-host who spun weird and ghastly stories about her time as a Satanic high priestess, and an entire host of viewers enamored of their weekly catharsis of Bible and Beelzebub. It was "The Rocky Horror Picture Show" for Christians. The Salmons had a three month run on Landers' show and now were traveling the world exhorting Christians everywhere to be on the lookout for the devil's disciples in high places. In Manila they had been persuaded by Philip's uncle to take an idyllic side trip to Ilusan to share their story with the BTM missionaries.

They spoke at the Wednesday night prayer meeting. The meeting hall was packed and the audience hummed with anticipation. Philip's seventh and eighth grade students were all there, but the younger children had been left at home. They were too young to hear the "sensational true story" of the couple "bred for Satanism." Philip and Joseph Haaf sat together in a back pew. Kari and Celia refused to sit with them, because, as Celia put it, "you're just here to mock." And, in fact, Celia was right. Although Philip at least felt a bit guilty for his initial skepticism and was trying to keep an open mind, Joseph was in full and fabulous flower. He sat proudly in the seat of the scornful and dared anyone to dislodge him. Philip and Kari had just come from dinner at the Haaf house, and Joseph had infuriated Celia with his rant against gullible evangelicals and their penchant for embracing and stuffing money into the pockets of "every fakir with a good story." Having grown up in the Bible churches of his father, Philip knew Joseph was right. He had seen these sorts of folk come and go, and never once had anyone in his church questioned their fantastic accounts. And he thought he knew why. To be an evangelical was to be a believer. It was as simple as that.

And the Salmons' account was truly fantastic. They were both stunning specimens of humanity. In some ways the devil was like a spoiled high school coed. He preferred the beautiful people. Philip supposed Satan didn't choose ugly people because they were already living through hell. Hell as destination spot would simply be Hollywood on fire, the final cruel trick on mortal expectations. Heaven would be filled with the homely and personality disordered, no mirrors and a willing but socially unobservant conversation partner on every corner.

The Salmons had been raised in Satanism, chosen from birth as special breeders and named appropriately to mock the holy couple. Joseph whispered to Philip, "When your advertising slogan in the yellow pages is 'The best we can offer you is hell,' no wonder you have to breed your own kids to grow any kind of decent-sized church." The two children were first brought together for stud purposes when they were six years old. Joseph groaned, but the rest of the audience was appropriately horrified. "Is that even possible?" Joseph muttered. They were bred periodically after that. Mary was sent to Catholic schools so she could learn all about the enemy. "So what are we, chopped liver?" growled Joseph. "Why don't Satanists ever infiltrate Protestant churches? I demand equal treatment. I want an honest-to-goodness Satanist love child sitting next to me in the pew."

Joseph's whispers were getting louder. Philip shushed him with a nervous glare.

Mary stole supplies from the Catholic Church to use in satanic rituals. "That explains it," said Joseph. "Protestants don't have enough cool stuff." Mary, a better speaker than her husband, announced to the hushed audience that she had witnessed numerous rituals involving human sacrifice. She saw a demon crush a man's neck while the victim knelt in a Pentagram.

Philip looked for Kari. She turned and found him. Her eyes were shocked. Philip shook his head at her, trying to communicate a warning not to take this too seriously. But Kari was beyond such discernment. There were moments when her attachment to the subculture was almost childlike. He scanned the rest of the crowd. They were transfixed. Sally was staring hard at the couple up front. Then she too caught Philip's eye. She looked at him a moment and smiled. Then she whispered something to her mother, got up, looked at Philip again, and exited out the back. She was gone just a moment before she slipped quietly into the pew beside him.

"I told my Mom I had to go to the bathroom," she whispered. She glanced over to see if her mother had noticed her return. She had not. "Do you believe them Mr. Andrews?"

"What do you think about their story?"

"There's something wrong. But I don't know what."

"I agree with you. Let's listen to the rest of it and then we'll talk afterward."

Mary was narrating how both she and Joseph had managed to escape from the Satanists separately, how they became Christians (the audience cheered loudly), and then ran into each other at a church. They married and began to have children. But then the Satanists found them and took their revenge. They captured Mary and her child. They asked her where her husband was. When she refused to say, they killed her baby in front of her eyes. The audience gasped. Sally stiffened. Philip touched her arm and shook his head. She nodded. Beside them Joseph had sunk into a stupor. His head was down, his hands over his eyes, and he was moaning softly.

Two more of their children were kidnapped. The couple believed their lives were even now constantly in danger. That's why they had never gone to the authorities with their story. "Listen carefully here," Philip said to Sally. The couple concluded by declaring that the upper level Satanists weren't the weirdoes seen on television. (Nobody in the room seemed to notice the self-indictment implicit in that statement. Joseph was beyond noticing much of anything.) They had high positions in world leadership, "white collar Satanists." They were never caught, never associated with Satanism.

Mary said, "They know they are going to hell, so this world is their slice of heaven. Power is what they seek." Ba-da boom, said a voice in Philip's head. What a great close.

It was an amazing story. The meeting ended as several offered fervent spontaneous prayers. But it didn't finally end before the offering basket was passed. Philip held it in front of Sally and shook it. "No thanks," she said.

"Good girl. Let's see how much Uncle Joseph puts in." He held it in front of Joseph, but Joseph had not changed his posture for the last fifteen minutes. Philip handed the basket to the usher.

Afterward Joseph was about to launch into a tirade, or at least that's what Philip suspected, but he was cut short when his wife and Kari joined them at the back of the room. Celia had tears in her eyes. "Those poor children," she said. Joseph threw up his hands in disgust and stomped out of the building.

"What's the matter with him?" said Kari.

"Uncle Joseph, Mr. Andrews, and I think they weren't telling the truth," said Sally.

"Sally, how could you say that?" Celia looked at the girl, then at Philip.

"If you saw one of your girls murdered in front of your eyes and had the other two kidnapped, what would you do?" Philip looked from Celia to Kari to Sally. Sally smiled.

Celia looked puzzled. Then she looked to the front of the room where the ex-Satanists were surrounded by adoring missionaries. "I guess I'd go to the police and make sure those people all wound up dead or in jail."

"Of course you would," said Philip. "And it would lead the nightly news for weeks. Maybe months. And you probably wouldn't travel the world turning your children's deaths into riveting speeches."

"But they didn't do anything because they were afraid of the Satanists," said Kari.

Fossia had been making her way toward them and she arrived in time to overhear Kari's remark. She smacked her housemate lightly on the back of the head. "Don't Satanists watch TV?" she asked. "Maybe they don't watch Christian television where these two have been spilling their guts for months. Come on girl, you're going to give brains a bad name. Actually I'm expecting a squad of Satanists riding demon-possessed monkeys to come charging through the door any second now. We better arm ourselves."

They all gaped at her. Philip was gratified to have the principal on his side, but astonished that she would so quickly dismiss the testimony of fellow Christians and in such glib terms. "And all these white collar powerful world leader Satanists," said Fossia. "Did they name one of them?"

"No they didn't," said Kari. She sounded a bit put out.

"We rest our case," said Sally. The adults looked at her. The girl had a huge smile on her face.

Fossia turned to the front of the room where missionaries still crowded around the Salmons. "Baaaa," she said. She bleated like a sheep twice more. When she turned back she caught Philip's eye. He must have still looked astonished. She slapped his arm. "Come on Philip. Lighten up. Have a sense of humor. It was an entertaining evening." She laughed as cheerful a laugh as Philip had ever heard from her, gave Kari an affectionate but firm Dutch rub, which caused the librarian to wince, then, still chuckling, headed for the front of the room.

"Is she going to cause trouble?" Philip asked Kari.

"You never know with her," said Kari, still rubbing her head.

"I'm never going to hear the end of this from Joseph," said Celia.

"Don't tell him if you put anything in the offering," said Philip.

"Oh no!" Celia covered her face with her hands. "Maybe I can get it back out."

"I still can't believe they'd make it up," said Kari. "Why would anyone do that?"

"Mr. Andrews," said Sally. She looked concerned. "I don't think you should tell the class tomorrow about this. Some of their parents," here she looked at him and made a face, "won't like you saying anything bad about the Satanists. Let me do it. That way you won't get into trouble."

It was sweet to see the girl protecting him. "Thank you Sally! I'll let you take care of the debunking."

"I don't know that word. Would you write it down for me please?" Sally dug a pencil out of her pocket and handed it to Philip.

Philip and Jerry were golfing when the demon possessed man arrived at Ilusan in a Helio. He arrived in dramatic fashion, with his hands around Tom Jacobsen's neck as the airplane bounced hard onto the runway in front of the golfers. It veered sharply toward the corn field before Tom managed to wrest himself free from Madong and cut the engine in the middle of the strip. Lillian Troyer was in the back seat with the possessed man and she tried to calm him as he clawed for the door.

Lillian had been out to her allocation for a short visit and had decided to bring Madong, the older brother of the chief of the tribe, to Ilusan to see if the doctors or prayer warriors could help him. "He went nuts when he saw your golf course on the runway," Tom later said to Jerry after they got the man under control. "Lillian said he kept yelling about the eyes of the spirit of the earth. We might have to come up with a new mission policy for flying demoniacs into runways that double as golf courses."

"I'm guessing this was a unique incident," said Jerry, "which suggests that your desire for a new policy might be a trifle supererogatory at the moment. It probably calls for a footnote at best."

But that conversation was still about fifteen minutes in the future as Philip and Jerry ran for the airplane. Tom was already out and opening the back door when they arrived. Philip's initial curiosity turned to genuine concern when a small wizened half-naked brown man leapt through the door and knocked Tom off his feet. The man was snarling and appeared to entertain the notion of relieving Tom of a hunk of his neck with his teeth. Philip leapt on him and they both rolled off of the pilot. Philip had an immediate impression of tremendous strength, and, despite his tight grip around the man's chest, would certainly have lost him if George Donahoe and Oscar Platt had not arrived just then on a dead run. They, along with Jerry and Tom, each grabbed an appendage and hung on for dear life. The man gave one blood-curdling shriek and then went limp as a sleeping kitten. Five minutes later he was chattering happily with Lillian while the men eyed him warily and rubbed their bruises. "He's really a very nice man," said Lillian. "He's just got a devil in him."

Half an hour later, after Tom restarted the Helio and taxied it to the hangar, and after Lillian took Madong to their home, and after Philip fetched Matt St. Clair, the men huddled and discussed what to do. They all agreed the situation was a bit outside of their fields of expertise. "But I don't like the idea of that fellow being alone with the Troyers in their home," said Matt. "I think one of you should fetch Doc Lyman from Malaybalay," he said to Tom and George, "and I'll go get Aunt Hortense and see what she thinks."

Horace and Hortense Balfour were the oldest couple at Ilusan. They were the dorm parents for Happy Holler where the youngest of the center's children boarded. Horace was fast sliding into senility. He spent his days getting lost in the banana orchard and, at times, his nights crawling into bed beside one or another of the first and second grade children. The children wouldn't have minded so much except that he snored like the end of days and indulged in great heaves of windy flatulence that liked to have set linens on fire.

Hortense, on the other hand, was entirely to be reckoned with. If anyone at Ilusan achieved sainthood, it would be this wizened old woman with her steady get-the-job-done manner. She could be found most days in her rocking chair with a Bible the size of a small goat in her lap and a beaded necklace in her hands dispensing instructions to the house girls whenever they dared to meekly approach. She had grown up Catholic and loved the feel of beads between her fingers when she prayed. And, although there was no cross on the necklace in order to allay the suspicions of her Protestant community, the beads were worn to a nub. Many a sick child took comfort from the sound of Aunt Hortense's voice and the click of her beads as she kept lonely vigil during dark fevered nights.

She was known in the surrounding communities for her good works, and may well have been the most loved westerner in all of Mindanao.

And she was certainly the most feared of all of Christ's Ilusan followers in the echoing chambers of hell. When Hortense Balfour arranged herself to pray, the underworld's mightiest demons battened down the hatches and hoped to ride out the storm. And if she addressed a devil directly, well it had better keep its heads about it or a herd of pigs would be far too nice a fate. If Hortense had been disposed toward such sentiment, she might, as she walked bent over with her eyes on the ground toward the Troyer house, have said, "They'll be burning by nightfall." But she never said anything of the sort. Instead she said to Matt St. Clair, after refusing a ride on his motorcycle, "Have someone bring my rocking chair, see if one of the ladies can look after Horace, and make sure to fetch Ruth Sorenson. I suppose Carnley will have to come too. Make sure a few other men are there, strong ones, to help when the poor man gets agitated. But instruct them not to get in the way. Ruthie and I will do the talking, but you all can help with the praying."

Matt filled Philip in on what was taking place when he walked over to ask him to come to the Troyers to provide muscle if needed. Philip could hear the hymn singing coming from two houses down and had already figured something was up. He was nervous but intensely curious. He wanted to ask Matt if he thought Madong was really demon possessed, but was afraid such a transparent question would demonstrate a telling lack of faith. So he kept his mouth shut.

The scene that presented itself when they arrived at the Troyers' wasn't anything like what Philip expected. He had seen "The Exorcist," and William Friedkin had cast nobody close to Aunt Hortense. She sat in her rocking chair with her Bible on her lap and her beads in her hand in front of Madong and Lillian who were placed on the couch with their backs to the wall. Ruth Sorenson sat next to Aunt Hortense. There was no way out for Madong except through the two ladies. Evelyn and her mother sat together on the far side of the room next to the bedroom. Carnley, Matt, Oscar Platt and Tom Jacobsen were standing against various walls. Philip eased in next to the door. He tried to avoid Carnley's glare. The man clearly didn't think Philip could be of any help in the supernatural realm.

When Philip entered, Aunt Hortense was reading Bible passages that described Jesus casting out demons. Although Lillian translated as best she could, the missionaries seemed to operate under the assumption that demons spoke English. Aunt Hortense and Ruth both addressed Madong directly as if they were speaking through him to an urbane, if recalcitrant, truant English schoolboy. "So you see," Aunt Hortense was saying, "Jesus has power over you and when we speak in his name you must obey us." Madong stared around the room uneasily. He clearly hadn't kicked into demon gear yet. Philip couldn't imagine what the poor guy thought was about to happen.

Just then Dorothy, who had been squinting through her watering eyes at Philip, said loudly, "Jesus is here."

"Oh yes dear," said Ruth, "do you sense his presence too? Let's call on his name together."

"No need to call," said Dorothy. "He's right here." It was the most coherent sentence Philip had ever heard her speak.

"Why yes dear, that's right. Why don't you pray quietly with the rest of us? Jesus is always right with us." Ruth turned back to Madong.

"No he's not always here," said Dorothy. "But he's here now." Lillian shot a look at Philip and then Evelyn. Evelyn quietly took Dorothy into the bedroom.

The room hushed as Aunt Hortense began to invoke the name of Jesus and command whoever was troubling Madong to reveal himself. Philip wondered what playbook Aunt Hortense was operating by, but figured her relaxed manner indicated long experience. Maybe she wrote the playbook. Probably it came from long study of Bible passages relating to exorcism. Nothing much happened for the next half hour or so. Aunt Hortense and Ruth took turns reading passages of Scripture and addressing whatever was inside Madong.

All that changed when Ruth asked Lillian to tell Madong to repeat after her, "Jesus is God's son. Jesus is Lord." Lillian addressed Madong. Madong had just begun to compliantly reply when his body stiffened. He was quiet for a long second, then he leaned toward the women in front of him and barked loudly three times. Philip felt every muscle in his body tense. He glanced at Matt, but Matt was riveted on the scene before him. Madong stood, his voice dropped an octave, and he growled something. Lillian's voice quavered as she said, "He says he does not recognize your Jesus." Every man in the room was poised to leap into action, although Philip felt even more prepared to lunge for the door. But Aunt Hortense calmly said, "Sit down," and Madong sat down.

"What is your name?" Aunt Hortense barely moved, although Philip thought she was leaning forward slightly.

Madong spat a word at her. Lillian translated. "I think he said the word for rage."

While Ruth prayed next to her, Aunt Hortense began to command the demon named Rage to leave the body of Madong. Her voice was quietly insistent. Madong twisted on the couch. He growled and spat. Suddenly he lurched sideways. He sensed an opening. He leapt over the side of the couch and charged for the door. Matt lunged at him, but was shoved aside. Then he was in front of Philip. Philip stepped in his way. Madong hit him in the face with what felt like the force of three men. Philip went down in a tangle of body and legs, but Madong tripped over him and came down with him. Then the rest of the men were on top of them. It was like being under a hungry mountain lion. The man would have torn him apart except that he had to deal with four other men. Philip was kicked, bitten, and stomped on. Later he couldn't be sure by whom; he rather uncharitably thought Carnley might have gotten in some free shots. As at the airstrip, Madong eventually went limp and placidly returned to the couch. Philip groaned and crawled for the door. Not for the first time he wondered if he was a son of Sceva.

Philip sat on the porch the rest of the afternoon. Evelyn came out and attended to his wounds. She left him with a bag of ice to hold over his rapidly swelling eye. Matt poked his head out and asked him to sit tight, to be the last line of defense if they needed him. So Philip sat, his head aching, and listened to the battle going on inside the house. He never got to see what it was like when a demon actually left a man, but he was forced to assume they actually did. At one point Matt came outside and said, "Rage and Lust have left the building. Now we're dealing with Jealousy." There were no more physical scrapes, although voices were raised quite a few times. At one point Philip heard Aunt Hortense telling Pride that no, he most definitely could not be the last one to leave. It sounded like Pride broke down sobbing, although that might have been Lack-of-Self-Control.

It was Carnley who finally came outside and told Philip he was free to go. The man actually smiled at him. He asked to see Philip's eye. "That's quite a shiner," he said. He looked at Philip for a long moment, quiet in his victory. Philip thought he had the weary glow of a man just emerged from long physical combat. "This is no place for genteel sophisticated Christians," Carnley said. "Over here you have to choose sides."

Later that night Kari snugged herself against him on the couch on his porch. He told her the entire story. She was fascinated, but all she said at the end was, "Now you're going to have a black eye when my parents get here."

They were silent, listening to Bumbles purring. He was stretched across both their laps.

"Do you think that man was really demon possessed?" Kari finally asked.

"Rage made a believer out of me," said Philip.

The next week was Thanksgiving week. Of more importance to Kari and Philip, it was the week of Kari's parents' visit. They arrived Monday afternoon after school. Philip sat with Kari on his porch waiting for the announcement of their flight. Kari was on pins and needles. She was tense, listening. Philip eyed her from where he sat leaning back with his legs on the porch rail. She had dressed for the occasion and put on more makeup than usual. The effect was altogether lovely. She got up and scanned the sky again. Then she looked Philip over. "You're way too relaxed," she said.

"How could your parents not like me?" He grinned at her. "Don't worry so much. I'm a likeable guy."

"That's not the problem. They'll probably like you more than they like me." She was only half teasing.

"Don't be ridiculous," he said.

"I wish your poor eye didn't look so terrible." It was true. His right eye had turned jaundice yellow. Worse, the greater portion of the white of his eye, where capillaries had shattered by the thousands at the force of Madong's blow, had turned a deep red. The effect was eerie, like a drunk werewolf.

"Should I wear a patch?"

She didn't answer, just gave him a look. "Don't tell my parents you were beaten up by a demon possessed man."

"You don't think it'll give me a certain cachet?"

"No. They'll wonder why you didn't have the power of the Spirit to overcome him. Why didn't you have the power of the Spirit to overcome him?"

"I was thinking about you, how beautiful you are and how much I love you, and the devil caught me off guard. You can't be thinking about beautiful women when you're dealing with the devil."

Kari laughed, then came over and brushed him with a kiss. "Good answer. You are very quick on your feet aren't you?"

"That's why I'm such a likeable guy." He caught her arm and pulled her onto his lap.

"Don't mess up my makeup," she said, but then they were interrupted by the distant announcement from the radio shack.

"The flight from Cagayan will be arriving in ten minutes. On board are Mr. and Mrs. Saul Trainor, the parents of our very own school librarian, Kari Trainor. Once again the flight from Cagayan will arrive in ten minutes. Mr. and Mrs. Saul Trainor on board."

Philip was about to compliment Julia St. Clair's nod to Kari in her announcement, but Kari was already off his lap. She dashed into his bedroom to check herself in the large mirror over the bureau. Over the past month familiarity with Philip's porch had turned into familiarity with the rest of his house as they both gradually laid aside the conventions of Ilusan courtship. As long as no one was around to be offended, it seemed absurd to stay out of the house. They were already alone. What difference did it make?

He followed her into the bedroom. She stared at herself with a skeptical eye. "Do I look like a daughter you'd be proud of?"

"You look like the woman of my dreams."

"Touché again," she said. "I almost believe you." She touched him lightly on the cheek before heading for the door. Over her shoulder she said, "But right now it's my parents I'm worried about. You haven't had to forgive as much as they have."

A line from Scripture popped into Philip's head. "From whom much is forgiven, much is required." It was only a slight mangling of the text, but it seemed at that moment to explain a great deal.

~~~

Saul Trainor was an extraordinarily tall man. His wife, Doris, was short. Philip's first thought on seeing them was that any size influence they might have on their grandchildren's gene pool was probably a wash. That he thought of their grandchildren at all indicated the trend of his dreams for him and Kari. Philip understood perfectly what Kari meant when she said several weeks prior that "When you make that decision, I'll say yes." And although he had not yet popped the question, he and Kari had begun to talk about the future as if it naturally included the other. They had even indulged in a conversation about children. Two, Philip said. Seven, Kari countered. They bargained their way down to four, with an option for three or five depending on how things went.

Philip wore sunglasses to his first meeting with the Trainors on the hangar tarmac. He thought it might make for a better first impression. Kari introduced him and he shook hands. "Welcome to Ilusan," he said.

Saul was an outgoing warm-hearted man. He said what was on his mind, but rarely meant any harm. Perhaps because he was so tall and spent most of his time talking to the top of other people's heads, he had never closely observed the tell-tale facial reactions that indicated a less than welcome reception for his words. And his ears were too far from his wife's mouth to register her disapproving grunts. Consequently he continued to live his life with the notion that everyone was as happy as he and that they enjoyed his witty remarks as much as he enjoyed dispensing them. Now he looked Philip over and said, "Kari, your boyfriend looks like he ought to be in a rock-and-roll band. He's prettier than you are."

Doris Trainor lived at a much more earth-bound level. She was like a cat that learns the hard way, after being tromped on a few times, that humans don't see well in the dark. While her husband blundered happily through life, she moved carefully, sizing up situations and people before speaking, often staying out of the way entirely when she thought someone of her stature and personality could make no difference. But she loved her husband and daughter fiercely and would have thrown herself into a tornado to save them from harm. She was prepared to be equally as loyal to her daughter's husband when that time came. Now she squeezed her husband's hand hard and said, "I think handsome is the word you're looking for honey."
~~~

Kari was a veteran of years of negotiating her parents' divergent personalities. She deftly exploited the opportunity presented her by her father's humor to introduce Philip's wounded eye. "I wonder if you'll still think he's pretty Daddy after seeing what he really looks like." She reached up and took off Philip's glasses.

Saul said, "Well would you look at that?" He leaned down and looked at that. "I see my daughter has learned from her mother how to keep a man in line."

"That's not true Daddy," said Kari. "Mom doesn't hit nearly as hard as I do."

Saul roared with laughter and enveloped his daughter in a big hug. He planted a kiss on the top of her head.

"Actually," said Philip, "I was hit by the older brother of a tribal chief. He's a bit crazy and they brought him in for treatment. He's fine now, but when he first got here, the plane ride had shaken him up and it took several of us to subdue him. I got the worst of it." It was the story they had agreed to tell. It satisfied Saul for the moment. He looked around at the hangar and the small crowd gathered to greet them. Most of the windows in the facility had been repaired, but the two facing the tarmac were still boarded up.

"Did you have a bad storm?" Saul asked.

"Actually Daddy that was Philip's fault too. A bull chased him and it ran full speed into the hangar. Broke most of the windows."

"I was golfing." Philip smiled sheepishly.

"He could have been killed," said Kari.

Saul was choking with laughter again. "Philip," he said, "you might look like a long-haired ne're-do-well, but I see you're a man who leaves a mark on his world. I like that. Why don't you and Kari show us around this mission base of yours and let's see what other damage you've done."

Jerry and Mary had given the Trainors their entire first floor to use during their visit, so it was only natural that Thanksgiving dinner for the clan was also at their home. Although Philip figured he would be invited too, Jerry enjoyed toying with him throughout the week. On Monday he popped over to Philip's classroom during recess and asked, "Where are you going for Thanksgiving Philip?" When Philip replied that he had no plans as yet, Jerry shook his head and said, "You'd think on a mission center a single guy could get an invitation for Thanksgiving dinner. Sometimes Ilusan folk really disappoint me." Then he walked out still shaking his head. On Tuesday, arriving back at his classroom early after lunch, he found Philip and Kari sitting on the stairs eating sandwiches. Jerry calmly discussed Thursday's menu with Kari, going over it in great detail, then went into his classroom without ever saying a word to Philip. On Wednesday at recess, from his window he idly watched Philip playing foursquare with the kids. At one point he asked, "Still batching it tomorrow Philip?" When Philip nodded, he said, "I saw canned chicken on sale at the commissary. You might scoop some up before it sells out."

That afternoon as school let out, Mary poked her head in his classroom. "Philip, has Jerry not invited you yet for Thanksgiving dinner?" She sounded indignant.

Philip heard Jerry's voice from the stairs. "Are you forgetting the water balloons on our porch Mary? The man's a menace. We want to provide a nice atmosphere for our guests."

Philip saw Kari approaching from her building. He called out, "I'll come only if you promise to let me sit next to that Trainor chick. But I was really looking forward to my creamed chicken."

Mary laughed her music box laugh. "Believe me, my girls will whip up something a lot better than that."

The girls she referred to were the Domitro twins, the house girls she hired to cook and clean. They usually only came one at a time, but on Thanksgiving they were both going to be there. Mary was one of the few wives smart enough to let her house girls plan menus and cook on their own. Consequently dinners at the Van Kleek household were routinely off-the-charts delicious. Many of the missionary women, from a fear of worms, insisted on teaching their house girls western germ avoidance techniques, techniques which primarily involved overcooking everything. Philip remembered the horrified look on one poor girl's face as she was given careful instructions on how to cook one particularly tasty vegetable to death. "Oh maam," she said, "oh maam." Philip thought he saw tears in her eyes. But by the time it landed on Philip's plate, there wasn't a germ or worm left within striking distance of the soggy mess.

When Philip entered the Van Kleek home at 2:00 on Thanksgiving afternoon, the house smelled like pure gold, that is if gold smelled like chicken adobo. It had rained hard all morning and Philip had rolled up his pant legs to keep clear of the mud. The ground squished beneath him as he walked. His shoes were a mess, so he left them with his umbrella at the door. The Trainors were already there. Fossia and Gordon Lundy arrived just a few minutes later. Mary and Kari served kalimansi juice, and the feast was on. And the feast was extraordinary, heaping helpings of rice, chicken adobo, corn on the cob, sweet potatoes, tomato salad, watercress, pandesal, and a choice of banana crème pie or caramelized camote for dessert. The Domitro twins had outdone themselves.

Philip settled in, enjoyed the food, and observed his friends. He didn't talk as much as he usually did. He didn't need to, what with Saul and Gordon around. Philip had quickly decided that he liked Saul and Doris. Saul was hilarious, if mostly clueless. Doris was serious and didn't miss a trick. She trimmed Saul's sails when they needed trimming, paddled hard on the right or the left when he needed steering, fed him his best lines, and all the while let him believe he was a jocular and benevolent Captain Ahab totally in charge of his own life and fate. They were an ideal couple.

They both were devoted to Kari in their own way. Philip tried to help Kari see this, and thought in fact that she did, at least intellectually, but he noticed that often when she was with them she appeared to mistrust the evidence before her. It was as if she believed her father's jocularity was forced, a false, if loving, cover-up of the deep wound she had inflicted by her failure to live the perfect Christian life. And when her mother was quiet, she must have been remembering the pain Kari had caused. As much as Philip gently disagreed, and as much as Kari earnestly agreed with his disagreement, he knew that she didn't feel it in her bones. And it worried him. He wondered if her inability to free herself from the perceived failures of her past might eventually cost him as well. He had never quite understood how it could be that while grace and forgiveness were at the very heart of the Christian gospel, and while evangelicals loved to freely dispense it to repentant sinners, when it came to one of their own it was as if the universe of grace was confined to an eye dropper. It was often with themselves that they were the most parsimonious in their dispersal of life's most necessary medicine.

Philip was thinking about this as conversation swirled about him, when Saul suddenly said, "So, Philip, is this true?" And when Philip admitted that he had no idea what they were talking about, Saul laughed and said, "I'm going to charitably assume that you were daydreaming about my daughter. Shall we catch Philip up? Gordon has just claimed that he had you and Kari pegged as a couple almost from the moment you arrived. And, and this is even more significant, that he was one of your earliest champions in that role."

Philip agreed that it was true and mentioned how Gordon used to invite them over and then arrange to leave them alone.

"You left that rascal alone with my daughter," exclaimed Saul. "You're a more trusting man than I am." And he was off and running again with a story about Kari and her first boyfriend away back in grammar school. Kari laughed, but Philip thought he saw the briefest flicker of something behind her smile. It might have been worry, might have been anger, might have been grief, might have been nothing.

After dinner everyone migrated to the verandah. The rain had ceased, the sky had cleared except for an indistinct cloud or two, and a hazy heat settled over the afternoon. It was wonderful to relax with a full stomach. Philip began to feel like a nap. He closed his eyes. He felt his skin prickle and begin a light sweat. He heard Saul suggest a swim. Then he heard Jerry say, "Mary, what are the rules for postprandial swimming?"

"I never know what you're talking about," said Mary.

Saul laughed loudly. Then he said, "Of course I have no idea what you said either professor."

"I merely expressed concern about swimming too soon after eating," said Jerry.

"An old wives' tale," said Saul. "No truth to it at all. But we'll let Philip go in first just in case."

On Saturday afternoon Philip, Kari and a dozen of the Trainors' new friends gathered at the hangar to see them off. Saul watched Oscar Platt stow their baggage. "Push that seat back as far as you can," he said to Oscar. "These airplanes aren't built for men like me."

"You can sit up front," said Oscar. "There'll be more room for you up there. Only one pilot on this trip." The prospect of sitting up by the pilot fascinated Saul and he began to follow Tom around asking questions.

"Daddy is easily entertained." Kari was standing with Philip while her mother said goodbye to the Van Kleeks. "I should grab him and make sure he thanks Jerry and Mary. He's liable to forget completely." Then she lowered her voice and leaned close to Philip's ear. "I love my parents, but I'm looking forward to getting back to just me and you. I've felt on stage all week." She squeezed his hand hard, but, still self-conscious about public displays of affection, quickly released him. She smiled wistfully and left to corral her father.

On Sunday afternoon Philip sat on his porch with Sally, Bobby and Mr. Bumbles. Mr. Bumbles was lying on his back on Philip's lap enjoying a tummy rub. He kept one paw hooked around Philip's wrist and whenever Philip tired of rubbing, a purposeful extension of claws got him back on task. Sally and Bobby were working on their math homework. Over the past month the two had developed a good working relationship. As long as they limited their conversation to homework they carried on with the relaxed animation of old friends. But let the conversation stray from neutral tasks and the two were as tongue-tied and uncomfortable as a couple of inexperienced young lovers. Philip thought he knew what was going on and he tried to be a quiet conversation facilitator whenever his young charges got stuck.

Bobby was explaining to Sally how to figure the area of a triangle when Mr. Bumbles suddenly sat straight up in Philip's lap. Then he leapt to the porch, pattered quickly down the stairs and looked under the house. Sally was the first to react. She got up and peered under the house as well. It was the quickest way to check all the angles of approach. "Bobby, it's your father." She sounded alarmed.

Philip jerked his head toward the door and Bobby quickly darted inside and hid in the kitchen. When Carnley walked around the corner, Sally was back in her spot demurely studying her books. Bobby's books were behind her back. Philip had resumed his relaxed pose with his legs on the rail. Mr. Bumbles sat rigidly at the head of the stairs. His tail slowly swished and curled behind him. Philip had seen that look before. The swift death of one of Ilusan's smaller creatures usually followed.

Carnley seemed startled to find Philip's porch so crowded. He looked at Sally, then Philip, back to Sally, back to Philip. Philip let him conjure whatever dark image he wished to savor. He offered no explanations. Finally he said, "Hello Carnley. What can we do for you?" His feet were still resting on the rail. Mr. Bumbles had begun a soft moaning.

"I have some news for you," said Carnley. "I thought I'd do you the courtesy of letting you know about it before I alert the others." His eyes continued to dart around the porch. Philip followed his eyes. They both noticed Bobby's book bag leaning against a chair. Philip saw a question begin to form in Carnley's mind. The man took a step forward to get a closer look.

It was then that Mr. Bumbles saved them from catastrophe. With a piercing howl the cat launched himself at Bobby's father. Bumbles landed on Carnley's shoulder, dug in his claws to gain purchase, and took a vicious swipe at his face. Carnley yelled, jumped back, and swung hard at the spitting cat. He succeeded in knocking Bumbles off his shoulder; the cat left a nasty scratch all the way down his left arm as he fell. As soon as Mr. Bumbles hit the ground he leapt for Carnley's leg and began a rapid climb back toward the man's face. Carnley screamed, swatted at him again, then bolted from the yard. The cat followed in huge bounds, concluding his pursuit by streaking up a tree and snarling at the retreating man from a low branch. Carnley ran all the way to the barbwire fence before stopping.

Philip, who had watched the scene with shock and amusement, strolled toward him. "I don't think my cat likes you," he said. "Maybe you better tell me your news out here."

Philip, of course, knew exactly what Carnley had come to tell him. He had been expecting it ever since the day Carnley warned him that he was nosing around in his background. And he had already decided what he would say when the time came.

"That cat has a devil," Carnley gasped.

"I prefer to think of it as the gift of discernment," said Philip. The two men glared at each other. Philip felt a warning throb from his conscience, but he had determined in advance to ignore it this time. He was going to enjoy saying what he had planned.

"All right," said Carnley. "I think I have the gift of discernment too. And I discerned from the moment I saw you that you were a fraud. And now I have proof." He paused to relish his triumph.

"I'm sure you do," said Philip. "Go ahead. And please enjoy it. You have my permission."

Carnley appeared puzzled only for a second or two. But he too had long savored the thought of this moment and he was not to be deterred. "My brother knows some people from your father's church. They told him you went to the Bible College of San Diego." He waited to let that name sink in.

"I did," said Philip, "all too briefly. But I made quite an impression before I left."

Carnley's face flickered with doubt. But there was no direction to go but forward. He dabbed at the wounds on his face with his handkerchief. "Yes, you were there only briefly. You were kicked out when your sexual sin was exposed. You're the worst kind of hypocrite, and it's my duty to relay this information to the base authority." He waited, then proceeded slowly for dramatic effect. "I wonder what your girlfriend will think of your deception." His tone of voice said all that needed to be said about how he viewed that relationship.

That last bit surprised even Philip. Did Carnley think he wouldn't have shared his past with Kari? But of course he would think that. Premarital sex was such a black hole of shame for evangelicals that someone like Carnley would not be able to imagine that a man would freely divulge such information to a woman. He would of course be immediately rejected, and rightly so.

Philip had to smile. "Your news will be a surprise to the base authority, as you put it, but it won't be a surprise to Ms. Trainor. She's known the details of my past history for months. No deception there I'm afraid." Now Philip paused for dramatic effect. "And the amazing thing is that she loves me despite my sin and hypocrisy. Funny how that works. Young love; there's no explaining it."

Carnley's face worked. He wiped the blood off his arm, then snarled, "Well the base authority will view it another way I assure you. I know they won't want you near our children. I shall inform them immediately. The works of darkness must be exposed."

Philip had carefully rehearsed his next lines. He kept his face blank. "Yes," he said, "indeed they must. I am ready to answer to anyone for my past." He took a deep breath and looked directly into Carnley's eyes. "Maybe we should go together. Maybe we should let the base authority judge both of us. Maybe the bruises and cuts that I see regularly on your boys ought also to be brought into the light. I'm ashamed I haven't said something earlier. It's time I said something now."

Carnley paled. "My boys are none of your business," he spat.

"And perhaps my past, which after all is past, is none of yours." Philip felt his voice flirt with the line between control and fury. "Your boys are present, and I have an investment in them. And whether or not you tell the base authority about my past, if I ever see another bruise on one of them, I will tell the base authority about your present."

Carnley took a step back, then another. Philip recognized the hate in the man's eyes, recognized it because he knew it was welling over in his own. "Do we understand each other?" he said.

Carnley was breathing hard. Finally he hissed, "You will go to hell."

Philip felt the emotion begin to drain from him. "Perhaps," he said. "Perhaps I will. But my sins stem from a lack of self-control; yours come from an overflow of hate. Which one of us do you think will sink to a lower spot in hell?"

They stared at each other, the gray-haired, iron-willed fundamentalist and the long-haired, weak-willed pseudo-evangelical. The fundamentalist blinked first. "Once saved, always saved," he said. Then he turned and walked rapidly away.

Philip watched him go. Then he leaned against a fence post and looked back toward his house. Sally was standing on the stairs holding Mr. Bumbles. She was staring hard in his direction. Philip supposed she'd been like that the entire time. She sat back down when he began to walk toward the porch. He thought that would make a wonderful picture, Sally sitting with Mr. Bumbles on his porch. He determined to get his camera and shoot it before she left. By the time he got back to his yard, Bobby had emerged from the house. Philip sat on the steps and looked at the two children. "Well kids," he said, "that was that."

Sally's face was drawn with concern. "I was really frightened," she said.

"So was I," said Philip. He collected his thoughts for a minute, then said, "Your father really doesn't like me Bobby. He'd like to get me sent home. And he just might do that."

"He can't do that, can he?" Both kids spoke at once.

"I don't know. I think I persuaded him to back off, but I can't be sure. At any rate, I better be careful. I don't want to give him any more ammunition. Your father is a dangerous man Bobby."

"I hate him," said Bobby. "I really hate him."

Philip was too tired to be guarded. "If I'm not careful, I just might join you in that sentiment."

Sally said, "Uncle Carnley can't send you home. You're already home. Your home is right here." He wanted to hug her.

"You're absolutely right Sally. I'm not going anywhere." He reached up and squeezed both of the children's arms. "And I think we have Mr. Bumbles to thank for defending our home, don't we?"

"I love Mr. Bumbles," exclaimed Sally. She gave the cat a hug. She began to describe Mr. Bumbles' attack on Carnley to Bobby. The sound of children laughing and talking reclaimed the afternoon. Mr. Bumbles purred and purred.

That night Philip had a dream that even by his standards ranked as unusual. He and Mr. Bumbles were sitting in a room together. The room was dimly lit; perhaps it was dusk. Both Philip and the cat perceived the presence of something else in the room, but Philip could see nothing. Mr. Bumbles, however, had better eyes. He began leaping into the air and when he came down there were tufts of hair in his claws. Philip began swinging at the empty room. In a panic he shouted, "Reveal yourself." He saw ghostly catlike faces with glowing eyes. He thought they must be evil. He thought they must be demonic. He thought he should be afraid. But they only wanted to play. So he played.

# Chapter Ten

EVERY TWO YEARS THE Philippine branch of the Bible Translation Mission came together for conference. Conference was held during the two weeks around Christmas and New Year's. Everyone looked forward to it. It was the only time the missionaries stationed in Luzon and other of the northern islands got to enjoy the luxuries of Ilusan. When they weren't in their allocations, they were either in Manila or the tiny northern center of Bagabag. Neither compared to Ilusan. And it was the only time that all the mission personnel were together in the same place. Allocations emptied, and every inch of available space on the center was occupied by missionary families. Those who owned homes on the base shared with those who didn't. The houses next to Philip's filled up. Philip would have been required to take in boarders as well, except that Celia Haaf, the base hostess, remembered that during fall break Philip's home had become the late night gathering point for the Faith kids and older Ilusan kids. She couldn't think of a family that would be able to endure those kind of hours, so she left Philip's spare room empty, saying, "You'll probably have more people crammed into your place most of the day and night than any of the rest of us anyway." Philip stocked up on soft drinks and snacks and counted his blessings that he didn't have to share his home with strangers.

Philip spent the weeks prior to conference preparing his kids for their end of the semester exams. The kids were on sensory overload, what with the month-long break, Christmas, conference, and the return of the Faith kids all approaching at once. It was hard to keep them on task. He also spent several evenings a week at the St. Clairs' where he, Matt, and Oscar Platt planned the various tournaments and activities that would keep kids and quite a few of the adults intensely active for the better part of two weeks.

Along with the downriver trip which they scheduled for the first sunny day after New Year's, there would be volleyball, softball, tennis and ping pong tournaments, game nights, skit nights, movie nights and the Christmas pageant which the fifth through eighth grade children had been practicing for the past month. Bobby Sorenson was Jesus. Sally was Mary Magdalene. The script which Jerry and Philip inherited had a literal if New International Version flavor to it. As none of the kids seemed to have any acting talent whatsoever, the two teachers had decided to play it for laughs as much as anything else. Together they rewrote the dialog into an over-the-top King James English that was almost indecipherable. There were moments when the actors had little clue as to what they were saying, all of which Jerry and Philip found hilarious, although Mary and Kari, when treated to a sneak preview, simply found the whole thing incomprehensible. "You two will be the only ones laughing," prophesied Mary.

"And your point is?" said Philip. The two women had shaken their heads and left early. The pageant sets were constructed next to the basketball court. If the weather cooperated, "Jesus of Nazareth" would go off on Christmas Eve.

Of course conference was primarily designed for policy and decision making, and for serious attention to the dozens of translation projects. The mission's top linguists flew in from around the world to assist the Bible translators with their work. It would be a busy two weeks for Joseph Haaf, but as Philip wasn't a full member of the mission and had no expertise in Scripture translation, he wasn't required to attend these meetings. He would spend his time with the kids, an assignment for which he was exceedingly grateful.

He would, however, attend the spiritual emphasis meetings, and so he found himself that first Monday evening sitting on a table in the back of the meeting hall between Kari and Derek Sorenson. James Montgomery and the Platt girls were also crowded onto the table. There were no seats left in the pews. The bus from Cagayan filled with Faith kids had rolled into Ilusan just a few hours ago, and now the jam-packed meeting hall throbbed with anticipation for the launching of conference. The entire branch was present except for Tom Jacobson and George Donahoe, both of whom, exhausted from three days of round the daylight hours flying, had collapsed into bed when the last of the Philippine missionaries had been safely offloaded from the steaming overworked Helios.

Every conference the branch invited a special speaker from the United States to fill the spiritual emphasis side of the program. "I wonder who Dr. Dynamic will be this year," Derek muttered to James, and everyone on the table snickered appreciatively. As Derek spoke, this year's Dr. Dynamic was being introduced by a missionary unknown to Philip. The missionary was stationed in Luzon, and the special speaker was his pastor. Reverend Randy Rothooft was a tall man of Dutch extraction, pastor of a large Christian Reformed church in Grand Rapids, Michigan. That few of the BTM missionaries were strictly Reformed bothered no one. Nobody was anti-Reformed either. Virtually everyone believed absolutely in the sovereignty of God and absolutely in the free will of man. It was the rare person at Ilusan who saw any contradiction between the two.

Pastor Rothooft came billed as a skillful Scriptural exegete and excellent preacher. What nobody knew at the time, in fact what nobody except perhaps Randy's wife, Josephine, could have known, was that Pastor Randy had already begun his slow trek toward insanity, the journey that would occupy him and his family and congregation for the next several years. Eventually Reverend Rothooft would be committed to the Calvary Christian Home for Insane Pastors in Grand Rapids, a ministry founded by Tom DeSos of Amway money when his own pastor, the Reverend Spencer Vander Lee, shaved off all his hair, married an artist, and went quietly crackers in 1975. The CCHIR had not had an empty bed since 1976. But there were no prophets in the audience that Monday night to warn the good Ilusan missionaries against the tall pale man on the platform.

The only prophet there that night, as a matter of fact, was already on the stage. About a year ago Pastor Randy had attended a Pentecostal revival. He was deeply impacted by the cacophonous piety on display there and by the end-times exegesis of a particularly powerful speaker. By the time he left the building he was a Spirit-baptized pre-tribulation rapture dispensationalist Calvinist. Which was all well and good except that he had also somewhere acquired the notion that he was a prophet. It was this that eventually drove him insane. Or perhaps it was the other way around. At any rate, by the time he stood on the platform in the meeting hall at Ilusan he was convinced he could do no wrong, speak no wrong, think no wrong. Every notion he entertained came directly from the mouth of God.

His wife was the first to feel the effects of his newfound prophetic status when he announced one night during their bi-monthly coupling that from now on they would not face each other when making love. "This is the way Adam knew Eve," he pronounced with ringing authority. When she asked him how he could possibly know such a thing, he ordered her not to question the prophet. But that was barked in the throes of passion. Later he informed her that when God revealed himself to Moses he showed him only his backside, and that God had revealed to him, Randy, that men, made in the image of God, should, in like manner, not permit their faces to be seen during moments of intimate revelation. Josephine hadn't faced him during intercourse since. Later that week Jenny Moran, his Thursday a.m. appointment, was puzzled to find her chair facing away from Pastor Randy when they reviewed the progress she was making in overcoming a debilitating lack of self-esteem. "I would prefer not to look at you," said Reverend Randy, and Jenny's budding confidence took a nosedive. Prophets tended to do better with groups than one-on-one.

Now Reverend Rothooft raised his hands grandly and gestured toward the children's recorder choir which had just played an opening song. "Thank you for that welcome of wind," he said. The man was clearly a connoisseur of words. "It bespeaks an admirable love of the lung and nurture of the note." Philip's eyes shot open with alarm.

Kari must have felt him stiffen, because she looked at him and said, "Be careful or your face will freeze in that position." But Philip couldn't seem to bring his eyebrows back down from the middle of his forehead. He knew that somewhere in the audience Joseph Haaf's face must have a similar expression, and, in fact, he noticed just then that Joseph had risen half out of his seat and seemed frozen in place. What followed did little to ease the state of Philip's eyebrows or Joseph's posture.

It turned out that Pastor Randy was master of the grand gesture, bard of the nonsensical truism, user and abuser of every evangelical chestnut imaginable. He trotted out ancient bons mots as if he were the first to think of them and as if this audience were the first to hear. "If you were arrested for being a Christian, would there be enough evidence to convict you?" he asked during one especially egregious run of wearying clichés, and then paused, postured, and twinkled during a long moment of spiritual bonhomie during which he clearly expected his dazzled audience to puzzle over the immaculately phrased challenge. "Garbage in, garbage out," he opined during another gripping, if incomprehensible, sermon, and he gestured grandly in, grandly out. "Jesus is the reason for the season," he announced as Christmas drew near, and then repeated it twice to make sure everyone in the audience captured the clever rhyme.

Somewhere the good pastor had read that props helped an audience attend, and Pastor Randy never met a visual idea he didn't try out at least once. During the garbage in, garbage out sermon he spilled a bucket of banana peels and tangerine rinds on the stage. He sent stones winging around the auditorium during a sermon on David and Goliath. He pulled a fish from his pocket to multiply the loaves and fishes.

He took no notes into the pulpit with him, preferring to rely on the direct inspiration of the Holy Spirit. The Spirit's wind came from all points of the compass that week, and Pastor Rothooft's messages hung together by only the slenderest of threads. To discover a thesis in them was to search for El Dorado; a core truth, even a central point, was always just over the next horizon.

His message that first Monday night appeared to be on the text "And by his stripes you are healed." At least he read that text by way of an opening gambit. But then he told a story about serving in a soup kitchen in New York, chatted for a bit about the kind of whale that swallowed Jonah, mused about what Daniel thought while sitting in the lions' den, before finally seeming to re-approach the subject of healing by discussing the woman with an issue of blood. His eventual exegesis of the passage issued in the grand announcement, "You are already healed. Past tense. You have to believe it and receive it by faith." But he followed that encouraging line of thinking with "Of course we have to understand that sometimes it takes time. It can be a process. It may take years. Some don't receive healing until they die and get their new bodies." By the time he finished unpacking the implications of the verse, it meant virtually nothing for either the here-and-now or the hereafter.

He closed by pulling a stethoscope from his jacket pocket, listening for a long silent moment to his heart, and saying, "The pure in heart shall see God. You won't need a stethoscope then." Then? Then when? Philip wasn't sure. And why wouldn't you need a stethoscope? For that matter why would you have needed one in the first place? Nobody knew. At first Philip thought the stethoscope was meant to connect the healing bit of the sermon to the seeing God bit. You'll see clearly, won't have to fumble about trying to hear. But he eventually came to the conclusion that the stethoscope was a leftover prop. Pastor Randy had meant to use it earlier, forgot it, pulled it out at the end, and simply voiced the wind of the Spirit. That the Spirit could on occasion be incomprehensible seemed a reasonable notion to Philip. After all, theoretically at least, the same Spirit had more or less written the Book of Revelation.

After the message Josephine Rothooft rose to announce some special programming for the ladies. She was every bit as tall as Pastor Randy. The "girls" would meet two afternoons a week. The hour and a half long sessions would begin with forty-five minutes of crafts. They would first discover their season and then would make earrings in line with this newly discerned bit of wisdom. The experience would be "really fun" and "super neat" and would provide "lots of neat fellowship."

Kari leaned close to Philip and whispered, "Goody! Crafts!"

"Don't you love doing crafts with the girls?" said Philip. She punched him hard in the shoulder.

"Then," said Josephine, and to her credit she sounded pretty excited about her husband's role in the women's groups, "Pastor Randy will teach us about personal prayer. My husband is really good at bringing the Bible down to our level. Because that's what we girls need, someone to bring Scripture to our level." It felt to Philip like his grin would tumble off the edge of his face. He turned triumphantly to Kari. Her eyebrows had rocketed almost to her hairline. Her expression, when she finally looked at Philip, said she knew very well that he would never let her hear the end of this.

Philip was up early the next day. He had decided to try to get in shape over the month-long break, so now he put on his tennis shoes and went for a jog on the airstrip. He started running as soon as he ducked through the fence by the water tower. He crossed the road, navigated the ditch on the other side, then broke into a fast trot when he reached the north-south runway. He was already puffing when he passed Jerry's first tee box. He jogged at a decent clip past the hangar and through the intersection of the two strips. He was heaving hard now, but a quick check over his shoulder revealed that if Jerry or Mary were up, or Kari if she happened to be upstairs in Fossia's house, they might still be able to see him, so he didn't dare stop. But as soon as he felt safely out of sight he slowed to a walk and then went down on one knee. He walked the rest of the way to the end of the strip and only resumed running when he came back in sight of the houses. "I am a hypocrite," he thought as he jogged by Kari's window, "but I wouldn't be if there weren't so many people I had to fool." It felt good to realize what a genuine human being he could be if only he lived entirely alone.

After a shower he lingered over his cup-of-coffee devotions with Mr. Bumbles. The world seemed an extraordinarily beautiful place. And he was glad after all that he didn't live entirely alone. He realized that no matter in what direction he jogged on the center, no matter what route he took, that he could imagine with some accuracy what was going on in almost every house he passed as the people within slowly roused themselves to their day. He knew every Ilusan face, every adult up with the dawn, every sleepy-eyed child who rolled over and untucked their mosquito net. He knew the pets. He thought he might even be able to hazard a guess as to the tenor of the comments, the temperature of the moods.

Gordon Lundy, alone on his porch, thrilled at the influx of old friends for conference, but missing his wife even more keenly for all that. Matt and Julia up early so as not to miss a moment with Benjamin, Matt wincing and flustered over the additional responsibilities of conference, Julia assuring him he was up to the job. Jerry and Mary almost certainly hovering over coffee on their verandah, listening to see if their downstairs guests had awakened, Mary wondering when to start breakfast, Jerry hoping against hope the rain held off so he could get in a little golf. Joseph and Celia, Joseph probably surly at Celia's early morning good cheer and the stampede of girlish feet through the house, Celia giddy with anticipation for the weeks ahead. Horace Balfour still sleeping, his nose billowing on the pillow. Hortense in her rocking chair with her Bible and beads outlining the day's agenda to her house girls. Annabel undoubtedly kneeling by her bed in prayer, Bible open, misty eyed. Perhaps Gordon was also praying now face first on his rug. Peggy Margaret, well it was always a gamble to pick her mood. Samuel and Virginia in from their allocation, Virginia more than likely prodding her husband with a sharp comment or two, Samuel fending her off while trying to figure out how to sneak a hit from his pipe. The Platt household filled again with kids. Sally having a quiet breakfast with her parents, her mother trying to engage her while her father read a book. The Sorensons up early feeling for Carnley's mood, taking their cues from him, the children wondering how soon they could leave the house and relax.

And Kari, sweet Kari. Philip wondered what she looked like when she first woke up. He wondered what she wore to bed. He wondered what it would feel like to wake up next to her, to reach over and touch her body. He shook his head. Better to leave that line of thinking or he'd be distracted for hours. He heard movement from the houses next door. He'd forgotten the Troyer sisters and their mother. He smiled as he imagined Dorothy rising, wondering if she'd see Jesus today. A powerful feeling welled up in Philip. It felt good to know and be known. "I do love this place Mr. Bumbles," he said.

After breakfast he finished putting together the brackets for the tennis and ping pong tournaments. There had been a few late entries the night before. Then he hurried down to the meeting hall to post the brackets, times, and locations before the morning meetings began at 9:00. He stayed for the opening devotions, thankfully led by a missionary, not Pastor Randy, but then hurried home again. He would have a few hours every morning to himself before the meetings broke up and the afternoon and evening activities dominated his attention.

But time to himself was not to be. He had just finished reading the assigned section in the "Journals of John Woolman" when Derek and Bobby Sorenson, James Montgomery, and the Platt girls showed up in his yard. Reverend Rothooft was something of a Woolman specialist, and he was leading a men's group which would focus its discussion on the life of the Quaker saint. Philip doubted he would attend, but he had heard of Woolman and thought he might at least do the reading. Perusing the "Journals" now he realized why he preferred his saints in a book. Woolman must have been insufferable to actually live with, always "not wanting" to correct his brethren for their faults, but then upon "further urging" in his spirit, correcting the brethren anyway. From Woolman's point of view God always gave him "grace in their eyes" so he wasn't poorly received. Right!

Philip thought there were probably at least two kinds of saint. *Every* saint was somehow an affront, challenging human complacencies, human compromise. Saints like Woolman, however, never lived heartily, intentionally blind to the fact that mankind's designed home is the world and all in it. Philip preferred saints like Augustine, who refused to become a Christian for years because he enjoyed sex, or Luther, who lived heartily and sinned boldly. Woolman reflected on his youthful backslidings, while at the same time thanking God that he had been "preserved from profane language or scandalous conduct." What else was there? Philip thought that a saint who had never lived was worth less than a saint who had tasted of life's bawdy joys, but then decided to lay them aside in pursuit of better things. The second saint was not as likely to be parsimonious. Such a saint might remember that life's sensual pleasures were not inherently evil and might be less apt to judge others who were freely enjoying the sun. At any rate Philip was glad now for the interruption. He laid Woolman aside and never picked him up again.

The kids wanted to talk about the end of the semester at Faith Academy, so that is what they did. Later someone suggested a swim. The long, full, but still lazy days of conference had begun.

It rained hard for the next two days. The runoff ditches raged in flood, the low area by the basketball court filled with knee-deep water, and the sound of giddy bullfrogs echoed through the sticky nights. The volleyball tournament was postponed until after Christmas, and the high school ringleaders organized a Risk marathon to take its place. They set up at Philip's house and there were as many as four games going at once. Heated arguments broke out from time to time. The Ilusan regulars seemed to think the kids from Luzon cheated too blatantly, and Philip was eventually forced to agree after losing a match to a short blond Canadian whose armies seemed to spontaneously regenerate every time Philip turned his back. At one point Benjamin St. Clair stalked out of the house yelling, "What is it about Luzon that breeds cheaters?"

"I think it's proximity to Marcos," Derek yelled after him.

The tournament was eventually won at 1:00 a.m. on Christmas Eve morning by little Drew Sorenson, who, it turned out, was a silent cheater of Nixonian proportions. Nobody suspected the cherub-cheeked boy of foul play until he'd smashed the last army on the last day. "I don't believe it," muttered Delbert Meyer, the last opponent left on the board. Drew might have pulled off his triumph unscathed if he had remembered to stay seated until everybody left the room or at least turned away. Instead he stood up in a paroxysm of childish triumph, and extra cards and armies rained from his sleeves, pant legs, indeed virtually every available bodily orifice. He received a dunking in the pool for his hubris, but then the high school kids, in grudging admiration for his prowess, and, to be honest, in grateful recognition that at least none of the Luzon kids had won, gave him the trophy anyway.

It was probably fitting that the trophy would never be displayed publicly. It had been purchased in Manila by Derek and James and smuggled south in their luggage. It was the ten inch version of the ubiquitous man-in-a-barrel, found all over the Philippines in sizes ranging from three inches to three feet. It was exactly that, a man standing in a barrel. The whole thing was admittedly quite tame until curiosity overcame the viewer and he or she lifted the barrel. At that point a spring-loaded and anatomically correct giant penis snapped into full salute, and the tourist collapsed into gales of laughter or died of embarrassment. The three foot version could knock the unsuspecting barrel-peeper over. It was like being hit in the chops by a Joe Frazier uppercut. Drew asked Philip to keep it for him, and Philip agreed, knowing full well the price to be paid if Carnley caught the boy with the offending trophy.

After grabbing a few quick hours of sleep, Philip joined Jerry and the cast of "Jesus of Nazareth" for one last rehearsal. They walked through the play in Jerry's classroom. There was some thought given to canceling the life of Christ, but during the afternoon Philip and several of the men managed to get the water swept off the basketball court and the bleachers set up. There was still a good bit of standing water on the field of drama, but Jerry rearranged a few scenes to play directly in front of the bleachers where the kids would remain dry, if muddy. Golgotha presented a larger problem. The hill was now surrounded by water. Some thought it might actually enhance the drama to have the procession move through the water, and Jerry and Philip quickly agreed. They reinforced the base into which the Roman centurions would set the cross and hoped for the best.

The rain held off the rest of the day, and at 4:00 p.m. the entire Philippine branch of the Bible Translation Mission gathered to watch Ilusan's fifth through eighth grade children re-enact the life of their Lord and Savior. It turned out to be an abbreviated edition of the life of Christ which tragically left off the blessed hope of the resurrection. But before the abrupt end, there were a few high points. Timmy Mullen, egged on by Charlie Pilarski, kicked off the unusual rendition of Christ's life by hurling a live chicken at Bobby during Jesus' baptism. Donny Meyer, splendidly outfitted in an extremely itchy monkey-skin shirt as John the Baptist, had just anointed Bobby with muddy water, easy to do as there was plenty of it about, and Bobby was standing with arms raised staring beatifically into the heavens. Jerry, in charge of narration, was solemnly intoning, "Behold the heavens opened and the Spirit of God descended upon him in likeness of a dove," when the squawking chicken smacked hard into the back of Bobby's head, bounced into the air for a long breathtaking second, then landed all fluffed and out of sorts on his still outstretched arm. As the audience stared goggle-eyed at this desecration of the Gospel story, Jerry, without missing a beat and without the smallest change in intonation, said, "But to others gathered there he appeared in likeness as a chicken," and even the crustiest old inerrantists had to laugh.

There were a few other minor gaffes before the final colossal crackup. Drew Sorenson, the man born blind, had not been adequately briefed on the change of location for his scene, and he walked with eyes closed smack into the basketball backstop. He went down hard in the mud, and a brief intermission ensued while he was revived. Sally, the woman who anointed Jesus' feet with her tears (and perfume) and washed them with her hair, in a fit of method acting cried so many real tears that she couldn't clearly make out the correct set of feet. She started washing three pairs of feet too far to the right, feet that happened to belong to Donny, now playing Judas, all of which made no theological sense at all. And Judas appeared extra churlish for complaining that the expensive perfume might have been sold and the money given to the poor, when, after all, he had just gotten his feet bathed in the stuff. Then Timmy, as Pontius Pilate, couldn't stop laughing when Bobby addressed him with one of Jerry's King James masterpieces. Pilate asks Jesus if he was really King of the Jews. Jesus was supposed to say, "Are you asking this on your own, or did you hear about me from someone else?" Jerry had changed the line to "Sayest thou this thing of thyself or did others tell it thee of me?" Bobby had a hard time wrapping his mouth around the line, and by the time he got it out correctly, Timmy was bubbling over. Mary Michaels, incongruously present as Pilate's wife throughout the entire scene, had to feed Timmy his next few lines. She had memorized the entire script.

But all of these incidents paled next to the crucifixion debacle. Philip had designed a gripping penultimate scene in which Bobby would actually be raised up on a cross before the gathered multitudes. Actually Philip had just insisted on it and encouraged Jerry to design it. Philip could no more have figured out how to get a kid on a cross than he could have created an internal combustion engine. So Jerry, with help from Matt St. Clair, had rigged a seat on the cross for Bobby to crouch on, ropes to hold him up, and a reinforced stand in which to place the cross. Unfortunately nobody counted on two days of rain. As the kids marched through the knee deep water to the muddy rise of Golgotha, Philip edged next to Jerry. He wanted to be next to his co-creator when the audience gasped its appreciation. They watched as Donny, now a centurion, led the rest of the boys as they ripped off Bobby's robe to reveal a loincloth. They roughly laid him on the cross, simulated pounding nails as they slipped ropes around him, then hoisted the cross up and plunked it into its reinforced hole. Philip glanced at the crowd. They seemed appropriately appreciative. "Pretty cool," he said to Jerry.

Bobby's lines from the cross had to be shouted, as the only dry spot for Golgotha was about thirty yards from the bleachers. But, as it turned out, he only had the opportunity to get one line out anyway. "Father forgive them," he shouted, and Philip noticed the cross shift subtly forward.

"Oh-oh," he said to Jerry. But it was too late. Whether the boys had failed to seat the cross properly or whether the ground was simply too saturated to support it was never accurately determined. What was quite accurately agreed upon by everyone present was that Jesus' catastrophic tumble from the cross was a lastingly memorable moment. Good Friday sermons would never be the same. If only Philip noticed the first subtle shift forward, everyone present saw the next alarming movement. The cross tipped suddenly toward the audience. Bobby was now clearly leaning at a precipitous angle. The centurions started forward to prop him up, but it was too late. Slowly, almost majestically, the cross with Bobby transfixed upon it first slipped, then hurtled, toward the ground. Fortunately Golgotha was surrounded by water. Bobby, with the cross at his back, smacked face first into the deep. For a heart-stopping moment the entire ensemble disappeared beneath a geyser of water. Then the cross reappeared. It floated slowly away from Golgotha, rocking ever so slightly as the stunned Bobby struggled to right himself.

Philip, Jerry, Derek, James, Matt and a few other men all leapt into the water. They quickly reached the cross and flipped it over. Now another unusual sight greeted them. As expected, Bobby was red-faced, muddy and gasping for air. The unexpected twist was that he was clad only in his briefs. Somehow his loincloth had come loose. With his arms still roped to the cross, the boy could hardly cover himself. Philip ripped his shirt off and quickly threw it over him. "Find his loincloth," he hissed.

Derek splashed around for a bit, but couldn't find it. Neither could James. They rejoined the group around Bobby. Derek nervously glanced at the hushed crowd. He whispered, "It's too muddy. It's got to be right here somewhere, but I can't find it." The men looked at each other.

"I think your show is over," said Matt.

"Quite a finish," said Jerry. "Almost biblical in proportion."

"Is someone going to untie me?" said Bobby.

"If you were really Jesus, you'd get off the cross yourself," said Derek. That was when one of them started laughing. Then they were all laughing. When the audience saw that the crisis was over, they stood and applauded.

"Well that was a fresh spin on the Gospel story," said Joseph to Celia and Kari. "If this were the Middle Ages, they'd burn your boyfriend for a heretic."

On the other side of the bleachers Samuel Clayton calmly surveyed the scene before him. "They don't make missionaries like they used to," he said to his wife.

As it turned out the Christmas day service was the last to be led by Reverend Rothooft at Ilusan. The service began with a special number worked up by Josephine Rothooft with the children's choir. "I always have a special place in my heart for our Jewish friends around Christmas," Josephine announced. "They're good people and they try so hard, but they just won't open their hearts to Jesus. I wrote this song as a special appeal to them."

Philip felt every nerve in his body begin to thrum with alarm. He glanced at Kari. She was craning her head to see all the cute kids. "This is going to be monumentally embarrassing," he whispered to her.

"Don't be such a poop," she said. "Kids are cute."

"That's not my point. I like singing children as much as the next guy."

It turned out Josephine only wrote the lyrics to her song. The Beatles wrote the tune, but she could hardly admit that to a bunch of missionaries most of whom considered the Beatles only a step below the four horsemen of the Apocalypse. The tune the children would sing was "Hey Jude." Josephine had turned the song into the evangelistically overwrought "Hey Jew." It went like this.

"Hey Jew, don't keep bein' bad/Take your sad heart and make it better/Remember to let Jesus into your heart/ Then you can start on the way to heaven./Hey Jew, don't be afraid/You were made to be God's children/The minute you let Jesus into your heart/Then God will begin to make you better."

The children sang with remarkable aplomb. After the second verse Josephine picked up a guitar. She invited the audience to sing along. "Hey Jew, don't let Jesus down/He has loved you, now go and follow him/so force sin out, and let Jesus in/Remember, to let Jesus into your heart . . . ." The missionaries sang hesitantly along. They didn't look at each other, perhaps afraid that in their neighbor's eyes they would see reflected their own doubt. But none of them could put their finger on what bothered them. Philip stared straight ahead, willing himself to continue existing for a few more precious seconds.

He came out of his trance when Pastor Randy mounted the pulpit. "Thank you Josephine for that lovely Christmas message," said Randy. Philip looked carefully about him. Kari was still there. The room appeared normal. He looked outside. The sun shone. He thought he heard a bird singing.

"Did we survive?" he whispered to Kari.

"Yes we did, although you were kind of whimpering." She patted his arm. He desperately hoped she was in on the joke.

Pastor Randy was dressed like a shepherd. He even carried a shepherd's staff. Philip sighed and prepared to be browbeaten. Reverend Rothooft's sermons had taken an ominous turn a few evenings into his tenure as this year's Dr. Dynamic. His prophetic urge got the best of him. He began to lash out at what he saw as the complacency of the missionaries. He began to demand greater sacrifice. "You might even consider going to the foreign field," he bellowed late one evening. His audience, accustomed as they were to respecting the pulpit, nodded along. He probably means it metaphorically they assured themselves. "You'll never confront the devil on the front lines sitting in your comfortable homes and driving your fancy cars," he said another night. Philip thought of the weapons carrier, admittedly pretty fancy for central Mindanao. He remembered getting his eye blacked by Rage. He wondered if Reverend

Randy had ever been punched out by a demon. Seemed pretty close to front line action to him.

Now on Christmas morning the prophet was in full flower. He rambled on about how God didn't come to the high and mighty but to a group of shepherds. "If all your friends are the powerful and wealthy, you're not like Jesus," he shouted. "Have you ever spent even one minute with the truly poor, with the naked stranger?" Pastor Randy paused, then seemed to momentarily remember whom he was addressing. Naked strangers were the missionary *raison-d'être*. Philip could see his mind scrambling to recover. He needed a down-and-out group that these missionaries might not have stooped to help.

"Prostitutes," he said. "Do you know any prostitutes?" The room hushed. "I've met them." The Reverend paused, his spirit on the brink of prophetic climax. "I've known them. Come with me sometime and I'll introduce you to some." He strode to the front of the stage. "I'll give them the shirt off my back. That's what Jesus would do." He began to tug at his shepherd's robe. He had it halfway over his head when his wife's voice cut through the silence like a cleaver.

"Randy." Then louder still. "Randy."

The prophet sagged against the pulpit. His robe slipped back down. It covered him haphazardly. He appeared dazed. He muttered, "The prophet needs rest," and sat suddenly on the edge of the stage. The tension in the room threatened to pop Philip's eyeballs. Kari's fingernails drew blood on his arm. If Philip could have chosen, he would have willed himself to some distant point in the universe, but at the same time he couldn't take his eyes off Reverend Randy. It was like rubbernecking on a slow drive by a particularly gruesome accident.

Reverend Randy sat for a long moment staring at the floor, then slowly turned and looked back at the pulpit. When at long last he spoke, his voice cracked with emotion. "I've always wanted to be a preacher," he said, then again, almost whispering, "I just want to preach." He lurched to his feet. His eyes did a slow pass over the hushed audience. "I'll take that for a yes," he said. He took two steps onto the stage, then turned again toward the missionaries. His left hand grasped the pulpit. "Now hear this carefully," he said. The extraordinarily long index finger on his right hand jabbed at the room. Philip couldn't imagine a speaker ever having an audience's more undivided attention. "When the dam breaks, ride the wave," said the prophet. "Ride it like it matters." And with that

Reverend Randy closed his Ilusan conference ministry and sat down next to his tall wife on the front row.

The room exhaled as if nobody dared acknowledge their breath. Not a head turned to look at their fellows. Philip knew everyone was thinking one thought. Now what?! Then Philip noticed Matt St. Clair, from his seat near the front, surreptitiously survey the room. Philip silently willed him to take over. Matt stood and walked to the front. The center superintendent looked flustered for just a moment. Then he said, "Let's all stand and sing 'Hark the Herald Angels Sing.'"

As they began to sing, Kari said to Philip, "But what does it mean?"

Philip honestly wasn't sure. "This is one wild and wacky Christmas," he said.

If someone had told Philip at that moment that the Christmas service would turn into one of the most meaningful of his life, he might have been forgiven a bit of skepticism. Memorable certainly, but hardly meaningful. But somehow someone still had to pull off a communion service. The table at the front of the room stacked with trays filled with broken Nabisco crackers and tiny cups of grape juice wasn't going to just disappear. Everyone had stopped singing and was looking at Matt. The man was clearly nervous, but he went to the table and offered a brief prayer and then read the Last Supper passage from the Gospel. Then he said, "Would those who were going to help with communion please come forward." A moment later it was obvious they were one server short. Reverend Randy was in another world. He was clearly in no shape to serve communion. Matt scanned the room then said, "Philip would you lend us a hand?"

Philip sat bolt upright. The shot of adrenalin that surged through him threatened to escape his mouth in an embarrassing squeak. He looked at Kari, but she was no help. She was smiling as if he'd just been elected president. She actually wants me to do this, he thought. He looked around the room. He expected hands to shoot up, voices of denunciation to be raised, figures from his past to appear and declare his unworthiness to serve. At the very least Carnley would stand and shout his tale of Philip's fornications and rebellions. But no hands or voices were raised. Matt was staring at him expectantly. In a moment people would begin to turn and look. Philip had to act. He stood and went to the front of the room. Every fiber of his body tingled with shame. If they knew who he really was they would reject the Eucharist from his hand. Perhaps they still would.

Philip took his tray of ruby red grape juice and went to a station next to Gordon Lundy. Gordon beamed at him and squeezed his shoulder with the hand that wasn't holding his tray of crackers. "It's a privilege brother," he said. When Matt saw that all the stations were ready he invited the congregation forward. Philip hardly dared look up as the lines began to form. With his head down he risked a peek. He noticed Kari walk all the way across the room to get into his line. Then Sally whispered something to her mother and they both switched lines as well. Then Bobby, Donny, and several of the high school kids made their way to his line. An emotion he had never felt before began to slowly tingle its way up from his belly. But he had to concentrate on what he was doing. Nobody had offered any instruction. Oscar Platt paused in front of Gordon. "The body of Christ broken for you Oscar," said Gordon. Oscar took a piece of cracker and ate. Then he was standing expectantly in front of Philip.

"The blood of Christ broken for you Oscar," Philip said.

"Amen," Oscar said. He drank the cup, then leaned over and whispered, "I think the blood is shed, not broken." He winked at Philip and returned to his seat.

Philip concentrated fiercely on the next few communicants. He knew most of the names, but if he didn't, he picked them up from Gordon. "The blood of Christ shed for you. The blood of Christ shed for you." He said it over and over. And the more he said it, the more he almost dared believe it, that somehow there might be a connection between the life of this man who lived so long ago and the lives of the community that passed before him. Indeed with his own life. He felt, as the words tumbled from his lips again and again, that he ought to find a new way to live, a new manner of being. And as he served Kari and then the children and young men and women he had come to know so well, something stirred in him that threatened to overwhelm his defenses. He struggled to keep his eyes from filling with tears. It was the kind of emotion that called for dramatic action, that might compel someone to give up their life if need be to save another. It felt, he thought later, a little bit like love.

That afternoon Philip struggled to find words to write on the Christmas card he had selected for Kari. He had finished wrapping the few small gifts he had had sent from either Cagayan or Manila. The teachers were all getting together for dinner at Jerry and Mary's, and Philip intended to stop on the way and exchange a few presents with his girlfriend. He searched for just the right words for his card. He was in the middle of deciding between poetry and prose, when he heard a soft "maayo" at the door. He recognized Sally's voice.

"I brought you a present," she said when he emerged onto the porch. They sat together on the stairs and she handed him a small parcel tied with string.

"Should I open it now?"

"Yes, but you don't have to read it all now."

"So it's a book is it?" He began to undo the string.

The girl smiled. "Sort of," she said. "It's not a real book."

The book consisted of about twenty sheets of notebook paper, three-hole punched and tied together with red braid. The cover proclaimed it a "Report on the Life of Sally Fraser." Pasted on the pages, in chronological order, was every report card the girl had ever received from kindergarten through the first semester of eighth grade. The early grades were filled with a mix of U's and S's alongside teacher comments such as "Sally has a hard time concentrating" or "Sally doesn't seem interested in group activities" or "Sally doesn't apply herself." Always "Sally doesn't apply herself." It was the favorite bit of teacherly wisdom to explain youthful bad grades. One teacher put a brave face on it. "Sally is a sweet girl, but if she doesn't start applying herself, she'll never amount to much academically." In the later grades, where the letters of the alphabet weighed in more definitively, Sally's report cards were filled with C's and D's. There was even an F or two. Philip recognized the card on the second to last page. He had filled it out himself just over a week ago. He had done his best to show no favoritism, to grade her straight up, and she had still earned all A's with one B+ in Math. On the last page of Sally's book she had written a simple note. "I like school now. Thank you. I'm glad you came to Ilusan. Merry Christmas! Sally Fraser."

When he looked at her, he remembered the girl who climbed out of his tree over five months ago. "Merry Christmas to you too Sally," he said. "I'm so proud of you." And although he felt awkward doing it, he gave her a long hug.

The next week passed rapidly. It rained intermittently, but they managed to get in all the outdoor tournaments. As conference rolled along, Matt St. Clair continued his quiet competence, Joseph Haaf, who led numerous linguistic sessions, managed to look both satisfied with his own brilliance and harassed by the dullness of his fellows, while Celia reveled in her role as base hostess because it required her to show hospitality, something she was good at so long as her guests liked to talk. And most missionaries, who could spend months in semi-isolation, enjoyed a good conversation at conference. Philip was so busy running the various tournaments, and his house was so crowded with kids late into the night, that he and Kari found little time to be alone. But they were together almost constantly working to ensure a good time was had by anyone who sought a bit of fun, and Philip found the week exhilarating. Kari was a joy to work with, and he got secret pleasure observing her quick repartee with the high school boys. They were all clearly in love. He didn't blame them a bit.

The rest of the spiritual emphasis meetings were canceled, but nobody seemed to miss them. Having spiritual emphasis meetings for missionaries seemed a bit redundant to Philip anyway, sort of like having a pool party for a swim team. The Rothoofts retreated to their house by the pool, the best guest house Ilusan could offer. Josephine was rarely seen, but Reverend Randy routinely lounged on the porch overlooking the swimming hole. He wore his shepherd's robe. He enjoyed calling out to the swimmers and engaging them in conversation. It was rumored that someone had seen him skinny-dipping late one night, but the source of the allegation could not be tracked down, and nobody believed it.

Two evenings stood out to Philip. The first was a skit night on the Friday before New Year's. All the skits were very funny. Philip was impressed with the talent on display. But the one that brought down the house was an ingenious mix of talent with its horrific absence. Someone came up with the brilliant idea to gather twelve of Ilusan's bravest to sing "The Twelve Days of Christmas." They alternated beautiful voices, Annabel and Gordon Lundy for example, with clueless voices, Joseph Haaf and Hortense Balfour for example. Philip could not believe that Joseph, for one, played along with such good humor. It seemed entirely out of character. As Joseph flatlined the fourth day immediately after

Annabel's stunning third day, or Hortense squeaked "six geese a-laying" after Gordon's lovely tenor rendition of "five golden rings," the meeting hall stormed with laughter. When Philip shook Joseph's hand afterward he said, "That was very brave, and very funny."

Joseph replied, "Yea, but who told Aunt Hortense she could sing?"

The second stand-out evening stretched into the early morning. On New Year's Eve the Faith kids commandeered Jerry's and Philip's school rooms for their all-night party. Games, games and more games all night long. At midnight they shot off bamboo cannons, and Benjamin St. Clair, who had removed the muffler from his father's motorcycle, roared around the base wishing every house a happy New Year. Then more games, including something called Coastguards and Smugglers that involved packs of smugglers attempting to transport money to the opposite end of the center before getting killed by the coastguard watchdogs (signified by the breaking of their yarn wrist band). The game was rough and some very real blood was exacted along with the treasure. Kari was kept busy cleaning scratches and putting ice on bruises. By the time Philip tumbled into bed next to Mr. Bumbles he was too tired to notice the cat's disapproving glare. Mr. Bumbles did not like to sleep alone. He considered giving Philip a swat or two, but decided not to waste a cool morning on petulance. He calmly surveyed Philip's position, then took advantage of the greatest possible generated warmth by wedging himself snuggly between Philip's arm and chest. In a moment he was fast asleep and snoring loudly.

The first Tuesday of the new year dawned cloudless and warm. All the kids had been told to be ready to leave on the downriver trip at a moment's notice as soon as the perfect day revealed itself. Inner tubes of all sizes had already been collected at the shop. There were individual tubes small and large, and giant tractor tubes that could carry four or five. Early Tuesday morning Matt St. Clair decided today was the day and by 7:00 a.m. Benjamin had alerted every household with children above the fifth grade to be at the shop by 8:00. Quite a few parents gathered to see their kids off. A downriver trip was the most popular outing for Ilusan's children, and the morning felt festive. Philip couldn't wait and even Kari didn't need to be forced along just because she knew first aid. Although some of the rapids made her nervous, she enjoyed the trip almost as much as the children.

Once again Beverly Fraser took Philip aside and asked him to look after Sally, and once again Philip assured her he would. "I'll keep her right in front of me," he said. "If she falls off her tube I'll yank her up by her hair." Sally, standing within earshot, smiled. He helped her select her ride. It didn't surprise him that she wanted a tube all to herself. While some of the other girls claimed the tractor tires for themselves and their friends, Sally found a small well-worn tube that fit her body perfectly. Philip checked the patches with Matt. They were secure.

Matt had enlisted Oscar and Jerry to drive the weapons carrier and the Toyota. They would drop the group off well up the river and then pick them up three hours later on the far side of Bancud. It took an hour to drive to where they would put in, mostly on single-track grassy back roads, and it was almost 9:30 when the group assembled on the bank of the Eho River.

Philip recognized immediately that this was not Kulasihan Creek. It was a broad river, and with the heavy rains over the last month the brown-green water swirled by at a fair clip. The high school boys were ecstatic. "It's high which means it's going to be rocking and rolling downstream a bit," said Derek. "This is going to be wild." Philip looked around at the rest of the group. The girls and the grade school kids seemed just as excited as the older boys.

After Oscar and Jerry drove away, Matt organized the group. He and Benjamin would go first. "I don't care about the next ten or so," he said, "but then I want James and Delbert in the middle. Philip, you and Derek and Kari come last."

He then ordered each of the kids to choose a buddy. When it came Sally's turn she looked hesitantly at Philip. He nodded, and she said, "I'll take Mr. Andrews."

"O.K. Sally," Matt said, "I'll expect you to rescue Mr. Andrews when he starts drowning." He and Benjamin waded into the river. "Always know where your buddy is," he said to the group on the bank. Then they were on their tubes and the river whirled them away.

"Come on," yelled Benjamin. Five minutes later the bank was empty. Thirty missionary kids on tubes were strung out along the muddy waterway shouting and laughing.

For Philip the next two hours were a blur of good feeling interspersed with regular shots of adrenalin. The Platt girls and Lizzie Sorenson had corralled one of the tractor tubes. They floated next to Philip, Kari, Sally and Derek. Bobby and Donny hung back to ride with them as well. The Platt girls always made for noisy good fun and their shrieks were the truest signal that the approaching rapids were large. When they dropped into the first set, Derek told Philip, "The number one rule is butts up. Keep your butt above the tube line so you don't bang it on the rocks. And use your feet to steer off of rocks you can see."

But the river was so high, Derek's advice was rarely needed. There was usually plenty of clearance where the water rushed over the rocks. Each set of rapids presented its own unique collage of white water, tossing tubes, shrieking kids, and pure adrenalin. Matt always halted the column below the fiercest stretches. As soon as he was convinced everyone was accounted for and still smiling, the group took off again.

Sally approached each challenge with her usual focus. She never once cried out, but she shot Philip a smile at the bottom of the whitest sets. Philip kept her in front of him and tried to keep an eye on her, although it wasn't always possible. There were moments when he had to mind his own business to stay afloat. The kids all seemed more adept at rapids running than he was anyway, and they all swam like fish. It seemed silly to worry.

It wasn't all white water and heart in his mouth. There were long placid stretches during which they hooked up into tight trains, warmed themselves in the sun, snacked, chatted, and, when they drifted close to shore, dodged the occasional water buffalo that emerged suddenly from beneath the surface. During the moments of almost peaceful silence Philip examined the surrounding landscape. It was mostly flat, long stretches of cane, a few cultivated fields, every now and then a small house, with children running along the banks waving. Then the trees might close in and the river would shoot through a small canyon. That always signaled rough water.

Philip got hung up on a rock at one point and when the girls on the tractor tire floated by, Jenny Platt grabbed at his leg to pull him free. All she succeeded in doing was yanking off his right shoe which she then promptly lost when they hit a rock and capsized. Derek caught their tube down below and the girls had to walk and swim to where he clung to a tree next to the bank. But Philip got off his rock and the girls were reunited with their tube and nobody was the worse for wear and tear. "I see why you all love this trip so much," he said to Derek during one quiet warm stretch.

They were more than two hours into the trip when Philip noticed Matt halting the column about two hundred yards ahead in a shallow spot next to the bank on the left hand side.

Philip was drifting next to Kari, Sally and Derek. Derek said, "This coming up is the wildest stretch."

"I don't like this part," said Kari.

Philip could see that just ahead the river dropped a bit down through a small gorge. He could hear it too. Derek explained that if you stayed to the far right next to the canyon wall you got a wild ride. At one point the water carried you under a tree growing out from the side of the bank. The boys enjoyed grabbing a branch and seeing who could hang on the longest as the white water tore at their bodies. "We shoot it one at a time," said Derek. "The first person through collects the tubes at the bottom. Most people lose their ride at some point. It's really cool!"

They paddled over and joined the entire group standing in the shallows looking down the river. "O.k. folks, you know the drill here," said Matt. He spoke loudly over the tumble of the water. "It's roughest on the right. If you go left it's actually pretty easy. If you go down the middle it's quick and rocky. But right is real big. As high as it is now, it'll be very tall and quick. And it looks like the water is actually in the tree branches, so anyone going right will hit the tree. Benjamin and I will go first to collect the tubes of those going through the tree. The rest of you make up your minds and we'll see you down below."

Everyone watched as father and son paddled hard to reach the far current. Once it caught them, they accelerated. When they hit the first big bump they rode it up and then almost completely disappeared on the back side. Then they were shooting up another small wall of water and vanishing again. Philip could hear them shouting with excitement. They were moving fast when they hit the tree. Benjamin kicked hard left off a branch and managed to stay on his tube. Matt tangled completely. His tube shot out below him. He clung for a long moment in the tree, almost submerged, battling the water while the high school boys cheered. Then he let go, disappeared for a second, then reappeared bobbing in tall water before shooting out the bottom where Benjamin waited with his tube, floating on water almost immediately deep and serene. They both waved and called.

"I'm going left," said Kari. Some of the younger girls joined her. Nobody picked the middle. It seemed to be all or nothing. All the boys chose all. The team on the tractor tire chose the right as well.

"I'm going to do what you do," said Sally. She was looking at Philip.

"Have you done this before?"

She nodded that she had.

"Unbelievable," said Philip. "All right, but I go first and then you wait until I've walked back up the middle to where I'm across from the tree. I want to be able to watch you all the way down." The girl agreed and seemed pleased at the care he took.

One by one they launched into the river. One by one they whooped and screamed and wiped out in the tree with varying spectacular results. The girls on the tractor tire stuck in the branches in their tube for a long minute before they managed to work their way free. Donny and Bobby shot the rapid together and both clung to the tree as long as any of the high school boys. Finally only three of them were left. Philip asked Derek to wait with Sally while he rode down. If he had been alone he might have taken the middle route, but with everyone watching there was no choice.

It was a struggle just to work his way out of the eddy into the hard current on the right. As soon as it caught him he knew he was in for a wild ride. When he dropped over the first fall his tube spun around and he shot into the swiftest current facing backward. The next plunge headfirst and backward down into the water took his breath away. He managed to turn halfway back around but with the water so big he had a difficult time seeing where he was going. He hung onto the tube and gave himself over to the river. It was all wet noise and falling and un-yielding water.

Then the river drove him into the tree. The current immediately grabbed the trailing edge of the tube and pushed it violently under while the lead edge rode up a branch. Philip was under water and off his ride before he made sense of what had happened. He pulled his right leg up beneath him afraid of bashing his bare foot on a rock. He felt himself strike hard against a branch and managed to pull his head above water. For a long strange almost quiet moment he clung to the tree against the full force of the rapid. He saw Derek and Sally watching above and the faces of several dozen adults and kids down below. It looked like some were cheering. Then he could hold himself no more and he released into the current. He expected to be crushed against rocks, but the river was so high that he shot over the crest of any that lurked below. Before he knew it he seemed to come off the end of a slide into slow water, and James and Benjamin were grabbing him and pulling him upright. All he found to say was, "Wow."

Leaving his tube with the girls on the tractor tire, he immediately swam to where he could walk in the middle of the river and began making his way back upstream. It was difficult without his shoe, but he tried to keep most of his weight on his left foot. By trending all the way to the side opposite the tree where the water was slow, he managed to reach a position level with the tree in about five minutes.

He looked up to see where Derek and Sally were. Derek was already at the bottom of the run. He looked for Sally. He didn't see her anywhere. He waved down to the group at the bottom and shouted to ask if Sally was there. They didn't seem to register what he was saying over the rush of the water. He looked again toward the top of the run. It was empty now. Then he saw an individual tube floating alone at the bottom. Matt collected it, then looked back at Philip. Philip shouted again. Both he and Matt had the same hard thought. Philip stared into the tree. Nothing. Then what appeared to be a tangle of light hair just below the surface. The girl was caught in the tree, held fast below the water, and the day, the week, the year that had been so wonderfully light turned instantly dark.

Philip shouted down at Matt and saw both him and Benjamin lunge for the shore. It would be their fastest route up. But Philip would have to be quicker. He realized with a kind of terrible instinct that unless he entered the current above the tree he would never reach her. He would be swept helplessly by. He turned and lunged back up the river. He fought his way through thigh deep water. He leapt forward when he could, clung to boulders when he slipped, struggling always against a current that willed him back. That his legs were tearing on rocks, he knew but hardly felt. But when his right foot caught between two rocks and twisted, he yelled in pain and frustration. Then he was above the tree and he threw himself into the deep water.

Almost instantly he slammed hard into the branches and was pulled under. He grabbed desperately for something large enough to give him purchase while he felt beneath the water for Sally. He only had strength to hold for a moment, but just before he was torn away he felt the girl in front of him and to his left. When he lost his grip on the tree he lunged for her and clung desperately to her body. Then they were both torn away. As the current caught him again, he lost his grip about her waist. The river pulled him under and he felt her dead weight tumble over top of him and surge away. He grasped blindly and when he came to the surface he had her hair in a death grip in his right hand. He pulled her to him and together they swept toward the horrified group waiting below.

He had never been more grateful for others stronger and more competent than himself. James took the girl from him and carried her up the bank. He heard Matt yelling for Kari and saw Benjamin haul her from the water and rush her to where a small group clustered around Sally. Philip made it to the bank, but was too exhausted to pull himself out. Derek manhandled him out of the water. Desperate, he hobbled to where the adults hovered over Sally. He grabbed at Matt.

"What should I do?"

"Let Kari do it," Matt said.

Kari shot him an agonized look. "I don't know how to do this very well." She was almost sobbing.

Matt seized her by the shoulders. "Just follow your training. Don't think about possibilities. Just work. And tell us how we can help you."

Kari took a deep breath and began to give instructions in a shaking voice. A sharp pain stabbed up through Philip's leg and he sat suddenly down a few paces away. Blood was running down his right shin, and his ankle throbbed. He watched Kari begin to work on Sally's still chest for a few seconds, then was overwhelmed with fear. He rolled onto his back. He was aware of the other children gathering round, staring horrified at the scene. He knew he should do something, but he couldn't move. He was conscious of his chest heaving. He realized his right leg was jerking spasmodically and that his hands were clutching at the earth as if he might be hurled off. He tried to focus on what was going on next to him, tried to listen, but was only aware of a frantic movement. Then he heard a girl's voice. She was weeping and desperately praying. "God save her," she wailed over and over again.

He knew that he should pray. He opened his mouth, but all that came out was a wild moan. It sounded like a shriek in his ears. He tried to stifle the sound, but the ache in his chest burst out around his hand. He opened his mouth again, and again felt only a gasp escape him. But then around the gasps, he heard his own voice repeating over and over, "You must do this, you must do this." He forced himself to focus on the sky above and lost himself in his body's desperate prayer. You must do this.

How much time passed Philip would never be able to accurately reconstruct. He became dimly aware of a mood change in the hysterical children around him. At some point fear transformed into hope. He managed to sit upright. Kari was still on the ground, but now she was holding Sally's head in her arms. Then Matt was kneeling next to him. "Sally's breathing again, but we've got to get her out of here. If we take turns carrying her and strike out directly across that field, I think we'll hit the highway before too long. We'll pick up a ride from someone. We've got to get her to Ilusan and then fly her into the clinic in Malaybalay."

Philip felt his body flood with relief. But all he could do was point at his foot. His right ankle was swelling rapidly.

"Shoot," said Matt. Then, "O.k. I'll take Kari and Benjamin and Derek. The three guys will take turns carrying Sally and we'll go as fast as we can to the road. I'll leave James and Delbert with you. You'll have to go pretty slow anyway from the look of your leg, so you guys bring the rest of the kids and the tubes. Make for the highway. When we get to Ilusan we'll send the trucks back for you."

Matt explained the plan to the group. Benjamin picked up Sally, and he and Derek started across the field. "Catch up Dad," he called. Matt gave James and Delbert a few more instructions. Kari only had time to tell Philip that "we'll need to get your leg looked at," before she and Matt were jogging after the two boys.

The next hour and a half was a nightmare for Philip. As the adrenalin drained out of him, his body sagged with weariness. Worse his foot could bear almost no weight. James and Delbert and then some of the high school girls had to take turns helping him walk. The large group was somber as they slowly rolled their tubes across the plain toward the highway. They soon reached a plowed field which made the going a bit easier. Then they found a small footpath. But long before they reached the highway Philip was soaked in sweat and his leg was on fire. His ankle was twice its normal size.

Bobby was the first to spot the weapons carrier and the Toyota. "That's a good sign," said James. "That means Uncle Matt got Sally back to the base in good time. They've probably already flown her to Malaybalay."

When they arrived at the highway, Jerry and Oscar informed them that Sally was indeed already in Malaybalay. They had flown her parents and Kari in with her. "She seemed very likely to recover," Jerry assured Philip. "And we have instructions to take you directly to the hangar as well. They want to get you into the clinic right away." He took a good look at Philip's leg and then remarked with the smallest of smiles, "But I think they're just babying the hero."

That the story might take a turn that direction had not yet occurred to Philip. But when the two trucks pulled onto the center and drove directly to the hangar, and when he saw a Helio primed to go on the tarmac with over thirty people gathered to see him off, he realized that the good folk of Ilusan were indeed very grateful for his actions. As filthy as he was he had to make it through a gauntlet of hugs and well wishes before Tom could strap him into the front seat of the airplane. Many of the women had tears in their eyes. "Nothing a little tincture of merthiolate wouldn't fix," Virginia Clayton said as she hugged him, but even she looked a little misty eyed.

"Our boy's finally becoming a real missionary," said Samuel. "We'll make a man out of him yet."

"When they take that leg off, tell them you want a whalebone stump like Captain Ahab." Trust Joseph to keep everything in perspective.

An hour later Philip stood next to Sally's bed and watched her sleep. The flight to Malaybalay only lasted five minutes. The doctor had stitched one gash on his leg, cleaned out the other, and soaked his ankle in ice before wrapping it tight. Then a nurse wheeled him down to Sally's room. Beverly Fraser had clung to him for almost five minutes, and even Robert appeared shaken. Now they all watched Sally. She looked pale, and there were long scratches on her arms and legs, but she would be fine.

"I never should have let her go on the right side," said Philip. "But the other kids were doing it, and Sally said she'd done it before."

Beverly looked at him astonished. "Philip, Sally has never even been downriver before. She's never wanted to go until today."

It was Philip's turn to be surprised. He looked at the girl lying so peacefully in the bed. "But why would she have insisted on taking the hardest route?"

Beverly sighed. "Don't you realize by now that my daughter takes her cues from you?" Robert shot Philip a glance, but then resumed looking at Sally. Beverly touched Philip's arm. "I've been waiting a long time for someone to reach Sally and pull her into the world. Her other teachers gave up too easily."

"I got lucky," said Philip. "I had a tree on my front lawn."

"I think you were honest with her," said Beverly. "That's what she was waiting for."

It was twilight when Tom flew Philip back to Ilusan. Matt was waiting on the tarmac to give him a ride home on his motorcycle. "I see they gave you crutches," he said. "But this will be quicker."

As they passed Fossia's house, the principal stepped out and flagged them down. Philip had not yet seen Kari, because George had flown her back to the center in one Helio even as Tom was transporting Philip to the clinic in the other. "Kari insisted I wake her up when you got back," Fossia said, "but she's so exhausted. I think I better let her sleep."

Philip agreed. "I'll probably do the same," he said. "Tell her I'll see her tomorrow. Tell her I'm glad she was there today."

Philip would later think that if they hadn't seen each other until the morning, all that next transpired might have been avoided.

Late that night after the generator had gone silent plunging Ilusan into darkness, Philip sat on his porch, his leg elevated on a chair in front of him. Mr. Bumbles lounged watchfully on the rail flicking his ears at the night. A full moon was up and a glow that seemed to come from the earth itself illuminated the yard and the fields beyond. The trees cast shadows. It was eerie and beautiful and Philip felt intensely alive. He longed to hold the moment, indeed the entire day, before him to be examined, re-experienced, sensualized, caught forever in the dream of memory. He was conscious of the feel of the bamboo chair beneath his arms and fingers. Mr. Bumbles began to purr and in one of the nearby trees two birds chirruped sleepily to each other. The golden scene before him might have been from another planet, it felt so strange and unreal, yet Philip possessed it with his eyes and knew it for home. And always playing before his inward eye was the rush of high water, a slow churning against the current, a leap of love and hope, and a desperate clinging to a body that felt like death. But then there was life. There was sweetness, affirmation, and love. There was laughter. There was a resurrected community of joy. He lingered long in the memory.

The Troyer sisters and their mother had dropped by shortly before lights out. They brought him a pitcher of kalimansi juice and a container of pansit. Dorothy stared rapturously at her Jesus as they sat on the porch, apparently untroubled that the Son of God appeared unable to walk without the aid of crutches. As they left Lillian said, "Now we know at least one reason why God brought you here. Where would we have been today if you hadn't been on that river?" Philip couldn't bring himself to accept the logic of sovereignty that easily. For one thing, Sally probably wouldn't even have been out there if not for him. Still it was nice to think that God might have a purpose for his life, that God might use him to impact other lives in ways large and small. Perhaps simply getting Sally out onto the river was the more important thing.

His ankle had begun to throb and he decided to take a few aspirin. He left his crutches on the porch and hopped into the kitchen. He poured a glass of kalimansi juice and took two pills. He lingered by the sink a moment enjoying the ice cold drink. Then he turned and hopped toward the door into the living room. When he reached the doorjamb he caught himself and rested against the wall. It was then that he heard light footsteps hurrying on the stairs. He knew immediately it was Kari. Who else would it be?

The figure stopped in the doorway. Philip stepped forward to show her where he was. The girl was backlit against the moonlight, a ghostly fire playing around her hair. She rushed to him and drove herself into him so hard that he was knocked back against the wall. Then her mouth was pressed, no, jammed into his. Her chest was heaving. Philip wrapped his arms around her and pulled her into him hard. He felt fierce with longing and relief.

She tore her mouth from his and then her face was against his chest, her hands gripping his shirt. She might have been weeping. He couldn't be sure. He held her for what seemed a long time. Then she pushed herself away. She continued gripping his shirt with her left hand. In the pale reflected light Philip could just make out her eyes regarding him.

What passed between them at that moment he would never be able to clearly articulate. Nothing was spoken. It happened in their eyes, and then in the movement of her right hand, slowly, as if born aloft on a sudden breeze, to the top button of her shirt. Her fingers rested lightly on the button for what seemed long toning seconds, then her thumb and forefinger pushed the button through the eye. Philip felt strangled. At that moment, with that gesture, he loved her utterly. He would risk everything. He would tear wild beasts to shreds to protect her. But to protect her from Philip Andrews, to protect her from herself, that was too much to ask.

He led her, or she led him, or together they walked and hopped into the guest bedroom. There was no mosquito net over the queen bed that rested there so inviting. It would be easier. How had they both known that so instinctively?

There was one more moment when he might have stopped it. She turned her back to him and he saw she was undoing her blouse and then her bra. But then she leaned back into him and he held her from behind as they both took long slow breaths. He kissed her ear. He thought briefly of speaking of what they were about to do and perhaps in the speaking they might have come to their senses. But instead he dropped his head and kissed her throat. He saw before him her open blouse and the gift of her breasts only partially covered now by the loose bra. She knew what he was looking at. Philip felt her breath catch and then she arched her shoulders into him. The thin material still covering her slipped to her sides, holding for just a second against the crest of her small breasts, then tumbling completely free.

She held herself before him, willing him to see her. It was her gift to give. He was helpless to refuse it. The desire to touch that intimate stretch of pale skin was too great. He slid his hand up her body. She caught his hand at her ribcage, lifted it to her mouth and kissed it, and then guided it the rest of the way herself. And their lovemaking began.

But what began so beautifully ended in tears. Her shallow breathing turned to an almost fevered moan, and finally a savagely suppressed outburst. But that exultant gasp was a false ending. The true ending was the tears.

She did not turn away from him and he held her. Neither of them had yet spoken since she entered the house. He could hardly breathe, both from the expenditure of passion and from fear. How would she respond as her heart stilled and the flood of powerful emotion which had built throughout the day ebbed away? His own feelings were inscrutable to him. He felt almost too full. He only had room to be puzzled by her tears. He would later remember how odd it felt, the warm liquid catching at the hair on his chest before pooling in the hollow of his ribs. Finally she said in the tiniest of voices, "I better go."

"Have we ruined everything?" He had to ask.

"No," she said.

But of course they had. He watched her dress in the pale light. She didn't cower as she dressed or hide herself. Every glimpse of her was like a stab. He wanted to say, "Wait." He wanted to say, "Please." He wanted to see her. There was no question of that. But most of all he wanted to understand. But all he knew, deep in his heart, was that every recovering was a removal. It was as if the gift of sight were being torn from him. He felt bitter blindness.

He made no protest when she kissed him and silently left.

He dreamed again that night. He was in a hot smoky room. He was playing poker. The devil dealt the cards. Across from him Carnley looked smug. The man grinned at the devil and then flashed Philip his hand. He was holding five aces. But that's not right, Philip wanted to say. But how did you complain to the devil that your opponent was cheating? "That hand's going to be pretty hard to beat," said the devil.

# Chapter Eleven

THE END CAME MORE quickly than Philip could ever have anticipated. He supposed it was a tribute to the tenderness of Kari's conscience. He knew he had to talk to her and when she didn't come by the next morning, he hobbled to Fossia's house on his crutches, but Kari was out. Fossia gave him a strange look, like she suspected something was amiss, but it wasn't anywhere close to the looks he would soon receive. Still to come were the sidelong glances of horror, suspicion and fear, mixed, in some, with a dash of pity. Mixed, in others, with a healthy dose of triumph. He was about to become the outsider again, pinned like a disease on the wall. He would be cut out, cast off; the body of Christ would be cleansed of his disease. He'd been here before. He knew the drill. He knew that when it came to the intimate transgressions of love or passion, for some reason judgment always trumped mercy. Love was swallowed up by loathing.

He would be reminded over the next twenty-four hours that, while what happened last night between him and Kari might seem to be nobody's business but his and Kari's, acts of sexual intimacy, when mixed with religion, quickly became everybody's business and usually with devastating consequences. God is love, toned the evangelist, but that didn't mean the church had a soft spot for young lovers. God might be love and grace, but his most ardent pursuers often found those qualities difficult to wield, those paths impossible to follow. Fear drew a clearer line on the map.

Philip knew what was coming when Matt pulled into his yard on his motorcycle that afternoon. The distress on the man's face told him everything he needed to know. "What have you done Philip? What have you done?" Matt had difficulty meeting his eye.

Philip felt the blood drain from his body. His hands began to tremble. Oh Kari, what have you done? How have you destroyed us? These were his thoughts, as he could imagine no other activating cause for the horror before him, but even as he thought them he knew they weren't fair. His lover was a child of her community, as was he. They knew the rules, and they had transgressed. That he could sublimate his guilt and go forward, was that an indication of strength? That she could not, was that an indication of weakness? The community would perceive it otherwise.

The word had gone out; a summit had been convened of the leading men. Philip's presence was required. He felt the deep weight of the forgone conclusion drag at his spirit. The old bitterness welled up within him. He considered refusing to go; he would ride out the storm on his porch with his cat come hell or high water. Mr. Bumbles was all he needed. But when he looked at Matt he couldn't do it. When he thought of all of the people on the center he had grown to love, he wanted to pound his head against the porch rail. Perhaps there was still hope.

As he rode with Matt down to the office building Philip glanced around at the familiar houses. The air was bright and hot. Everything looked normal. But he already felt the sense of catastrophe that brooded over the center where so recently there had been such joy. When they got off the motorcycle, Philip asked Matt to wait a moment. "Will Kari be in there?"

Matt shook his head. "No. She's with some of the women."

"How did this all happen? How did you find out?" It was hard for him to vocalize the question. He hoped that maybe someone had seen them, that Kari hadn't betrayed them. The thought crossed his mind that maybe Ben had observed Kari enter his house, had lingered outside and heard their lovemaking, and then reported them. But he knew that Ben was probably the least likely person on the entire center to do him harm.

Matt looked down at the ground. "As far as I know, Kari confessed to Annabel. Annabel came to me. She thought something should be done. So here we are."

"Yes, here we are," said Philip. He mounted his crutches and walked into the building. Matt held the door to the familiar room, and Philip entered. He smiled wryly as he observed the usual men gathered around the table. Carnley was twitching like a piece of popcorn about to explode. Matt took his seat looking hangdog and forlorn. Don Barker was there and William Mullen and Oscar Platt. None of the school staff was there. He supposed Fossia was with Kari. Then with genuine surprise he noticed Joseph in the far corner. Joseph's arms were crossed tightly over his chest and he was staring at the table in front of him. Nobody spoke.

Philip leaned his crutches in the corner and hopped to his seat by the door. It struck him as amusing that he thought of it as his seat. He'd sat in the same place twice before. But then he'd been defending other people. Now he was defending himself. But then he decided that was precisely what he would not do. Why give anyone here the satisfaction of the gory details? He hadn't even had time to process the experience himself. It felt precious to him. All the events of yesterday were precious. And they were his to treasure, to keep private and intact, even sacred. Why cast his pearls on the table?

When nobody said anything, Philip said, "Well gentlemen we all know why we're here. Let's get it over with."

Matt said, "Is it true?"

Philip raised his eyebrows but said nothing.

Matt tried again. "It has come to our attention that you had a sexual relationship with Kari Trainor. Is that true?"

The past tense struck Philip as odd. Did Matt think it was over, that there was no future sexual relationship to be had between him and Kari? He considered commenting on that, but realized that might not be wise. Then he pondered the term relationship. Did one sex act make a relationship? Had their entire relationship been sexual in some sense even though they'd only engaged in the act once? He considered pursuing that line of reasoning, but discarded that idea also in its turn. Instead he simply said, "Kari and I made love last night, yes."

Carnley popped. "Made love?! Made love?!" He rose out of his chair and leaned across the table. "This man did what he's always done. I recently discovered that he was thrown out of Bible college for seducing the daughter of an evangelist. I've known since I first saw him that he was a wolf in sheep's clothing. I warned some of you, but you wouldn't listen. Now you know. He is a seducer of women, the worst kind of sinner. And you turned him loose on our children."

It was unclear who exactly was meant by Carnley's use of "you." No matter. The men's eyes were startled, even alarmed. They all looked at Philip. Joseph was smiling slightly.

"Is this true?" said Don.

Philip wondered. The facts were correct. He had been thrown out of Bible college for having sex with the daughter of an evangelist. But the characterizations? Seducer? Wolf in sheep's clothing? A danger to women and children? Perhaps he was. Perhaps he did seduce women. That he had rarely initiated the act of sex or asked a woman for sex meant little in the long run. Perhaps he seduced with a smile, a kind word, and his drifting amiable availability. Perhaps he was a danger to children with his suggestions implicit and explicit that their community might not be quite right in every particular, that they should think outside the lines. Maybe his precious outside-the-lines thinking was just emblematic of his own failure to live up to community standards. A wolf in sheep's clothing? He doubted that. A bad seed? At the very least.

He realized he had been quiet a long time. The men were restless. "Yes," he said, "I suppose that's true."

The men gaped at him for a long silent moment and then Carnley started in again. Soon others were talking. The tension in the room roiled and snapped between Carnley's hubris and hate and the more reasoned suggestions of Oscar and Matt. For thirty minutes they decided his fate. From time to time someone asked Philip another question. They probed for details. They waited for him to speak. But he sat quietly. He heard as from a great distance the swirling conversation, but his mind was elsewhere. His grief for what he was losing drifted over him like a great blanket. He tried to keep it at bay. He would deal with it later when he was alone. But as much as he pushed it away, it slowly settled back.

He didn't really wake up until the meeting was over. All the men were looking at him when Matt said, "O.k. Philip. We'll get you on a plane to Manila, hopefully tomorrow. We would like for you not to try to contact Kari. In fact we think it would be best if you stayed as much as possible at your house." Carnley had won that point. He didn't want any of Ilusan's innocents coming into contact with the wolf.

"There are some things in my classroom I'd like to get," said Philip.

"I'll walk with him to school." It was Joseph. It was the only time he spoke.

"Thanks for all your help in there." It wasn't as bitter as it sounded.

"I said everything possible before you arrived," said Joseph. "Besides, we both know the die was cast."

"Yes I suppose we did," said Philip.

"Let's stop by my house on the way to school. Celia wants to say goodbye."

"That's what this is going to be like, isn't it?" It was beginning to dawn on Philip that a sudden ending bell had been rung.

"Not really," said Joseph, "most people won't want to say goodbye."

The comment didn't take Philip aback. He had grown up in these communities. He knew Joseph spoke the truth. "Amazing, what did it take me . . . thirty-five seconds . . . to go from hero to pariah?"

"You may have set a record," said Joseph.

"I think I hold most of the records," said Philip.

Philip spent half an hour at the Haaf house. After Celia finished weeping and scolding they sat together on the porch overlooking the pool. Celia insisted they have a snack together.

"What are you and Kari going to do?" Celia's eyes were filled with pity.

"I don't know that there is a me and Kari anymore," said Philip. There seemed a finality to his young life, as if he were on a ship slowly sliding beneath cold waters. "You know what the odd thing about it all is? What Kari and I did wasn't really even an act of lust. I think it was just two people overcome with the emotions of the day. It had been an amazing day. Neither of us intended to pull a David and Bathsheba."

"That wouldn't matter to folks," said Joseph. "Sex drives Christians crazy in some sort of elemental way that I'm not sure I understand. I knew a guy once in church who found out his girlfriend wasn't a virgin. His entire world crumbled. Evangelicalism has an us versus them quality about it, and he suddenly figured that all this time she was one of them. Or at least that's how it felt to him. It shattered him. Sex is the tree of knowledge of good and evil to evangelicals. Once you eat from that tree, somehow you can't go back. You are expelled from Eden. It was like his girlfriend had deliberately pulled one over on him, like she now held more cards, like she was an initiate into some dark society that he wasn't a part of. After that he'd badger a girl on the first date about whether or not she was a virgin." Here Joseph cackled hysterically for a few seconds.

Celia said, "And? What did the girls do?"

"Most girls didn't care for it. But his feeling was, if you were a virgin, you should proudly own up to it. On the first date. It was part of your bloodline."

"Did he ever marry?" Philip was curious.

"I think he eventually married a nun. If you were going to have a lover in your past, it had better be God."

"I don't think I believe anything you say anymore," said Celia.

When they said goodbye, Philip reminded Joseph of what the linguist had once jokingly accused him of being. "So am I a bad seed after all?"

Joseph thought for a minute and then said, "There's a reason Jesus told that parable. Seeds grow into plants and it takes a long time to discover what they're eventually going to be. Ask me again in thirty years."

"I probably was a fraud when I first came here," said Philip. "Now I'm closer to being the genuine article than I've ever been in my life. And they choose this moment to cast me aside. Where's the sense in that?"

When Philip hobbled into his classroom the emotion that he had struggled to bottle up ever since Matt pulled into his yard threatened to overwhelm him. His classroom was far enough from the generator that its hum barely made a dent in the warm silence that settled over the center by mid-afternoon. But everywhere Philip turned, his room, and it felt very much like *his* room, was populated with the memory of childish voices and laughter. There in the center were Bobby and Donny, always smiling, Bobby smart and attentive, Donny all a-tumble in testosterone and mad growth, both of them the stars around which the rest of the small planets whirled. Timmy Mullen next to them complaining about some assignment or other, reveling in his role as class clown. Charlie Pilarski chirping belligerently from his perch with the seventh graders. Drew quietly nesting next to him, politely raising his hand to voice a hesitant question, glancing at the older boys to see if his words garnered a reaction, desperately hoping for approval, but fearing derision, or worse, apathy. Madeline dazzling the boys with her height and beauty. Mary attempting to win the approval of all with her brilliance, especially the attention of a teacher whose manner both charmed and frightened her.

And then Sally. Philip paused by her desk in the corner by the window, always, like its owner, slightly removed from the others. But what a transformation! Philip slumped into Sally's chair. He opened her desk.

He glanced briefly through her books and the folders of assignments. He remembered now that Matt had said that an urgent request would be sent to Miss Morgan, the regular seventh and eighth grade teacher, a severe woman who had taught at Ilusan for a decade, asking her to return early from furlough to take Philip's place. Philip imagined Sally sitting at her desk in a couple of weeks as this apparition patrolled his classroom. And he felt keenly what was being taken from him, and from them. He felt the magnitude of his failure. He knew it for what it was, a betrayal.

As he sat there he heard Julia St. Clair's announcement from the radio shack. "Arriving in ten minutes from Malaybalay, the Fraser family with Sally. Everyone is well." Julia repeated the announcement. Philip could almost hear the center exhale with relief. In another minute he heard first one motorcycle, then another, making its way toward the hangar. Of course that's how it would be. He got up and went to a window. For the next five minutes he watched as a steady stream of people, walking, on bicycles and motorcycles, hurried, some just in front of his classroom, toward the hangar. By rights he should be there. He wanted to be there. Instead he sank into the shadows and watched.

He imagined the conversation that would take place very soon. Maybe it had already occurred on the plane. An adult would approach Beverly Fraser. They would be guarded, not wanting to speak openly in front of Sally. How would they phrase Philip's demise when they spoke to her? How would Beverly, in turn, put it when she spoke to Sally? He felt slightly nauseated. However they said it, the message would be plain. Your teacher is excommunicated, persona non grata, guilty of a sin so disturbing that he must be rushed away as soon as a flight to Manila can be booked. How does an innocent eighth grade girl process something like that?

It occurred to him that now, while everyone was gathered at the hangar, would be a good time to make his laborious journey back to his house. He didn't want to risk running into anyone. He hurriedly looked through his desk, located a few personal belongings, took one last look around, grabbed his crutches and hobbled out the door.

Jerry was sitting alone on the steps. He was looking toward the hangar. Philip wondered how long the man had been sitting there. He sat beside him. "I'm sorry Jerry," he said.

Jerry's face was impassive. "Yes," he said, "it's disappointing." Philip knew that was as close as Jerry could get to saying, "I'm disappointed in you." He patted Philip's knee. "Going to be hard to work up a foursome without you." Since they had never managed more than a twosome, Philip knew that Jerry was doomed now to golf alone.

They sat in silence for a few minutes. Finally Jerry said, "When I was young I spent a lot of time outdoors. I loved to golf. Perhaps I've mentioned that."

He looked at Philip for the first time since Philip sat beside him. A very small smile played briefly over his face. "I had been warned to use sunscreen but I never did. I didn't think anything bad could happen to someone on the golf course, other than a bogey or two. Too beautiful out there. So of course I got a spot of skin cancer on my face. Oddly enough I felt guilty more than anything. I apologized to my doctor for not heeding his warning. He was looking through some sort of magnifying glass at my face and he said, 'Jerry, I never expected for a minute that you'd heed my warning. You are young. It doesn't make you a bad person. We'll just cut this spot out, and it'll hurt a bit, but there's no lasting damage. And maybe now you'll listen.'"

Jerry paused. Philip thought he understood. "So I started wearing a hat and sunscreen."

The sound of the approaching airplane could be heard in the distance. Jerry stood up. "I should go welcome Sally home."

He held out his hand and when they shook, his grip was strong. "Mary and I will miss you Philip. I suppose it helps to remember what it was like to be young. The problem with so many of these good people is that they think cancer is contagious." He began walking toward the hangar. He turned one last time at the corner of the building. "Put on sunscreen. Especially when you're young. They say the fate of your skin has been decided by the time you reach thirty or so."

Philip received several visitors that afternoon and evening. The Troyers had come and gone while he was at his classroom. They left some food, a pitcher of kalimansi juice, and a note that simply said, "We'll pray for you."

Joseph stopped by about 4:30. Philip had given him a note for Kari. It was short. He wanted to argue with her, to plead that she find a way to transcend her upbringing and address the situation in a rational way. He wanted to argue that God had more important things on his plate than punishing two young lovers. Surely reading the prophets told her that.

He wanted to say that in all his time spent in the Gospels over the past few months, he had never once read of Jesus condemning lovers. Jesus had made little mention of sex even as he welcomed prostitutes and what were probably serial philanderers into his entourage. Jesus seemed consumed with addressing exploitation, hypocrisy, and all manner of social evil. Surely a beautiful relationship didn't have to be destroyed because they had made love. Jesus had never thrown over any of his followers, no matter how stupid they were or how egregiously they behaved. He hadn't even exiled Judas, just politely invited him to proceed down the path he had chosen. But Philip hadn't the time to write all that. Instead he just asked her to meet with him. Begged her.

The note Joseph carried in return held little hope. It simply said, "I'm sorry. It was my fault. I just wanted Annabel to pray with me. I don't want you to leave. But how can God bless our love now?" She signed it formally, "love Kari." There was no indication that she would meet with him. Perhaps they wouldn't let her. He doubted they would physically stop her, but they would certainly encourage her to stay far away from the source of her temptation. How better to demonstrate the seriousness of her repentance than to cut the cause of her sin loose? He could almost hear Kari's thought process. God forgave me once before. How can he forgive me again after committing the same sin? Jesus had once ordered his disciples to forgive someone who sinned against them not seven times, but "seventy times seven." By Philip's count he had over four hundred love-making sessions to go before he ought to run out of rope.

About 5:30 as he was idly starting to pack, he heard the sound of Matt's motorcycle in the yard. Matt was all business, friendship replaced by formality. He had secured a ticket on tomorrow's "Night Mercury" flight from Cagayan to Manila. He had charged it to Philip's uncle's account. They would fly Philip to Cagayan tomorrow afternoon at 3:00 p.m. Matt would stop by to give him a ride to the hangar at 2:30. Philip thanked him and Matt quickly left.

His final visitor that evening was Gordon Lundy. After Matt left, night had fallen and then deepened in eerie silence. The center was full. Conference was not yet over. But, at least at Philip's corner of the base, all was still. He had been sitting for several hours on his porch, brooding and hoping desperately for the sudden appearance of Kari out of the night, when the old man walked around the corner of his house. "May I join you?" Gordon was unfailingly polite.

Philip tried to keep the disappointment out of his face. If Kari didn't come, he preferred to be alone. But he nodded, and Gordon sat next to him. "I thought you could use some company." The old man squeezed Philip's knee hard.

They sat together silently. Philip began to relax. He got up and brought Gordon a drink. Gordon sighed with pleasure at the taste of the sweet kalimansi, but never spoke. After another five minutes, Philip glanced at him. The old man's eyes were closed. He might have been praying. He might have been sleeping. Philip gazed at him for a long time. Gordon's face was deeply lined. Decades in the tropics had burned him to a leathery brown. Gray barbs sprouted from his ears. His eyebrows looked like a wizard's. His hair, even carefully oiled, appeared coarse, the ends desiccated and crumbling. But there was a vast quiet about his eyes.

"What am I going to do Gordon?" When he asked the question, the old man's eyes blinked open. They fastened on him as if he'd been watching Philip through his lids the entire time.

"There are many things you can do. But only one thing is important." Gordon leaned forward and grabbed Philip's arm. "You must forgive. That is the heart of any true religion, because forgiveness is the very lifeblood of love." He didn't elaborate. He didn't say whom Philip must forgive. Kari? The community? Himself? Philip thought for a second that the hardest person for him to forgive might be God. Philip always seemed to come out on the wrong end of his blessed Scripture. Dangerous stuff in the hands of impressionable human beings.

"Besides," Gordon said, "I'm not too worried about you and Kari. You two are adults. She can get on the next plane after this all calms down if she wants. She can write you. But your kids? They worry me. They adore you brother, and what they will make of all this I have no idea. But they'll be talking about you for a long time to come."

"I've thought about that," said Philip, "but I have no idea what to do."

The two men were sitting like that when the lights flickered. They were still there when the generator whined into silence. Philip stood and mentioned that he had better turn in. Gordon shook his hand and said, "I'll pray for you brother." Philip knew he would, face first on his living room rug, the smell of vanilla teasing his nose.

❧❧❧

After Gordon left, Philip returned to the porch. He hadn't intentionally deceived the old man. Well maybe he had. His countdown clock was already under twenty-four hours. He needed time alone. Sleep would be difficult tonight anyway. His emotions were running too high. Might as well take a deep breath and enjoy the night.

Was it just yesterday that he threw his inner tube into the water of the Eho River and caught the ride that would set his life on a dramatically new course? Was it just last night that Kari ran up these stairs with the light touch of an elf and threw herself into his arms? He relived the entire day in his mind. How utterly precious it was. Strange how two incidents that happened so fast could remain frozen in time, affecting lives for eternity.

When his mind turned to the events of this day, the pain, anger and humiliation made him tired and ugly. He knew there was more to come. There was his uncle to face in Manila, the curious glances of other missionaries wondering why he was headed home halfway through his assignment. Then his stepmom. Then his friends. How wide would the story circulate? There probably wasn't a real big population of missionaries kicked off the field for sleeping with their girlfriends. He would be notorious.

The night deepened around him. The moon emerged from behind a steep cloud bank and saturated the high plain with its pale light. Mr. Bumbles, who had jumped into bed when Philip first went inside, finally realized he wasn't returning and came outside to join him. He nosed into Philip's lap and rammed his head into his chest. Philip hugged the cat fiercely for a moment, smelling his clean fur, feeling his body vibrate with the effort of his purr. After a moment, Bumbles heard something and leapt to the rail. His body stilled. His every sense came alert as he focused on the night.

Philip stood beside him. He placed his hands carefully on the rail. He closed his eyes and leaned forward into the darkness. He willed himself to be still. He willed himself to become part of the world around him, first with his ears, listening to every offbeat sound playing beneath the insect chorus, then with his nose, smelling the cool night breeze off the fields, then with his hands, outlining every knot in the wood with his fingers, and finally, opening his eyes again and seeing the moon-drenched night. Where he couldn't see he imagined. The world opened before him, stirring, vibrant, alive.

He looked at the cat beside him, equally locked into the moment. And he began to laugh softly. Let them come. Let them judge. Let them howl and tear their hair. It would never change the deep essential truth. "It just doesn't matter, does it Bumbles? It just doesn't matter." The cat looked at him. "But then you've always known that haven't you?"

The sun in his face was what finally woke him up. He had fallen asleep in the chair on the porch. He moved slightly and groaned. He felt stiff and old. I feel like Gordon looks, he thought. He sat for a moment clearing his head, but the sun was already high and hot. He hobbled inside and put on a pot of coffee. Then into the bathroom where he splashed cold water on his face. He didn't spend any extra time looking at himself in the mirror. When he went back into the bedroom he noticed the suitcases. He remembered and he momentarily lost his equilibrium. But then he shook his head. It just didn't matter.

He resumed packing. He had never been a good packer. He tried to fold his clothes, but when he failed, settled for gentle wadding. If need be he'd sit on the suitcase and force it shut. He went into the living room to look for stray objects to pack. He noticed his Bible thrown casually on a chair. He picked it up and went back out onto the porch. He found some shade in the corner and sat. He idly flipped the pages. He noticed the stain in the shape of an exclamation point. He smiled at the memory. He read the highlighted verse. "Friend your sins are forgiven." Jesus said that. He wondered if it were really true. Could sins really be so lightly forgiven? Jesus seemed to dismiss failure with a wave of his hand. Grace spilled out of him in such abundance that it was freely wasted. There's more where that came from, he seemed to say. The well won't run dry. Philip wondered what it felt like to be forgiven. In the religious communities in which he had lived it happened so rarely.

He limped back inside and threw the Bible into a suitcase. He still had about four hours. He gathered a few things out of the bathroom. He noticed his swim suit thrown over the shower curtain rod. He took it down. It was dry. He thought of the pool. Should he do it? Of course he should. What did it really matter? Why protect their feelings? He put on his suit. He grabbed a towel and walked through the kitchen onto the front porch. He was looking toward the heart of the center. He looked carefully around. He didn't see anyone moving. Of course, most of them would be in the meeting hall or dispersed into some office around the base. With any luck he wouldn't meet anyone. But if he did? No matter. He could deal with it.

He sat down on the stairs. He unwrapped his ankle. The swelling was almost gone. He took a few careful steps. The ankle twinged, but he could make it. After a few more steps he was confident it would bear his weight. Soon he was moving between the houses in his plaza. He kept his eyes straight ahead. He would walk on the far side of the office, thereby avoiding the meeting hall.

As he approached the central road, he saw people streaming from the hall. They must be breaking for merienda. He noticed some of them notice him. He took a deep breath and kept on going. He crossed the road. He ducked behind the office. He was now out of sight of the hall. When he re-emerged from behind the office, he had to cross an open green space, then another road, then he would disappear down the stairs into the pool. He felt as if a dozen rifles were trained on his back as he slowly, forcing himself to keep a measured pace, walked toward those blessed stairs. He didn't look back.

Then he was on the stairs, enveloped by the welcoming trees and the damp mossy smell. The cement steps were cool on his feet. What a relief, there was no one swimming at this hour. He dropped his towel on the bench and walked to the edge of the pier. The water was shaded a pale blue. Minnows darted by the dozens beneath the surface. Moss grew on the legs of the pier. Monet should have painted this pool. He took a deep breath and plunged into the water. That cold shock and then all was silent. It felt good on his leg and foot. His body glided smoothly. Nothing existed outside of cool water and peace.

He broke the surface and began swimming toward the far spillway. He felt the slippery seaweed on his legs, but he easily kicked through. When he neared the spillway he switched to the breaststroke, enjoying the sight of the rushing water and the tall trees. He stood and looked out into the creek beyond. With the center behind him now he might have been alone deep in the jungle. He walked into the spillway. He could almost span the entire breadth of it with his arms. He felt the tug of fast water. He knew that feeling. He reached for the sides of the bank but couldn't quite touch them. He looked again into the creek and the dense growth beyond. Then he gazed into the high blue sky. He raised his arms over his head. The skin on his back and arms was already dry. He felt the day's pleasant heat playing over him. He closed his eyes toward the heavens. He took a long breath. It felt like worship.

When, finally, he turned back toward the central swimming area, there were several men standing on the pier. They were staring toward him. Even from this distance, Philip could make out Carnley and Matt. He wasn't sure about the others. He groaned. He could climb out here, go around, try to avoid them. But why bother? It just didn't matter in the long run.

He eased his way into the water and began to swim back toward the pier. He detoured into the deeper hole with the rope swing. If they wanted him so badly, they could wait. He sat for a moment on the fallen tree as he had first done so many months before. He walked down it until it left his feet and he was floating again over that deep dark cavern. He slipped beneath the surface. He let his air out. It bubbled up past his face and he began to sink. He looked up following his bubbles as they moved toward the light above.

As he sank the water grew dark. He looked down. He stretched with his toes. He let out more air. Still he felt no bottom. He let out more air. The light receded above him. His lungs burned. It would be a hard pull to the surface with no air left in his lungs. He could see seaweed and fish on the muddy walls of the cavern, but still there was no floor beneath him. His arms began to feel weak. He took one last look down. All dark emptiness. He pulled hard for the surface. The mystery would remain, the depth uncharted. He floated on his back for a few minutes catching his breath. Then he reluctantly rolled over and began to stroke toward the pier.

He kept his head down, reaching toward the pier in a long lazy crawl. There was seaweed below him. Then the growth dropped away again and he was in the central swimming area. He felt for the cement steps. Only then did he bring his head up.

Carnley started into him before he was completely out of the water. "I thought we told you to stay at your house. What if there had been children swimming? You have no right to be here any longer. You're just waiting for your flight." On and on.

Philip walked up the stairs and stepped onto the pier. He picked up his towel. He kept his back to the men as he slowly toweled off. His peripheral vision told him that some of the high school boys had gathered by the diving board. They were watching silently. Gordon had said they would talk about him for a long time. He might as well add some more to the conversation. He finished drying himself and then slowly turned to the gathered men. Carnley was standing between Philip and the water. It seemed an invitation arranged by powers beyond himself.

"You know Carnley," he said, "yesterday you called me a wolf in sheep's clothing. I assume from that metaphor that you are a sheep. Well what do you suppose a wolf does when faced with a sheep?"

Carnley caught the warning in his eye and voice. He stepped back away from him. It was the wrong way to move. It simply meant he was closer to the water when Philip hit him. Hard. Harder than he'd ever swung a fist in his life. That Carnley was an older man, that they were Christian missionaries, that he might be somehow placing a seal of failure on his future life, none of these things registered with Philip until long afterward. All he felt was fury. Only later, as he dressed for his flight, did he realize that Carnley must have landed some blows as well. There were deep red splotches on his face and chest. Philip remembered nothing now until Carnley was sailing in sun-dappled splendor toward the water. If such moments kept one out of heaven, Philip would later think, this moment would almost be worth surrendering his passport. The man's mouth opened in surprise. His arms and legs flailed for purchase in the empty air. He struck the water flat on his back, before disappearing in a geyser of cold spray. Philip thought he heard a whoop from the high school boys. He turned to Matt. "Tell Gordon I'll start forgiving tomorrow."

A man's voice called, "Well played. Well played indeed." They all looked up toward the guest house. Reverend Randy was standing on the porch. He laughed his loud rolling laugh. "Pharaoh vanished into the sea," he shouted. "And the waters closed over his head."

Philip picked up his towel and walked up the stairs. The sun had never felt so good. The center was busy. The missionaries were on their morning break. They parted for him like he had the plague. Philip hobbled between them with a forced smile on his face. If he had to play the wolf, he'd play the wolf.

He had just set his suitcases on the porch when he noticed Beverly Fraser walking slowly up the fence line toward his house. Sally wasn't with her.

Philip sat on the steps and waited for her. He wasn't looking forward to the interview but he had to get a goodbye message to Sally. This would be the best way to do it.

It was easy to measure the distress on the woman's face. Her expression stabbed at him. He didn't trust his voice. He motioned toward a chair on the porch, but she shook her head. "I won't be long."

They looked at each other a moment. Philip looked away first. Finally he said, "How's Sally?"

"She's fine. She's out of bed."

"That's great. That's really wonderful news."

"I hoped she would come say goodbye to you." The news stunned Philip. Most of the parents were keeping their kids away. He assumed Sally was still bedridden. That she might have come, but had chosen not to, was a nasty surprise. He couldn't believe it.

"Do you mean . . . ?" He didn't know quite how to finish the sentence.

"She's very upset Philip." Beverly twisted her hands, then grasped them tightly at her waist. "She doesn't understand of course. She's just a girl and very innocent. But I'm afraid it feels like rejection to her, like she's being cast aside. She'll understand when she's an adult, but right now she's not an adult."

Philip remembered thinking that he owed nothing to anyone but himself and Kari. He realized how terribly wrong he had been. His head slumped into his hands.

"I've never really understood my daughter. She's alone, but not really lonely. She doesn't smile a lot, but she's never seemed terribly sad. When we told her how you and then Kari and the others had saved her, she hardly said a thing. She just lay there and looked so at peace. That's the only way I can describe it. I could hardly bear to tell her, the very next day, that now you're leaving. She can't process it. She just kept asking 'But what did he do?' And I didn't know how to tell her. How would you tell her?" The woman looked at him helplessly.

Philip shook his head. "You just don't think," he murmured, "when you're caught up in a moment what the repercussions will be. It's like when I went into the river to rescue Sally. I didn't think. I just acted." He searched for words. "You know what your daughter means to me. Don't you?" Beverly nodded. "Well Sally knows it too. She must know it. Ask her to remember that." Beverly nodded again.

They heard a motorcycle approaching.

"This will be my ride to the hangar," said Philip. He stood and then reached for Beverly and grasped her arm. "Above all tell her I'm sorry. Tell her that. Tell her I want to ask her to forgive me." He thought of something else. "And will you let her take Mr. Bumbles back? She should have him. And will you let him sleep with her? I think that will mean a lot to her."

"I'll send Sally up to get him."

Beverly was already walking away when Matt pulled in. As Philip looked after her he knew that playing at wolf was a game for adults. Where children were concerned, he should have been a shepherd.

"Will you be able to balance those cases on the bike?" Matt was briskly efficient.

"Don't rush me Matt," said Philip. "The cases are small. We'll be fine." Mr. Bumbles had heard the motorcycle. He wandered sleepily onto the porch. Philip picked him up. He hugged the cat for a long time. Before he set Bumbles down he whispered into his ear, "I'm sorry kiddo. I wish I could take you with me. You've been a good friend." How did you explain to a cat that this good thing was abruptly coming to an end?

He took a last look around, then climbed with his suitcases onto the back of Matt's motorcycle. Mr. Bumbles watched them go from the porch rail. He knew the cat would expect him back before lights out.

Only a few people came to the hangar to see him off. Kari wasn't one of them. Joseph Haaf was there, and Jerry and Mary. Gordon Lundy was there with a big hug. Philip was surprised to see Samuel and Virginia Clayton. There had always been something a bit iconoclastic about that couple. But he was truly stunned to see Derek Sorenson with Bobby and Donny. They hung back from the adults. Philip approached them and they solemnly shook hands.

"My Dad was really fuming when he got home this morning," said Derek. "Lizzie started laughing and he threw a book at her. I think it was from an encyclopedia set." All the boys smiled.

"Your father is not a good man," was all Philip could find to say.

He thought he might have gone too far. But the boys were nodding in agreement.

"He told us he'd whip us if we came to see you off," said Derek. "But I told him exactly where we were going. I'm through hiding from him. And I told him that if I ever saw another bruise on one of my brothers that I'd reproduce them on him. He almost hit me right then. And I was ready to have it out with him." Philip could see from the tension on his face the toll the act had taken on him.

"You did the right thing. Don't let anybody tell you different. I had a similar deal with your Dad you know. That's one thing he understands. Sudden violent judgment."

He turned to the two eighth grade boys. "I'm sorry for how this turned out guys. I really hate to leave you in the middle of the year. Tell everyone goodbye for me. Tell them I'm sorry."

"The others should be here," said Donny.

"Don't hold it against them. Not everybody has a big brother looking out for them."

Tom Jacobson had finished loading his suitcases. He was curt. "Time to go Philip." Philip shook hands again with the boys, then with the adults. Nobody said much. Without asking Tom he climbed into the front seat and fastened himself in. Tom didn't object. He never said a word to Philip as he went through his preflight check. Then he was yelling "Clear" out the window. The propeller turned over and the engine fired hard. Almost immediately he spun the plane on its tail wheel and headed for the runway.

The wind was coming from the south, so Tom taxied to the extreme northern end of the north-south strip. They would be taking off over Philip's house. As Tom twice ran up the engine, Philip remembered that on this very spot he and Kari had waited on their bicycles for an advancing storm. The memory made him wince. As the Helio slowly started its roll back toward the hangar Philip looked into the corn field and another memory came to mind. Somewhere out there was a bull with a nasty scar and a grudge thinking, Good riddance.

The airplane was already in the air as it passed the hangar. Philip waved at the small group standing there. They waved back. Then they were over Fossia and Kari's house. There was no sign of life. The water tower shot below him. He would have one last glimpse of his home. He pressed against the window. There it was, the rusty roof, the rain barrel. And sitting on his porch steps a young girl and a large gray cat. They were looking up. He waved frantically. The girl stood. She remained motionless for a moment. Then she stretched first one hand, then the other, toward the airplane. Philip's last memory of Ilusan was of the girl with outstretched arms receding rapidly into the distance until she and then the house and then the center itself was gone.

They flew in silence for a few minutes and then Tom banked the Helio hard and they wheeled away north toward Cagayan. For a moment, during the steep turn, Philip felt as if the plane might plummet from the sky. He almost wished it would.

Philip looked at the pilot. "You drew the short straw huh?"

"Yep."

"That about sums it up," said Philip. But he wasn't thinking of the pilot. His eyes, blurry with tears, were seeing the girl and the cat and their upturned faces.

Tom glanced at him. "You brought it on yourself," he muttered.

Philip turned away. A storm was rolling in from the east. Ilusan was in for a hard rain. "You got that right," he said. "You got that right."

The End